# PERFECT ARMENIAN

*A Novel*

Keri Topouzian

HYEVAN
PUBLISHING

A PERFECT ARMENIAN
Topouzian, Keri
ISBN-13: 978-0-9854124-0-1
ISBN-10: 0-9854124-0-2

Jacket design by Mark Stegeman, Stegeman Creative & Elisabeth Veltman, Blue Pearl
    Customer Stategies, LLC
Interior design by Troy Scott Parker, Cimarron Design

Published by
Hyevan Publishing
1900 South Telegraph Road
Suite 102
Bloomfield Hills, Michigan 48302, USA
aperfectarmenian@gmail.com
www.aperfectarmenian.com

For more information, please visit www.aperfectarmenian.com

Printed in the United States of America by Thomson-Shore

10  9  8  7  6  5  4  3  2  1

*I dedicate this book to my mother,*
*Veronica Norma Topouzian, whom if alive would*
*have been my biggest critic and staunchest fan.*

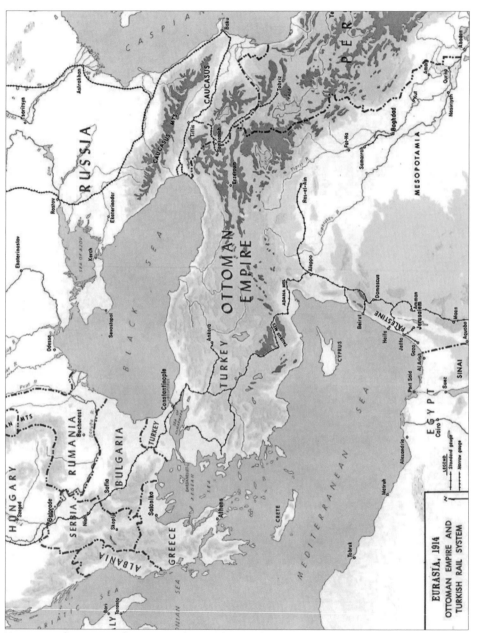

Map courtesy of Department of History, United States Military Academy

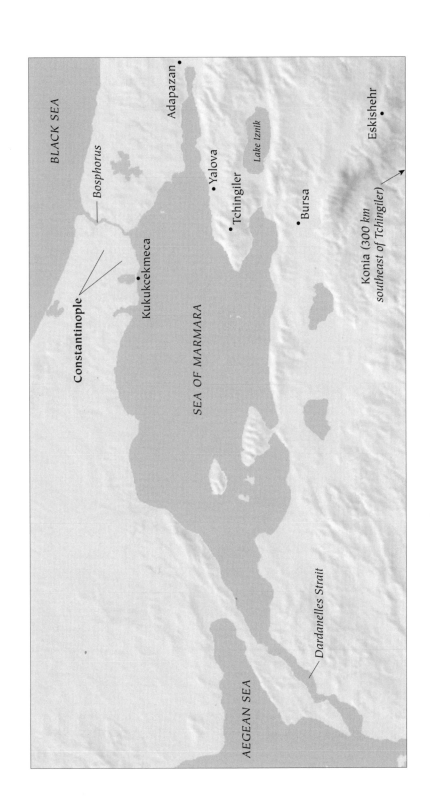

BLACK SEA

Bosphorus

Constantinople

Kukukcekmeca

Adapazan

Yalova

Tchingiler

Lake Iznik

Eskishehr

Bursa

Konia (300 km southeast of Tchingiler)

SEA OF MARMARA

Dardanelles Strait

AEGEAN SEA

# A WORD FROM THE AUTHOR

Reader Notes:

"Chapter of Remembrance" after the Epilogue is in commemoration of April 24th, Armenian Martyrs Day.

My hope is that the maps found in the front of the book will be of interest to those of you who appreciate details.

To expand awareness of Armenian culture, food, language and more, I have compiled a glossary and a character list located in the back of the book.

For more background on the novel, visit our website at www.aperfectarmenian.com.

Thank you.

– Keri Topouzian

# INTRODUCTION

My grandfather died the day before I was born.

I was born on June 25th at 12:12 AM and my grandfather was pronounced dead at 11:11 PM June 24th after suffering lethal wounds from a motor vehicle accident. He was driving to the hospital after hearing that his first grandchild was to be born.

Some tell me that this was a very sad time for my mother because she knew how much her father was looking forward to seeing his first grandchild. But I tell you the truth, I remember my grandfather better than I remember a lot of other people. For when I was in the womb and coming into this world, I saw him as he was passing through to the other side. He was so happy, full of love and gratefulness that he had died on this day because he was able to see and know me and at the same time place his mark on me. I will never be able to forget him or his soul; his consciousness will always be within mine.

My mother believes me but that's about it. Others smirk or say, *awww that's so sweet,* when I tell this story.

But I know what I saw. It's not a dream. It's as real to me as anything else in this world. And I am looking forward to seeing him again when I die. But in the meantime, let me tell you what else has happened to bring this book into being.

My grandfather died almost a year to the day after my grandmother had passed. My parents were in charge of sifting through all of his belongings, discarding what was deemed to be of no use and salvaging what was in some cases to be cherished. This coincidentally included several weapons including handguns, blackjacks and some knives.

But let's go back further to when my grandmother died. During the requiem dinner after the funeral there was a reading of her last requests. One of these was that my grandfather promised to give my mother an old manuscript of his past writings. A project my grandfather had nearly forgotten and which was infrequently discussed. Weeks later, my grandfather fulfilled this wish and brought to my parents' house a large and somewhat filthy cardboard box filled with manuscript-like documents all in my grandfather's handwriting. Hundreds of pages.

"Do what you will with this, but it is from the past and I feel it should stay there where it belongs," my grandfather stated. "Obviously my wife disagrees. Thinks it would be a good project for you…as if you don't have enough to do, eh? I hope you enjoy the journey. I know I have."

Over the years, my mother had slowly sifted through the writings, all of which were handwritten in Armenian. Initially with some help from her father, she compiled the papers and began translating them into English. During this initial year when my grandfather was still alive, there was confusion as to where this story really came from. Was it my grandfather's memoirs or was it fictitious? When asked, my grandfather always said, "It's a story. Some of it is true and some of it…well, you decide."

But the names were of no one my mother had known, yet the places, dates and events she had recalled from the past. Had he changed the names for some reason? And if so, why? Years later we concluded that he was either playing a joke or was concerned that if these writings got into the wrong hands some of his old friends or their relatives could be put in harm's way. My grandfather was always very careful. Some say he was just plain paranoid. I say he was *thorough*.

When my mother became pregnant with me, the translation of the writings was put on the back burner. Then came my birth and my grandfather's death, and the manuscript sat untouched for years. Like an old Tavloo[1] board that had lost one of its masters.

On one of my grandfather's birthdays, she decided to finally reawaken her work and again started to piece together the story. There were times when you could hear her swearing in Turkish while going over the writings. My father would ask her what was wrong. She would always say, "I think it's all true but I'm just not sure. I should have made him tell me! I hate not knowing!"

---

[1] Armenian: backgammon.

Smudged carbon handwritings, water damage, and poor penmanship made this journey for her long and frustrating. And unfortunately, my mother never completed the translation of my grandfather's writings; I inherited this responsibility after she passed away.

It took me seven years to get through half of the papers and have them translated. What I am telling you is this is only half of the story.

Tavid Kaloustian, the main character of this book, was born in 1893. Funny thing. So was my grandfather.

*Being an Armenian is a merciless task and a heroic enterprise.*
*It is a commandment, a mission, and a destiny that history*
*has imposed on us from the depths of centuries. We are the*
*shock troops of the struggle between light and darkness....*
*And we are charged with an awesome responsibility.*

– GOSTAN ZARIAN (1885-1969)

"Do not go as a lamb into a den of wolves. That is for the prophets and the martyrs to endure. The same holds true if strolling into a Turkish village dressed as an Armenian peasant. You might as well just throw yourself off a cliff."
   – Yervant Yacoubian

# CHAPTER 1

# Do You Know Me?

September 7, 1914, Constantinople, Turkey. 0930 Hours

AN ORNAMENTAL DOOR OPENED WITH a whine, as if directed toward its present patron. In walked a tall, white-bearded Kurdish Tribesman wearing a colored palto[1] and fez. From his dress he was a man of stature, at least within his clan. He had walked into a fine goods shop in the northwest sector of Constantinople where silks and fine fabrics were sold, bartered, and in some cases given away to protect the shop's owner.

"May Allah bless this fine shop," the Kurd slowly said, in a raspy voice.

"And may you be blessed with long life and many wives," the shop owner replied from behind a display counter of silks near the back end of the shop.

The Kurd shook the dust off his clothes and shoes from his ride through the city and began perusing the shop. He then purposely inhaled to catch the scents that permeated from the walls lined with merchandise, almost erotic in aroma. However, something else had caught his attention. There were two other men in the shop sitting at a carved stone table adjacent to the front display window, drinking amber liquor from a local yet discreet distillery and playing Tavloo.[2] Both were dressed as Europeans but it was

---

[1] Turkish: robe or a long wool overcoat.
[2] Armenian: backgammon.

apparent to the Kurd that they were Turkish gendarmes. At first, they scrutinized the Kurd when he walked in, then continued with their drink and game.

*Gendarmes are here in this shop?,* the newcomer thought to himself, and then spoke. "Still it is early morning and you two are drinking already! Ahhh, if only I had the time to join you, but I have important business today," exclaimed the Kurd. The two gendarmes tried to ignore him.

"What is the occasion?" the shop owner asked. "A grandson coming of age? A birthday? Marriage of one of your children?"

The Kurd looked at the owner and slowly walked over to the table where they were playing Tavloo. "No, my friends, I am to take another wife! And it is by no means the first. This will be my ninth bride and the youngest of all!"

The gendarmes looked up; half sneered and again tried to ignore the old-looking Kurd.

"That is why I am here today. I am in need of many things, many beautiful things to please my future bride."

The eyes of the uglier of the two gendarmes glistened; he looked up at the old Kurd. "Nothing left underneath that palto to please her, eh?" Both gendarmes laughed and toasted to his wit.

The Kurd just smiled. "Ahhh, but it is not easy being an elder, my half-toothless friend. I have many responsibilities, including producing many offspring. It is a difficult task at my age so I have chosen a younger bride to help me with my duties." Looking at the shop owner he said, "I would first like to look at some of your softest feather pillows."

"On the left by the door," pointed the owner. As the Kurd walked over to the merchandise, the gendarmes went back to their game.

No one noticed that as the Kurd was testing the softness and texture of the fine pillows, he had discreetly reached under his palto, brought out a metallic object and placed it under a pillow. He folded the pillow around his left hand, quickly looked out of the windowed door and walked towards the gendarmes while talking to the shop owner. "This is what I am looking for. How many colors does this fine pillow come in?"

*Poofb! Poofb!*

Before the owner could answer, there were two quick pops and a flurry of feathers flew into the air. One of the gendarmes fell to the floor. The other just stared at his comrade as he fell. Then his face whirled around to look at the Kurd.

*Poofb!*

Another muffled pop followed by more feathers. They were both dead.

"Aldo!" The elderly-appearing Kurd grumbled to the shop owner. "Call in the third one that is across at the distillery. Tell him one of his friends is not feeling well and needs another drink."

In reality, this was not a Kurd at all who had entered this fine goods shop but an Armenian by the name of Tavid Kaloustian, disguised to evade detection. Underneath the disguise was a powerfully-built young man barely in his twenties. His face was covered by a dyed white beard and mustache, but without the disguise Tavid could easily have been mistaken for any of the dark-complected races: Southern European, Greek, Arab, even a Turk.

Again Tavid inhaled, this time to take in the smell of gunpowder and blood as they eclipsed the now weaker scents of the shop's merchandise.

Aldo smiled at Tavid. "A pity that the last thing these Turks had to see was your ugly face. And look what you have done to my pillow and the silks! And the Tavloo board!"

Aldo was Tavid's older Romanian liaison to Constantinople's black market. Dwarfed in stature next to Tavid, his features were remarkably similar but faded as if bleached by the sun.

The Tavloo board was covered with blood as were the silks hanging on the wall behind where the gendarmes had been sitting. Tavid had picked one of the largest pillows to muffle the shots of the revolver as he shot both gendarmes in the head.

"My apologies. The board I will clean up. Can you wash blood out of the fabrics?"

"Never mind!" Aldo ripped. "I will be right back with their comrade."

"Make sure you are not standing next to him when he walks in the door. I do not want the bullet to go through him and hit you as well," Tavid remarked.

"Yes, yes. You are always thinking of me. God bless you, Tavid. Could you not have been thinking of me when you ruined those silks?"

Tavid shook his head.

"Hurry, Aldo! We have much to do, today you must die."

Aldo gave Tavid a questioning look and left for the third gendarme. Tavid grabbed a sheet and wrapped it like a blanket around the gendarmes' bodies. Then took two small linens and placed them on their head wounds to catch the escaping blood.

*Their hearts are still alive,* he thought to himself. Then, quickly he retreated to the opposite corner, out of sight. As the third gendarme opened the door and walked in, he froze at the site of his two comrades on the floor.

*Come...walk in a little further,* Tavid thought. Aldo, who walked in behind the Turk, seeing that he had stopped in the doorway lunged forward, pushing him into the room where he lost balance and fell in front of his fallen comrades.

*Poofb! Poofb!* The gendarme jerked and groaned, his eyes locked onto his dead comrades. Then his head slowly dropped, his eyes closed, and they were a threesome once more.

"Lock the door and let us get to work," Tavid commanded.

Aldo obeyed and closed the shade on the door and front curtains.

"It is a good thing you came on a Friday morning when business is slow. Someone could have easily seen you with all these windows open. And that costume you have on!" Aldo exclaimed. "I have to admit when I saw you walk in I almost thought you were a Kurd. A very ugly one at that. Come now and take it off."

"How did you know it was me?" Tavid asked, disgusted.

"Your eyes, of course. Your black eyes. Besides, I have known you and your grandfather Yervant Yacoubian for years. And I could have been blind and known it was you walking in by your scent. I can smell the opium, you know. Even through the chemen[3] and garlic, I can smell the opium. Now then, you mentioned something about killing me as well?"

---

[3] Turkish: a thick and pungent mixture of hot spices used to cure meats.

"Aldo was a rare find. One of my few contacts that I could
trust. He was open to new ideas, trustworthy and a good friend.
I even taught him how to speak Armenian over the years."
– Yervant Yacoubian

CHAPTER 2

# Informer

"THEY KNEW, ALDO! HOW DID they know I was coming here?" Tavid
questioned, but continued before Aldo could answer. "Now, I know you
did not tell them. Unless they tortured you. But you do not look like you
have been tortured; just short and irritable as usual."

Aldo shook his head.

"I did tell them, but they already knew. Let me tell you what happened."

Aldo proceeded to tell the tentative young Armenian, still dressed in his
Kurdish outfit, what had transpired over the past three weeks.

"For months now the Turkish port commander on the Northern
Bosporus has been trying to find the sources of the opium exports. Not
to stop the flow of opium mind you, but to profit from it. He does not
have the manpower to search every ship and cargo, and he suspects some
of his gendarmes are taking bribes. So he has changed his strategy to find
the growers and their delivery routes. Tavid, he knew you were coming.
He has a source from your village or at least someone that is familiar with
your village."

"How did you know this?" Tavid asked, disgusted.

"I have a relationship with one of the port commander's lieutenants. He was given orders to find the drop off point for the opium in the city. They knew that the contact in Constantinople was Romani.[1]"

"What shit is this you say?" Tavid retorted. "I can tell when you are making up a fairy tale!" he added, hoping to be right.

Aldo ignored Tavid and continued. "The lieutenant came to me that night to let me know what had happened. He knew I would pay him well for the information, which I did. But I also told him to come back to the shop the next day with three gendarmes and question me about the opium. Threaten to burn my shop down or, better yet, I told him to suggest that if I did not tell him what he wanted to know that he would have the gendarmes strip me down and hold me while he had his way with me. I told him to put on a good show, just do not break anything in the shop and do not even think about actually taking off my clothes."

"I am listening," Tavid snapped.

Aldo continued. "The next morning he came with three gendarmes. The two of us put on a good act and afterwards he ordered his men to watch the shop, two inside and one outside. The lieutenant reported his actions back to the commander, and we have been awaiting your arrival."

"So what did you tell them about me?" Tavid pressed.

"That the delivery was due in about two weeks and you were coming from Tchingiler.[2] But they already knew that. I just confirmed their information. They did not ask me who you were or what your name was. They already knew."

Tavid thought about what he had just been told and whether Aldo, one of his closest contacts in Constantinople, was lying.

"God damn you! Why did you not try and warn me then?"

Aldo laughed, then paused. "I was not worried about you, you untrusting Ermeni.[3] I was sure you would sneak around before coming into the shop to make sure it was safe," Aldo said with confidence.

"Well, what if I had not this one time, Aldo? What if I assumed that I have known you long enough and I did not have to make sure it was safe? What if I just walked into your shop?"

"Who are you kidding? You would never do that. Never! I know you too well. But just as insurance, I had two of my cousins on the roof across the

[1] Turkish: Romanian.
[2] Pronounced "Cheen-geh-lehr." Tavid's home village just southeast of the Sea of Marmara.
[3] Turkish: Armenian.

way, with rifles." Aldo pointed out the window. "They were instructed to kill the gendarmes, only the gendarmes mind you. And even if something went wrong, your eerie luck would have saved you. Just like your grandfather, Yervant. I have never seen such luck within a family."

Tavid peered up to the flat roofs with their colorful façades.

"Ohf! Romani gunmen on the roof? That is a relief! They cannot see straight let alone shoot straight. Always drunk." He continued to think of any flaw in Aldo's story. He smirked, "Why did the Turks not try to take me in Tchingiler?"

Aldo smiled, showing surprisingly white teeth though partially camouflaged by his mustache. "This is a good question, my young partner. Apparently the port commander was told the village of Tchingiler is off limits."

"What? By whom?"

"Well, by a Turkish commander in Bursa.[4] I believe his name is Kalkim Bey.[5]"

"Bahbahm![6] Again you are speaking with shit in your mouth," Tavid muttered.

"Oh yes! Apparently Kalkim Bey told the commander that you were off limits in his territories. You were a spy working for him and if he entered Bursa's jurisdiction against his authority, the Bey would have the port commander removed from his post. Well, that did not sit well at all. He ignored the threat and sent half a dozen disguised gendarmes to retrieve you. However, they never made it to Tchingiler. They are all dead."

"Oh? A Turkish commander had a band of Turks killed to save an Ermeni? Not even in Jehennem[7] and you know it!" Tavid exclaimed.

"No. You are right; he did not have them killed. We killed them as soon as they reached the outskirts of Constantinople. My men and I. Buried the bodies, took the horses and guns, sold them at market three weeks ago. But the commander thinks Kalkim Bey had them killed and now he wants retribution," Aldo said beaming with satisfaction.

Tavid wanted to reach out and grab his Romanian partner by the neck, but forced himself to subdue his rage and contemplate Aldo's words.

---

[4] A large city in western Turkey not far from Tchingiler.
[5] Turkish: "Bey" is used at ends of names to signify a provincial governor or officer of high ranking.
[6] Turkish/Armenian slang: "my father!" Used in the same way as "oh my God!"
[7] Turkish: hell.

"So it seems I am going to have to kill the port commander too," Tavid finally resolved.

"That would be a good idea. Especially if you are working for the Bey."

"Ahmahn![8] Do not even try! You and I both know that the Turk knows as long as I am alive, he will keep getting his share."

Aldo smiled, "Can I not play with your head like you do with mine? Can I not have some fun with you on occasion as you do with me, Tavid?"

Tavid could not hold back a smile.

"Now I have a question for you, my young friend. How did they know to look for a Romani?" Aldo asked.

"I do not know. The informer told them this?" Tavid asked.

"Yes."

"Hmmm. I will have to give that some thought. Maybe this will be of help to me in finding him. Or her."

Tavid then looked down at the floor where puddles of blood had formed. It seemed to relax him. As Aldo viewed the chaos, his anger began to erupt.

"What a damn mess you have made! Why could you not have just strangled them or bashed them on the head with a piece of iron?"

Tavid ignored Aldo and knelt down beside the three dead gendarmes, deftly taking their concealed revolvers and ammunition belts, rifling through their pockets for anything worth keeping or selling. He found some tobacco, a few paper lire, some coins, but best of all identification papers.

"Dead men have no honor with you, do they? How many guns do you need, Tavid?"

Tavid looked up at Aldo, "You never know when they will be needed. Many Ermenis will buy guns and bury them for safekeeping. Besides, why let all this go to waste? I can always sell them if I don't need them. Here, help me take off their uniforms."

"What? I will not! What are you going to do, sell their uniforms too?"

"No, no. Not sell them, keep them, and maybe wear one, if I need a disguise to get out of the city. Why do you think I shot them in the head?"

Aldo shook his head. Even though he outwardly disapproved, he accepted the Armenian's resourcefulness.

"Let's take care of business, Aldo. Then we can talk about what to do with you and your shop."

---

[8] Translates as "oh" or "oh my."

"I remember the first time I made Tavid dress in a disguise.
We had to travel through a predominantly Turkish sector of
Constantinople. Gendarmes stopped us not once but twice.
Afterwards, his mischievous grin revealed that he now understood
the necessity to be invisible. And now you cannot get him to stop!"
– Yervant Yacoubian

# CHAPTER 3

# Resin

"ARE YOU GOING TO TAKE off that Kurdish costume now?" Aldo asked again.

"Not yet. I will soon." Tavid walked around to behind the glass counter. He removed two three-inch leathered wooden blocks from the bottom of his boots.

"Handcrafted! Made me over six feet tall."

"A giant for an Ermeni," Aldo laughed.

"Look who is talking!"

Tavid then took off a sheepskin inner cloak. On the inside of the cloak were dozens of small glass vials, about twelve centimeters in length and nearly two in diameter. Each vial was in its own little pocket sewn into the inside of the cloak and lined with sheep's wool for protection.

"Like babies in their womb," Aldo said. "It was a good harvest this year?"

"Of course! Plentiful and stout. Here, look at the color, the consistency." Tavid pulled out one of the vials from its pocket. Thick auburn-tinted liquid filled the vial. It was resin that had been extracted and purified from opium plants. He turned the vial on its side, then upside down to show Aldo the consistency of the liquid. It barely moved. Turning it upright, he unscrewed the cap.

"Smell how strong it is."

He handed the vial to Aldo whose fixated eyes mimicked that of a child being given candy. Aldo smelled the opium resin and almost choked, then smiled.

"God's perfume. Stronger than any liquor. Tavid, can you imagine the state of the church if Christ were born in Armenia two millennia ago and you were one of his disciples? Ha! When He gave thanks, broke bread with you and the rest of his disciples, then dipped the bread in your resin instead of wine, what a wonderful place the world would be, eh? The Turks would be lining up to be baptized!"

Tavid took the vial from Aldo who was too busy laughing at his own wit to pay attention to the open vial.

"Careful! You are talking stupid! Have you been selling all of the resin or keeping some of it for yourself?"

Aldo shrugged his shoulders and smiled.

"I have twenty-eight vials. Each with fifty milliliters of resin. Can you pay me in the usual way?" Tavid asked.

"Of course. Do you want it split up in equal amounts?"

"No. I will need more gold lire this time," Tavid replied.

Aldo opened one of the glass doors on the display counter and fumbled through the fine silks to find a piece of carbon and some old paper.

"Alright now. Fifty times twenty-eight…3,200 Swiss francs…forty-six gold lire and sixteen diamonds, one carat each. Agreed?"

Tavid thought for a moment and nodded. "Tell me, what's your price? Who are your buyers? Do you dilute, like many resin sellers these days?"

Aldo did not answer.

"It's better that I do not know these things. Right, Aldo, my friend?"

Aldo nodded. "Help me move this over. And pick it up so there are no slide marks on the floor."

The two picked up and moved a heavy display cabinet. Then Aldo reached into his pocket and pulled out a small knife, knelt down on his knees and began prying out two of the wood floor planks. Underneath the planks were the stone foundation blocks of the building. One of the blocks had a barely discernable opening.

Aldo reached into the display cabinet, and pulled out a long key-like metal tool. He placed the key into the small opening, turned and pulled the block out and placed it onto the shop floor.

"Layers to protect layers," Aldo remarked.

Under the block was payment for the opium, or at least part of it—the gold lire and diamonds. Aldo counted out lire and sixteen dusty diamonds, placed them in a purple silk cloth and handed it to Tavid, who in turn stashed them in a small leather pouch. Aldo quickly took the remaining valuables, placed them in a small bag which he placed in a vest pocket under his coat, and buttoned it closed. There was also a small dusty envelope in the hole. Aldo paused before retrieving it and slipped it in his vest pocket. Methodically, he resealed the enclosure and they moved the display cabinet back.

"Love letter, Aldo? Must be very important if you hide it with your wealth."

Aldo gave half a smile. "Yes, a dear letter from a friend. Now, we can stop at Bank Switzeria before we go to the eastern port. Costel has been there now for almost a month. He has been waiting for me."

Tavid nodded.

"And now, what do you want to do with these bodies? And for that matter, my shop?" Aldo asked.

Tavid looked around the shop. "If we leave everything as is, the Turks will turn the city upside down until they find us. They will search every ship going out the Bosporus especially any Romanian vessel. We have to make them think we are dead. And then we have to kill the port commander. This could be enjoyable," Tavid said matter of factly.

"Enjoyable for you perhaps. What is your brilliant plan?" Aldo was displeased.

"Do you have explosives?" Tavid asked.

"Explosives? What are you thinking? No, not the shop!"

"Listen! We need to make it look like you were shot and then we will need a diversion. Now, how much, and how many detonators? I will need the plunger and enough wire to be about two shops away," Tavid explained.

Aldo mumbled about his poor shop and led Tavid into the darkness of the back storage room. Aldo again knelt to the floor and pulled out his knife to reveal a second concealed chamber under the shop, this one larger than the first. Aldo pulled out a large filthy wool blanket and placed it with a *clunk* on top of an old marble table. Opening the blanket, Tavid saw all he had requested and more.

"Eleven sticks left. Only five detonators though. Here is the plunger and wire. I paid a fortune for these, you know!" Aldo hissed.

"Are you giving me these as well?" Tavid asked, pointing to two revolvers and a box of ammunition.

"No! I need those to protect myself from you." Taking the revolvers and ammo from the blanket he placed them on one of the shelves, then took an elongated item out of the blanket which was wrapped in its own thick cloth.

"Here. This was your grandfather's. He asked me to give it to you when I thought you were ready."

Tavid looked at Aldo, and grabbed the bundle. Inside were parts to a rifle: stock, firing mechanism, three clips, barrel, scope and three large boxes of ammunition.

"Careful! Do not drop it. Let me show you how to put it together. I had to take it apart so it would fit under the flooring," Aldo explained.

Tavid nodded, still staring at the rifle. As he watched Aldo assemble it he stood, remembering his grandfather Yervant. How much he missed him. It had been months since Yervant Yacoubian was killed in Bursa by two Turkish lieutenants greedy for more than what his grandfather was bribing them.

*God damn them,* he thought. He remembered finding his grandfather's body. Tavid hated the Turks. They had taken away his grandfather, his mentor, his companion.

Aldo softened his gaze. "I miss him too."

Tavid nodded. "At least the Turks who killed him got their just reward when their commander found out that my grandfather was dead. No more bribes, no gold, no opium for the commander. I wonder how long it took before the two of them died in Adapazari prison? For treason, yes? Treason." Tavid smiled to himself.

Aldo looked up at Tavid while reconfiguring the rifle.

"Yervant is…was one of a kind. A trustworthy brother, a wonderful kindhearted man and a son of a bitch all at the same time."

Tavid looked at Aldo, hesitated then grinned.

"You mean a shrewd businessman."

"Yes, but son of a bitch sounds better."

Aldo finished assembling the rifle.

"Here it is. German made. Uses these 7.9 millimeter shells." Aldo held one in his hand. "Take good care of it. Your grandfather paid a small fortune for this rifle."

As Tavid picked it up, he checked the weight then tried looking through the range scope.

"Never used a scope. What is the range of accuracy? How much of a kick does it have? Is the ammunition fresh? How loud is…"

"Wait! Just wait a minute; I do not know. I have never fired it. However, from your grandfather's bragging it sounds like it was accurate up to eight hundred meters. Besides that, I only know the name of the rifle and how to put it back together. I am sure you will have a chance to play with it later."

Tavid examined the lettering on the rifle.

"Ahhh! A Mauser like my own. But it's more modern, and called a Karabiner.[1] That must be its name. Almost sounds Ermeni."

Aldo smirked, "Yes, of course. Armenians are always trying to take credit for everything."

Tavid ignored him. He took the rifle's strap and swung it over his right shoulder. He then took the ammunition and placed it in pockets on the inside of his overcoat. Next the explosives. He took out three sticks, blasting caps, the wire and the plunger from the blanket, and rolled the rest back up and tied it tightly.

"Alright, here is my plan," Tavid proceeded. "First, we cover you with blood from those three on the floor. I fire a few shots; you stumble out of the front door wounded in the head and the chest yelling for help. Make sure you are at least two shops away on the other side of the street. I will be two shops down on the opposite side watching for you. Then I will blow up the shop."

"No, not my shop!" Aldo sighed. "My poor shop. This is your fault!"

"It is no one's fault, Aldo! Now, you will have to put on a good show. And what about your two cousins on the roof? We need to let them know what is going to happen."

"Yes, yes, I will call them down, but you will help me load up my goods into the wagon out back. I am not going to let you destroy everything."

Aldo walked to the window at the front door and signaled to his two comrades to come down. He went to the back door of the shop, unlocked it and watched for them. When they arrived, Aldo explained the plan and instructed them to stand guard while he and Tavid loaded the wagon.

---

[1] The Karabiner was a German rifle introduced into general service in 1898. It was manufactured by the Mauser armory in huge quantities until it became obsolete after WWII.

Twenty minutes later Aldo's goods were wrapped and loaded on the wagon. Aldo also took out a change of clothes and placed it behind the wagon seat. He found his gunbelt, put it on under his coat and retrieved the two revolvers he had placed on the shelf previously. Tavid rigged the explosives, connecting the wires and passing them through the back door. He ran them forty meters down the alleyway into an abandoned shop. Satisfied with his view of the shop, he ran back.

Once back inside, Tavid walked over to the three dead men and retrieved the blood-soaked linens. "Squeeze this one by your heart and then I will squeeze the other one on the back of your head."

Tavid made Aldo open his shirt and shoved the bloody towel inside.

"Ugh! Disgusting! Even their blood smells like it has not bathed in weeks." Tavid grinned and twisted the other towel so the blood ran out onto the back of Aldo's head with most of it running down his back. "Uuuuhhhh!" Aldo started to shiver. "It is going down too far!"

"What?"

"It is going down into my pants, God damn it!"

Tavid froze then exploded with laughter.

"Well if anyone asks, tell them I shot you in the ass!"

"Sikishmek[2] Ermeni!" Aldo cursed.

Tavid tried to stop laughing. "Alright, it is time now. Tell your cousins to get back into position and signal when they are ready."

Ten minutes went by and Aldo, standing in the middle of his shop, bent down so he could see the top of the roof across the street where his cousins would signal. After seeing them pop their heads up, he signaled to Tavid.

"They are ready. Let us get this over so we can have breakfast."

Aldo did not notice through the half-curtained window that his cousins did not wave; instead, they were pushing their hands forward and shaking their heads. Aldo only saw that they were in place. He did not notice their warning.

Tavid picked up the plunger, pulled out a revolver, held it in the air and erratically fired six shots.

"Go!" Tavid yelled as he ran out the back door of the shop. Aldo walked to the front door clutching his chest, dropped his head, and staggered out of the shop and started to cross the street.

---

[2] Turkish profanity.

"Help! Help me! I am shot!" He yelled in Turkish. As he was halfway across the hard-packed dirt street he heard his cousins on the roof yelling at him, but before he could discern what they were saying he heard a group of horses. He looked to his left just enough to see about half a dozen Turkish gendarmes riding toward him. Aldo tried to keep walking to the other side of the street but the gendarmes were yelling at him to stop. He was about three meters from a storefront on the other side of his shop when he stopped abruptly, pretending to fall dead. When the gendarmes got to him, one jumped off his horse and crouched down to see if he was still alive, turning him over onto his back. Dust and dirt covered Aldo's face and overcoat. He lifted his head, pointing to his shop and repeating in a raspy voice, "I shot him. He is in the shop. He still has the gold."

The Turks turned to the shop, then looked at each other. One of the Turks looked at Aldo. "Is the Ermeni dead?"

Aldo did not answer.

"Is he dead?" the Turk yelled.

Aldo kept his eyes closed and nodded.

"Shot. Him. In. The. Head. Shot. Him. In. The. Head."

Smiling, the Turks left Aldo and slowly started toward the shop.

Aldo had collapsed in front of a carpentry shop owned by two elderly Romanians. Seeing Aldo bloodied in the street, they rushed out and knelt down beside him. One of the men started to weep at the sight of Aldo lying in the street.

"Pick me up and take me inside," Aldo whispered. The weeping stopped as the two men just stared at him. "Now! Quickly!" he said through gritted teeth.

At that, the two older men dragged Aldo with difficulty into their shop.

The gendarmes were too busy watching the other side of the street to notice Aldo anymore. All of them had dismounted their horses and moved slowly to Aldo's storefront. One of the Turks appeared to be giving orders to the others, pointing to the shop. Revolvers and rifles were pulled, cocked and ready as two of the gendarmes entered the shop.

"I thank Jesus that I was not present for some of the fiascos that occurred after my death. Yet through these events, my grandson severely matured. He has surpassed even my expectations. But on the other hand with a teardrop from my eye, I also regret not being there to see these things come to pass."
– Yervant Yacoubian

CHAPTER 4

# Detonation

THE BLAST ROARED THROUGH THE streets like a lightning strike. It was deafening. Taking the path of least resistance fragments of glass, wood and other debris flew out of Aldo's storefront windows with a concomitant shockwave that instantly killed all of the gendarmes and their horses. The buildings directly across from the blast took the worst hit, blowing out windows and sending debris into the shops. After the blast, Aldo's shop imploded, collapsing onto itself followed by a huge ball of dust and smoke mushrooming into the air. Then there was silence.

"Der Voghormiah!¹" *Maybe I should have used just one stick,* Tavid pondered. He saw Aldo poke his head out of a blown-out window and felt relieved to see him emerge and approach the carriage and horses.

"Son of a bitch! Stupid sikishmek Ermeni!" Aldo muttered to himself. He quickly looked around outside, looking up and down the street to make sure there were no more gendarmes coming to surprise him. He bustled out the back door of the carpenter's shop, neglecting to thank the two puzzled old men for pulling him to safety. Five minutes later he met up with his two cousins and Tavid. Aldo spoke with his cousins in Romanian, slipped them a few lire, and sent them quickly on their way.

¹ Armenian: "Lord have mercy."

"If they are your cousins why do you have to pay them?" Tavid asked.

"Never mind! You almost killed me and half of the sector. Get in the carriage and let us be off!"

Both slung themselves onto the old wooden carriage. After retrieving Tavid's horse the two headed northeast toward the port, the vast waterfront district of Constantinople.

Constantinople's port area was like a city within itself, with numerous ships entering and exiting through the Bosporus[2] importing or exporting goods to other countries. Passenger boats and a few smaller military vessels were also anchored close to shore. With the coolness of autumn, the stale odors of over-ripened cargos from overdue voyages rose into the air.

Aldo's brother was a captain of a smaller merchant ship that flew a Romanian flag. He had been in Constantinople for a month, waiting for Aldo. His brother was the last cargo. All other purchases, deals and transactions had been completed; they were headed back to Romania where the goods would be sold. To elude suspicion from the local authorities, the ship was docked in one of the least bustling and desirable areas of the waterfront district.

Aldo's adrenalin began to subside. "Well, I bet you're sorry right now. Not because you almost killed me, but because you blew up all those precious uniforms that you could have had! Ha!"

"You are right. It makes me sick. Well, the day is young. I still have to take care of the port commander."

"Ahhh, I have news for you, my lucky Ermeni. You just killed him!" Aldo remarked.

"What?"

"He was the one in front of the shop giving orders before you blew it up! That was him. A little surprise visit I assume he was going to give us."

Tavid paused. "You are right. That was convenient. It could have easily gone the wrong way. Maybe we need to be more careful."

"Well I am not that worried anymore, Tavid. Everyone who was informed about us is dead. I doubt that they would have told anyone else, the selfish pigs. Now then, I need to change and bathe before this Turkish

---

[2] An ancient strait connecting the Black Sea and the Sea of Marmara and separating Turkey in Asia from Turkey from Europe; 32 kilometers long and ranging from one to two and a half kilometers wide.

blood starts to seep through my skin. Then we can go see my dear patient brother, drop the goods off then go to the bank."

"Aldo, we will go to Bank Switzeria first before we see your brother."

Aldo was annoyed.

"I do not know if I should smile or be angry that you trust no one including me. Your parents should have named you after your grandfather Yervant."

"And after we see your brother we will go out to breakfast? I am starving. Maybe your brother will come join us."

"Are you buying breakfast?" Aldo asked.

"Absolutely! We can go to Eftendelians. I can taste the food already! Fresh warm bread, choreg,[3] farm cheese, thick butter, large brown eggs, fresh cream, basterma,[4] bourma[5] for dessert and…"

"Ahhh?" Aldo interrupted. "The place we went to last spring? Yes, I remember. Was there something else you wanted that was not on the menu? Perhaps I should say you liked someone more than the food?" Aldo's smile grew wider.

"What? No! We're just friends. They have been friends of the family for years. They are almost relatives. I love seeing them all."

"I thought only Turks intermarried," Aldo muttered.

"Aldo! I am not getting married! She is only sixteen."

"What do you want to marry, an old lady?" Aldo remarked.

"I. Am. Not. Getting. Married!"

"Alright, my friend. Say, I have a better idea. I know of another place we could go to for breakfast that has just as magnificent food but the women are a bit old and wrinkled."

Tavid smiled. "Shut up. We are going to Eftendelians."

---

[3] Armenian: a delicious braided bread made with eggs, sesame seeds and spices.
[4] Turkish: a type of cured spicy meat.
[5] Armenian: a lighter adaptation of baklava that is rolled.

"I was by no means a perfect father or grandfather and made many mistakes throughout my life. But my father, who was a rebel in his time, once told me the following: *'Victory in life is the result of good decisions. Good decisions are the result of experience. Experience is the result of bad decisions.'* I can only hope that the decisions my children make are not as lethal as were my own."
– Yervant Yacoubian

CHAPTER 5

# Wish Come True

ALDO WAS IN DIRE NEED of a bath and change of clothes. As they pulled up to the bathhouse Aldo drove the carriage off to the side, grabbing an old cotton bag that he had put under the seat. "Wait," he told Tavid, disappearing into the place.

After Aldo was out of sight, Tavid took a sack he had stashed under the seat and jumped off the cart. Hiding behind the large wheel he exchanged the Kurdish outfit for a uniform from the sack, and neatly rewrapped his previous disguise. He used a rag to wipe the white ash from his face that had made his beard appear grey. Then he stowed the bag back on the cart and waited for Aldo.

The bathhouse was empty except for the elderly female caretaker. Aldo hastily apologized for his appearance and gave her five lire. She bowed her head to avoid looking at him and quickly offered him a couple of tattered towels.

Twenty minutes later, Aldo left the bathhouse carrying the bag with his bloody clothes. As he walked outside and turned toward his carriage, he looked up and saw a Turkish gendarme. Without hesitation, Aldo quickly turned around and started to walk back into the bathhouse.

"Aldo! Did you forget something?"

Aldo slowed down before turning to march right past the gendarme. He climbed onto the carriage, as did the gendarme.

"Not funny, Tavid! Not funny at all!" Aldo showed frustration.

"But Aldo, I thought this way I could protect you until you were safely on your way with Costel."

"Again, always thinking of me."

They were off. Barring the events of the morning, the city was having a peaceful day. The relaxed sun reflected the cooler colors of the beginning of autumn against the crisp and decorative architecture of Constantinople. Bank Switzeria was only twenty minutes away. It was a pleasant ride without incident except for the occasional lopsided stone-paved streets.

Arriving at the bank, there were two authentic gendarmes standing at the front door. Aldo gave Tavid a look. Usually, gendarmes would station themselves in areas where bribes could easily be obtained.

"How is your accent?" Aldo asked.

"Perfect." They disembarked.

"How are the profits today, comrades?" Tavid said in his best Turkish. The gendarmes looked at Tavid for a moment, then looked at each other.

"Agh. Not good. No one is coming to the bank today," one of the Turks replied.

"And do not think you can come and replace us here. This is our bank," the other Turk piped up.

"No, no. I am escorting the effendi[1] only, and I believe he has something for both of you." Prompted, Aldo reached into his overcoat pocket and pulled out five paper lire for each of the Turks.

"That is all? Five lire?" Tavid asked. "They deserve ten each, dear effendi!" Aldo said nothing, reached into his pocket again and gave the Turks each five more paper lire. More than satisfied, the Turks thanked Aldo and smiled at Tavid, opening the doors for both.

"Life is one big joke with you, is it not?" Aldo whispered.

"If you cannot enjoy life why live at all?" Tavid quipped. "Besides, how many Ermeni opium chemists do you know? One. And most of my village thinks I was born from dirt, except for the ones that knew my grandfather. Somehow, he was able to make them understand why he changed from the silk trade. I must make fun of life."

Aldo's glare cut deeper.

---

[1] Turkish: a name given to a man of property, authority, or education.

"I do hear what you are saying. If you hated what you do and wanted to change, you could. I know you could. Do not ever think that life has to be one way or another. You can change it. Just put your mind to it like you do now with your perfection with the opium. The same is true for me. I know I can change my life, get out of the black market if I want. And now, that is what I am going to do."

"Yes, but you have somewhere to escape. You can go back home to Romania. Where can I go?" Tavid asked.

Aldo paused. "You would be surprised."

The bank was empty as they approached the counter. Aldo transferred 3,200 Swiss francs into Tavid's bank account. Tavid knew this money offered him possibilities. Choices he may need some day.

As they left the gendarmes opened the doors for them, bid them farewell and invited them to come back soon.

They headed toward the port. Aldo was anxious to see his brother, and he wanted to load his merchandise and belongings onto the ship. As they approached the port more suspicious gendarmes eyed them, despite Tavid's uniform. Tavid would just return the stare, winning each standoff.

Aldo was greatly relieved to find his brother's ship. His brother Costel, was on deck, sitting in a lounge chair playing cards with one of his crew members. Aldo whistled. Seeing his brother, Costel smiled immediately, but it quickly faded when saw the would-be gendarme. Aldo quickly put his arm around Tavid.

Costel and his crew came down to the dock to greet them. There were many embraces and laughs but Tavid had no idea what they were saying. He could speak Armenian, Turkish, French and even some Greek but not Romanian. *"No need,"* his grandfather used to tell him. Though Aldo was fluent in Armenian. Taught by Tavid's grandfather years ago.

After loading his things onto the ship, Aldo returned and gave Tavid a bag of silks and blankets. But something had changed. Aldo had a look of unease.

"Give these to your mother, Tavid, with my blessings. It has been a long time since I have seen her and God knows if I will ever see her again." Aldo paused. "We cannot leave."

"What?"

"We cannot leave port. They have closed down the Bosporus."

Profanities issued from his lips followed by a heavy sigh. Then he continued. "It is the goddamn war. We should have left weeks ago. They have shut down all passage except for military vessels."

"For how long?"

"No way of telling right now. Weeks. Maybe months depending on where the war accelerates."

"Well, worse things have happened. I do not see why it is a big problem for you."

Aldo, disgusted, stared at Tavid but said nothing.

Costel came from the ship and they headed for breakfast.

The Eftendelians restaurant was in the Protestant Armenian sector of Constantinople, not far from the port. They entered through the rear via the kitchen. Tavid had never walked in through the front door; his grandfather Yervant had always taken him through the back. *"It is safer,"* he would say. The Eftendelians never seemed to mind. As they entered the mixture of aromas from freshly cut wild basil, garlic, cilantro and slowly simmering basterma was intoxicating.

"Paree Looees![2]" Tavid said in Armenian to the cooks, whose mouths gaped as they gasped in shock at the visitors. But one young boy ran from the kitchen into the dining hall, where his soft high-pitched voice was soon lost amidst the clatter and chatter.

Tavid continued into the dining room, amused. As the restaurant patrons spotted Tavid coming from the kitchen a wave of uneasiness swept from the front to the back of the hall, where again one could hear only the same young boy's high-pitched voice warning the proprietor of the uniformed gendarme. Turks in general did not come to this sector, let alone into the restaurant.

Eftendelians was not just a restaurant; it was a social meeting place for the local Protestant Armenians. As Protestants they were subject to protection from gendarmes or other official hooligans due to the close relationship of the German and Ottoman governments, allied during the war.

"Attention! The restaurant is surrounded! You are all under arrest for eating Armenian food without permission under a new enacted law by his eminence, Mehmet Pasha![3]" Tavid roared in Armenian.

---

[2] Armenian: "Good morning."

[3] Talaat (Mehmet Talaat Pasha 1874-1921), Minister of the Interior of Ottoman Turkey, 1913-1917 and Grand Vizier (Prime Minister) 1917-1918.

"Under arrest? What have we done, sir?" one elderly Armenian woman asked.

Mrs. Eftendelian walked over to Tavid, turned and addressed her patrons. "Do you not recognize Yervant Yacoubian's grandson? He is a prankster, not a real gendarme!"

Turning to Tavid she said, "Are you trying to ruin my business? What kind of greeting do you expect me to give you looking like that? A warm hug and a bachig?⁴"

"I am too old for that anyway," Tavid said.

"Not I!" pressed Aldo. "Seta, remember me? Aldo Petrescu?"

"Of course, Aldo," She embraced Aldo and kissed him on each cheek. "But why do you wait so long to come visit? Tavid has an excuse but you, you should come by more often. Promise me?" Seta Eftendelian was a tall beautiful woman and Aldo could never deny her.

"Now, sit down all of you."

The men sat at an open table near the back of the restaurant. There was no menu; Seta knew what to bring them for breakfast. When the food was served, Tavid's eyes lit up. The delectable dishes were just as Tavid had remembered: warm breads, fresh cheese, hot choreg, thick and cooled fresh cream, spiced tea and coffee. This was followed by fresh eggs mixed with thinly-sliced cured meats, spinach, onions and olive oil.

"How am I going to eat dessert after all of this?" Tavid asked.

"You will find a way. How is it that you are not a fat pig, the way you eat all the time?" Aldo smirked.

In spite of his athletic frame, Tavid was known for his voracious appetite and intense love for food, usually found only in the portliest of men. His dark facial features, softened only by his eyes, matched the hardness of his stature. Fire burned so hot and pure in his belly that not even poisons could survive, his mother claimed.

Tavid looked over to Aldo's brother. "You have been very quiet, Costel."

Costel looked at both his brother and Tavid, "I am worried about this war."

"What? The Germans and Austrians? Why? Just another war!" Tavid remarked.

"No, not just another war. This one looks bad. The Germans have already declared war on the Russians and the French. The Turks are in bed

---

⁴ Armenian: kiss.

with the Germans. It is becoming unsafe to sail the Black Sea, let alone the Mediterranean. Not that we can go anywhere right now."

Aldo added, "I have heard Great Britain has also declared war on the Germans. You hear many things here in the city."

"Yes, and we have seen many dead bodies floating along the coast and hearing horrible rumors down through the Dardanelles that the Turks are clearing out all the Greeks, pushing them out of Western Turkey, drafting them into the army to fight or work in labor battalions. They put them on death ships or work them until they drop," Costel exclaimed.

"Who is telling you these things?" Tavid demanded.

"Merchants, sailors on other ships tell me things they are not supposed to see or hear. I do not like it. The Turks hate everyone: Greeks, Romanians, too. But I feel they hate your people the most."

Tavid said nothing.

"What do you think about coming with us, Tavid?" insisted Costel. "Come and get the hell out of here when they open up the Bosporus."

"Leave and go where? Romania? Without my family? What would I do there? How do they treat Ermenis?"

"Tavid, Romania is not for you," Aldo interrupted, then started stroking his mustache nervously.

Costel turned to his brother. "Why not, Aldo, we could take care of him. There are other Ermenis. They would have…"

"Costel!" Aldo said harshly, then sighed. For a moment Aldo paused, put his hand across his forehead and looked down at the table. He looked up at Tavid trying to find the words to explain.

"There is something I have to tell you. Something you do not know." Aldo's face hardened as he pulled out the envelope that Tavid had seen hidden under the floorboards in his shop.

"Ahhh, your love letter," Tavid said.

"Not mine, yours," Aldo replied. Shaking his head, Aldo nervously tapped the envelope's still crisp edge on the table, looking at it then at Tavid.

"Your grandfather is not dead…"

Tavid's face froze, then outrage set in. Grabbing Aldo's shirt he pulled him close. "Why are you being an idiot? Just because I blew up your shop?"

Aldo, frustrated yet unfazed, built up the courage to repeat his confession.

"No, listen to me, damn it," Aldo said sternly, then whispered urgently, "Yervant is alive!"

Tavid was about to pick him up and throw him across the room when he noticed that Aldo was not looking at him anymore but gazing off behind Tavid with an entranced smile.

"Are you ready for dessert, my dear men?" Seta interrupted with a tray of desserts. "Madzoon with fresh Toot,⁵ Paghlava, Bourma?⁶ And stop talking so much business!" Without waiting for an answer, she walked off to take care of another table.

Tavid used every ounce of strength to blurt a calm *"thank you"* toward the retreating Seta, then reviewed the desserts before his eyes snapped back to Aldo. Though he wanted to yell at the top of his lungs, Tavid somehow managed a deadly whisper.

"What the hell do you mean, he is alive?"

Costel nervously surveyed the two; he'd be no match for either if the situation escalated. He hedged his bets, siding with Tavid. "Aldo, how can Yervant be alive? They killed him almost a year ago. You told me they found his b…"

"Costel, just listen! Tavid, that was not your grandfather's body!"

"Not his body? Not. His. Body?" He paused. "Where in Jehennem is he? What is in that letter?"

"He is in Cyprus. He has been there the entire time. But something must have gone wrong."

Tavid began to stand up from the table, enraged.

"Why are you trying to play this stupid joke on me?"

"Let me explain! I can see I need to start from the beginning. Remember about a year ago, there was that bastard Yesil? That Turkish piece of shit that was commanding the regiment in Bursa? Well, your grandfather was paying him off, remember?"

Tavid nodded, still standing, ready to pounce.

Aldo continued, "Yesil became greedy and threatened your grandfather that your mother would be put into a harem if he did not get all the gold from the sale of the opium resin. He also threatened to do some other things I would rather not mention. Your grandfather being as maniacal as you had this idea to dress up as a doctor and go to a hospital here in

---

⁵ Armenian yogurt with mulberry.
⁶ Armenian sweet pastries.

Constantinople. He was looking for someone who was dead or dying who
might look like him."

"Look like him?"

"Yes, yes. And it only took him three days. Three days! There was an
older Yahudi[7] who had just died and the family was poor. Your grandfather
told them that if the hospital could use the body for teaching younger
Turkish doctors, he could pay them seven gold lire. Well, they settled
for ten, took the money and the next thing you know your grandfather
showed up at the back of my shop with the dead body dressed in his
clothes. Then he wanted to go all the way to Bursa with a body that was
starting to smell very badly. And he wanted me to help him."

"Wait. Wait. Wait! Stop! Are you telling me that you are not joking
about this? My grandfather Yervant really is alive! Why would he…" It was
too much for Tavid to take in.

"I swore not to tell you! Please just let me finish."

"Swore to whom?"

Aldo sighed, then continued. "Anyway, he wanted me to help him with
the body. What was I going to say, no? I asked him why he did not go to
Bursa to find a body instead of having to drag this one all the way there.
But arguing with him is like…like arguing with you!" Aldo tried to smile
faintly.

Tavid was breathing deeply as he tried to stay in control.

"So we wrapped the body up, went to Bursa, and at night laid the body
in a trench near Yesil's command post. We made some knife wounds on
the body, put some gold coins and a forgery of your grandfather's Turkish
citizenship papers on the body and left. We waited until he was found
the next day. When Yesil found out, he went crazy and blamed two of his
lieutenants, had them both disciplined." Aldo paused.

"That is it?" Tavid hissed.

Aldo held up his hand. "If you could just sit down and eat, maybe I
could finish."

Tavid reluctantly sat, but did not touch the sweets.

"Yesil showed up dead a few days later. Kalkim Bey took over command,
named two new lieutenants—one being his son of course—and charged
the other lieutenants with murder and treason. And you know what
happened to them. So, as far as the Turks were concerned, Yervant was
dead. He could not stay here and risk being found out. So he left for

---

[7] Arabic/Hebrew: Jew.

Cyprus. He was supposed to have returned long ago to retrieve you and your family."

"That is ridiculous! Grandfather would not leave without us," Tavid protested.

Aldo paused. "We talked about that and I told him it was crazy to leave his family behind. I asked him why not take you and the rest of the family. But he was worried what the Turks would think or do if suddenly the entire family disappeared. He was certain that repercussions would have come down on your village. Plus, he told me he knew you'd be able to handle it. He had this idea that he wanted you to grow on your own...it would make you stronger."

Tavid said nothing as he silently reached for some dessert. Aldo and Costel allowed the young man to process this stunning news. He ate in silence. A first piece. Then another. And another. The brothers respectfully let it sink in, leaving the rest of the sweets to Tavid's recovery. Finally, he lifted his eyes.

"Grandfather is alive...and he is testing me again. Hmm. Always testing. Should have known. I should have known. Sikishmek![8]"

Tavid looked at Aldo then grabbed another crispy bourma.

"Why are you telling me this now? Why did you not tell me this months ago? How could he let us suffer? What is in the envelope? And why did he go to Cyprus?"

Aldo thrust the envelope at Tavid.

"Many questions, yes. I do not believe things went as he planned. I received this envelope about a month ago from another Romanian ship that was delivering goods to Cyprus. I believe it is from your grandfather. Something must have happened."

Tavid took the envelope and opened it slowly. Inside were four visas to Cyprus. One for each member of Tavid's family. There was also a letter in his grandfather's handwriting. It read: *Nareg Armenian School. Larnaca, Cyprus SE.* The letter read: *"Dear Baron[9] Tavid, you have been invited with your family to come to Larnaca and become a part of our community in Cyprus. Enclosed are your visas. May you have a safe journey."*

"What is he doing in Cyprus, Aldo? Is he a schoolteacher selling opium?" Tavid pranked.

---

[8] Turkish profanity.

[9] Armenian: formal greeting to a man, as in Mister. Pronounced "bah-rone."

Aldo laughed nervously and shook his head. "He was going to buy a vineyard. To grow grapes and produce wine. They have many plantations there. He wanted to try something different, to have it ready for all of you."

"You are joking this time?"

"Yes. I mean no! No more opium resin. No need for that in Cyprus. Oh, I forgot to tell you what happened to Yesil. Your grandfather took care of him. Not the lieutenants like Kalkim Bey had thought."

Tavid pressed his hands to his temples. This was too much at one time. He noticed Aldo and Costel smiling. Tavid turned around and his head and eyes seemed to clear. He, too, began to smile.

"It was common for Armenians like myself to arrange our children's marriages. To pick and blend our race as we saw fit. Always saying it was for their benefit. Some day, Tavid will learn that I did this to him as well. Not just for his benefit though, for mine."

– Yervant Yacoubian

# CHAPTER 6

# Siroon Karoun[1]
# (Sweet Spring)

"Mayrig[2] told me to come over and tell you that you are all being too serious," Seta's daughter said with a half smile.

"Karoun! How are you? Come, come!" Aldo said, motioning the girl to join them.

"I, I do not know if I am allowed," she murmured as she glanced over to her mother for some type of permission.

"It is fine. We are old friends. Come, please sit with us for a moment," Aldo insisted.

"Only if you are going to start being happy and enjoying yourselves. Most people come here to enjoy themselves. Why cannot you do the same?" Karoun asked sternly.

"Oh, I am sure if you sit with us for a moment, that will all change, Karoun." Aldo glanced knowingly at Tavid.

Tavid's mind was a blank now, partly from Aldo's confession and partly from seeing Karoun. He could not think of anything to say to her; he was happy just to gaze at her. He was amused by her attempt to be stern with them, how she was trying to have the manner of authority her mother

---

[1] Armenian: "sweet spring," pronounced "see-roon kah-roon."
[2] Armenian: mother.

wielded. She sat down at the table next to Tavid and across from Aldo. She was dressed for work wearing a blue blouse covered by a white apron. A matching scarf covered most of her dark brown braided hair. Her features were youthful yet dark, petite yet strong with distinct almond eyes.

"Karoun, I do not know if you remember my brother Costel?"

"Yes, of course. It has been a long time, but very nice to see you here. I do not know if I remember this boy though. He does look vaguely familiar." Karoun looked at Tavid. Tavid still just gazed at her and smiled.

"Ha! Now I know how to shut him up. Your Achilles' heel, Tavid!" Aldo laughed.

"May I ask, what is in the envelope? A love letter from someone? Or is it for me?" Karoun asked, then blushed.

"Ahmahn!³" the Romanian brothers sang in harmony.

"It is a letter from Cyprus inviting me to visit," Tavid replied. "I have some…some distant relatives there. We were discussing whether I should go or not."

"Really? We have relatives there too! My aunt Satenig lives there with her family."

"You? You have relatives there, too? Do you know where in Cyprus? What city?" Aldo inquired.

"I am not sure," Karoun turned around. "Mayrig!" she called to her mother.

"Mayrig, do you remember where in Cyprus Aunt Satenig lives?"

"Ehhh, the town name starts with an L. Oh, I cannot remember. Why do you ask?"

"Is it Larnaca?" Aldo asked.

"Yes, Larnaca. Beautiful place."

Someone else called to Seta from another table. Then Aldo started to laugh.

"I love coincidence!" exclaimed Aldo. "Larnaca is where Tavid's relatives are."

"Really, Tavid? Do you think you will go? May I see the letter?"

Tavid handed her the letter minus the visas.

"I do not know." Tavid was lying.

"This letter is from a school," declared Karoun. "Does this mean they are inviting you to come and live there?"

There was disappointment in her voice.

---

³ Translates as "oh my" or "uh oh."

"I am jealous. I wish I could go. I am tired of Constantinople, always having to watch where I go, whom I go with. Cyprus is supposed to be safe. Safe for us," Karoun said earnestly.

"Would you miss your friends? The restaurant? Anything?" Tavid asked.

"Maybe I would. However, I would like to live somewhere where I do not always have to hide from the Turks when I go out. My mother does not trust any of them. And you better not come in here again dressed like a gendarme or else she...we might not let you back in here!"

Seta called Karoun, who rose to leave the table.

"Karoun do you have to work all day?" Tavid asked.

"No, why?" she said smiling and blushed again.

"I have some things to take care of with Aldo, but later I would like to come back and visit."

"You better ask mother first. I will put in a good word for you." Smiling still, she thanked Aldo and Costel for coming and left the table to help her mother.

"Tavid, where are your courting skills?" Costel chided.

"He has a few other things on his mind right now, Costel. So, what do you think Tavid?" Aldo asked.

"What?"

"Come now! Cyprus? Larnaca? The Eftendelians? I figure Yervant is working on your wedding over there right now!" Aldo exclaimed.

"Well, I can think of worse things that grandfather has arranged for me," Tavid said matter of factly.

"My friend, you may change your mind after you have been married for awhile! Ha!" Costel and Aldo both laughed as Tavid just sneered at them.

"Well I am glad to see things have lightened up over here." Seta had just returned to their table and sat down next to Tavid. "Karoun asked me if you could come by and visit later. Did she ask you or was that your idea?"

"My idea, of course."

Although their families had been good friends for a long time, this was the first time Tavid had asked to visit with Karoun; such a request was viewed by Armenians as having serious intentions.

"I do not know if I want someone like you visiting my daughter. Look at you, dressed like a gendarme. Are you still selling opium? Guns too? What kind of future is that for my daughter? One day you will show up dead like your grandfather Yervant. Then what? Then what? Give me one reason why I should let you visit with my daughter?"

Tavid looked straight at Seta. "Good men get killed more than the bad ones. Not that I am a bad one but look at my father, who tried to break up a fight between two of his friends, got shot in the leg, died in the hospital from blood poisoning. What did he do to deserve that? Eh? Who is to say who is going to die and who is going to live? All I know is that I can take care of myself and I would always take care of the ones close to me."

"Do not forget he is goodlooking!" Costel added.

"And he is not poor!" Aldo said with a smile.

Tavid's face gleamed. "And I love your cooking," he said, polishing the ending.

"My cooking? You better love it!" Seta grabbed Tavid's hair. "Alright, her father is not going to like this but you can come over around seven o'clock. Dress nice and do not make me sorry!" Seta left the table.

Tavid looked over to Karoun and caught her watching. She looked away but then looked back at Tavid. Tavid frowned and shook his head at her, as if her mother had said no. Karoun quickly sidled up to her mother and a moment later was giving Tavid the evil eye. Tavid just smiled and winked.

Then, as if waking from a beautiful dream and realizing the hell he was in, Tavid whirled at Aldo. "We have to leave now, for Cyprus!"

"Without your family? You are not thinking straight. Besides we cannot leave Constantinople now. It is impossible!"

"Nothing is impossible," Tavid retorted.

Costel laughed, "This is impossible right now. We cannot even sail out through the Dardanelles. The British are sinking anything that tries to escape through the straits. It is a bad situation, but things will change."

"When? When will they change?" Tavid insisted.

Costel just shook his head.

"I could go back to Tchingiler, take my family and travel south by horseback along the railways to where it is only a few hundred kilometers to Cyp…"

"That would be suicide!" Aldo cried in a whispered yell. "Alone maybe you could make it, but with your family? Your mother and sister? How old is she now?"

Tavid did not answer.

"That is where all the shit is happening. That is the last place you want to take your family," Costel insisted.

"So what am I supposed to do, just sit around and wait for him to show up? For the war to end?"

Aldo shook his head. "I do not understand why he has not contacted us other than this letter. I am worried that something may have happened to him."

"Tavid, will you take some advice from an old friend?" Costel sighed as Tavid looked at him. "You do need to get out of this country, and the sooner the better. But I think you have some time yet. Assuming I can get back to Romania, I will be back in early spring and will be sailing to Athens, but first I can take you and your family to Cyprus. Who knows, maybe even Aldo will come along just to see your grandfather again."

Tavid was in shock, "You want me to wait until the spring? Are you serious?"

Costel held back his frustration. "Tavid, please listen to me. There is another problem; the winds this time of year are starting to come out of the northeast. Even if there was no war it would be nearly impossible to sail to Cyprus without an engine. And then there is the problem of finding petrol. We have to wait until early spring when the winds shift and come from the northwest. In the meantime I would suggest you focus on who you might take with you to Cyprus, and plan your return here from Tchingiler in the spring if not earlier."

"What are you talking about. Who I would take?" Tavid asked.

Aldo smirked and looked in the direction of Karoun.

Tavid sat back in his chair, folded his arms and stared at the Romanian. "If I find out this was all just a joke..."

"It is not, Tavid. I am sorry that I did not tell you earlier but your grandfather was very specific. And yes I would be glad to come along" he said, teeth glistening through his thick blonde mustache.

He continued, "Now if I was you, I would take some time and stay in Constantinople. Visit with Karoun. I want to get out of here just as badly as you, but we must keep our heads and be sensible."

Reluctantly, Tavid conceded and leaned back in his chair. "Damn your advice."

"And when you go back home, do not let anyone know of your plan to leave. No one. If the Turks you are paying off get wind of it..."

"Yes, yes. I know. So, when exactly will you be back, Costel?" Tavid asked.

"In late March, early April. The winds from the northwest are strong then. We can make good time to Cyprus. Maybe eight, ten days."

"How will I know you are coming for sure?" Tavid insisted.

"I am telling you now, I will be here. That is it!" Costel assured Tavid, who nodded.

"Alright then. In the spring. In the sweet spring."

"I miss my family intensely. But at times I am almost
leery of seeing them again. Especially Tavid. What will he
think of his grandfather now? Will they understand?"
– Yervant Yacoubian

# CHAPTER 7

# Second Home

THE THREE FRIENDS STOOD UP to leave Eftendelians. Tavid left a gold lira and
three piasters[1] on the table to pay for breakfast. They waved goodbye to
Seta and Karoun and exited through the kitchen as they had come.

The three talked for some time outside, Tavid asking even more
questions about his grandfather while Costel brainstormed on how and
when they would be able to sail to Cyprus.

"Maybe in a few days we will meet and go over this some more. I am
still not happy with having to wait until the spring to leave. Tonight I will
go to Eftendelians and fight with her father. Tomorrow night I am going to
see our old friend Aleksandar."

"Ahhh, my competitor. Be careful with him, Tavid. He pretends to be
your friend yet he can be a cutthroat."

"I am the one that told you that, Aldo. You think he is your brother!"

The three tussled their words for awhile longer then departed, Tavid to
his apartment and the Romanians to their ship. Tavid waved them off and
watched until they disappeared within the city. It was always sad to say
goodbye even for short periods of time.

---

[1] Lira (plural lire) and piasters are units of Turkish currency.

Tavid felt at ease with the Romanians and at times yearned for a bond like theirs, compared to his fragmented relationships back in Tchingiler. Most seemed to despise him or appeared jealous for what he did and with whom he associated. He was an enigma to them. Only the villagers who knew his grandfather well treated Tavid with respect. Then, for a moment, Tavid's mind raced back to his village Tchingiler and to the old vartabed.[2]

Tavid climbed back into the carriage and headed for his apartment. It had belonged to Yervant and Tavid had inherited it, so he thought. The irony of Aldo's strange revelation struck Tavid as he reached the cobblestone street and saw the caretaker talking to neighbors. As he approached, the group paused. Even though this was a safe haven for foreigners, most people still deferred to Turkish gendarmes to minimize any chance of harassment.

"Good afternoon," Tavid greeted them, smiling at the caretaker.

The woman realized that this was her Armenian tenant, raised her hands in the air and shook her head.

"My boy! I did not recognize you in that uniform. Welcome back!"

Tavid jumped off the carriage and embraced Ana. A stout woman with jet-black hair, she was always happy to see Tavid for not many of her tenants paid rent a year in advance and brought her gifts.

"What are you doing in that uniform?" said as she she eyed his costume.

"Working for the government, spying on officials, looking for blackmailers and thieves," Tavid spun his alibi.

"Ha, then you have been very busy! Come, let us get your horses fed and into the stables so we can visit." Tavid helped her onto the carriage and then climbed up himself as they rode toward the back of the residence where the stables were located. Ana helped Tavid tend to the horses. He removed a small parcel from the carriage and placed it in his pocket, also taking one of his shoulder bags from the carriage. There were no other horses in the stables and Tavid wondered if any of the other tenants were in.

"Come! Would you like some tea?" Ana asked.

"Yes, thank you." Tavid sat at a table behind the apartments near the stables while Ana went inside and returned with a tray of tea and fresh cream, honey, warm bread, butter and apricot preserves.

---

[2] Armenian celibate high priest.

Ana was not Armenian but she knew a thing or two about them, especially Tavid with his love of fresh foods. "Oh Ana, tea would have been more than enough. You are too kind."

"This is nothing and I know you enjoy it. I do not get many visitors these days you know with this war starting. None of my tenants are here. I am afraid I will not see them for quite awhile."

"Yes, I noticed there were no other horses in the stable."

"Hopefully this war will not last long. I am afraid to say that in a few years, Gorge will be old enough to be in the army and I am not looking forward to it. Losing a husband is one thing, but my son…I think I would kill myself."

"Ana! Do not think like that. Nothing is going to happen to him. Why not send him to Bulgaria to live with your father?"

"You are a mindreader, Tavid. We have been talking about it, but my son does not want to leave his friends."

"Does he like girls yet? If he does, find a nice Bulgarian to lure him away," Tavid said with a smile.

Ana laughed. "That is not a bad idea. I know his grandfather would enjoy looking for a girl for him. The problem is he might keep her for himself!"

"Ha! So he has not changed, eh?" Tavid laughed.

"No! The same adorable old man, my father is. And what about you? Have you found a girl yet?"

"I am not looking. But, I am going to see someone tonight."

"Ohhh! You are not looking, eh? Well if you are half as nice to her as you are to me, she will melt in your arms."

The two sipped their tea and Tavid let Ana talk. He had so much on his own mind and knew she relished the chance to chat. She was also important to him to help keep his belongings and secrets safe while he was away. While he was there she protected him from prying travelers or bounty hunters looking for certain opium dealers.

Cups empty, Tavid opened the shoulder bag he took from the carriage and retrieved a finely-wrapped package that he had obtained from Aldo's shop. He gave it to Ana. When she opened it she found a beautiful silk tablecloth with matching napkins made from linen.

"Tavid, this is lovely! Why do you bring me such things? You should save this for your mother, or at least I hope you think of her and buy her such beautiful things."

"Listen! You are the one who does too much. I am indebted to you. You watch over my residence and you take care of me as if I were your own son. It is the least I can do."

"And I will always treat you like a son. So get used to it! Thank you so much!"

"Now I have to ask you something and tell me the truth," Tavid said. "Are you still having your headaches?"

Ana nodded. "With the tenants gone I have had fewer worries around here, but occasionally yes, my head aches. Not as often, honestly. But I have used all of the Afyon.[3]"

Tavid reached into his pocket, pulled out the other small parcel he had taken from the carriage and handed it to Ana.

"Use these wisely, my caretaker. And use them sparingly. Remember these are not sweets to be…" Tavid stopped, then smiled at Ana.

"Yes, of course. But when my head feels like it could burst I thank God that you have helped me."

She put the parcel in her pocket and began to clean up the table.

"I am going to get another load and then rest for awhile," Tavid said.

"Alright, and make sure you change into something nice. Do not go visiting in that." Ana pointed and waved him off in his gendarme uniform.

Tavid nodded and started back toward the stables. Making sure he was alone, he went to the inside corner of the stable and pushed away the old straw. Grabbing a manure shovel, he dug down to reach a large wooden box. This was one of his grandfather's special hiding places. Tavid cleared away the excess dirt and removed the top cover. Inside were ammunition and two spare revolvers wrapped in hemp. He checked to make sure the hemp was dry and see if the guns showed any signs of rust. He removed the old straw in the box and replaced it with new straw just as his grandfather had taught him in the past. He started to think about how, up until this morning, these little things triggered memories of his grandfather, memories that would overwhelm him with sadness. He had trained himself to think of something else, someone he loved, his mother, younger brother and sister, but today he did not. Instead, he thought of his grandfather Yervant, alive in Cyprus. Could it be? For the first time in months, he felt anger toward his grandfather.

Walking over to the carriage, he again made sure no one was within sight. He removed his grandfather's rifle, partially dismantled it. He took

---

[3] Turkish: opium.

out the ammunition and cache of weapons he had collected this day, including the dynamite, and placed them all in the underground box. He covered it, replaced the dirt and straw, and then went up to his apartment with the rest of his belongings. Ana had already started a small fire for him in the stove and had left him some fresh coal to burn. She also had a pot of water heating on the stove.

The apartment was just two rooms, with a wash area and an old bathtub. It was more than adequate for Tavid. He changed out of his Turkish gendarme garb and washed up. Finally, even though it was still mid-day, he lay down on a cot, thought of Yervant then Karoun, of bringing this news to his mother and fell fast asleep.

"Karoun Eftendelian is a gem. The first time I saw her I dreamed a plan. Satenig, her aunt, had the same dream. But Armen Eftendelian, her father, well, we do not agree on most things, especially my dream. But deep down he is still a good Armenian. Maybe not perfect, but perfect in his own way."
– Yervant Yacoubian

CHAPTER 8

# Eftendelians

WHEN TAVID AWOKE, HE WAS disoriented. A moment later, remembering where he was he lit one of the lamps, checking the time with a Swiss watch he had purchased from a merchant in Constantinople. He made himself presentable for the visit to Karoun.

As was his ritual before traveling anywhere, he checked both of his revolvers, placed extra rounds in his pocket and a wickedly long dagger in one of his boots where a scabbard was sewn on the inside. He snatched his coat and a gift and went to the stables. Shaking off a chill, he saddled up his horse and rode off to the Armenian sector. Used to being the master of his circumstances, he was surprised at his apprehension over visiting Karoun. Smiling to himself, he wondered what he was getting into.

The Eftendelians lived in a flat directly above their restaurant. Tavid secured his horse and ascended the stairs. Before he could knock on the door, Karoun opened it.

"You are on time. Welcome."

As soon as she opened the door, he could smell the familiar scents emerging from an Armenian home. With the heady fragrance and her beautiful smile, his trepidation vanished. Karoun was far from the working girl he had seen earlier. No scarf covered her now unbraided hair, and in place of her apron was a beautiful burgundy, black and green dress.

"You look...different. Of course, I am on time," Tavid said tensely. Her hair was thick, dark and captivating.

"Different. Hmm! Do you like my dress? I made it myself."

"Yes, it is beautiful. But, well..."

"But what?"

"You have beautiful hair."

Tavid's face became a boyish grin.

"Yes, your eyes, your smile, your skin. All beautiful."

Karoun blushed.

"But is that a poppy seed between your teeth?" he added and pretended he was going to remove it with his hand. Instead he touched her cheek.

He caught Karoun offguard and at first she did not realize he was joking. Then she got that look on her face, the same look his mother would give him when he played one of his tricks.

"I only said that so I could touch you, Karoun," Tavid said quickly to neutralize his misstep.

Karoun blushed even deeper, then looked back to see if her parents were watching.

Tavid put his hands over hers and did not say another word.

"Hello, Tavid. Hrammetzek![1] What are you doing standing in the doorway? Close the door, it is cold out there!" Karoun's father bellowed.

Tavid and Karoun dropped their hands, embarrassed, and turned around.

"Hello Baron,[2]" Tavid said.

"Hello to you, Tavid! It is a good thing I was not at the restaurant this morning when you came in dressed in that uniform. I would have thrown you straight out. Tell me, did you kill a gendarme for his clothes or buy it on the black market from your Romanian friends?"

"Killed him, Baron, of course."

Karoun's eyes flew open. Baron Eftendelian stared at him, shaking his head. Tavid winked at Karoun, trying to ignore her father's bellowing.

---

[1] Armenian saying: "Come in, welcome," as when a meal is to be served or a guest comes to visit.
[2] Armenian: formal greeting to a man, as in Mister. Pronounced "bah-rone."

"You know, it is Armenians like you that make life a Jehennem³ for the rest of us. Whom do you think the Turks punish when one of their comrades comes up dead on the street? Eh?"

Looking at Karoun, Tavid answered.

"The Turks hate us, Baron. They hate…"

"No! Not all of us! Just the ones like you that do not follow the laws."

"Baba,⁴" Karoun said, looking anxiously at her father.

"Yes, yes. Let us not engage in battle until after dinner," Baron mused. "But I tell you the truth, he is lucky he is even here tonight after that stunt in the restaurant!"

Seta came from the kitchen and greeted Tavid after an approving look at his clothing. Tavid handed her a gift, a silk tablecloth. Seta thanked him with a hesitant kiss on the forehead. The four of them sat down at the dinner table.

"Where is your brother, Karoun?" Tavid asked.

Karoun looked at her father. "Shant is with some of his friends."

"That is too bad. I would have liked to see him. Is he still planning on studying to be a chemist?"

"No. He decided to take a job at the government building. He is working as an apprentice with one of the top Armenian representatives there," Baron interjected.

"He did? What made him change?"

"You mean who," Karoun whispered.

"He came to his senses," Baron paused. "Working in the government building will offer him more opportunities in the future. Possibly even moving up in politics as a community leader. We need influential people in the government and the Young Turks Party⁵ is encouraging this. That is the only way we can live at peace in the future," he lectured. "As a chemist, what can be his future? Work in the silk industry? Or become like you?"

"I see," Tavid replied. "Well I hope he is as excited about working with a gang of bashibazouks⁶ as he was about being a chemist. I suppose he is not here tonight because you were worried that I might try to change his mind. I would never let Shant follow my lifestyle. And if he ever tried, I

³ Turkish: hell.
⁴ Another Armenian way of saying Father.
⁵ The political party controlling the Ottoman Empire at this time.
⁶ Turkish: hooligan.

would show him the dark side of it. I am not proud of what I do. But it is all I know right now. It helps me and my family survive."

"I think you do what you need to do, and sometimes you seem to enjoy it. I cannot say I always approve of your ways. You are so much like your grandfather Yervant!"

Tavid did not respond to Baron because he was partially correct. There was a certain thrill from selling opium. He thrilled in being able to influence people who, under other circumstances, would not even notice him. And the killing, he did not mind that part either.

"Tavid, give me your plate," Seta said. Tavid noticed that she had cooked some of his favorite foods, including a tomato pie.[7] He felt Baron's judgment. To calm himself he again glanced at Karoun and studied her eyes.

"I think there are a lot of other things you could do, Tavid. Mayrig says if you put your mind to it, you could do almost anything," Karoun said.

Tavid looked at Seta, "You said that about me?"

"Maybe. Maybe my daughter is mixing you up with some other Armenian boy." She handed him his dish. Doing the same for her husband, she lightly patted his shoulder and he visibly relaxed at her touch.

As they ate, conversation bounced from Tavid talking about Tchingiler and his family to Karoun talking about the restaurant. Then Seta remembered something about Cyprus.

"Karoun, why did you ask me about Cyprus this morning?"

"Oh! Tavid has relatives there. He received a letter from…from Larnaca, I believe. They invited him to come there."

"Larnaca? That is where Seta's sister Satenig lives. So you have relatives there too, Tavid?" Baron inquired.

"Ehhh…from my mother's side. Cousins."

"Come to think of it, I have not heard from my sister in months. Usually we will receive a letter from her from time to time. Nothing since…are you considering going there, Tavid? I would love to go. It is supposed to be a beautiful island."

"Too many Greeks! Nothing like our city here," chortled Baron.

"I think we are going to go in early spring. I am going to take my mother, brother and sister," Tavid said with marked hesitation.

"Take me with you, too? They can watch the restaurant while I am gone," Seta pleaded, pointing to Baron and Karoun.

---

[7] Fresh baked bread covered with a rich tomato sauce with garlic, parsley and basil.

"Maybe Karoun could come too and Baron could handle the restaurant himself," Tavid said wishfully.

"Very funny. No one is going anywhere. It is too dangerous to be in the open seas with this new war going on," Baron uttered decisively.

After dinner, Baron and Tavid retired to the sitting room for dessert. Seta and Karoun brought out Armenian coffee, sweet braided bread and sliced melons. Tavid wanted to speak with Karoun alone, but knew it was not likely.

"You said your sister was here a few months ago?" Tavid asked Seta.

"It was closer to a year. I remember because it was when your grandfather died. She was a good friend of your grandfather's."

"How did she know him?"

"When she lived here before she married, she worked with my father at the restaurant. Your grandfather always came to visit with my father. They would sit and drink coffee and nibble on sweets for hours. He would always bring something for Satenig. Over the years your grandfather was like one of the family."

"I am sorry about your grandfather, Tavid. I wish I could have met him," Karoun said.

Tavid nodded. His eyes grew distant. He ate his dessert without a word.

The Baron eyed Tavid closely. Holding back from something.

The conversation then turned quite general. Tavid, like any other visitor, was not allowed to sit and visit with Karoun by herself; it was custom to sit with the entire family. Yet, Karoun and Tavid were able to communicate shyly through their indulgent, lingering gazes.

Finally, the evening was gone. Seta kissed him on both cheeks as did Karoun, the highlight of his visit. Baron waved him off, not even rising from his chair.

"You are welcome back anytime, Tavid," Seta said apprehensively, looking back at her husband for support.

"If you come by for breakfast again, Tavid, come early. It is not as busy and…the service is better." Karoun blushed.

"Ehhh? We have good service all the time; what nonsense are you speaking, daughter?" Baron bellowed once again.

"Yes. I will come early next time."

Tavid hurried down the stairs into the clear black night. The chill seemed gone, chased away by the memory of her lips on his cheek and the silky touch of her hair. Yes, he thought, an early breakfast without Baron's opinions. Thoughts of leaving for Cyprus seemed closer than they did before meeting with the Eftendelians. Tavid imagined taking Karoun and her family, even Baron with him.

Back at the apartment, Tavid stayed awake for hours pondering Yervant, Karoun, and his shifting plans.

"I am going to put it bluntly. Sometimes Armen Eftendelian
has his head up his ass. Now, some people do not even realize
they have this affliction; always being in the dark so to speak.
But at least with Armen, once he arrives at this destination
he will realize his mistake and try to find a suitable way out.
Trying to repeal the action but still not smelling like a rose."
    – Yervant Yacoubian

# CHAPTER 9

# Beautiful Girl

THE MUSTY ROOM WAS WARM and dark, but its inhabitant had a flame-red
blush on half her face and shivered uncontrollably. Hands wet and tingling
from wiping tears and hyperventilating. Slowly, she calmed her breathing
and ceased the flow of tears that were burning the left side of her face.
A final sigh altered her mood from panic to a pure depression. She sat
on the side of her bed, trying unsuccessfully to make sense of what had
just happened. The walls were closing in tight on her and soon she felt
she would die if nothing was done to alter the future. A final sigh raised
Karoun to her feet. She cleaned up and changed her clothes to work in the
restaurant.

As she entered the restaurant her mood and face were stoic, but soon
the tasks at hand within the restaurant buried Karoun's depression. Until
she saw Aldo and his brother Costel enter the restaurant. She experienced
a flush that nearly weakened her to the point of collapse, but then a flicker
of light flashed within her as she went to greet the two men and sat them
at a table off in a corner of the restaurant.

"Karoun, must we sit way over here? Put us closer to the kitchen where
we can feel and hear the soul of your restaurant!"

"This is a much better table for speaking of secrets." Karoun's hands were shaking. Aldo noticed.

"What is wrong, Karoun?" Aldo asked abruptly.

"What has happened to your face, Karoun?" Costel pressed.

"I, I must find Tavid. Do you know where I can find him?" She held her hands tightly to try and stop trembling.

"Sit down, Karoun. What has happened?" Costel repeated urgently.

Karoun quickly scanned the restaurant for her parents, then sat with the Romanians.

"Can you help me find Tavid? Tonight perhaps?"

Aldo and Costel eyed each other and nodded.

"We can have him come by the restaurant or to your apartment."

"No! No. Please. Can you take me to him?"

Aldo paused, "Beautiful girl, are you going to tell us what has happened?"

The tears flowed, as did her story of the morning's events. She explained how her father had returned late that morning to announce that he had finally secured a suitor for her. That the parents were well-respected in the Armenian Protestant community and their son of eighteen years was being bred and prepared for a vocation in the field of medicine. Possibly through the University of Constantinople. And tomorrow, both our families would be meeting at the Protestant church for an engagement ceremony!

"He told me that I would not see Tavid anymore. That he was a bad influence on me and the entire family. That this was for my own good, that I would thank him some day, that I would grow to love and respect this suitor, that life is safe here in the Armenian sector of Constantinople, and on and on he went. Until I could not take it any more and, and I...I yelled at my own father! I yelled at him." Her head dropped into her hands as she continued to weep.

"Karoun, did your father do that to your face?" Aldo asked.

Karoun could not answer.

Aldo continued, "Karoun, Tavid is going to be at a place called Aleksandar's tonight. I can take you there."

"You are going to take her where? Are you crazy? That is not a good idea and Tavid is, well, not going to like it!" Costel cautioned.

"Considering the circumstances I think it is the only thing to do right now. What do you think Tavid will say if we do not take her to him and he finds out after the ceremony? And do not worry, nothing will happen to her. I will be there with her."

"We will, brother. I am coming along too. Who says you get to have all the fun? I want to see this for myself."

They made plans to meet Karoun outside the restaurant after closing, and a very nervous Karoun left the Romanians, forgetting to take their food orders.

"Same thing happened to our own sister, remember, Aldo?"

Aldo paused. "Oh yes, I remember. That did not work out very well either. God rest his soul."

"Aleksandar, my Bulgarian contact, is quite the character. Most think he is a ruthless cutthroat, but in reality he rules his establishment with kindness and a warm heart even though he runs a brothel. Such scruples he has!"

– Yervant Yacoubian

# CHAPTER 10

# One Too Many

TAVID SLEPT ALMOST UNTIL NOON, thanks to the unusual quiet. He felt rested for a change, with no other tenants around. He lay on his cot for a few moments thinking of Karoun and last night's dinner, and wondered what the future would bring. He drifted off to a half-sleep as he dreamed of life on Cyprus with her and his family. At the realization he had missed his opportunity for an early breakfast with her, he jumped out of bed.

Tavid dressed as a Turkish merchant, complete with dress fez and a patch over one eye. It was a perfect costume for today's business. All his disguises were acquired from his grandfather. Yervant Yacoubian had some friends in Constantinople but had also acquired enough enemies to change his appearance frequently. How he dressed depended on the area of the city he was visiting. Today, Tavid felt momentarily giddy as he adjusted the fez. If Aldo's revelation about his grandfather were true, it would be truly astonishing.

Tavid would go visit Aldo's Bulgarian competitor Aleksandar and trade opium resin for weapons to sell back in Tchingiler. He spent most of the day looking for a horse to buy, but by evening he had come up empty-handed. He found plenty of short-haired black Friesians but not the pure ebony perfection he sought. He decided to visit Aleksandar and at least accomplish something for the day.

Tavid did not always enjoy visiting with Aleksandar. Frankly, he did not trust the Bulgarian, but Aleksandar had the best black market weapons and would trade at premium for the resin.

It was dusk when Tavid arrived at a cluster of deteriorating, mosaic-laden buildings. All but one was uninhabited. Strong scents and music filled the street from this place. He would find Aleksandar inside.

The street was nearly empty as he dismounted, tied his horse to a rail and approached the two short, stocky Bulgarian gatekeepers.

"Hay Allah!" Tavid bellowed. "Tell Aleksandar that his friend is here to see him."

"He is not available. But…for the right price we might be able to talk to him and see if he will consent to an…"

Tavid pulled out a revolver and put it to the guard's neck before he could finish.

"I promised Allah that I would kill at least one infidel a day, but today I have not fulfilled my promise. I suppose killing an eshek[1] like you would be just as good, eh?" Tavid threatened calmly, gritting his teeth with a smile. He then looked over at the other guard.

"If you are trying to decide what to do, I would suggest you go inside and tell Aleksandar that his old friend is here before I shoot off your comrade's head."

The guard thought for a moment then indignantly walked inside. Tavid then frisked the second guard, removing two revolvers and a large knife strapped to the back of his belt. He then grabbed the guard by the neck and shoved the barrel of his revolver into the guard's left cheek.

"What were the gendarmes doing here?" Tavid demanded.

The guard looked at him in horror.

"The gendarmes! What did they want?"

"No gendarmes here. Never!" The guard pleaded.

"Last chance, my almost dead friend. Why were the gendarmes here?" Tavid cocked the hammer back on the revolver.

"I swear! No gendarmes here ever! They do not come here!"

In reality, Tavid had not seen or heard of any gendarmes at Aleksandar's. He just wanted to make sure that all was safe within.

---

[1] Turkish: jackass.

Tavid then let go of the guard and moved off to the side so that he was not standing in front of the door, then crouched down.

"For your sake I hope your boss does not decide to just try and kill me by shooting through the door," he said, stifling a smile. The guard looked back at the door then started to move off to the side.

"And if you try to move away from the door I will shoot you first!"

The guard looked visibly shaken and in a few moments a group of people walked toward the door from inside. With a bang, the door burst open and out came Aleksandar with two bodyguards. Just as fast, the guard that was with Tavid dove for the ground, holding his head.

Aleksandar looked at him. "Sersem![2] What are you doing? Get up!" Then Aleksandar turned towards Tavid. "What are you standing out here for, my friend? Come in! Come in! Welcome!" Aleksandar put his arm around Tavid's shoulder and led him inside. One of the bodyguards stayed while the other followed behind Tavid.

"No wonder they did not want to let you in. You look like a Turk!"

Tavid removed his eyepatch and fez.

Aleksandar's private club was full of smoke reeking of opium, tobacco and perfumes. Music cut the thick air and there were plenty of young women for dance and companionship. For Tavid, being here was like entering a dream or nightmare, depending how matters went. Aleksandar took him to a large sitting room where he had Tavid recline on large sheepskin pillows. Aleksandar also sat next to him as a bodyguard waited by the door.

"Have Ivanka bring us something to eat and drink," he ordered the bodyguard.

"Tavid! Tavid, it is good to see you! We thought you were dead along with the Romani. How did you escape? What happened?"

For a moment, Tavid forgot that Aldo was supposed to be dead.

"The Turks were waiting for my shipment. They shot Aldo in the head and chest, but before he died he set off some dynamite. Blew them all to Jehennem. I was lucky. I got out just in time."

"Greedy Turks. They want everything from everyone. Bulgarians, Romanians, Armenians, everyone. Our women, our money, even our souls. Did all the opium go up in the blast?"

"Almost all of it. I do have some to trade if you are interested?"

---

[2] Turkish: idiot or stupid.

"Interested? Ahhh, of course I am! What are you looking for in trade? Something different this time? Maybe a young companion? You are old enough now," he laughed.

"I am looking for pistols and rifles. About a dozen or so. And only good ones. Not that shit you sell to others."

Tavid pulled out two small vials.

"Do you have anything worth trading for this?"

"Well, well! If it is as pure as the last lot, we should be able to do some good business tonight."

"It is better, my friend," Tavid replied. "Better every year."

Ivanka came in with a tray of dried fruit, chestnuts, pecans and a carafe of burgundy wine. She also brought Aleksandar's water pipe.

"Ah! Bless you my dear! Bless you. Tavid, you do not mind if I try the resin first?"

Tavid opened one of the vials of resin and placed one thick drop onto some hashish that was already in the pipe.

"Enjoy," he said.

"You are going to smoke with me, are you not, my young Ermeni?"

"You know me better than that, Aleksandar. Besides, I do not have any bodyguards that I can rely on like you."

"Nonsense! You are as safe as if you were my own son!" Aleksandar exclaimed. Aleksandar lit the water pipe, inhaled deeply, then a moment later exhaled the bluish-tinged smoke of the resin.

"Very smooth, yet the scent is so heavy...ahhh...yes, very potent, very intoxicating," he said, glassy-eyed with a faint smile. "How do you do it, Tavid?" He handed him the pipe, but again Tavid would not accept.

"Family secret," Tavid smiled.

Tavid would have had an advantage over the Bulgarian when it came to being able to handle the effects of the opium resin. From harvest time in late summer until after distribution of all the opium resin, Tavid's clothes and skin were contaminated. Initially during this time, Tavid would feel mildly intoxicated, but after a week or so the effect of the resin on his body would dissipate. Once all the resin was sold or traded and his clothes and skin had been cleansed, Tavid's body would go through an unfortunate withdrawal. He would drink special teas during this time to help cleanse his body and soul; after several days, Tavid's body would be free of all remnants of the opium. But for tonight at Aleksandar's, he would be able to smoke enough resin to make any other man lose consciousness yet still keep his wits about him. Aleksandar soon sent Ivanka out to fetch one of his men to bring in a cache of guns for Tavid to examine. A moment later, three large wooden boxes were placed in the room.

"Would you believe I bought these from an Ermeni?" Aleksandar said pointing to one of the crates.

"Oh? Who?"

"I do not know. I met him briefly but did not deal with him. My nephew heard that he was looking for a buyer. We met with him, inspected his merchandise and came to an understanding."

"I see. Is he still alive?"

"Ha! Yes of course. I am not in the habit of killing priests or ministers. At least he appeared to…"

"What? He was a priest?"

"Well, he was dressed like one, wore a collar, had the beard and wore a large silver cross. It would have been odd to ask. Besides, it did not matter."

"What was his name?"

"We did not ask, and he did not ask of ours. And now you are asking too many questions. Let us now get back to the business at hand."

Tavid got up from the pillows, opened up the crates and inspected the contents. A moment later, he smiled and looked at Aleksandar.

"Nice try you crafty old Bulgarian. Even the Ermeni's weapons are junk. Now can you have them bring out something worth trading for?"

Aleksandar shrugged, pretended to play dumb and then said something in Bulgarian to a bodyguard. A few minutes later he returned with a tattered old heavy rolled-up Oriental rug and dropped it on the floor in front of Tavid.

"What is rolled up inside? Your last customer that did not want to buy these guns?" Tavid said.

"No, no, no! Roll it open. You will see," Aleksandar urged.

"Ahhh, finally!" Tavid said as he perused the firearms inside the rug. He selected revolvers, pistols of differing calibers and some Russian Mosin rifles, all in good condition.

"I will trade for these if you have fresh ammunition that can be used with them."

Aleksandar gestured to the guard again, who a moment later brought out a smaller wooden crate filled with ammunition. Tavid inspected the ammunition and placed them with the guns.

"Fair trade, Aleksandar?" asked Tavid, handing him the vials of resin.

"A good trade. Though if you want, I would be willing to give you all three of the first crates for the resin. Why not? Take them and sell them back at your village. Most of those peasants will never even fire these guns. Why sell them these and have them go to waste?" As he pointed to the guns, Tavid decided to make the trade.

"You are right. God willing they may never have to use them. But just as I will not sell shit to you, I will not sell it to them."

"Ha! Yes. I see. Scruples you have, eh? Good. Very good. Now if we are done with business let us enjoy the rest of the evening!"

Aleksandar sent Ivanka to bring more food and some dancers, and then he took the water pipe and began to inhale.

Ivanka returned, followed by two young women carrying more trays of fruits and cheeses. Dressed in long white blouses with matching aprons, they placed these trays in front of Aleksandar and Tavid. A moment later, they tossed aside their outer garments to reveal flimsy dancing attire. Tavid eyed the food and the dancers. The resin mixed with the hashish in the air had a strange effect on all appetites.

Aleksandar signaled to one of the dancers to sit with Tavid. The perfumes of thick lavender and tart citrus were intoxicating as she cuddled next to him, stroking his hair affectionately. Tavid was having difficulty holding back the urge to accept Aleksandar's hospitality. Then the dancer moved over and straddled Tavid's lap.

"Do you like my little Tatiana?" asked Aleksandar.

Tavid shook his head at Aleksandar as he thought of Karoun.

Tatiana, not giving up, arched her back, reaching out to one of the trays of food and snatching some fruits. She then began feeding them to Tavid as she swiveled sensuously on his lap.

"Why not keep her for the night? Longer if you so please. The first night is my gift."

Tavid flashed back to last night's visit with Karoun. "Thank you, but I am not here for that. Such a gracious host you are."

"Agh! Always the same excuse. I do not offer my hospitality to everyone you know. You will be sorry some day, my Ermeni friend."

### Same Time, Eftendelian's Restaurant

Eftendelian's restaurant was closing as Karoun had slipped outside with a large shoulder bag to secretly meet the Romanians. As she waited, someone came from behind and placed a hand on her shoulder. Karoun started but when she saw it was her brother Shant she relaxed.

"What are you doing? Leaving without saying goodbye to your brother?"

"You do not understand. I was too scared to..."

"I do understand, Karoun. I am glad you are leaving. You are stronger than me. I should have left a long time ago. Are you going to try and find Tavid?"

"Yes, the Romanians will take me to him."

"Good. Tell Tavid I am on his side and I am going to tell our father off tomorrow after they figure out that you are gone."

"Do not say anything! You will just get yourself in trou..."

"I do not care. I am tired of it! Let him try and hit me too. I will..." Shant paused.

Karoun embraced her brother. "Leave me now. Make sure no one else sneaks up behind me, eh? Take care of yourself. I love you."

Shant returned her embrace and walked back into the restaurant.

It was not long before Aldo and Costel arrived. Seeing Karoun and her luggage, Aldo became apprehensive but said nothing. The three slipped through the corridors of Constantinople to eventually find themselves within sight of Aleksandar's.

"What kind of place is Tavid at? Why does he come here?" Karoun asked.

"Tavid trades with the owner. A Bulgarian. It, it is a place of song, women, good food and..."

"It is a brothel, Karoun." Costel interrupted his brother. "Make no mistake. But your Tavid is there only to trade. You can believe that."

The right side of Karoun's face now matched her left and she asked no more questions.

"Do you still want to go see him?" Costel added.

Karoun nodded.

When the three presented themselves to the entrance of Aleksandar's, the same two guards were present. But with this encounter Aldo offered them a bribe, finding out there was a Armenian that had just arrived who was meeting with their boss. Following a second bribe they were ushered in and escorted to the sitting room that Aleksandar and Tavid were in.

As they entered the room and Karoun saw Tavid initially she felt a fraction of relief until she realized that a half-naked woman was sitting on his lap. As Tavid looked up and saw Karoun, his breath stopped, his heart hesitated and his skin turned cold with sweat. Karoun was dumbstruck. The events of her day flashed before her and the reasons she had come to this place were fading rapidly. Anger started to build within her until the pressure was too great. She walked into the room, picked up one of the trays of food and hurled it at Tavid. Biting her lip she ran out of the room.

Tavid had managed to push the young woman on his lap out of the way from the flying saucer but was unable to dodge Karoun's wrath. The tray had sliced open Tavid's upper arm.

Quickly he sprung up to chase after her. Out in the hall he found her hyperventilating, tears flowing uncontrollably though she was desperately trying to get control of herself. Tavid grabbed her hands, but Karoun pulled them angrily away.

Behind Tavid was the complete entourage from the sitting room as well as the surrounding rooms seeking to ascertain what the commotion was. While Aleksandar was questioning his guards, Tavid tried desperately to get through to Karoun.

"What are you doing here?" Then looking over to the Romanians, "What are you doing here?" he yelled.

Finally, Karoun had enough composure to speak. "I asked them to bring me here. I thought I wanted to see you. But now…what have I done? Is this what you do? Who is that woman you were with? How could my father be right? How could you let him be right!" At that she began pounding her fist on Tavid's chest. Tavid let her finish, then slowly wrapped his hands around her and held her tight as the tears returned.

"This is not what it seems to be, Karoun." Tavid knew not what to say and just shook his head, almost to the point of tears himself.

"I am sorry Karoun, Please forgive me. But this is not what it seems to be," he repeated. He brought her face up to his. "Really. Please tell me what has happened that you are here."

Karoun shook her head and did not speak.

"Alright then, maybe someone else will tell me why you are here." Tavid slowly released Karoun and stepped back.

"Aldo, my dear friend! You are back from the dead, eh? Ha! It looks like Tavid has not told me the truth about you. We were just talking of you and, well your bullet wounds seem to have healed!" Aleksandar chuckled.

Tavid did not answer and continued to stare at the Romanian brothers.

"It was necessary to have most people think I was dead. Eventually the more intelligent people like yourself would realize that this was not true. It was only a matter of time," Aldo explained nonchalantly.

Aleksandar then shifted his attention on Karoun.

"And who is this beautiful woman that you have brought with you? And why is she so sad? Aleksandar's is a place of happiness and joy for most people and yet you are so sad."

"My name is Karoun and I came here to…" but she hesitated.

"Find Tavid? Ahhh, and now you are not so sure because of what you have seen, eh? Well, I tell you the truth, you are a very lucky woman, Karoun. Oh yes. Tavid only comes here to trade. Oh, he has some drink and I force him to indulge in the resin with me occasionally, and I also try to entice him with my women. You see I am always trying to get more money out of him or to try to get a better deal with our trades. But he does not bite. He does not fall for my traps," Aleksandar whispered in her ear. He followed with a chuckle, then continued.

"Yes. Yes, what you have seen here is distressing to you, I understand. But you have to make a decision now, my beautiful girl. Either you trust your Tavid or you do not. If you do, you must forgive him. If you do not, you must leave with your Romanian friends and I suspect never see him again. What is your decision, my child?"

Karoun looked at Tavid, then at the Romanians followed by the rest of the crowd.

"That is not a fair choice. I have to forgive him," Karoun said angrily.

"Ha! You have to, eh? That is good news! Now tell me, why are you here? What has happened that you have even brought a bag containing your belongings with you? Are you going on a trip? Maybe with Tavid?"

With that, the faces of Karoun, Tavid and even the Romanians began to glow. Karoun then told the story to Aleksandar as Tavid and the rest of the crowd listening tentatively.

"Ahhh, such a story! I see now why you have come here. But what is it that you expect Tavid to do? Take you away? To escape, the two of you? Where will you go? Back to his village? Are you willing to leave your family for Tavid?"

Karoun looked at Tavid for answers.

"Karoun, I have to take you back to your family and speak to your father." Karoun shook her head.

"Wrong answer, Tavid," Aleksandar whispered.

"I do not care what your damn father thinks, but your mother will never forgive me if I do not take you home," Tavid insisted.

"Do you care more about what her mother thinks, Tavid? She has left her family to be with you. Can you imagine how difficult it would be for her to do this thing? And you want to take her back? My friend, you do not always take my advice but I am going to give it to you one last time. If you take this young beautiful girl back to her parents you will have lost her forever, but if you take her with you, you just might fall in love." Aleksandar paused, "I tell you the truth. Do not worry about her parents. They will come around in time. And do not be too angry with your Romanian friends. They were trying to help you, eh?" Aleksandar smiled at Tavid.

"Tavid, anything you would like to say now to this wonderful girl?"

Tavid, realizing the wisdom of Aleksandar's words and also that he had just saved his life, looked over to Karoun and again asked for her forgiveness. Karoun walked up to Tavid and embraced him as he clutched her in return. The crowd applauded.

"Ahhh, nothing like a sad tale with a happy ending to sober one up, eh, Tavid? I will have my men help load up your horse when you are ready and maybe I will see you both again soon?"

"It appears anything is possible, Aleksander." With that, Tavid returned to the sitting room followed by Karoun and the rest. Tavid began loading his newly-purchased guns and ammunition into a large sack. Karoun watched him intensely. She wanted to ask about the guns. Tavid instinctively knew what was going through her mind.

"I sell these weapons to Armenians back at my village."

"But why? Why do they need guns?"

"Hopefully they will never need to use these. But many would like to have something just in case," he paused.

Karoun nodded in understanding.

Picking up his bag of weapons, Tavid gestured to Aleksandar to lead them out. Tavid offered his hand to Karoun and she accepted. The two Romanians fell on either side of the young couple, putting their arms around their respective shoulders.

"See Costel, I told you this was a good idea." Aldo smiled and looked at Tavid.

"Yes, it was his idea. I came along just in case." Costel looked at Tavid and smiled brightly.

Tavid shook his head and smiled back.

"A few minutes ago I was ready to throw both of you through a wall. But now, I can say that I would have done the same for you." He then whispered in Aldo's ear, "But I would have given you some warning."

Outside, Tavid and Aleksandar said their farewells. Tavid approached the guard he had held at gunpoint earlier. "I am sorry," he said, putting a gold lira in the palm of the guard's hand—more than a month's earnings for the man. Tavid and Aldo decided that they would meet up in a few days to go over their plans for the spring and maybe discuss how the Eftendelian family could be a part of this.

As they went into their separate directions, Tavid helped a still nervous Karoun onto his horse.

"I think I am scared."

"Do not be. I will not let anything happen to you. I promise."

Through her young and innocent eyes, she saw only the darkness of the night and her strange surroundings. Never had she ventured into this part of Constantinople.

To keep Karoun's mind off things, Tavid continued to talk to her while walking. It was late in the evening now and the only light came from the rising crescent moon and kerosene lamps shining through windows from within dwellings they passed.

They had only walked for about five minutes when two men came quietly from behind. Tavid did not hear them as he was still talking aloud to Karoun, trying to keep her mind at ease. Without warning the two silhouettes came upon Tavid, one striking him on the head with the butt end of a revolver. The other quickly grabbed the reins of the horse and violently yanked Karoun down. Tavid fell to the ground, knocked unconscious. As his face hit the ground he could just hear a stifled scream from Karoun and some distant laughing. Then there was silence.

"When Tavid was younger and I was teaching him the skills to protect himself, I would never brag or even talk about people that I had killed. This was not something to be discussed openly. It was private. Between you and God and not to be openly displayed with friends or at a dinner table. Even though his ferocity at times was more intense than my own, he has still obeyed this principle."

– Yervant Yacoubian

CHAPTER 11

# Bounty

"I TOLD YOU I COULD kill him with one blow, you sersem![1] said the one figure.

"Sikme![2] Alright, you get her first," the other said as they dragged Karoun kicking and screaming into a dwelling a few meters from the attack. The door opened, the three entered and the door slammed shut behind them.

Tavid stood in front of a beautiful waterfall, towering about three stories high. The skies were clear and peaceful with a warm and intermittent wind. He could feel the spray of the water on his face but the water was hot and not refreshing at all, almost like steam. For a moment, he felt at peace but then something started to bother him. He could hear and feel the waterfalls were alive and breathing life onto him. At the top of the falls was his grandfather, standing there with his hands on his head. His face came closer and closer to Tavid until it was right in front of him and his grandfather whispered, "Wake up…wake up, Hyevan![3]"

---

[1] Turkish: idiot.
[2] Turkish profanity.
[3] Turkish: wild animal.

Tavid first started to hear distant sounds but could not comprehend them. His eyes opened. Blood was dripping down his face, his horse inches away snorting a heavy mist onto his face.

*Where am I?* Tavid thought. *Why am I laying on the ground?* He felt the pain from the blow to his head and heard the muffled screams of Karoun. What had taken place all came back in a rush. The rage filled inside of him. He got up slowly on one knee and reached under the cuff of his pants to the boot where he kept his dagger.

With blade in hand, he stood up, wiped the blood off his face and ran into the closed door shoulder-first like a battering ram where the muffled sounds could be heard. The door flew open with a bang, like a detonation. Two meters in front of him was the first assailant, laughing with his hands on his hips and his back to Tavid while the second was on his knees trying to tie Karoun's hands and feet. Tavid hurled himself at the first and drove his blade through the assailant's upper back into his heart.

The blade was long enough that it escaped through the front of the man's chest, which he could see. The sheer horror of seeing the end of a knife coming through his skin froze any movement the man could have made. Still holding onto the embedded dagger, Tavid grabbed the man's roped pant belt with his other hand, and as the second assailant turned and stood Tavid drove the body of his comrade into him, pushing them both up against the wall. The exposed end of the dagger found its way into the second assailant's chest and the two were pinned face to face with one dagger, both comparing looks of terror. Tavid twisted the dagger hard, breaking ribs, then retrieved it from the two bodies.

With a gasp and moan, the two slid down the wall and dropped to the floor. Tavid took a quick sweep around the room then outside to make sure that there was no one else, cleaned his dagger off on one of the men's pants and grabbed each of the almost dead assailants' heads by the hair and violently snapped them to break their necks. Putting his dagger away, he looked at Karoun who was still screaming, trembling and trying to back away from Tavid on the floor. She did not realize it was him. His face was covered with his own blood and there was only a small kerosene lamp on a table in the room making the lighting dim.

"Soos[4] Karoun! They cannot hurt you now. They are dead."

---

[4] Armenian: "Be quiet!"

Tavid grabbed a kerchief from his pocket, wiped the blood from his face and tried to put pressure on the gaping wound on the top of his scalp. He cut Karoun loose and held his hand out to her but she just stared at him.

"Karoun! It is me, Tavid!"

Karoun reached out with trembling hand and Tavid pulled her to her feet.

"Are you alright?" he asked.

Karoun did not answer, staring at him with wide open eyes. Tears began to flow and she nodded her head. As she looked down at the two bodies, she began to tremble again.

"They are dead, Karoun," Tavid declared, kicking one of the bodies.

"Stand by the door and let me know if you see anyone coming or if you hear anything."

Tavid decided not to leave the bodies so close to Aleksandar's. He rifled through the dead men's pockets and found one hundred paper lire. He took their revolvers and ammunition, placing them with the cache from Aleksandar's. Rolling the bodies in some bedding he found, he hoisted them and tied them securely onto his horse. He considered setting the room afire but knew the flames could have easily spread to nearby places.

*I have a conscience,* he thought to himself. At that realization, he seemed surprised and amused. He closed the door and headed back to Aleksandar's, Karoun by his side and the two bodies on his horse.

"Where are we going?" Karoun asked, barely able to speak.

"Back to Aleksandar's. He will know where to dispose of the bodies. And maybe someone can tend to my head."

"You have not changed your mind, have you? You are not going to take me back home?" Karoun asked.

"Khentes eenches?[5] No, you are stuck with me now."

As they approached Aleksandar's the guards saw Tavid, and one went inside. A moment later, Aleksandar ran through the doors shaking his head and pointing his finger at Tavid.

"What are you doing? You cannot change your mind that easily," he exclaimed. Then he saw the blood still dripping down Tavid's face, Karoun's torn clothes and two wrapped bundles on the horse.

"We were attacked. I didn't know what to do with this garbage," Tavid said, gesturing toward the bodies.

---

[5] Armenian: "Are you crazy?"

"Yes, yes, my men will take care of that. Are you hurt, beautiful girl? Come inside and let us get you cleaned up. And you, Tavid? Forgot what part of the city you were in, eh?"

"I think I am going to need some needlework on my scalp. Do you have a good seamstress?"

"Yes, yes of course. Come inside."

In Bulgarian, Aleksandar called his men to come and take the bodies. As he did, Tavid noticed the horses at the stable, one of which appeared to be a black Friesian, a beauty. But Aleksandar quickly escorted Tavid and Karoun back inside.

"Ivanka! Come and take care of Karoun, quickly!" Aleksandar bellowed. "And get Mariam from the kitchen. We have a customer for her."

"Here, sit down, sit down. Tell me now what happened."

Tavid sighed. "We were only five minutes away. Two men jumped me from behind and knocked me unconscious, I think with a revolver. When I woke up, they were inside a nearby dwelling trying to rape her...so I killed them."

As Tavid told the story, an elderly woman walked into the room with a sewing basket and steaming towels. Aleksandar told her what had happened. The seamstress bowed her head, greeting Tavid, and examined his wound.

"O'ho! That's quite a gash," she said as she called another woman for more towels, distilled spirits and hot water.

Tavid sat as if praying, elbows resting on his thighs. The seamstress tore off strips of towel, placing them in the hot water and then squeezing them out. Carefully she cleaned and examined Tavid's wound.

"Ahhh. Down to the bone. You are lucky it did not crack like an egg. You must have a strong head, my dear Ermeni."

"You mean a thick skull. Ha!" Aleksandar laughed, sitting down in one of the other chairs.

After cleaning the wound with alcohol, she reached into her bag, pulling out a curved needle and some white thread. She began to sew Tavid's wound. He felt some pulling and an occasional sharp pain; mostly he tolerated Mariam's needlework.

At the back of the building, Aleksandar's men pulled the bodies from Tavid's horse and unfurled them from the sheets. When they saw the faces of the two dead men, they froze. Reflexively, they pulled their revolvers.

"Go get Aleksandar. I will stay here," one guard said to the other, before putting his gun away. "Quick. Go!"

The guard upon finding Aleksandar excused himself and whispered his urgent message. Wide-eyed, Aleksandar ran out of the room. Tavid tried to sit up to see where he was going.

"Please, young man. Do not move unless you do not care where this needle goes," warned the seamstress.

At the back of the building, Aleksandar could not believe what he saw, instinctively pulling his gun out as well. He kicked each of the bodies to make sure they were dead.

"Master, they are dead. I, too, kicked them to make sure," the one guard said.

Aleksandar just stood there and stared at the two bodies.

"You know what to do with them?" Aleksandar asked.

The two guards nodded.

"Make it quick then!" He handed each of the guards a gold coin.

Aleksandar walked back into his establishment and into the room where Tavid was being treated. Ivanka and Karoun had returned as well. Karoun had bathed and changed her clothes. Tavid could tell Aleksandar had walked back in and something was amiss.

"What is it, Aleksandar? Did I kill a friend? Relative maybe?" Tavid asked.

Aleksandar just paced the room, looking down at the floor and occasionally at Tavid.

"You killed…you killed the Gemlik brothers…the goddamn Gemliks!" Everyone stopped and looked at Aleksandar, everyone except Tavid who had been instructed not to move. He could feel what he thought was tension in the air.

"Is someone going to tell me if I am about to get shot?" Tavid said.

"My young customer here killed them, Aleksandar?" Mariam asked.

Aleksandar nodded.

Mariam sighed, then laughed, "God bless your mother for having you, my child."

Everyone smiled, laughed and praised God. Everyone except Aleksandar.

"You are lucky you have only this wound to show after encountering those two devils. They have been terrorizing our neighborhood for months. Gemliks killed one of our guards, beat and raped one of my girls," Mariam explained.

She continued while looking at Aleksandar. "And there is something else too. They tried to kill our Master. For that, he put a bounty on their heads."

Tavid's eyes widened. He could not help but raise his head to see Aleksandar's expression.

"Bounty? How much bounty?"

"Uhhh," Aleksandar mumbled some numbers under his breath.

"What? How much?" Tavid repeated.

"A thousand lire for each," Mariam said. Aleksandar was still looking down at his feet.

"Ho! Two thousand lire. No wonder you are not smiling!"

Aleksandar tried to smile, "I am not sure what is more shocking. The fact that these two bastards are finally dead and out of my hair, or that I am two thousand lire poorer." Again, Aleksandar tried to smile, leaving the room again.

"It is a good ending for a bad night, eh? And I am just about finished with you here. Quite the headache you will have tomorrow, my young customer," Mariam cautioned Tavid. She completed her embroidery work, and again cleaned the outside of the wound with distilled spirits.

"Ahhh now, finished! I tell the truth, a doctor could not have done as good of a repair. Now, do not touch it. And if it starts to itch, do not yield to the temptation! With the spirits in this bottle, clean the wound twice a day, otherwise keep the wound dry for at least five days. You can have someone take out the threads in two weeks or come back here if you like. I like to see how my work ends up," Mariam said, handing Tavid the bottle of spirits.

Aleksandar walked back in with another sigh. "On my word, here you are my friend. Two thousand lire. Half in coin, half in paper. Well worth it. Well worth it," he tried convincing himself as he handed Tavid the bounty.

"Aleksandar, I believe I saw a horse outside that one of your men had, a pure black Friesian. Were my eyes correct?"

"Yes...yes, of course, a bull of a horse he is. Too large for you to ride though."

"I am in need of a young strong Friesian and I would be willing to give you half of my reward here for that horse."

"A thousand lire?" Aleksandar played with his mustache and shook his head. "I do not know. That horse was a special gift to me from one of my closest friends. It would not be right. I would not feel...comfortable selling such a..."

"Fifteen hundred lire," Tavid interrupted.

"Two thousand lire and I will also let you have the bridle as well," Aleksandar offered.

"It is done! But I must inspect the horse first."

"Ha, ha hahhh!" Aleksandar hooted, patting Tavid on the back. "It is always a pleasure to see you, always a pleasure! The Gemlik brothers for a black Friesian! I will have sweet dreams from this trade. Sweet dreams! Come, let us go inspect your new prize!"

The two went outside and Aleksandar commanded one of his men to bring the black Friesian around to the front. As he did, Tavid inspected the horse's gait and posture. She appeared to be a young Friesian of good stature and of pure black hue, even on her long mane. Tavid first tried to sense the horse's disposition; he checked the horse's hoofs, teeth and stroked its legs, checking their girth and strength.

Tavid nodded to Aleksandar and handed him back the bounty he had collected for the Gemlik brothers. Aleksandar chuckled and laughed aloud while embracing Tavid.

"Stay the night, Tavid. Stay here and leave in the morning," Aleksandar offered.

"Thank you, my friend, but I will sleep better in my own bed."

Ivanka then whispered something in Aleksandar's ear.

"Hmmm. Yes but perhaps it is not safe to travel at this time of night alone. If you must leave tonight, will you let my men and I escort you back home?"

"To the northeast sector. The rest of the way will be safe," Tavid replied.

Aleksandar smiled and laughed to himself. "Yes, just to the sector."

He then rounded up some of his men to get ready for a midnight ride.

Tavid thanked Mariam and handed her one hundred and fifty piasters. At first she refused to take it, but Tavid insisted. He also gave Ivanka an additional fifty piasters and thanked her for her hospitality.

"What are you going to do with the bodies, Aleksandar? Dump them in the Bosporus?" Tavid inquired.

"No. Too messy. The bodies can float back up after awhile from the currents. No, we burn them."

"Burn them? Where?"

"Mmm, I have a friend. A blacksmith by trade. Very hot furnace. Burns everything, even the bones. So there is no trace left, just dust in the wind. Very clean but he charges me a gold piece for every body. I tell him his prices are outrageous and he just smiles at me and says, "Yes, they are!" We both laugh and I pay him his fee."

Tavid nodded his head slowly in agreement. He put his hand up to his scalp but remembered what Mariam had told him and brought his hand back down.

They walked out to the front of Aleksandar's where his horse and escort were waiting. Tavid checked to make sure all of his newly-acquired weapons were still in place. The men brought an additional smaller horse for Karoun. The farewells were short this time.

Except for the encounter with the now-dead Gemlik brothers, it was a beautiful night. Clear skies with a waning gibbous moon revealed just enough light streaming from the houses to see one's way through the streets. The air was crisp and clear.

It was an uneventful ride back to Tavid's neighborhood; the entire group was getting tired and there was only some small talk between them. When they neared the apartment, Tavid had Aleksandar's men take Karoun's horse and gave each of the escorts a few piasters. Tavid waved them on and headed with Karoun back to the apartment, checking behind occasionally to make sure he was not being followed.

"Let us see if we can make it back this time in one piece, eh, Karoun?"

"Please, do not joke like that."

"This is a safe neighborhood. But I will keep my eyes and ears open until we get there," said Tavid while Karoun did the same.

Upon arriving at the apartments he went around back and settled the two horses in the stables. Too tired to secure his weapons in the underground hiding place, he removed the bags and the two of them went inside. Once there he lit a kerosene lantern and started a fire in the stove to heat some water for tea and warm up the apartment. He brought out additional bedding and placed it near the stove where Karoun could sleep.

"I hope this will be comfortable for you. Tomorrow we can go to a local store and buy additional bedding," Tavid said apologetically.

"This is fine. I can sleep here."

"There is another room if you need to change or anything else," Tavid said, pointing to the room with the bath. Karoun nodded. Her hands were shaking.

"Would you like some tea?" Tavid asked.

Karoun just nodded.

Out of the cupboard Tavid took some mild tea leaves, honey and a sifter. For himself, he took some dried willow tree leaf, placing this in another sifter for tea. In the past his mother had taught him to use this type of tea for pains. Tavid did not want to take anything stronger for his worsening headache.

The two sat and drank their tea, both tired and saying little. After a few minutes Tavid took off his shoes and settled into his bedding; Karoun did the same. As he lay down his head began to throb so much that he doubled up his feathered pillows to raise his head.

As drifted off he heard Karoun's quiet sobbing. He rose, went to her and gently put his hand on her head, softly stroking her hair. She reached for his hand, clutching it tightly until she was asleep. Falling back into his own space in the quiet room, he was asleep in an instant.

"I introduced Tavid to Malachi early on in his youth. I wanted to get him used to dealing with people other than Armenians. I also knew that if anything should ever happen to me that Malachi would be one soul Tavid could trust in a time of need."
– Yervant Yacoubian

# CHAPTER 12

# The Messenger

THE ROOM FILLED WITH THE bright morning sun and awoke Karoun. As her eyes opened she looked around, not recognizing her surroundings but flashing back to the events of the day before, although these events seemed very far away. She got up and put more coal in the stove.

She sat in a chair waiting for Tavid to awaken but then sleepiness returned to her eyes. She quietly laid down on the floor next to Tavid making sure not to disturb him and soon she again fell back asleep. When Tavid finally awoke, he saw her fast asleep on the hard floor. Her face, an arms-reach away. How wonderful it would be, he thought to be able to wake up to this every morning. Then slowly his head began to ache from his head wound but he lay still just gazing at Karoun. Eventually she woke, first startled at seeing Tavid gazing at her, then smiled.

"Paree Looees,[1]" Tavid whispered. "Are you alright?"

Karoun smiled and nodded. "How is your head?"

"Mmmm, not too bad. Not too bad. I thought it would be worse."

Karoun started to wrinkle her nose, smelling the dried blood on Tavid's scalp.

---

[1] Armenian: "Good morning."

"You killed those two pretty easily last night. Have you done that a lot? Does it bother you?"

Tavid shook his head, then winced in pain. "What else was I to do last night with those two? Scold them for trying to kill me and what they were about to do to you? No. There was only one thing to do with them. And no, it does not bother me. I cannot let it bother me."

"Who taught you these things, your father?"

"My grandfather."

Karoun's stomach began to growl. "Are you hungry? There are some cracker breads and jams in the cupboard. But we can also go out for some breakfast."

She slowly got up off the floor and went to the cupboard and took some bread, heating it on the stove and adding some apricot preserves. She made more tea and again looked around her new dwelling.

"I am sorry about what happened with your parents, and what happened last night. Do you want to talk about it?" Tavid asked.

"Sometime. Maybe. But not now."

"Is this your father?" Karoun pointed to a picture on the wall.

"No, that is my grandfather. My father is to the right." Karoun looked intently at the photo, at Tavid's mother and his siblings, trying to imagine what they would be like.

"Do you think they will like me?" she asked.

"Well, as long as you do not throw a tray of food at them," Tavid teased as he slowly got up, putting his boots and coat on.

"Where are you going?" Karoun asked nervously.

Tavid laughed. "Just to get some water from the well. Do you want to come along? Or why not get it for me?"

He continued. "The well is to the right of the stables. And if you see a woman out there, her name is Ana. Introduce yourself to her. She is my very kind landlady." Tavid gave Karoun his coat and as she put it on her arms were swallowed in its size. They both laughed as she went out.

Still feeling tired, Tavid thought he would lie back down for a moment and as he did, he fell back into a light intermittent sleep. As he dreamed, it occurred to him that Karoun had not returned. His eyes opened as he jumped up to look outside. With a sigh of relief, he saw her sitting with Ana. He lay back down again to stop his head from pounding. Putting his boots on, he stumbled outside towards the two, looking as if he had a little too many spirits the night before.

"My, how you look this morning!" Ana said to him.

Tavid just smiled and sat down at the table. Ana had already brought out tea and breakfast for Karoun.

"How long have you two been out here?" Tavid asked, still squinting his eyes from the bright late morning sun.

"Long enough to know what happened last night. Are you ready for some breakfast?"

Tavid nodded and Ana went into her apartment to get some fresh breakfast and teas.

"I usually do not sleep this late, Karoun. Must be the hit on the head."

"And the opium?" Karoun added.

Tavid hesitated, "I did not have any last night."

Karoun snickered at Tavid's reply.

While waiting for breakfast, Tavid took the cache of guns he had purchased from Aleksandar's the night before and secured them in the stables with the rest of his weapons. He fed and watered the horses, finishing up just in time as Ana came back out and he started to eat his breakfast.

"You really need to get cleaned up, Tavid. You still have dried blood everywhere and you smell of death. Karoun, can you take the water and start to heat it on the stove so Tavid can bathe after breakfast?" Ana asked.

Without hesitation Karoun took the two pails to Tavid's apartment.

"How much did she tell you again?" Tavid asked.

"Everything I believe. Do you have any plans for today?"

"I thought I would take her to market with me. I have to buy some spices for mother and some additional bedding for the apartment."

"Ohf! Do not worry about the bedding. I will take care of that. Tavid, do you have medicine to help treat your wounds?"

"Ah. Good question. I will have to stop at an apothecary today as well."

After finishing his breakfast, he returned to the apartment. Karoun had just finished heating the water, poured it into the bath and was about to go get more water. They exchanged smiles and Tavid proceeded to the bath. Tavid had started to grow his beard and heavy mustache before coming to Constantinople. Now looking into the mirror, he decided not to shave but to let it grow in thicker.

Painstakingly, he tried to clean out all the dried blood from his hair without wetting the wound. Karoun returned with more hot water and placed it just inside the door. After his bath, Tavid opened up one of the

trunks of clothes that his grandfather had at the apartment and changed
into a more traditional Turkish outfit with Salvor,[2] a cloth belt and a jacket.
He topped his head with a fez.[3]

"I am going to an apothecary and to market to pick up some spices.
Would you like to come along?"

"Yes, of course!"

Rarely had Karoun had a chance to go anywhere, making the errand at
hand seem like an adventure. Tavid would be dressed as a Turk. Karoun's
dress was neutral with a European style.

It was another sunny but cool day in Constantinople. A slight wind
blew from the northwest, bringing with it the scent of the Bosporus. The
cobblestone streets were quiet this day. Peaceful.

After a while, Karoun asked Tavid, "You do not mind me being here?"

"Mind? Mind that I get to spend more time with you? Without having
to listen to your father's insults? Without seeing the worried look on your
mother's face as she wonders if I am the right one for you? I could not be
happier," he said with sincerity. Karoun beamed.

Their first destination was an apothecary at which Tavid knew the
owner. In the past, he had purchased willow leaf for aches and pains, witch
hazel for skin irritations whether for himself or his horse, bandages for
wounds and other items. Once inside, Tavid saw the chemist in the back
helping another customer.

"Yahudi[4] Malachi![5]" Tavid called.

The chemist winced and turned around. Even though it was a knee jerk
reaction to turn and see who was bellowing in his store, he already knew
who it was.

"Agh, Kaloustian. Just a minute, please," Malachi said.

Finishing with his customer, he came to greet Tavid. He was an older
man, nearly the age of Tavid's grandfather Yervant, with pure white
hair, thick as a youth's, complemented by a matching goatee. Malachi's
dress and accent were European but Tavid knew him as a Jew. Malachi
did not reveal that to everyone. Putting his hands out, he grasped Tavid's
shoulders.

---

[2] Turkish: full baggy pant.
[3] Traditional Turkish hat.
[4] Hebrew: men from Judea.
[5] Hebrew: "my messenger," pronounced "mal-a-kie."

"So you have come again to irritate me? Why do you insist on advertising to the whole city what tribe I come from?"

"Why does it have to be a secret? This is a safe sector. All Europeans. No one is going to give you any trouble here."

"Please, as a favor to an old man?"

Tavid smiled mischievously. Then, Malachi greeted Karoun.

"What can I do for you today, Tavid?"

"Since you usually like to give me advice, what do you think of this?" Tavid took off his fez.

"Oh-ho! What do we have here? How did this happen?" he said, examining Tavid's scalp.

"Butt of a pistol I believe. The seamstress gave me some alcohol spirits to put on it once a day," Tavid said.

"She did well for you. Yes, use the spirits once a day. Let me get you some ointments."

Malachi found the ointments and instructed Tavid to place on his head wound once a day.

"Here you are, Kaloustian. Now then, do you have time to sit with an old man and visit over some coffee and sweets?"

Tavid looked at Karoun. "Yes of course."

They sat down in the back of the apothecary with Malachi.

"So now, this is quite a change with you, Tavid. You usually come by yourself or in the past with your grandfather, God rest his soul. Now you show up with this beautiful girl. How are you related to Tavid?" Malachi switched to Karoun.

"She is not related to me, yet," Tavid paused, eyeing Malachi.

Karoun blushed and kicked Tavid under the table. A smirk erupted into a full smile from Tavid and became contagious throughout the table.

"That can be a wonderful thing. A wonderful thing. Now, let us first talk of this new war and what consequences it will have for you as well as me."

Tavid started, "There are more soldiers in Constantinople. It will be harder, if not impossible, for those inclined to leave or escape the country. They will try to draft more men into the military including Greeks, Jews, Ermenis; they will probably raise the taxes."

Malachi sighed. "Those are the obvious! Is that all you see, my young and naïve friend? Remember, I have lived with the Turk all my life. Whether it was here or in Palestine, I see the same things happening over and over. History repeats itself. Let me tell you about the Turk when there is a war," Malachi sighed. "What better time to eliminate political opponents and so-called insurgents under the label of traitor, conspirator or spy. And the many Greeks, Jews, and Ermenis. What better time to eliminate these, these infidels, these troublemakers, under the guise of quelling a rebellion. Yes, kill the women and children too for they are all the same. Draft the men into the military and they will never return after the war; they are either killed or put into labor battalions never to return unless the occasional man escapes by his own cunning or luck. I am not looking forward to this new war."

"Why not leave then? Escape to some other country. Maybe the Americas?" Tavid suggested.

"Ahhh…novel idea. But where is it safe for a Yahudi, eh? No, my best strategy is to stay right here, invisible. Here only the occasional Turk comes into my store. Mostly they are European. And when the Turk does come, either I will not charge him for my services or I give him twice what he needs. Yes, to stay invisible to the Turk but visible in the eyes of the Europeans. That is how I will stay safe during this war."

"Free? You are giving away your goods for free? Why not add a little arsenic to their medicines for free then?" Tavid mocked.

Malachi frowned.

Tavid continued, "That reminds me of a tale my grandfather used to tell me in Ermeni. It loses something in the translation but it goes something like this: Once there was a Yahudi merchant who was a great businessman and prospered. One day a poor Ermeni merchant opened his business next to the great merchant. And within a short time, the Ermeni ran the Yahudi out of business. He must have been giving his goods away, too!" Tavid exclaimed.

"Hmmm. That may be a true story, my young friend, but let me finish the tale for you. The Ermeni Merchant ran the Yahudi out of business because he extended credit to his customers including the poor Turk where the Yahudi would not. And before long, the Turk was in quite a bit of debt to the Ermeni. Then, one day with a little prodding from the Turkish Village Chief and his retainers, the Turks kill the Ermeni merchant and wiped out their debt. Then they take all of the Ermeni's possessions including his family. A little while later when all is quiet, the Yahudi merchant returns, opens shop again and as before prospers silently and extends no credit."

Malachi was not smiling. Neither was Tavid.

"Tavid, the Turks delight in these types of things you know. It gives them a chance to divide up unearned property. And during a war it can happen on a massive scale as in recent years gone by."

"Why do you enjoy telling me these things, Malachi?" Tavid asked.

"Enjoy? I do not enjoy telling you or even thinking these things. But they cannot be forgotten. I will enjoy seeing you survive and hope you will remember and respect what I have told you."

Realizing the wisdom of the old Jew, Tavid nodded in affirmation. Karoun was listening intently; this was all a new experience for her. To be away from home and able to listen to conversations of men on topics that only she heard her father speak of.

"So, Tavid, I know you are the traveler. What have you heard on the war?"

"Hmmm. Yes. I believe the British have declared war on us now. I have also heard the Turks are clearing out all the Greeks, pushing them out of Western Turkey. Drafting them into the Turkish Army and something about labor battalions as you mentioned as well. I suppose we are next, eh?"

"I see," Malachi said. "They are going to pull everyone into this war, it looks like. Not good. Not good at all."

The three finished their coffee. Tavid ate most of the sweets.

A new customer walked into the apothecary. Malachi excused himself and Tavid stood up after a moment, preparing to leave the apothecary.

"Thank you for the ointments, Malachi." Malachi turned around, excused himself from the new customer for a moment and approached Tavid.

"The ointments are two lire, fifty piasters."

"What? Two lire? But I am a Turk today and you do not charge Turks, remember?" Tavid whispered with a big smile.

Malachi tried not to smile. "Two lire, fifty piasters."

Tavid reached into his pocket and paid Malachi.

"How long are you going to be in Constantinople?" Malachi asked.

"Two weeks about," Tavid replied.

"Good! We will get together next week. Wednesday around 5 o'clock? I will take you out to the Tokatlian Hotel for dinner with my grandson. He is working there now, you know? And bring this beautiful girl with you," Malachi insisted while walking back to his new customer.

"Are you paying for dinner?" Tavid asked.

"No. My grandson will," Malachi smiled. "See you then, Tavid?"

Tavid nodded and turned to leave the apothecary. He was not keen on the idea of going out to dinner with Malachi but the Tokatlian Hotel was well-known for its grandeur and cuisine. *How can I turn down a free meal,* he thought to himself as he resolved to go.

From there they walked to an outdoor marketplace that was not in a European sector but influenced and frequented by Europeans. There were Armenians as well as merchants from other ethnic backgrounds. Some merchants sold from handmade stands where others rented open storefronts along market streets. Across from these open shops was a park where additional merchants could sell their goods and where children would play. Since the summer and the start of the war, the military utilized these parks to set up camps for soldiers. These were often new recruits, as there were this day.

Tavid did not give their presence a second thought. He was dressed as a Turk and for the most part "invisible" as Malachi would say. He did however reach into his pocket and put his fake eyepatch over his left eye. The military did not draft men with poor or lost sight.

"There is an Armenian who has a place here. Let us go there first and see what he has," Tavid said to Karoun.

Karoun looked at him strangely. "Why do you have a patch on your eye?"

"I will tell you later. Follow me."

They walked down the street of merchants. Karoun was awed by the variety of vegetables, fruits, meats, and silk clothing for sale. They came to a baker and the two could smell the fresh baked bread.

"Ahhh, I cannot pass up this store. We have to stop here first," Tavid said, pointing to the bakery. "Are you hungry?" he asked Karoun; she nodded her head with a smile. As they entered the bakery, Tavid greeted the owner.

"Whatever bread is hot will do. Two loaves."

The baker pulled out two oval-shaped, hard-crusted loaves of bread and gave them to Tavid, who put them in a cotton shoulder bag he was carrying.

"Careful, very hot!" the baker said. "Eight piasters."

Tavid paid the man and the two left.

"Maybe some butter or cheese?" Karoun suggested.

Tavid remembered another merchant who sold all types of cheeses. He purchased some that would melt in the warm bread, along with some fresh buttermilk. After paying, Tavid ripped off a steaming piece of bread and cut pieces of cheese, placing them on the bread which he handed to Karoun, then did the same for himself.

"Mmmm! I hope they have bread in heaven," Tavid said smiling.

"I hope you do not find out for awhile," Karoun smiled wryly in return.

"Yes. Too much to do!" The two walked over, sat near the edge of the street on a patch of autumn clover, and enjoyed their small feast.

As they sat, a young girl no more than 7 years of age walked by with a man who was obviously her father. With one hand, she held onto his and with the other she was trying to cuddle a handmade doll. Karoun stared at the doll with a yearning, her eyes following the child even after they were out of sight.

"Aren't you too old for dolls?" Tavid asked jokingly.

Karoun frowned, and began eating again with much less enthusiasm.

Tavid then realized Karoun had probably been forced to grow up too quickly because of her father's iron rule and the need to have her work at the restaurant at a young age. There were probably no dolls and few toys growing up in her household.

Tavid stood up. "Come. We have another store to visit."

As he sped off in another direction, Karoun caught up as he entered another shop. Inside, her face flushed with astonishment; she had never seen a toymaker's shop before. It was small but impressive, with wooden toys displayed on small tables, Karagoz[6] puppets, and on the shelf in the back were beautiful handmade dolls. Tavid greeted the shop owner and walked straight to the back where the dolls were on display.

"Hmmm. This one looks like you a little, Karoun." Tavid pointed to one of the dolls with brown hair, dark complexion and coffee brown eyes. Karoun looked at Tavid and slowly walked to where he was standing, all the time looking throughout the store.

"Ahhh, that is one of my favorite dolls. If you do not like the Ermeni costume on it, I can change it to whatever you like," the shop owner stated.

"One of your favorites, eh? Well then, you are probably asking too much money for it. Come, Karoun, there is another shop that is not so expensive..."

---

[6] Traditional Turkish shadow play puppets.

"Expensive? All of my goods are modestly priced," protested the shop owner.

"Do you see anything you like here?" Tavid stopped and asked Karoun.

"I may have something from here?" she asked.

"Depending on whether he gives me a good price," Tavid said, looking at the shopkeeper. "Do you like this one?" he asked, pointing to the doll in question.

"She is beautiful. I have never had such a thing," she replied.

"Well then, it is up to the price."

The shop owner started to play with his long white mustache. "With that costume I can give you a good price. Three lire."

"That is a good price," Tavid hesitated. "Is there something wrong with the doll?"

The shop owner laughed. "No, no, no. But most do not want the Ermeni costume. I sell more of the European dress dolls of course."

Smiling to himself Tavid paid the shop owner who gave the doll to Karoun, her disbelief showing in her eyes. As they left, Karoun was like a mother with her first child, in complete awe.

"Now then, off to pick up some spices." The two walked down a dozen storefronts to where Tavid had purchased spices from an Armenian merchant in the past.

Once there, Tavid noticed that Karoun was still engulfed in her new child, so he instructed her to stay in front of the store while he made his purchase. Some of the items on his list for his mother were spices usually unavailable in his village of Tchingiler: cayenne, anise, maleb, cumin, salt from the Black Sea and a few other spices like chemen.[7]

Tavid greeted the Armenian merchant and gave him the grocery list. Within a short while, the two had gathered most if not all of the items, wrapped and tied them individually in tightly-woven hemp, paid the merchant and bid him farewell. Tavid had bought an inordinate amount of anise and chemen. He tucked the spices in his cotton shoulder bag and turned to find Karoun.

During the few moments Tavid had taken to purchase the spices, he was not aware of what was occurring in the street behind him where Karoun was standing. While admiring her doll, Karoun had wandered towards the park where the military was encamped. A lieutenant had eyed Karoun walking toward their small encampment and slowly walked towards her

---

[7] Turkish: a combination of spices used to cure meat.

like a hound slinking toward an innocent kitten. When Tavid turned and looked, all he saw was Karoun trying to back step away from the lieutenant who was looking around to see if Karoun was alone. He was gesturing, and then demanding her to come with him.

Tavid focused his attention to approach the lieutenant broadside. There was hint of a smile on Tavid's face.

*Do what they do not anticipate,* his grandfather would tell him. As he turned right and headed toward the lieutenant, some of the other soldiers saw Tavid coming but he did not ignore them; instead, he waved to them and pointed to something behind them. That gave him the few seconds he needed to come at the lieutenant broadside, running into him full force and knocking the soldier down to the ground. Tavid pulled out one of his revolvers and with the other hand grabbed the officer's coat near the neck, jerking him back to his feet.

"Lieutenant! Look at her! Do you not see who she is?" Tavid said, pushing his revolver into the man's scalp.

"Let go of..."

"Lieutenant! Look at her, you idiot! This is the Vizier's[8] daughter! Talaat's youngest child!"

The lieutenant stared at Tavid then looked at Karoun, trying to comprehend what was being said to him. Now, Tavid had a number of soldiers pointing their rifles and yelling to their lieutenant.

"Did you touch her? Did. You. Touch. Her?" Tavid roared.

"The Vizier has instructed me to cut the hand off of anyone that touches his daughter!"

Finally, the lieutenant muttered "What? Who are you?"

"I am your death sentence! I am Yeshid Pasha. Sentinel to the Young Turks[9] Trilogy. Vowed to pro..."

"You! You are Cheté?[10]" the lieutenant said with a now-increased expression of terror.

Tavid paused and smiled at the lieutenant, "So, you have heard of us, that is g..."

"I did not touch her!" the lieutenant interrupted.

---

[8] Talaat (Mehmet Talaat Pasha 1874-1921), Minister of the Interior 1913-1917 and Grand Vizier (Prime Minister) 1917-1918.

[9] The political party in power in the Ottoman Empire during WWI.

[10] Member of armed irregular forces employed by the Ottoman government to carry out atrocities against Armenians.

Tavid slowly looked back over at Karoun, who seemed surprisingly calm. She shook her head as if to say to Tavid that the lieutenant was telling the truth.

"But the doll, why does she have an Ermeni doll?" the lieutenant questioned with whatever authority he could muster.

"Ahhh. Yes, the Ermeni doll. The Vizier instructed her to bring one back today so he could show her how we torture the Giavoor.[11]" Tavid used his best evil smile. The lieutenant looked at Karoun then tried to smile and began to laugh nervously as Tavid cocked the revolver's hammer and pushed it harder into the lieutenant's head.

"We have a small problem, my friend. Your men are going to kill me if I put this gun down."

"Corporal! Corporal!" the lieutenant shouted nervously in a high-pitched voice. A young recruit holding a rifle slowly walked up to the two of them.

"Have my soldiers stand down," he instructed.

"Sir?"

"Eshek! He is a Cheté! And a friend! Take the men and go back to your posts."

The corporal did not move.

"Are you deaf? I gave you an order! Put your rifle down or I will personally cut off your thumbs!"

Obviously confused and disgusted, the corporal again hesitated, but then gave the order to stand down.

Tavid unlocked the hammer of his revolver and withdrew it.

"I am sorry to have had to do that," Tavid said as he straightened and cleaned off the dirt from the lieutenant's jacket. "I see you have good command of your troops. I will report to the Vizier that you are one to be watched in the future. What is your name?"

"Karagoz. But do not mention that this happened to the Vizier. Please."

"Karagoz? What a coincidence. And yes, sometimes it is best to be invisible. I agree. May Mohammed guide you through whispers in your dreams, Lieutenant. May we meet again under different circumstances, eh?" Tavid half-saluted the lieutenant and turned, gesturing to Karoun to lead the way out of the park.

---

[11] A name given by the Ottoman Turks to Armenians and other non-Turks meaning "ungodly," "infidel," "tolerated peoples," non-Moslems who were given low citizenship status while forced to pay high taxes.

*I hope I do not take a bullet in the back,* Tavid thought.

After they were out of earshot Tavid said, "You seemed to take that situation pretty well. When did you become so brave?"

"When I saw you coming. I knew you would take care of him, but I did not know how you were going to kill all those soldiers."

"Ha! Kill them all? No, no! Sometimes you have to enter the lion's den and hope he has just eaten."

"What?"

"Just think about it. Let us get back to the apartment."

"Do not tell me that it is not God-like to get angry or go into a fit of rage. God himself when enraged will grasp a star and hurl it through the heavens. And at night, you can see bits of the star flashing through the sky, fallen apart merely by the sheer force by which it was thrown. Know when He is angry and stay out of His way…. And the same holds true for my grandson."
— Yervant Yacoubian

CHAPTER 13

# A Second Black Day

Regional Ottoman Military Command Post,
Outskirts of Bursa[1]

"HE IS DEAD, CAPTAIN."

"What do you mean he is dead? Who killed him? Who killed him?" The captain yelled.

"Ehhh…apparently there was an explosion…" the soldier replied.

"Yes. Continue quickly. I am starting to lose my temper!"

"There was an explosion, a blast at the drop-off point. A shop in the northeast corridor of Constantinople. The buyer was shot. About a dozen regulars were also killed in the blast. All except one…w-we have obtained the story from him. He claims he shot the Ermeni twice, who then stumbled inside the shop just before it blew up."

"And our dear comrade, the port commander, investigated the incident no doubt?"

"Ehhh, no, Captain. The port commander was also killed in the blast." The captain thought for a moment.

"Well, at least you bring me some good news."

"Captain?"

"Never mind!"

---

[1] A city approximately 90 kilometers south of Constantinople across the Sea of Marmara (and 35 kilometers south of Tchingiler, a day's ride on horseback).

Captain Kalkim Bey's son, Tahir, and nephew Mustafa joined in the conversation. Both served as lieutenants in the Turkish army.

"Did they find the gold or the opium?" Lieutenant Mustafa asked.

"Nothing. It was all blown to Jehennem, Lieutenant. After the explosion, the store completely disintegrated. Nothing was left," the soldier reported.

"That Eshek! His family will pay for his stupidity!" the captain yelled.

Mustafa smiled. "Captain, with your permission I will take some horsemen, go into Tchingiler and bring Kaloustian's family to you. Or should I just kill them there and burn their home?"

"What? No! Not the Hyevan's family, you idiot! I am talking about finding the Eshek port commander's family! See if you can find the Cheté assassins we used last spring in Bursa," Kalkim Bey instructed.

"Tahir, you go to Tchingiler and tell his mother that her son was killed...killed in an explosion. No remains. And see if you can find out if Kaloustian taught anyone else in that family how to grow and extract the opium! Sikishmek! It is useless. Eshek port commander. Well, go, get out!" Kalkim Bey yelled.

The soldier and the two lieutenants quickly left.

"Tahir!" Mustafa ordered. "I will go to Tchingiler and you go into Bursa. You have frien..."

Tahir grabbed Mustafa by the neck and practically picked him up off the ground.

Tahir was a huge man with a dark complexion, still bearing the oriental features of his ancestors. He was unlike many Turks whose blood was mixed with other races. He was twice the size of his rival lieutenant and cousin Mustafa.

"Yes, maybe I should go to Bursa? After I go to Tchingiler. But first I am going to take care of you," Tahir said. "How long can you hold your br..."

"Tahir! Put him down. Now!" the captain ordered his son.

"If you two cannot stop bickering like women I will have to find two new lieutenants! Now get out of here!"

Tahir ordered three soldiers to mount up and ride with him to Tchingiler.

Tchingiler, a small Armenian village outside of Bursa and was known for its silk production as well as its olive, mulberry and chestnut groves. Tahir disliked the village and, for the most part, hated Armenians. However, he had a strange affinity for the renegade, Tavid Kaloustian.

Tahir knew exactly where Tavid's mother and family lived. He resented the responsibility of telling them that Tavid was dead.

He rode straight up to the Kaloustian home. A few Armenians on the street stopped what they were doing when they saw him ride up. Tahir called out toward the home to see if anyone was there. No one answered. He yelled again for any Kaloustian. A moment later, the door slowly opened and Tavid's mother Anoush stood at the door. Tall and willowy with waves of black hair flecked with strands of grey, she looked at the Turkish lieutenant with uncertainty as she waited for him to explain his presence. A look of anger came over her face. A Turkish officer meant nothing but trouble.

"I know you. You have been here before. You know my son," Anoush said.

"Have you come here to visit him? What have you come to tell me?" Tahir hesitated, and then fell silent.

"Is he dead?"

"Yes," Tahir finally said. "There was an explosion at a shop in Constantinople. There…there is nothing left of him."

Anoush hesitated. "If there is nothing left, how do you know he is dead?"

"We have a witness who saw him in the building before the explosion." Anoush stared at the Turk.

"So, you have finally killed him. First my father Yervant, now my son Tavid. Was he not paying you enough?"

"I had nothing to do with it," Tahir said with angst as if being scolded.

"Of course, you did! All of you killed him! Were you there to protect him? No. Maybe it is more your fault he is dead!" Anoush rebuked. "Stepan! Varsenig! Come and see the soldier that killed your bro…" but she was unable to finish as tears formed a veil of hatred and anguish.

From inside the house came out first a young girl, then a boy almost sixteen. Both looked at their mother, then slowly turned to look at Tahir. Tahir looked back at them and saw the resemblance to Tavid. "Murderer!" Anoush exclaimed with disgust.

"Murderer!" Anoush yelled again, picking up a rock and throwing it at Tahir as he was leaving. Stepan and Varsenig picked up rocks, tears now in their eyes as well, and threw them. Tahir rode to where he left his horsemen but did not stop, did not utter a word and just kept on riding.

By this time, the few villagers on the street or in their homes started to come out to comfort Anoush. Fighting against the tears, she looked at them with disgust.

"All they care about is gossip," she whispered under her breath.

"He is dead!" she yelled to everyone with tears in her eyes. "Tavid is dead!" Before anyone could ask her what had happened, she took her two children into the house and closed the door.

No one came to the house that day. No one dared. But the next day a small frail man dressed in black with pure white hair came to the front of the home. Putting out his pipe he called for Anoush, calling repeatedly until she opened the door.

"I do not know if I can handle this again," she said in a broken voice.

"You can and you will, for your sake and your two children. May I come in?" the vartabed asked.

Seeing Stepan and Varsenig, the vartabed smiled, and gestured to them to approach him.

"Come now. I am not a stranger," he said to them.

They saw the love still in his eyes though his face was worn from years of the stress of others. The vartabed hugged them both.

"God bless both of you, your mother and your home. May Tavid keep a place in heaven for us all. God bless his soul. Lord have mercy," he prayed in Armenian, and if one looked closely, a tear could be seen in his eye as well.

Anoush offered the vartabed a place to sit.

"Would you like some coffee, tea? I still have some dried toot² from this spring."

"No. No nothing please."

"Well, I am bringing some out anyway. It will only take a minute, and look at you. Skin and bones you are."

The vartabed looked down at himself. "I feel fine. I do not need to look like a fat cat. No one likes to see a fat vartabed," he said.

A moment later Anoush came out with strong steaming coffee, a plate of dried toot, and warm choreg sprinkled with sesame seeds that glistened like tiny frozen raindrops.

"Ahhh, why did you not tell me you had choreg. Then I would have said yes," the vartabed said, smiling.

"Now sit down with me, Anoush. Let us talk about a few things."

---

² Armenian: mulberry.

"I would rather not."

"I know. I know. But in memory of your son, we should have a holy mass for him. Forgive me; do you know what happened to him?"

Anoush hesitated. Her sadness heightened. "They blew him up in a store. They said there is nothing...nothing left of him."

"Hmmm. Please forgive me again. Your son is...was very smart. Cunning. Do you think the Turks are wrong?"

Anoush began to cry. "They said they saw him in the store before it exploded. It has been over a month now. He never stays away that long. He would have come back by now."

"Well then, it is so. We could hold the ceremony later this week. Is there anyone you do not want there? I could make sure of it for you."

Anoush looked at the vartabed. "Let them come. Let us see who will come. I think most people hated my Tavid."

"Hated, no. Jealous, yes. He was respected by more people than you realize. Maybe not openly here in the village but outside of Tchingiler. If you ask me, I would rather have a thousand Tavids over some of the people here."

"Now you are exaggerating," Anoush said, wiping her tears.

The vartabed shook his head and took some choreg, dipping it in his coffee before consuming it.

"Ahmahn! Is it dry? You should have said something, I will bring out another," Anoush insisted.

"No, it is fine. Very delicious."

"No, no. Whenever the choreg was too dry, my father used to dip it in his..."

"Hokees, please let an old man enjoy his choreg and coffee. It is fine."

The two discussed funeral services for Tavid, and an hour later, the vartabed left to make plans. But Anoush still felt empty.

"Am I next?" Stepan asked his mother.

"What?"

"Are they going to kill me next?"

"Never!" She held both children close, tears running down her cheeks once more. "Maybe it is time we left Tchingiler. For now, let us finish our chores and I will make some bastegh for you both."

"There is no such thing as pure luck. Luck is a mixture of preparation for future events and having a forward-thinking attitude. When these things are a part of your soul, then luck will follow you. If you are lazy and do not prepare for the complexities of life and are always complaining about your misfortune, well then luck will just not exist in your world."
— Yervant Yacoubian

# CHAPTER 14

# The Second Strike of the Informant

WAITING FOR MALACHI AND HIS grandson at the Tokatlian Hotel, Tavid's mind drifted to Karoun. This was the most he had ever seen or thought about any girl. He had decided not to bring her to this meeting and found himself missing her presence. He wondered if she felt the same.

The sight of Malachi broke his reverie. As they approached the dining room, he walked up and stood next to Malachi without saying a word.

"Ahhh, Kaloustian! You did not forget. Good, good. This is my grandson, Ari.[1]"

The ornate, high-ceilinged halls were opulent and noisy on a busy evening.

"Is this the man who is buying dinner?" Tavid asked as he looked at Malachi's grandson, who stood eye to eye with him in height.

"Is that the only reason you came. For a free meal?" asked Ari.

"It may not be the only reason, but possibly the best one," Tavid said with a gracious smile.

Off to the corner a man sitting on one of many hand-carved benches looked up when he heard Tavid's name. The man stared at Malachi, then

---

[1] Ari means lion in Hebrew.

quickly at Tavid. Wide-eyed he rose, quickly turning and walking out of the entrance hall.

At that moment, Tavid felt a soft breeze brush past his face and for a moment, he picked up the aroma of rosewater. Tavid turned to find its origin, only to catch a fleeting silhouette of a tall thin figure as it disappeared through the entranceway. There was an odd familiarity to this man and his scent, though Tavid could not remember why.

Malachi instructed his grandson to get a secluded table so they could talk freely. The maître d' took all three to a table near one of the ornamental fireplaces, an area usually reserved for government officials. The three sat down to enjoy what hopefully would be a delightful meal, however Ari looked glum, poorly concealing his disdain.

"So did your grandfather force you to set up this engagement?" Tavid probed.

"Yes, more or less," Ari answered.

"He seems to think we have much in common," Tavid said, looking at Malachi. "But I can already see one thing where we are quite different."

"Ohhh?" Malachi interjected.

"I am much better-looking than you are," Tavid said nonchalantly and laughed.

"Laugh at your own jokes, do you?" Ari retorted.

"Have you ever killed a man?" Tavid said while still chuckling.

"What?"

"Have you ever killed a man? Better yet, have you ever killed a Turk?"

"This is getting stupid. Now let us order dinner then we can..." Malachi was cut off by his grandson.

"Yes, I have."

"Hmmm. Did you shoot him, use a knife?"

"Guns are too loud and knives do not always kill on the first blow. Brick to the skull. Dead before you could say good night..."

"Enough!" Malachi said. "This is not what I had in mind!"

Now, Tavid and Ari were both smiling.

"This is exactly what you had in mind, Grandfather."

"I would have to agree with your grandson, Malachi," Tavid added.

"Be that as it may, we are going to discuss other similarities!"

Malachi tried to control the conversation and was successful for a while. Ari ordered dinner for the three of them as his father attempted to discuss other ethnic and entrepreneurial similarities. Somehow, Tavid was able to turn the conversation to areas that Malachi did not want to broach.

"Do you have many government officials staying here?" Tavid asked.

"Yes, of course," Ari said.

"Then you have a valuable resource here. Have you exploited it?"

"What are you up to now, Kaloustian?" Malachi asked pointedly.

"Information. With all these government officials coming and going, there is a wealth of information available here. Turkish officials, Europeans too."

Ari smiled.

"Such information—if obtained discreetly, setting up a network in the hotel to listen in on conversations—could be used for profit, political advancement or even bribes," Tavid observed.

"Are not profit and bribes the same thing?" Ari attempted to correct Tavid, and then continued.

"Yes, you are right, but it would be very dangerous. No mistakes could be made and strict secrecy within the network would be essential." Ari smiled, and looked away from Tavid.

"And to brag about it would be a flaw in security," Tavid whispered.

"Bragging?" Ari scoffed.

"What would it cost me to obtain information, Ari? Do you deal strictly with money or do you barter? As your grandfather may have told you, I have my own resources."

"Ah, but they are all dead, yes?" Ari asked bluntly.

Silence hit the table. Tavid was not ready to give out such information.

"I would like to know what the Turkish officials are saying about the Ermenis. Is there going to be another slaughter like there was with the Sultan back in the 90s?" Tavid pressed on.

Ari did not answer and looked down at the table.

"We have heard many disturbing conversations," Malachi answered.

Ari quickly looked at his grandfather with surprise, then at Tavid.

"Again, this is not what I had in mind," Malachi sighed and paused. "The Ittihad[2] is up to something. They come here for meetings and openly discuss and describe things between themselves, outrageous things. Different tortures that could be inflicted on Ermenis, Greeks, and I suppose my people as well. Whenever a new method of inflicting

---

[2] The political party in power in the Ottoman Empire during WWI. Also known as the "Young Turks."

pain is thought of at these discussions, it is hailed as a splendid discovery. We heard one mention that they had researched into the records of the Spanish Inquisition. At first, we thought they were making jokes, but it was apparent they were serious in their discussions."

"Spanish what? Torturing? By whom?" Tavid asked.

"By the Cheté[3] under the guise of the war."

"Cheté? I have heard this. Who are they, really?"

"Armed bandits as far as we can tell. Cheté are employed by the government to carry out its filthy wishes: looting, torturing, killing."

Tavid was silent.

"It is difficult being hated. The Turks hate everyone. Luckily, for me I do not have many relatives living here, but your people, Tavid…there are so many. Millions.

Malachi looked at his grandson, "It is not right not to tell him."

"I know, I know," Ari said. "But the others have not listened to us. What makes you think he will?"

"I do believe you, though some of what you have told me is not totally clear. And I already know what I am going to do. I just hope I have enough time."

Dinner arrived. Malachi returned to superficial pleasantries but the morbid mood was set. After dinner Tavid thanked his hosts and asked again how to become a part of their network.

Malachi and Ari did not answer. Malachi and Ari rose from the table and bid Tavid farewell, expressing the desire to get together again soon. Malachi was genuine in this desire but Tavid could not tell about Ari.

As Tavid left the dining room and walked through the entrance hall toward the front doors of the hotel, one of the servers came to Ari's table, and while pouring tea and coffee started to speak to Ari without looking at him.

"There are three gendarmes. Two dressed as Europeans waiting for your dinner associate at the front door."

"What! Why did you not tell me sooner?" Ari barked.

"We just spotted them. It is too late to do anything," the server said.

"God damn it!" Malachi said, as he got up and started toward the entrance hall, but Ari grabbed his arm and held his grandfather back.

---

[3] Member of armed irregular forces employed by the Ottoman government in carrying out atrocities against Armenians.

"Wait, Grandfather! We will walk over together and see what is happening. Do we have anyone who can trail them and look for an opportunity?" Ari asked his server.

"Yes. I will take care of it," the server said, then looked at Ari. "He is not a Turk?"

"Ermeni," Malachi replied.

The server nodded and quickly left.

As Tavid walked out the front door Malachi's statements clouded his mind. As he descended the steps he saw a reflection at the street, a glimmer of light surrounded by a thin silhouette. A man from behind called out his name.

"Kaloustian!" It was one of the plain-clothed gendarmes. Tavid turned and saw two men pointing pistols at him.

"Did I forget to pay for dinner?" Tavid asked.

The third man dressed as a gendarme came from in front and had Tavid hold his hands out to tie them with a thin but strong rope.

"You are wanted for the murder of Teshkil Bey," he said.

"Who?"

The gendarme backhanded Tavid in the face.

"Our port commander! And a dozen of our comrades." The two plain-clothed gendarmes then pulled out their uniform hats and put them on.

As Ari and Malachi got to the door the gendarmes were leading Tavid away. Ari saw two of the hotel's security following behind unnoticed, but no one noticed the man standing on the other side of the street signaling to the gendarmes as Tavid had walked out of the hotel.

"If this is a matter of gold I am sure we can…" One of the gendarmes kicked him in the back of the leg and Tavid went down to his knees. Another gendarme kicked him in the ribs. Tavid dropped.

"Get up and shut your mouth!" the gendarmes ordered.

Coming from the other direction was a unit of soldiers who had seen what was going on and approached.

"What is going on here?" the lieutenant asked sternly.

"Not your concern, Lieutenant. This is a port concern. Be on your way."

Just at that moment, Tavid stood back up and was face to face with the lieutenant.

"Karagoz?" Tavid started, but before he could say anything else the gendarmes grabbed him by the neck and started to drag him away.

"…Cheté?" Lieutenant Karagoz whispered to himself. Pulling out his pistol, he turned toward the departing gendarmes and ordered his men to stop them.

"Halt! I demand to know what you are doing with this man," the lieutenant yelled, his men pointing their rifles at the gendarmes.

"Are you crazy, Lieutenant? What do you think you are doing?"

"Be on your way! This is not your concern!" a gendarme yelled back.

"Karagoz, they are not gendarmes! They are Ermeni." Tavid felt a blow to the back of the neck and again dropped to the ground.

"Drop your pistols! Drop them now!" the lieutenant yelled, cocking the hammer on his pistol.

"What is the matter with you, Lieutenant? He is an opium dealer who has…"

"Karagoz!" Tavid groaned and yelled in Turkish, "They have kidnapped the Vizier's daughter. They are holding her for ransom and have killed her bodyguards. They've stolen their uniforms."

The gendarme's rage was fierce. He pointed his gun at Tavid, but before he could shoot the lieutenant fired and his men followed suit, dropping all three gendarmes. At first, Tavid did not move as he tried to discern if he had been shot. Then the lieutenant went over to Tavid and helped him to his feet.

"Can you stand?" The lieutenant asked Tavid.

"Yes." Tavid looked over and saw the three gendarmes. The one dressed in uniform was still alive.

"It appears there was a reason why we had met last week, Cheté," the lieutenant said.

Tavid nodded. "I need to talk to the one who is still alive; those are my pistols they have. I would like them back." One of the soldiers retrieved two of the gendarme's pistols and gave them to Tavid. Tavid got down on the ground where the gendarme was lying.

"Maybe I am not who you think I am, eh? Maybe the hotel security gave you a bad tip," he whispered in the dying gendarme's ear.

"Sikishmek hotel. We never get shit from them. No, that is not how we knew you were there," the gendarme panted.

Tavid was puzzled. He was sure it had to have been from the hotel.

"Ha!" The gendarme started to laugh. "You have an enemy. Someone that you know."

"Who is it, my dying fool?" Tavid asked.

The gendarme just spit on the stones where his face was pressed. "There! There is your answer."

Tavid smiled at him, then went through the pockets of all three gendarmes looking for clues but finding nothing. Just some lire and official papers.

"Here, Lieutenant, take this and give it to your men. I have no need for it." Tavid gave him the lire that he had pulled from their pockets.

"I must go quickly now and try to retrieve the Vizier's daughter before it is too late."

"We will come with you," Karagoz said.

"If they see us coming they will kill her. No, I must be invisible and surprise them. Overpower them before they can do her harm."

Tavid got down on one knee and kissed the lieutenant's hand. "I thank you again, Lieutenant."

As Tavid started to leave, Karagoz yelled out to him, "Cheté! What should I do with the one that is still alive?"

Tavid thought for a moment. "Kill him," he said and took off into the night. As he turned down a darkened street, he spit the scent of the lieutenant's hand out of his mouth, at the same time hearing a gunshot. Tavid ran and did not look back.

"Malachi would always profess that Jews and Armenians had many similarities in their history. And I suppose this is true. In ways we are very similar, but in others we are very different. The Jews in Constantinople are a tight-knit community. Their survival depends on it. But Armenians, well I would not describe us the same way. If you ask me, I feel we have a more chaotic community and it is amazing that we get anything done at all on the community level."
— Yervant Yacoubian

CHAPTER 15

# Bad Ideas

Tavid awoke to his new aches and pains. He should have been used to it, but never was. "I am still human then," he thought. His back and ribs ached where the gendarmes had brutalized him. But then he looked over at the cot where Karoun slept, his pain momentarily disappearing as he gazed at her face as she slept. Childlike in sleep, beautiful when awake. Quietly he arose and slipped into the next room to find some of the soothing menthol from the apothecary. Whitening his mustache with some ash mixed with clear oil, he put on the Kurdish outfit complete with the eyepatch. He needed to see Malachi again and quietly left the apartment.

It was still dark and only merchants were out walking to their shops. When Tavid arrived at Malachi's apothecary, no one was there. He walked around and waited for Malachi to come down from his flat above the shop to open for business. As the sun began its ascent over the horizon, he saw two men approach the shop and knock on Malachi's glass shop door. Moments later, a light appeared in the shop and Malachi let them in. Tavid remembered seeing these men at the Tokatlian Hotel. Tavid waited briefly before walking to the same glass door, then he knocked. The same two men came to see who was at the door followed by Malachi. However,

Malachi only glanced to see who it was and walked to the back of his store to prepare for the day.

"We are not open yet, old man. Come back in an hour," one of the men said with an Armenian accent.

"Please, I have not slept all night from my pains. Have pity on an old Kurd and let me in to see the chemist," Tavid pleaded, trying not to smile.

They looked at Malachi, who nodded and waved him in.

"Thank you, a thousand thank yous, kind men. Security now in this shop? Have you had problems with thieves? Burglars?"

"No, no. Nothing like that I can assure you." Malachi did not look at the old Kurd.

While Tavid was standing between Malachi and the men, he discreetly pulled out two pistols and pointed them at the two men.

"Then why do you need two men to protect you, Malachi? Did you betray a friend?"

Malachi and the two men quickly turned and looked at Tavid.

"Now, now. I am not going to shoot anyone unless you provoke me. I just want to talk to my good friend, Malachi, for a moment," Tavid said in Armenian to the two men.

"Is that possible, Malachi? May we talk?"

Malachi nodded, "We can talk. Why did you come dressed like that?"

"First, tell me why you need these two here? To protect you from whom? Me?"

"You? Ha! No, not you. The men who took you away yesterday."

"They are dead," Tavid said.

"I know. I know they are dead but someone told them you were at the hotel and they must have seen Ari and me with you."

Tavid hesitated.

"Do you have anything for breakfast?" Tavid asked as he put his pistols away keeping his eye on the two men.

"I am making some tea and coffee and I have some of the leftover sweets." Malachi answered.

"That is all? Maybe I should come back another..."

"Will you sit down, please?"

"Will they sit also?" Tavid asked about the two men.

Malachi gestured to them all to come and sit in the back while he brought out the limited breakfast.

"We saw what happened last night. We trailed you and the gendarmes," one of the men said in Armenian.

"Why were you following?"

"We were waiting for an opportunity to help you escape. But obviously, you did not need our help. You have the military on your side?" he said with a questioning smile.

Malachi came to the table. "Ari had these two men follow you when we found out you had been taken by the gendarmes."

"I know. They just told me."

Malachi sighed. "Well then this conversation needs to be in Turkish, not Ermeni."

Tavid smirked at Malachi.

"As I was saying, Ari had these two men follow you. Unfortunately, we found out too late that there were gendarmes hovering at the entrance. Someone in the hotel must have recognized you. Did you see anyone there who may have known you?"

Tavid hesitated, "No. I was hoping you might have some information on that. I saw no one."

"We tried to catch up to you after the soldiers shot the gendarmes but we lost you in the night. You took off like a soul escaping from hell."

"What happened, Tavid? The story these two tell sounds absurd. How is it possible? Are you some type of informant, or supplying them with opium?" Malachi questioned.

Tavid shrugged his shoulders. "Maybe all of that, maybe none. Either way you would not believe the story. I cannot believe it myself."

"Tell us anyway," said one of the Armenians.

The two Armenians shook their heads and laughed at the story. Malachi just looked on with astonishment.

"How lucky can someone be, eh? I have no choice but to believe you. Who could make up such a story and tell it straight-faced," Malachi said. "What will you do now?"

"I am going to leave Constantinople as soon as possible. It is not safe here until I can find out who the informant is. If you or anyone at the hotel has any information…"

"Yes, yes. We will try to see what we can do," Malachi promised.

"You could come back to the hotel," suggested one of the Armenians.

"Yes, I agree," Tavid interrupted. "Maybe I will do just that. Maybe I will get lucky and flush him out.

Tavid said goodbye to a frustrated Malachi and company, leaving cautiously making sure no one was following him back to the apartment. He found Karoun was visiting with Ana over a late breakfast. As Tavid approached, Ana rolled her eyes at his outfit.

"Who is this old man? And what is your obsession with being a master of disguises? It is in your blood!" She laughed.

Karoun, who was starting to understand, said softly, "You never know when it could save your life."

"Sit down with us and tell us of last night. Are you hungry?" Ana inquired.

"Always," Tavid smiled.

The women provided a spread of breads, cheeses, and fresh vegetables, and then sat down at the table with Tavid.

"So, tell us of the Tokatlian Hotel."

"Our people, Armenians I am speaking of.... We are our own worst enemy. United we are not. Therefore, our only chance for survival lies within pockets of solidarity and the individual accomplishments that shape our entire nation."
— Yervant Yacoubian

CHAPTER 16

# Sailing

"WHAT THE HELL IS WRONG with you? Blowing up a store! Taking a young girl away from her home! Did I not teach you anything?" Yervant yelled, white waves of his hair being blown about by a wind Tavid could not sense.

Tavid could not speak or move.

"Answer me!"

Tavid still could not.

The old man got closer to Tavid and grabbed his arm. "Find the traitor!"

"Tavid. Tavid, wake up. You told me to wake you up," Karoun said.

Tavid nodded his head, sat up and rubbed his face.

"Nothing is wrong with me, grandfather," he said under his breath.

"What?"

Tavid looked up at Karoun. "Nothing, hokees.[1] Nothing."

Tavid had an hour before he was expected back at the Tokatlian Hotel. As he got up, he started to itch his healing scalp wound, then remembering again the warning of the old Bulgarian seamstress.

Ana had also just approached a lower window.

"Tavid, I have to talk to you. May I come in?"

---

[1] Armenian: "my soul," an endearing name given to loved ones.

Tavid nodded, sleep still in his eyes. "Can you take these threads out of my head today, Ana?"

"Yes, of course, but I just came back from the eastern sector of Constantinople, near one of the Parliament buildings. There…there was a riot. Tavid, please, it is not safe to go to the hotel."

Tavid was fully awake now. "I see. I have also been having second thoughts about going back there. I think it is time to just go back home."

"You should just stay here. It is safe," Ana begged him not to leave.

"Yes, it is safe here, but I need to go home to Tchingiler. I have been here longer than planned. We will leave tonight. Karoun, can you be ready to leave by then?"

"I have nothing to do, just pack my things."

"Hm. Do you remember how you were dressed when we went to the market last week? Something like that," Tavid instructed.

Karoun hesitated.

"I have a letter that I would like to send to my parents. Explaining where I am, where I am going. Is there a way to get this to them?"

"I need to find Aldo and Costel before I leave. I can have them take the letter to your father. I think they would be glad to do this. Maybe even yell at your father for me."

Ana sighed, "I will get some fine scissors, then pack some food for you to take."

"Only food that will not spoil. It will take us some time to get back home."

Tavid left for the eastern waterfront but in the back of his mind he hoped that his Romanian comrades would not be there. At first hopeful that they would have been able to leave port. Perhaps a sign that they could escape to Cyprus earlier than the spring. But there the ship was as before.

Their reunion turned to the plan Tavid longed to see in motion—he must be back to the ship by late March with whomever would join him to set sail to Cyprus.

"I am tired of sitting here doing nothing," Aldo complained. "If we are stuck here much longer I may just come down to Tchingiler to visit your family!"

"Do not worry Tavid, we will be in Romania before he gets that desperate!" Costel reassured. "I have ways of getting out of here and I am working on them now. But no worrying, we will be back by early spring."

Tavid gave Aldo Karoun's letter for her parents with his recommen-
dation as to what profanities should be uttered to Baron Eftendelian, and
they said their goodbyes.

By evening, Tavid and Karoun were ready. He had fed and packed the
three horses and unearthed his cache of weapons that he then secured
to camouflaged bags on the lower sides of each horse. First he wrapped
the weapons in hemp, placing them in the side bags then adding chemen,
cayenne and other spices over them to hide the weapons by scent and
proximity. After removing the threads from Tavid's scalp Ana brought out
three large sacks of food, one to be placed on each horse. She looked as if
the world was sitting on her shoulders.

"Ana, stop worrying about us. Nothing is going to happen," Tavid tried
to assure her.

She took a deep breath and nodded. "I cannot help myself." She tied the
food sacks to his horse and hugged Karoun to say goodbye.

"I expect to see you again, my dear."

She held Karoun close kissing her on both cheeks.

"I am bringing everyone back with me next time, Ana," Tavid said.
"Everyone this early spring," he added.

"You know, it has been years since I have seen your mother. I will pray
for all of you to have a safe journey there and back." Ana kissed Tavid and
hugged him.

Tavid had Karoun get on one of the horses that had a lighter load and
led the other two horses himself on foot. Karoun turned to look at Ana,
smiled and waved goodbye. It would take them about an hour heading
southwest to reach the port city of Kukukcekmeca on the Sea of Marmara.
Once at Kukukcekmeca, they would take a three-day voyage by boat,
making two stops before finally arriving home in Tchingiler. A five-day
journey, if all went well.

The night was quiet in the residential quarter. No gendarmes or soldiers
appeared as they made it to the south end of the waterfront district of the
city without incident. There were several ships that ran the sea and Tavid
enlisted one in particular each time he crossed the Sea of Marmara. Even
though it was night, Tavid had no trouble finding the vessel for its skipper
always moored at the same location.

At first, Tavid kept Karoun and the horses out of sight. He walked
toward the vessel. Its skipper was sitting by a small fire at the edge
of the dock, just outside a small storage shack. Tavid eyed the figure

keeping warm while cleaning something vigorously in the firelight. Tavid approached from the dark.

"Paree eereegoon, uhngehr,[2]" Tavid spoke softly to the older man.

"Eh?" The old man turned his head towards Tavid, squinting his eyes to see who it was. However, Tavid's face was not yet visible.

"My brothers or friends do not sneak up on me at night. They know better. What is your business?" the man sneered.

"I used to be your friend, Haig Navasart. How quickly you have forgotten me, it has only been three…" As Tavid spoke and came forward the light of the fire illuminated his face. The old man's face went cold with fear. Trying to get away from Tavid, he stumbled and almost fell into the fire. Tavid caught his right arm.

"Ghost! You are dead! Dead they told me!" Haig screeched wide-eyed, then looking at his arm where Tavid was holding him. Tavid smiled at him but with a look of puzzlement, and fear left the man's face.

"But a ghost could not grab my arm! Sons of bitches, you are not dead!" The old man shook his head, smiled and embraced Tavid, kissing him on each cheek.

"Who told you I was dead?"

"The soldiers. Ferried some over to Bursa weeks ago. One was telling tall stories about an explosion in Constantinople and how you had been killed."

Tavid paused, "Everyone must think I am dead now. Even my mother."

"Yes, very possible," agreed Haig. "Damn soldiers. I should never have believed them."

"Should be interesting going back home. Can we leave before dawn?"

"We can leave now if you like. I have no interest in staying here tonight. I would rather be out at sea."

"I have three horses and another passenger. Do you have enough feed and water for the…"

"Another passenger? You? Since when do you travel with anyone? Is it a woman? Perhaps you got married in Constantinople?" Haig inquired quizzically.

"Well, yes, a woman it is," Tavid explained. He then brought Karoun and the three horses over to the fire.

"Karoun, this is Haig Navasart. He is going to take us with his boat over to the other side. Haig, this is Karoun."

---

[2] Armenian: "Good evening, comrade."

"Ah such a beautiful girl. It will be a pleasure traveling with you and Tavid. Hmmm. Three horses, eh? Yes, I have enough feed and water. Come let us load up. But what is that smell coming from the horses?"

"Smell? Oh, spices I am taking home to my mother. Chemen, cayenne, garlic."

"I hope you do not kill your horses." Haig smiled and helped Karoun off her horse then loaded the horses into the hold of the vessel. Tavid stashed all the bags in the ship's bow. An old steam engine plus sails powered the vessel. Haig started the old steam engine. In a few minutes, they were on their way.

The clear night revealed a half moon shining in the southeast, making the water's surface and other vessels anchored or buoyed clearly visible. The ship's reflection made a path to the horizon on the sea in the moonlight. Karoun sat near the bow to watch as they left shore. It was a cool night and Tavid gave her some blankets. With the night's fresh air, the mild rhythmic rumble of the engine, and the sound of the vessel cutting through the still waters, Karoun was asleep in minutes.

"The waters here put a trance on the young ones. The sea sings to them and rocks them to sleep," Haig explained proudly.

"Some day I would like to have a boat of my own," Tavid mused.

Haig nodded, keeping his eye on the horizon and stars for direction, "So tell me, what happened in Constantinople. How is it that you escaped death after being blown up and shot?"

Again, Tavid recounted the incident at Aldo's shop. With each new telling, the story seemed to get more dramatic as Tavid perfected his tale.

"I would like to meet this stupid Turk who is telling these tall stories and the ones that believe him. Stupid. All of them."

Haig took a deep breath, "If you do not mind me saying so, if they are all so stupid, how is it that they have been our masters for over 400 years? Remember, the Turk does not have to be smart, just cunning. Let the Armenians defeat themselves."

"Yes, yes, I know. Did you hear anything from these soldiers as to who the informer might be?" Tavid asked.

"No. I did not. Though I know he is from Tchingiler and has recently been to Constantinople."

"I knew that much. Anything else?"

"Just keep your eyes and ears open. I am sure you will be able find him. Pity the poor bastard when you do."

Tavid did not answer.

"You have never killed an Armenian, have you?" Haig asked. "Well, just make sure he is the right one. Nothing worse than going to a doctor with leg rot and he cuts off the wrong leg, eh?" Haig smiled.

"Go check on Karoun. Rest now. I will wake you at dawn to let you take the helm while I sleep for a few hours."

Tavid was tired. After checking on Karoun, he lay down in the small cabin, wrapped some blankets around his shoulders and fell fast asleep.

Next thing he knew, Haig was waking him with a wet rag of cold dripping seawater on Tavid's face.

"Wake up, Tavid. It is my turn to dream. Come, take the wheel."

As Tavid rose and took the helm, he saw the red sun rising almost behind them in the northeast. Karoun was still sleeping at the bow of the boat, curled up in her blankets and holding onto her precious doll. Even her face was half-covered using her breath to keep her warm.

"Make sure you stay awake and head parallel to the coast. I will probably only sleep for a few of hours," Haig said in a tired voice.

"What if the wind picks up? Do you want me to open the sails?" Tavid asked.

"Raise...not open the sails. No, leave them. If they are not blowing from the northwest you could get into trouble if I am not awake to help you."

Tavid scoffed at Haig Navasart's weak faith in his sailing abilities, but heeded his words.

"How far off the coast should I stay and what if we run out of steam?"

"At least two kilometers and do not worry about the steam. I have stoked the chamber. See you in a few hours," Haig saluted.

Tavid took the wheel tiller of the craft and as instructed pointed south along the coastline. In a few minutes Haig was asleep and the sun was completely visible in the northeast horizon. Beams of light shone on and through the ship's imperfections, casting a long shadow onto the waters, making the ship out to be a great vessel. The sun caressed Karoun, illuminating the beads that accentuated her clothes. Even as the sun grew brighter she ignored its presence and continued to sleep, rest, and dream of her new home.

The wind had started to pick up. He wondered what it would be like to sail under full wind power. What would it feel like, the speed and quiet of nature's force? He felt something on his shoulder. Tavid jerked around so fast that he forgot to let go of the wheel as the boat began to turn quickly to starboard.

"Karoun!" Tavid quickly turned back toward the bow and corrected the ship's course.

"I am sorry. I thought you heard me coming. I did not mean to…"

"I was dreaming. And the wind makes it hard to hear," Tavid smiled.

Karoun retrieved one of the sacks of food packed by Ana and pulled out flatbread, goat cheese, dried fruit, and small linens. She prepared a small breakfast for Tavid.

As Tavid steered with one hand and ate with the other he asked, "Do you miss your parents, your brother?"

"A little. But I am fine. I am happy and I feel safe when I am with you." Karoun paused. "Tell me about your village."

"Tchingiler? It is a beautiful place. Mountains, fruit trees everywhere. Most people there work with silkworms. If it were not for the Turks and Kurds in surrounding the villages, it might be a perfect place to live. Ah, but nothing is really perfect."

"Not wrecked my ship yet, eh?" Haig yelled out to Tavid. Haig came on deck and stretched trying to shake off the stiffness from his bones. "It is a good wind coming from the northwest." Haig walked up to the mast and readied the mainsail. "Turn her upwind a bit, Tavid."

"You mean turn right?" Tavid asked.

Haig smirked. As Tavid steered, Haig raised a large scruffy sail. As he did Tavid could feel the boat roll and pick up speed from the strength of the wind.

"Now turn her back on course. Hold her southwest as before," Haig yelled.

Tavid complied and the ship started to race along. Haig secured the mainsail and went below to curtail the unneeded power of the steam engine, then returned topside to the helm.

"This is what you have been waiting for, eh? Well from the looks of the clouds, the wind should pick up even more today. We will make good time."

Haig sat nearby for a few moments and had some breakfast before attending to Tavid's horses. He fed and watered them, stroking their faces telling them how beautiful they were as if he was talking to one of his past love affairs. Finally he cleaned up manure, threw it overboard—downwind of course—and gave the floors a dousing of seawater that drained down and out the sides of the ship.

Haig offered to take over the helm, but Tavid commanded with his hand to go away.

"Alright then. I am going back to my dreams," Haig said with a grin. He grabbed a blanket and stretched out near the bow of the boat.

"Wake me if you get tired."

Tavid did not. He relished the reality of his earlier musings. The rush of air and smooth seas were even more thrilling than he'd hoped as the wind picked up and travel was swift. The voyage to Cyprus could not come soon enough.

The following day went as the first: strong winds, the sky speckled with clouds. Sleepy Haig and Karoun allowed Tavid to sail and dream in his own way. As the sun rose in the northeast calling an end to the second night of travel, they were near their destination port of Yalova, a small fishing and export village north of Bursa. It would allow Tavid the freedom to unload his cargo discreetly and be on his way without inspection. Before they knew it they approached the shore; Haig lowered the sail to maneuver his ship into a slip. The three of them secured the boat and unloaded the horses and cargo. As they disembarked, Tavid turned.

"What do I owe you this time, my friend?"

"Well, two passengers this time. Have to charge you more. Three horses and...the sailing lesson," Haig smiled.

"Are you paying in gold or paper?"

"Gold," Tavid replied.

"Well then...five lire for each of you. Three lire for each horse," he said, with both hands facing up to the blue skies.

Tavid opened one of his bags, pulled out an overcoat and searched the pockets. He pulled out a small item wrapped in hemp, and from another pocket pulled out gold lire. Tavid returned to Haig Navasart and handed him the lire and the package.

"What is this?" Haig weighed the small yet heavy package.

"Something I want you to hold onto for me."

Haig opened the parcel. Inside was a small revolver and ammunition.

"I have told you before I have no need for guns. Here, take it back!"

"No, no. I am not giving it to you; I merely want you to hold onto it for me. You can hide it down below by the engine. Just make sure it does not get wet. I may need it the next time I see you."

Haig shook his head. "You are just trying to trick me into accepting it. Why do you need me to hold onto it for you?"

"Please. Just do this for me. Hold onto it until the spring when I return."

Haig weighed the pistol in his hand and quickly slid it in his overcoat pocket.

"Go in good health, Haig Navasart. I have to go see the big shot before we continue our travels to Tchingiler. Have you seen him lately?"

"Ismail? He was down here last week getting a shipment ready for Constantinople. I spoke to him about you. Told him you were dead. He was not happy about that. Said something about owing him money? Called you a few names I will not repeat." Haig grinned amiably.

"Who else have you told?" Tavid asked.

"Oh, just about everyone who knows you. Ismail is probably still up at his residence at this time in the morning. I would like to see the look on his face when he sees you, but I have some things to attend to." Haig turned towards the horses. "Come! Let us get you on your way now."

"Ermenis for the most part are meek, passive yet cling to their traditions and Christ. Fight us! Do not give in if you want our respect. Of course we will still hate your kind, though our respect you will have. And yes, every so often I suppose a desperate mother gives birth to a dark soul like Kaloustian. But there is only so much one boy turned man can do."
– Ismail Bey, Port Commander, Village of Yalova

# CHAPTER 17

# The Big Shot

TAVID WAS NOW VERY CLOSE to home. Though he was starting to feel an unfamiliar emotion. He felt angst over what his mother would say. Coming back from the dead, bringing Karoun Eftendelian with him. And then he would have to tell her about her father. He shook off the shroud that was starting to engulf him and headed up to see Ismail Bey.

All exports traveling to Constantinople via the village had to go through a chief Turkish official. On a small bluff overlooking the Marmara Sea, Ismail Bey lived in an estate which also served as the administrative building for the village. Tavid, Karoun, and the horses approached the front gate where a drowsy guard rose.

"What is your business…" the guard hesitated. With dawning recognition he continued, amazed.

"Kaloustian! You are dead!"

"Yes, yes, I am dead. But God threw me out of heaven. Told me to go back and pay all my debts first. That is why I am here."

"Ahhh! Smart God he is, eh?" The guard laughed.

The guard ushered Tavid inside. Tavid tied the horses to the gate.

"How much did I owe you from before?" asked Tavid.

"Five lire."

Tavid reached into his pocket and handed the guard seven lire. "I am paying you interest for my late payment. Is the big shot, Ismail, in?" Tavid asked.

"Of course. I will take you up there. Who is the girl, and where is that smell coming from?"

"She is my sister," Tavid replied. "And you must be smelling the horses."

"She can stay down here, but take the horses with you," ordered the guard.

Tavid walked up to the guard and spoke softly. "She has fits on occasion. If something happens can you retrieve me from the house?"

The guard eyed Karoun warily, snorted and escorted both of them to Ismail's residence, pounding on the door. No one came. The guard pounded harder. Footsteps were heard and one of Ismail's wives opened the door.

"They are here to see Ismail Bey," the guard announced.

"What is their business here?" asked the woman.

"Just tell Ismail that Kaloustian's ghost is here to see him." The guard roared with laughter and left to return to the gate.

The woman went back inside and called to Ismail, relaying the guard's message. Soon, Tavid heard a familiar voice.

"I do not believe in ghosts! Who has come to bother me this early in the morning?"

Tavid said nothing. He heard the door swing inward and a tall thin figure stood glaring at Tavid. From Ismail's face, Tavid could tell he had just awakened.

"Hay, Allah!" greeted Tavid.

Ismail shook his head, "Sikishmek!¹" he said, gritting his teeth. "I should have known. I should have known! Do you know how mad I was when I found out?" Ismail growled.

"Effendi, forgive me. But do you think I would let myself get killed without first paying off my debts?" Tavid said with mock innocence.

"Yes, how stupid of me. Alright, alright, come in. I suppose you are hungry as usual?"

"No, thank you. We can wait until you are done eating if you…"

"Whaaat? Kaloustian not hungry? Maybe you *are* a ghost. Or is my food not good enough for you anymore?"

Tavid rubbed his face with his hands then rubbed his hands together.

¹ Turkish profanity.

He was tiring of being respectful.

"Ismail Bey, the last time I was here you complained I ate like an animal."

Ismail smiled, then gestured to one of his wives to set a place for Tavid. Then he noticed Karoun hiding behind him.

"Who is this one clinging onto you?"

"One of my, sisters. I am bringing her back from Constantinople."

"Sister? Ha! She can eat in the kitchen if she is hungry."

Tavid bowed his head and prompted Karoun to leave with one of Ismail's wives. He followed Ismail into a large dining room where other wives were setting a table for Ismail's morning meal. Tavid waited for Ismail to sit first before seating himself.

"Go on sit down, sit down!" Ismail said. "But before we eat do you have them?"

From his coat pocket Tavid pulled out a small wrapped package tied thrice with thin strings. He handed them to Ismail.

"No surprises this time?" Ismail questioned.

"Only good surprises this time."

Ismail tightened his eyes, showing apprehension at Tavid's statement. He opened the small package. Carefully untying each string, he unfolded the hemp to reveal its contents. For a moment, there was silence while Ismail intently examined the contents.

"Well, a pleasing surprise indeed! Not five but seven diamonds. And all appear to be of good size and brilliance. Yes, now I am glad to see you, Ermeni! Let us eat if these women will ever bring out the food. How much longer must I wait?" Ismail shouted towards the kitchen. A few moments later, there was a stream of delicacies—flatbreads encrusted with crushed sesame seeds and olive oil, goat cheese, soujouk,[2] hot steamed eggs, fresh figs and thick coffee overtook the table. The wives had enlisted Karoun to help.

Tavid again waited for Ismail to begin.

"Eat, Kaloustian! Just this time save some for me, eh?" Ismail grinned. "And tell me now why you are not dead. How you have escaped?"

Once again, Tavid entertained Ismail event by event as Ismail listened and ate.

"He is an idiot, that port commander. Was an idiot, I should say. And greedy. A hundred, no a thousand times more wealth and influence

---

[2] Multicultural: a type of cured sausage.

than myself in Constantinople and he needed more? Maybe that is what happens with all these government big shots."

Tavid smirked.

Ismail started, "Last week your villagers came and sold their silk here. They all believe you to be dead as well. I have been told they had a funeral and even made up a gravestone for you. Then there is Kalkim Bey. What do you think he will do to you when he sees you are still alive?"

Tavid's angst returned at hearing these words. "I do not know, but I will find out today."

"Today? You are going there today?"

"I must. I have more debts to pay."

"Oh?" Ismail was curious. Tavid read Ismail's thoughts.

"We both know his greed well." Tavid paused. "And I wonder what Kalkim Bey would do to you if I was not to make it to Bursa and by some chance he found out?"

Ismail grinned and sipped his coffee. "Yes, the temptation is there." Ismail glanced toward the kitchen. "Hizmetçi![3] My coffee is cold!" One of the wives scurried for more.

"But I am happy with what I have."

Tavid looked directly into Ismail's eyes.

"Ismail, I am in need of information again."

"What? What is it this time?" Ismail questioned.

"It is of a different nature, a more personal question."

Ismail gestured for him to continue.

Tavid paused, "Why do Turks hate us?"

"Hate you? Who has told you I hate you?"

Tavid shook his head and tried to explain. "When you are with your friends or family and you talk of Ermenis, what do you and your family say about us?"

Ismail stared at Tavid, trying to decide whether he would answer and if he was going to be truthful.

"Why do you want to know such things?"

"You have always been truthful and exact. I am merely seeking information from you as I have in the past. This time I want information of a more personal nature. It is important to me." Tavid tried to manage a sincere smile.

---

[3] Turkish: servant.

A PERFECT ARMENIAN 121

But Ismail was not smiling. "The reasons are as numerous as there are Ermenis. Most will say that it is because you are cross worshippers, Christian infidels. Others believe you are simply inferior to us. When wealthy Ermeni merchants profit where our merchants are struggling, it enrages them. They say, 'How is it that an infidel can prosper and I cannot?' So we make your people pay higher taxes, we impose restrictions to trade. Yet you still seem to prosper in one way or another. Then of course violence erupts."

Tavid stared intently at Ismail.

"But that is not what you are asking of me is it? You want to know how I feel."

Ismail stopped eating and folded his hands in front of him, and paused.

"Ermenis think that they are better than us. Yes, and they think this is still their land. Even after hundreds of years under our rule! That infuriates others and me as well. They walk around like we are the guests, guests in our own country," Ismail fumed.

"And I act this way, too?" Tavid inquired apprehensively.

Ismail shook his head. "You are a strange one. Your own people seem to dislike you, which I do not completely understand. You have learned to blend with many other people. No, I do not see these things in you."

The two paused, then continued to eat to break up the uncomfortable silence.

After the meal, Tavid bowed his head and thanked Ismail for his honesty and hospitality. Karoun and Tavid left the house, escorted by a servant.

Ismail watched them nearing the gate and quickly opened the window to call out, "Ermeni! Good luck with Kalkim Bey. Do not be a fool and ask him the same question!"

They walked silently down to the gate, Tavid reflecting on what had just transpired. After Tavid collected the horses, they then headed southeast away from the small port village and towards Mount Olympus on the outskirts of Bursa.

"I heard what you asked him," declared Karoun. "Do you want to know why I hate them?"

"You were listening?"

"Yes, along with his wives."

"Were you listening when he asked to buy you? He was willing to take you instead of the seven diamonds for payment." Tavid said.

Karoun's eyes widened.

"I was tempted but I am sure that your father would hunt me down to the ends of the ear…" Tavid felt instant pain in his side as Karoun pinched him.

"You are making it up! Tell me!"

"Are you trying to rip my skin off? No! No. And, I know why you hate them. You do not have to tell me. Freedom, it does not exist. You must stay at home or be escorted everywhere you go. It would suffocate me… hokees,[4] just try not to enjoy the hate. Today we will fill my home with love and hope."

---

[4] Armenian: "my soul."

"Dealing with Turkish officers is like an addiction to the opium resin. Over the years the addiction becomes more severe until the only way to free yourself from it is through death itself. And if you try to cheat death, there will be new consequences. This was a difficult lesson to learn."
— Yervant Yacoubian

CHAPTER 18

# Dogs of War

Kalkim Bey

TAVID AND KAROUN TOOK THE road to Keles up the southern slopes of Mount Olympus. As Karoun gazed upwards she was awed by the snow-covered cliffs. Farther up the road there were mountain villages, beautiful farmlands, and a river flowing by the road. After they passed the town of Keles, the road twisted farther up to the small village of Sorgun where most of the inhabitants were originally Turcoman nomads. Entering the village, Tavid and Karoun could smell fresh-baked bread as they walked up the stony streets. Tavid's small secluded farm was on the far side of this village.

As they left Sorgun, Tavid stopped at one of the last farmhouses to talk to an old Turcoman. Turning to Karoun, Tavid told her not to say anything. Nothing at all.

"Sinasi! Hay, Allah!" Tavid shouted.

"Hay Allah, Tavid!" the Turcoman called back. Tavid spoke in only his best Turkish when in these mountain villages.

Tavid saw Sinasi's flocks grazing on the mountain grasses. "Your sheep are looking plump. How were the crops this year?"

"The rain was good for the strawberries and fruit trees, but too much for the potatoes. What brings you to us today?"

"I have come to plant a winter crop, and to see my children of course." Tavid smiled. "Any visitors to report?"

Karoun's face expressed confusion as she overheard his announcement and continued to listen.

"No one. No one comes up here. They know better than that."

Tavid nodded in agreement.

"Do you have any cured meats and milk I may buy?"

Sinasi gestured to him to come and follow him into the farmhouse. Tavid turned to Karoun. "Stay here. I will only be a moment." He disappeared with the Turcoman.

Karoun, overwhelmed with Tavid's unsettling statement, was suddenly and undeniably confronted with her love for this dangerous young man. Even in the face of possible betrayal, her biggest fear was of losing him. Yet as she took in her surroundings she could not miss the grandeur of the peaceful setting. Glancing about her surroundings, there were no other villagers within sight. But she could hear the distant shuffling of the goats, sheep feeding on the grassy slopes, and the wind passing through the fruit trees. It made her feel alive in a way she had never experienced before. Until this sudden immersion in the harsh, unpredictable world, Karoun had never been outside of Constantinople. Familiar city sounds, caustic smells and the semi-colorless landscape had been replaced by this beautiful freedom. She intently enjoyed the quiet moment while considering what she was about to face. Tavid broke her reverie, appearing with two large goat skins filled with milk and another bag filled with meats.

"I will bring you back the flasks today my friend," Tavid assured Sinasi.

The Turcoman shrugged his shoulders. "When you can, Tavid. When you can."

Still juggling the milk and meat in one hand, Tavid got on his horse, bowed his head toward Sinasi, and they headed farther up the road. Before reaching the end, Tavid turned into a wooded area and directed Karoun to follow him.

Karoun asked the question.

"You have...there are children up here?"

Tavid turned, smiled but said nothing. Karoun was afraid to ask again. The two traveled on a dark, poorly-marked path riding up and down the mountain's side for another kilometer. The old tall forest trees formed a canopy above them. Soon the trees ended and the sun shining in a clearing came into view. Through this window, Karoun saw an old stone farmhouse, small in comparison to what they had passed on the mountain road. As they rode closer, Karoun could see a small stream that ran right through the bottom of the farmhouse.

"Stay on your horse," Tavid said as he jumped off his horse and tied all three to a post near the farmhouse. "I am going to call my children."

Tavid put his fingers to his mouth and let out a long ear-piercing whistle. Soon, in the distance, Karoun could see a line in the high grasses and opium plants being trampled, but these grasses and plants concealed what was fast approaching. Tavid began to jump up and down and howl like an animal. The more Tavid howled, the faster the grasses moved. Karoun's heart raced. At fifty meters, the grasses and plants parted as two dark brown figures came racing towards Tavid.

"Wild dogs," Karoun whispered, now completely mesmerized.

At impact, the two shepherd-like canines knocked Tavid to the ground. He lay there with his hands in front of his face as the two dogs tried to smother him. Tavid rolled, got up on all fours, grabbed one of the dogs by the scruff of its neck and threw him about a meter. He turned and went for the other dog but she was too fast for him to grab. Tavid then crouched down, started talking to the dogs as if they were little babies and lunged after them, barely able to catch hold. They growled but Karoun saw that both of their tails were wagging incessantly.

"You are playing with them?" she whispered, amazed.

Tavid was playing hard, and it got so rough that the dogs were tearing his clothes with their teeth. As Tavid pulled away, so did his garments with a rip and a tear.

"Owooo!" Tavid fell to the ground pretending he was crying. The happy dogs licked the hands and face of their missed companion.

"Look what you have done to my clothes! Look what you have done!" Tavid scolded the dogs while they continued to maul him.

"Dzo! Dzo! Gahteeg goozess? Mees gooses?[1]" Tavid slowly got up and repeated his offer to the dogs, which excited them even more.

With the dogs at his side, Tavid quickly went over to one of the horses and grabbed the milk and meat he bought from the Turcoman, holding them up high until the two dogs settled down and sat before him.

He opened the bag of meats and threw two large pieces to each of them.

---

[1] Armenian: "Hey! Hey! Would you like milk? Would you like meat?"

"I am going to get your cups so you can drink your gahteeg," Tavid said while walking over to the side of the small farmhouse to retrieve two large metal bowls.

"Chobanig! Keil! Look!" Both the dogs quickly responded and started to drink even before Tavid had a chance to finish filling their bowls. Tavid stood up, covered with dirt and grass, sighed and glanced at Karoun. "These two I have had since they were pups."

"They are beautiful! Will they let me touch them?"

Tavid nodded. "But let them eat first."

"Where did you get them?"

"You can find them here and there. The shepherds have them sometimes to protect their flock. They are wolf killers."

"Who takes care of them up here?" Karoun asked.

"Ha! Takes care of them? They take care of themselves. They have everything they need up here. Food, water, companionship. And they watch to make sure no one comes into my fields."

"Do they eat wolves?"

Tavid shook his head and pointed toward the stream. "See the mice burrows here by the side of the stream? They love mice. Or squirrels. Rabbits if they can catch them. Anything small that they can catch."

Tavid threw some more cured meats to the dogs and walked over to Karoun.

"You can come down now. They will not bother you."

Karoun smiled and dismounted her horse. The dogs turned and pranced over to Tavid and Karoun, licking their muzzles and wagging their tails. Tavid put his hands out in front of him palms down and Karoun imitated him. Sniffing and licking their hands, the dogs let Tavid and Karoun stroke their heads and ears. Eventually Karoun was petting both Chobanig and Keil. Tavid stood aside.

"They can tell you are not afraid of them, Karoun."

"Afraid of them? Look how beautiful they are? How could I be afraid?"

Tavid rolled his eyes then walked over to Chobanig, gently grabbing his jaw and pulling back the skin to show the large canines, a good four centimeters in length.

"These are what I like about them. Look at the size."

"They have to have those if you are going to leave them up here all by themselves," Karoun said sternly.

Tavid's eyes widened, then he shrugged his shoulders. Karoun took a deep breath and took Tavid's arm as she led him to the stream. Tavid did not resist.

"You are filthy," she said. She dipped her hands into the stream and began to wash Tavid's face.

"I think you are more dangerous than they are. And I am not afraid of you."

Tavid placed his hands on hers as she was washing his face and kissed both her hands. Then approached her lips and kissed her softly. Karoun did not blush, but looked at him and confessed, "I was worried that you really had children. I am sorry for not trusting you."

Tavid smiled, and embraced her for a long long time.

Karoun then mimicked Tavid in saying, "That is quite a smell you have on you. I hope you do not always smell this way," and now she did blush.

Tavid let go of their embrace, eyed her with a smirk and got on all fours to wash his face and hair in the cold water, taking a long drink to quench his thirst.

"Ahhh. Always cold, always fresh."

Karoun helped Tavid comb his now tangled, medusa-like hair with their fingers. Tavid, holding Karoun's hand, strolled over to a small patch of garden separate from the poppy field, and the two pulled up clumps of carrots and radishes to feed the horses. They then went to the large boarded-up farmhouse door where Tavid pulled off some nailed boards with his clasp-knife.

"Karoun, I must go somewhere in a little while and leave you here for the rest of the day. Where I am going would not be safe for you. You must stay here. I will return before dusk."

"Can they stay with me?" Karoun asked.

"Of course. Here." Tavid handed her the milk-filled goatskins and bag of meats.

Tavid inspected his scant belongings in the farmhouse. On one side was an old roughed-out granite table with his chemist laboratory, including a distiller for refining opium, a large wood-burning stove that vented out through one of the walls, an old oblong wooden table, and chairs with blankets and bedding. On the other side of the farmhouse, separated by the flow of the crisp mountain stream, were stalls for horses during the night or severe weather. Years ago, Tavid and his grandfather had dug the streambed out under the farmhouse and placed stones on each side to prevent flooding. The sound of the flowing stream against the stones echoed within the farmhouse, and the freshness of the stream cleaned and almost purified the air. Tavid shook out the dust from the sheets and bedding and started a fire in the stove. Karoun walked into the farmhouse with Chobanig and Keil.

"Why is it built on top of this stream?" Karoun asked inquisitively.

"Keeps the farmhouse cool in the summer. And you can put milk, cheese or eggs in the water to keep them cool and fresh."

Karoun lowered the goatskins of milk in the stream.

"Did you notice anything about Keil?"

Karoun looked at the dogs. "Which is which?"

Tavid walked over to one of the dogs, "This is Keil and I think she is going to have pups."

Karoun's face lit up almost as bright as when Tavid walked her into the toy shop in Constantinople.

"When?"

"A month or two. Maybe sooner. The next time we come up here maybe we will see her babies."

Tavid walked outside to fetch Karoun's horse to settle into the stables and he unloaded the weapon bags tied to all three of the horses.

"The sooner I go, the sooner I may return. Stay in or near the farmhouse while I am gone," Tavid instructed Karoun as he untied the two remaining horses and mounted one.

"What if you do not come back?"

Tavid frowned. "I will come back. Do not worry about that..." He paused slightly, then rode back to Karoun to give additional instructions.

"See that opening in the woods? It is a path to my village. If I do not come back, take your horse and follow it for about three kilometers. You will come out of the forest and see the village in the distance. Go there and ask where I live...Kaloustian. Then go to my home. Do not worry about getting lost; your horse knows the way, too. But I will be back."

Karoun nodded, acknowledging Tavid's orders with a smile.

Tavid turned and headed down the same forest path, traveling through open fields back to Bursa. At one point he paralleled the road that would lead him directly to the military command post on Bursa's outskirts. There, he would have to deal with Captain Kalkim Bey and his lieutenants.

First, Tavid would stay off the road until he neared the post. Too many soldiers traveled the same road. After a three-hour ride, Tavid was a kilometer away from his destination. He chose the main road to travel this short distance. He stopped, dismounted and rubbed dirt and sand into his clothes, face and hair, then rolled and kicked around in the fields next to the road.

"How do I look, Kourkig?" he asked his horse. "Do I smell bad enough?" Kourkig snorted, sneezed, and turned his large head away from Tavid.

"Hm. Good! You disapprove. So will they."

Tavid was not on the road for more than a few moments when two soldiers approached from behind.

"Look at this animal on our roads! What should we do with it, eh?"

"Needs to be put in a cage, I say. But look at the horses," the second soldier scoffed.

Tavid kept riding and ignored the soldiers. The two rode past him and quickly turned into Tavid's path.

"Where do you think you are going..." The soldier stopped and stared at Tavid.

"Hyevan? Hyevan!"

"Sikishmek! You are dead!" said the other.

Tavid smiled. "Kalkim Bey is expecting me. May I pass?"

The two soldiers looked at each other, turned and galloped toward camp. Tavid followed slowly.

Back at camp, the two soldiers raced to beat each other to give word to Kalkim Bey. Jumping off their horses in front of the commander's quarters they raced for the door. Inside, Kalkim Bey was reprimanding his son, Lieutenant Tahir.

"Yes, the soldiers are terrified of me, but they know what I expect of them! They know they do not have to worry unless they do something stupid or against my rules! But you, Tahir, they do not know what you are going to do or when you are going to explode! Yes, I have told you that you must strike fear into their souls to lead them. But you must show some consistency! If they follow the rules, they will be rewarded. If they disobey, it should be like a Jehennem for them..." The two soldiers broke into the quarters, tripped and fell onto each other like circus clowns.

"Sarsakh! Eshek!² What are..."

---

² Turkish: idiot, jackass.

"Pasha![3] He is alive! We saw him! On the road coming here now!" one of the soldiers exclaimed.

Steam seemed to erupt from under the commander's collar.

"Who is so important that you come running in here like d…"

"The Hyevan! The Ermeni, Pasha! We both saw him."

"Whaaat?" said Tahir. "Kaloustian is alive? You saw him? Where?" He picked up one of the soldiers off the ground by his shirt. "Where did you see him?" he demanded from the soldier.

"On the road less than a kilometer away!"

Tahir looked at his father, who now suddenly had the glimmer of a smile on his face. Tahir bolted out through the door where he could see Tavid coming down the road at about 250 meters. As Kalkim Bey came out, Tahir started to sprint directly to Tavid.

"Tahir! Tahir! Get back here!" His father roared. Tahir did not even turn his head and raced ahead to Tavid.

"Eshek," Kalkim whispered to himself. From his jacket pocket he pulled out a pre-rolled tobacco leaf, licked and rolled the ends tight, lit one end and smiled.

"Alive, eh? Hope you have not come all this way empty-handed."

Kalkim watched his son running out to meet Tavid and then noticed many of his troops had stopped what they were doing to see what was causing the commotion.

"Kaloustian! Kaloustian!" Tahir yelled and cursed under his breath. When he had reached Tavid he stopped to catch his breath and stared in disbelief. He studied Tavid's appearance.

"You! You ugly piece of pislik![4] You are supposed to be dead!"

Tavid looked down from his horse with disgust. "Am I some long-lost girlfriend or relative that you come running out to meet me? Am I a woman from your harem you have not seen for weeks that you come out with such speed?"

Tahir's eyes tightened, nose flared.

"The entire regiment is watching you, Lieutenant! As is your father. Has he taught you nothing?"

Tahir's face hardened. "It is of no matter to me what they think. Pack of lazy cowards," Tahir retorted.

---

[3] Turkish: a man of high rank or office.
[4] Turkish: dung, manure.

"No matter? You are one of their leaders and need to be an example for them to follow. Or else your father may decide to make an example out of me! Pretend you are furious, pull me off my horse, and throw me on the ground. That way they will see it was not from happiness that you have run out to see me, but from anger."

"Happy to see you? You think I am happy again to smell your ugly stench, Ermeni?" Tahir grabbed Tavid's leg and yanked him off his horse. Tavid fell to the ground. Tahir then picked Tavid up with both hands and lifted him up in the air until they were eye to eye.

"It will be snowing in Jehennem before I am glad to see you!" With that, he smiled, as did Tavid.

"Then it is snowing now, you overgrown monkey."

Tahir became furious and threw Tavid about five meters through the air like a sack of rice. Tavid landed off to the side of the road and did not move. Tahir started for him, but stopped for he heard the regiment in the camp cheering and whistling. At first, he did not realize their praise was being directed at him.

"What are they all howling about?"

"They are cheering for their lieutenant," Tavid said in a muffled voice.

Tahir looked back at Tavid. "Maybe I should give them a better exhibition?"

"No need to overdo it. May I suggest you just throw me on my horse now and take me in to see your dear father?"

Tahir laughed, walked over to Tavid, picked him up by his pants and overcoat and threw him back on his horse sideways. Tavid hung to the foot straps of his horse's saddle. Tahir grabbed the reins of the two horses and led them into the encampment. He noticed one of the horses was a pure ebony Friesian with a long thick mane and tail.

"I see that you have found a horse for me as I required."

"The Friesian is young, strong and handsome like his new owner. But unlike you is level-headed."

Tahir shook his head and grinned through gritted teeth, "Most men are afraid to even talk to me. But you, you even *try* to enrage me!"

The soldiers continued to whistle and cheer from camp but Tahir waved them off.

"Afraid of you? No. I feel sorry for you having to be here in the shadow of your father. Being trained to be someone you do not want to be. Having to listen and work with soldiers for whom you have no respect. Anger is the only pure emotion I have ever seen in you. Everything else has been…"

"Shut up Kaloustian! No lectures today!"

Back outside the captain's quarters, Kalkim Bey and his second lieutenant Mustafa Kulhan observed the reaction of the troops while awaiting Tahir's return with a Kaloustian ghost in custody.

"Ahfedeem![5] I thought he was going to embarrass me again running out there like that. Maybe he is slowly learning," Kalkim praised.

"Pasha, what will you do with the Ermeni this time?" Mustafa asked.

"If he has brought payment, nothing. I will let him go as usual. But if he comes here with excuses, that is a different story." Kalkim took another pull from his rolled tobacco.

"He is a Hyevan. We should kill him if he does not pay us, Pasha."

"Perhaps. We shall see what comes to light. Maybe he will make a mistake today, Lieutenant. Maybe he will take advantage of my kindness toward him. Just once, I would like to see him dare to ask a favor of me. I would send him home with one less finger for each favor he dares to ask. Maybe more."

Mustafa smiled, "Yes, Pasha. I am looking forward to that day."

Tahir approached his father with Tavid and the two horses as a swarm of soldiers surrounded them like water around a peninsula. Tahir's irritation with them was growing and his father could see it.

"Mustafa! Have the soldiers return to their duties. We have private business to discuss," the captain ordered.

"As you wish, Pasha."

Mustafa yelled orders out to the troops.

Some of the soldiers did not move fast enough for the captain who suddenly took the rolled tobacco out of his mouth and studied some of the soldiers' faces.

"Afterwards, you know what to do with the ones that seem to be hard of hearing. I demand complete obedience, Lieutenant," an impatient Kalkim ordered Mustafa.

Tahir arrived in front of the quarters and roughly hauled Tavid off his horse.

"Lieutenant! Do not be so harsh with our young dead friend. We will conduct business under the tent. Come! Bring the horses." A tented area off to the side of the quarters had a large lofty table.

---

[5] Turkish: translated as praise towards someone.

Tavid stood, tried to brush the dust and dirt off his face and clothes, and followed the officers under the tent.

"You look pathetic, Kaloustian! As if you have come back from the dead! What happened to you? And how is it that you are alive after being shot and blown to Jehennem, as we were told?" the captain bellowed.

"Forgive my appearance, Captain, but I have traveled not like a man but an animal to return here alive with your payment and gifts. Regarding my death, Pasha, it was highly exaggerated."

The captain laughed, "Yes, exaggerated! And your village? They have buried you in tradition as well as in their minds. No matter. The past is the past. Let us move to the present. Show me what you have brought today."

Tavid bowed his head and went to one of the horses, where he untied a bag secured to the saddle. He walked over to the large table and removed the contents.

"Here is payment to you for your kindness in allowing me to grow my crops to sell in Stamboul.⁶" Tavid tried to hand the captain a small hemp bag.

The cautious captain demanded, "Open it on the table for me to see, Ermeni.

Tavid obeyed. On the table fell twenty gold lire, six diamonds, and five hundred paper lire. More than two years' pay for an Ottoman captain. Their enchantment was given away by their silence. The captain then examined the lire, tapped the coins, and rolled the diamonds between his thumb and forefinger,

"This is twice what you brought us last year. Have you been holding out on us, Ermeni?"

Tavid smiled. "It was a very good crop this year and the opium resin is very strong. With the war starting, there are fewer sellers. I hope you are pleased, Pasha."

Kalkim Bey studied Tavid's face and nodded his head as if he were still thinking.

"There is more." Tavid continued by pulling out a small glass tube of resin wrapped in sheepskin, placing it on the table.

"Ah! Very good. You have not forgotten anything."

Tavid pulled another bag tied to the saddle. It held a small container.

"What is this now?" asked the bemused captain.

---

⁶ A district in Constantinople. Later named Istanbul.

Tavid handed the small bag to the captain, "It is a gift. Something made for one of your stature. Please."

The captain took the bag, which was heavy for its size. The gift was wrapped in silk cloth and when this layer was removed, the captain's eyes revealed great pleasure.

"A merchant in Constantinople was desperately in need of some resin and was willing to trade anything. I believe that it was once owned by an Asian warrior."

Tavid had handed the captain a traditional crescent-shaped knife and scabbard etched with calligraphy. The blade was cut of jade, the handle and scabbard of silver.

"The merchant tells me jade is a very hard stone, Captain, and it was the tradition in his country for emperors and other men in high authority to bear such kni..."

"You are lying! That is not something that you can just buy on the streets in Stamboul! Who did you kill to steal that knife?" Mustafa accused.

"Lieutenant, the merchant I am speaking of was very desperate. Have you ever seen one addicted to the resin? He would have traded much more if I had insisted."

Tahir laughed under his breath. "Then you should have traded for three knives! One for each of us!" Tahir exclaimed. Both he and his father laughed uproariously. Mustafa looked irritated.

"Yes and what have you brought for my two lieutenants? I hope you have not forgotten them."

Tavid looked over to Tahir who was starting to be acquainted with his new horse, caressing his forehead and talking quietly to him.

"As directed, I brought a horse for Lieutenant Tahir. It is a young stallion and will have many good riding years. I hope it is acceptable."

"The horse will do fine. I approve. What else did you bring?" Tahir demanded.

Tavid pulled out two more bags. Bowing his head, he handed one to each of the lieutenants. Inside each bag were approximately a quarter of the gold and lire that the captain was given.

"Is that all?" Mustafa snarled. "No more payments for a year now, Ermeni?"

Tavid was ready for this question for he would need time and an excuse to go to Constantinople in the spring.

Tavid addressed the captain. "I have acquired special hybrid seeds for a spring crop this year."

"Oh?"

"Over the past few years I have seen that some of the Asian merchants have been selling resin in Constantinople, not only in the autumn but also in the late spring. How could they grow the poppies so fast? Finally, I learned that over the decades they have been able to produce a seed that could be planted in the autumn for a spring harvest. When the autumn frost would come, it would kill only the fresh leaves on the plants but not the deep roots. When spring came, the plants would bear their flowers early. The opium resin could be taken and processed by late spring. That is what I intend to do with these new seeds."

"A crop twice a year?" Tahir was incredulous.

"Just as they plant spring wheat in the autumn fields."

"This is good news if true. I am pleased with your payment. Perhaps it was destined for you to live. If only the rest of your village was as productive. And as appreciative."

"They do not always realize how fortunate they are to have you here." Tavid said, bowing his head again.

Kalkim Bey studied Tavid's words and nodded. "Yes, you do something about their insolence. So I do not have remind them. We shall see you in the spring then, Kaloustian?"

The captain thought, "Unless there is anything else?"

Tavid hesitated. "There is one thing, Captain, if I may ask a favor."

Mustafa's head turned, eyes widened and hand slowly crept to where he kept his knife.

"What did you say, Ermeni?"

"Pasha, as you know my father and grandfather are both dead. I have no stepfather, no one I can ask for advice on things. I have no experience. I trust very few people, respect even fewer. I am...in need of your advice."

Kalkim Bey was warily pleased at Tavid's brilliant stroke of his ego, not prepared for such a request. Then looked at his son and Mustafa and walked halfway around the table to address the Armenian.

"Advice you need. Advice I will give. What is it?"

Mustafa suddenly looked confused as he stared at the captain, saying nothing.

"There is a spy," Tavid started. "An informant was helping the port commander in Constantinople. Twice he has come close to having me killed. When I find him out, what should I do with him? What if he is a friend, or someone close to my family? Or he is a young boy or an old man, someone who was blackmailed into helping another?"

Kalkim Bey's eyes were fixed on Tavid as he walked up to him.

"I would kill him. No question," he answered.

Tavid glanced at Mustafa and asked, "But, Captain, what if he is not an Ermeni?"

The captain's eyes flashed. "Then you come to me, tell me who the dog is and I will kill him myself!"

Tavid bowed his head in apparent reverence but was attempting to hide a smile.

"Thank you, Captain. May I go now?"

"Go? Is there nothing else you would like to ask? Nothing at all?"

"No. Thank you. You have already given me too much."

"Go then, get out of here!" He seemed disappointed that there was no more.

Tavid slowly mounted his horse and rode off.

"Captain!" Mustafa pleaded. But Kalkim Bey just raised his hand gesturing him to shut up.

"You are dismissed, Mustafa!"

"Tahir, follow the Ermeni. Make sure he gets back to Tchingiler alive. He does not look very good."

Tahir smiled at his father.

Seeing this the captain added, "I just do not want to see some dead animal rotting on the side of one of my roads!"

Tahir saluted, changed saddles and followed Tavid.

"I give my daughter Anoush a lot of credit. Her husband died before his time, leaving her to put up with me and my influence on her children. But through the years she has found happiness and always sees the sun through the clouds. I may not have told her often but I love her dearly and am proud of her."
– Yervant Yacoubian

# CHAPTER 19

# Arrival of The Dead

THE SUN WAS LOW BUT clear in the northwest. In a few hours, it would be nightfall. Tavid hoped that Karoun would be safe until he was able to return. He looked back on the road and saw Tahir following, keeping his distance but in pace with him. Tavid did not slow or halt his horse and continued to Tchingiler. Once they were out of sight of the Turkish encampment Tahir galloped next to Tavid. Nothing was said at first. Tahir looked at Tavid's filthy clothes, tangled hair and dirty unkempt face and smirked.

"Asking my father for advice. Ha! You are more of a Tilki[1] than a Hyevan!"

Tavid, straight-faced, said nothing.

"Advice! He lives to advise us! We will not hear the end of how an animal knows better who to ask for advice than us!"

"Your father is a wise man," Tavid said without turning.

"What? Your mouth is full of shit! I see what you are doing. And I hate how it makes me like you even more! Bahbahm![2]"

---

[1] Turkish: fox.
[2] Turkish/Armenian slang: "my father!" Used in the same way as "oh my God!"

Tavid narrowed his eyes and stared at Tahir, said nothing while holding back a smile.

Tahir continued, "If only I had a young brother like you…someone that was not afraid to fight, to kill or to just be…until the ground could hold us no longer."

"If you were my brother, Lieutenant, I would have to kill you," Tavid replied, and then continued. "Brother or not. To release you from your misery."

"Sikishmek! What stupidities are coming from you now?"

"You are unhappy with your life and you take your anger out on everyone around you. Tell me I am wrong. You cannot stand any of your subordinates at camp including Mustafa, and you hate the military. You feel nothing but anger and rage when you wake up in the morning until you are asleep at night. And you feel trapped because of what your father wants you to become and you hate him for it."

Tahir was adamant, "I do not hate my father, and the times will change. I must wait for the right opportunity. Who are you, a prophet now that you are back from the dead?"

"Ahhh! You have hope! That is good. Many Ermenis have hope just like you that they will survive this coming war, that they will not be taxed more heavily than they are now, that they will not be taken away to fight."

"What do I care of them? Let them take care of themselves," Tahir interrupted.

Tavid showed disgust. "We could never be brothers. Not even friends."

"And you! Such a respectable citizen you are? Caring only for your village and for your brothers and sisters. Ha! You and I are much alike, whether you like it or not," Tahir retorted.

In response, Tavid spat on the ground.

Both became silent as a mild breeze blew in their faces as if to stop their argument. They continued on their way to Tchingiler and for a while said nothing, neither wanting to provoke the other. At least not while they were on their way to Tchingiler. Tahir remembered his last trip there, when he told the Kaloustian family of Tavid's demise.

"I was the one that told your mother you were dead…"

"You? Why?"

"My father sent me to find out if you had taught anyone else to harvest the opium. And I think he did not really believe you were dead. Wanted to find out how your family would react."

"How did they react?" Tavid asked.

"Told me that I should have been protecting you. Called me a murderer. Then your brother and sister threw rocks at me as I left."

Tavid laughed. Thinking of his two siblings and their apparent bravado toward a Turk that could have easily killed them. Tavid had not seen his family for over a month now. More than ever, he was looking forward to returning home.

"You let two young children chase you away? That must have been a horrible feeling. And being called a murderer…"

"I have been called much worse, Kaloustian."

"Yes, but I doubt that person is still alive."

The two rounded a bend in the dirt road and Tchingiler was in sight two kilometers ahead. White-capped Mount Olympus dwarfed the village. Forests with adjacent olive groves grew at its foothills. The road was empty of villagers and in the distance Tchingiler seemed asleep and peaceful with only the movement of white smoke from chimneys rising and drifting with the gusts of wind from the northwest. Tavid could see Tchingiler's cathedral, the largest structure in the center of the village. Its soul protected by the surrounding structures. Tavid knew he would be visiting the cathedral in a day or so, but not to pray. His thoughts moved to finding the spy.

"Has your cousin been to Constantinople this month?" Tavid asked.

"Mustafa? I do not believe so. He has been to Bursa twice this…ahhh, Mustafa!" Tahir paused, then continued.

"You think he could be the spy? No. He is not that stupid to betray my father."

"You are probably right. Nevertheless, you see how he hates me. I can see it in his eyes. Would probably kill me if he had the chance. It is fairly easy to get to Constantinople from Bursa."

Tahir shook his head, then thought of what Tavid said. "If you had told my father this…"

"Someone would be dead right now," Tavid finished. "But whom? Mustafa or me?"

"I will keep an eye on him. And if he goes into Bursa I will have him watched."

As they neared the edge of the village, Armenians slowly moved away from the streets and into their houses, seeing the Turkish soldier.

Tavid could see his own home now and prodded his horse into a gallop as Tahir followed. Tavid stopped in front of an unassuming half-wooden, half-stone house. A sun-bleached wooden fence built by his father surrounded the small front yard. Tavid had repeatedly repaired it with new wood from felled trees of the nearby forests. His mother had planted autumn flowers and herbs in the front of the house.

As Tavid dismounted from his horse he suddenly saw his mother in the doorway, tears streaming down her face utterly overtaken by emotion at the sight of her son. Tavid wanted to say something smart like *"Mother, the ghost of your son has returned."* Instead he quickly walked into her open arms and the two embraced wordlessly. Her hair drifted onto Tavid's face and the scent of it reminded him of his childhood, making him feel calm, warm and at peace. He continued to hold her tightly.

"I buried you. I…" Anoush could not finish without crying.

"Mayrig, I am sorry. I did not know. Oosh uhllah, anoush uhllah.[3]"

His joyous mother wiped and opened her eyes, and saw Tahir dismounting from his horse. At first she ignored him, holding onto Tavid. Eventually she faced him.

"You! Why do you stand there?"

Tavid looked around at Tahir. "To make sure I returned safely."

Anoush looked at her son's face, held it in her hands, kissed him then walked to Tahir, who appeared apprehensive.

"Why? Why are you the one to bring my son back?" She asked in Turkish.

Tahir took a deep breath, "Because I am the one that took him from you."

Anoush nodded her head while staring at the lieutenant then bowed her head.

"I am sorry for what I said to you on our last meeting. Thank you for watching over my son, Pasha."

Tavid walked up and put his arms around his mother, then whispered something in her ear. Anoush nodded and walked back into the house.

Tahir started to get back on his horse. "Farewell, Kaloustian. Maybe some of your neighbors will come…"

*"Herikeh![4]"* Tavid said, "Get off your horse and stay for a moment."

---

[3] Armenian: a saying translating as "better late than never."
[4] Turkish: "Enough!"

Anoush returned with a basket of fresh warm bread, butter and mulberry brandy.

"I do not like it when you drink, Tavid. It makes you crazy." Anoush reminded him in Armenian.

"One drink with this soldier. What can it hurt?" he answered in Armenian.

Anoush started to walk back into the house. "I am going to go find your brother."

Tavid took the basket and presented it to Tahir. "Let us eat and drink before you return to your Jehennem."

Tavid filled up the glasses with brandy, tore off a large piece of buttered bread for Tahir, who was hesitant to eat or drink.

"What is the matter? Do you think I am going to poison you? Or have you never eaten from the hands of an Ermeni before?"

Tavid drank his brandy and started to devour a large chunk of buttered bread. Tahir's mouth began to water. He took another deep breath, downed the brandy, smiled and began to eat. Tavid filled the glasses again, checking over his shoulder to see if his mother was watching.

"What type of drink is this?" Tahir asked, smacking his lips.

"Brandy from mulberries. Made here in the village. Strong and sweet... just like me."

Tahir choked. Bread, brandy, all at once. Eyes tearing, he could not stop coughing and sputtering, finally downing another shot of brandy to wash down the errant bread. When he recovered, the warmth of the sudden intake of brandy had hit home.

"Let us toast to...toast to your return home, to this pathetic village you live in."

"And to your father and all the brave soldiers in your encampment!" Tavid responded. "May they never have need to come to my pathetic village." The two drank again.

"You? Strong and sweet? Ha! You were not so strong when I picked you up at camp and threw you like a sack of olives. And you look and smell worse than...than the worn-out prostitutes in Bursa!" Tahir began to laugh uncontrollably.

Tavid laughed and stepped closer to Tahir. In one quick motion Tavid thrust his open hands full force into Tahir's chest, knocking him back and off balance. Almost simultaneously Tavid placed his foot behind Tahir's, guaranteeing his inability to recover. As Tahir was falling back Tavid followed almost on top of him until Tahir hit the ground. Just before impact Tavid reached down with one hand into his boot, retrieved his dagger and held it to Tahir's face, the steel shimmering in front of him. Tahir's eyes closed tight briefly, then opened wide. He did not speak, breathe nor move.

"Do not move," Tavid said in a low voice as he slowly touched the flat end of the steel blade to Tahir's face, smiled and quickly rolled off Tahir and stood up. Still stunned, Tahir took a breath and climbed to his feet.

"That dagger. It is forbidden for Ermenis to carry a weapon. No less into our encampment!"

"Forgive me I did not know that!" Tavid threw the dagger, blade first into the ground. He opened his overcoat, withdrew two pistols and dropped them next to his dagger. Tahir's eyes and mouth were now wide open.

"Pistols! You! Are they loaded?"

Tavid did not answer. He just glared at Tahir as if he were an idiot. "Take off your gunbelt, Lieutenant."

Still stunned from the fall and the sight of Tavid's weapons, Tahir stood staring at Tavid. He looked down at his gunbelt, smiled, looked back at Tavid and removed the belt. It was time to fight.

As they did, the villagers quietly came out of there homes to watch from a safe distance. The two fought and wrestled like two drunken friends. Tahir was taller and bigger, yet Tavid was quicker and their strength closely matched. The dirt-packed street swelled with the grunts and groans of the two men. Then a gunshot startled everyone.

Staying low to the ground, Tavid quickly turned to see where the shot came from. At first, he thought he was looking at a reflection of himself. However, this reflection was pointing one of his guns in the air.

"You are scaring Mayrig!" Tavid's brother Stepan yelled, eyes burning, body tense.

Tavid held his hand up towards Stepan while trying to catch his breath.

"Put that down!" Tavid yelled at his brother. He walked over to Tahir to help him off the ground.

"All right. It is time for you to go," Tavid said to Tahir, brushing the dust and dirt off the lieutenant's uniform. He patted his chest and handed him what was left of the bottle of brandy, brushing the dust off it and retrieving the cork that he picked up from the ground.

Trying to catch his breath, Tahir gazed at Tavid's brother, then focused on Tavid. "I will see you in the spring, Kaloustian, unless the war changes our fates." He took a pull from the bottle and mounted his horse.

"Take care of your new ride. I expect to see her also this spring, healthy and strong."

Tahir powered his horse to turn full circle while glaring at the villagers who now gathering and galloped away.

Tavid brushed off yet another layer of dust, dirt imbedded in his clothes and on his face, but realized the futility. His brother's position was still frozen, pistol in the air, eyes fixed on the soldier riding away. He glared at his older brother as he walked over to him. This was not the happiness Tavid had envisioned.

"Was this supposed to be another one of your jokes? Pretending to be dead?" Stepan said in an irritated voice.

Tavid shook his head, "Of course not. I had no idea until a few days ago. I am sorry, Stepan." Tavid looked at his pistol in his brother's hand.

"Finger off trigger, barrel pointing away," Tavid instructed him and reached for his pistol. Stepan responded but still kept his distance.

Tavid wanted to embrace his brother who stepped back again.

"You look like you have just crawled out of a grave," Stepan said.

Tavid grinned. "Yes, I know. Now come here once and for all and give me my gun." Stepan paused before handing the gun to Tavid and embraced his brother tightly.

"Good to see you starting to look more like me!"

Bending down he retrieved his dagger and remaining pistol. "Let us take my horse out back. Unload the bags later."

Suddenly, a voice from behind yelled out Tavid's name. "Kaloustian, how did you escape Jehennem? What kind of deal did you make with the Turkish devils this time?"

"Do not listen to him. He is an *aboush*,⁵" Stepan said as they walked into the house. "At your funeral he told me that it was a blessing that you were dead. So I hit him. You know, right here as hard as I could like you have showed me?" Stepan pointed to his lower ribs just above his stomach. Stepan laughed, "He was not expecting that. Then he fell in the hole they dug for your grave!" Tavid joined in the laughter as they entered the house.

---

⁵ Armenian: idiot.

"I wish I could have been th…" Tavid froze as he entered his home. Sitting at the table were two girls interacting. His sister Varsenig and Karoun. Yes, Karoun. Stepan expressed a contagious smile as he saw the surprised look on his brother's dirt-ground face. His mother stood next to the table where Karoun showed Varsenig her beautiful doll. Anoush's arms were folded in front of her with a look of discontentment. Anoush explained that Karoun had arrived at their doorstep a few hours before he arrived. Both girls looked up at Tavid, Varsenig with a angelic smile, Karoun with a look of worry.

"She has not stopped talking about you since she has arrived," Anoush grabbed Tavid's head to confirm Karoun's story through the now-healed scalp wound.

"Ahmahn, Asdvadz![6] It is all true!"

"What has she told you?"

"Everything! Yes, everything!" Shaking her head at Tavid, Anoush showed disdain.

Tavid was petrified. He could not look into his mother's eyes. He thought of his grandfather, Yervant, who had those same piercing clear eyes. Then took a deep breath.

"She has not told you everything, Mother."

Rolling her eyes, Anoush gestured toward Karoun and Varsenig. "They have been inseparable since she arrived. She is acting like this is her new home."

Tavid felt a lump in his throat. His face began to flush.

"What is this she tells me about some half-naked girl sitting on your lap?"

Stepan howled, grabbing his older brother's hips and thrusting them back and forth. His mother stopped him and slapped Stepan squarely on his scalp.

"No more trips to the city for you, Ahnbeedann![7] No, no. You are staying here for a long time, a very long time. And we will see about Karoun. Hassguhttsar![8]"

Tavid looked at his mother. "It is alright then for her to be here?"

"It was not right for her to leave her family the way she did. But what her father did… Well, we will see what is to happen. Her parents must be

---

[6] Armenian: "oh my God!"
[7] Armenian: mischievous child.
[8] Armenian: "Is that understood?"

worried sick about her, even if they do know she is with us. Enough of this for right now. Your smell is making me sick. Go get washed up in the back. Now!"

Tavid had his brother retrieve his horse and belongings and carry them to the back of the house. Tavid quickly walked into the only other room in their home where the family cooked, ate, washed and slept. In a corner was an old metal bathtub large enough for Tavid to bathe. Anoush had sewn curtains around the tub that hung from the ceiling from fabric her father had brought back years ago from Constantinople. Beside it, a fireplace large enough to heat pails of water. When Stepan returned, Anoush sent him to fetch more water for Tavid's bath while ordering Tavid to disrobe and throw his clothes into the fire. He argued at first and then conceded, seeing that his mother was becoming even more irritated.

Emptying out his pockets onto a wooden table Tavid stripped down, throwing his filthy clothes into the fire. Then checking the water, he slowly submerged himself into the tub. Stepan returned moments later and began heating additional water. The warm waters together with the mulberry brandy running through Tavid's veins gave him a pleasant euphoria until his mother remembered something he had said in the other room.

"What did you mean; she has not told me everything"?

Tavid popped out of his trance.

"Hahmeh?⁹"

"*Dzo!*¹⁰ What has she not told me?"

Tavid remembered and he hesitated again.

"What more could have happened? You come back from the dead and bring Eftendelian's only daughter with you. Are there others somewhere you have brought back with you from the dead? Others for whom you have promised sanctuary?" Anoush stared at her son, waiting for an answer.

Tavid wanted to sink into the tub and hide from his mother like a child. He looked around the room worried that any item could become a weapon in her hands. His heart raced as his eyes fixated on his pistols and knives sitting on the table.

"You are not going to believe me and you are going to get even more angry, Mayrig."

"Then let it happen! Tell me and be done with it!" she yelled.

---

⁹ Armenian: "What?" or "What did you say?"
¹⁰ Armenian/Turkish: "Hey!"

Tavid thought for a moment, then started to smile nervously. "Your father is alive."

"Stepan is a younger replica of Tavid. With a few differences: He would follow you into the depths of hell if he admired you. Loyalty, truth and purity are how I would describe him. And if you look very closely, you will find that there is a trace of slyness to his thoughts."
– Yervant Yacoubian

CHAPTER 20

# Resurrection Revealed

WITH OPEN HANDS, ANOUSH BATTED Tavid's head as he tried to dodge her blows by ducking under the water.

"Everything is a joke with you, *Sah-dan-nah*![1]"

Tavid could not help but laugh, even though he was gasping for breath from submerging into the bath water. His exposed scalp stung from his mother's blows.

"It is true! He is in Cyprus. Aldo has told me!"

Anoush stopped.

"Still you joke! Do you not know when to stop?" she said in a lower tone.

Tavid shook his head. "It is not a joke. I felt the same way. There is an envelope on the table. He sent it to Aldo to give to me."

"Who sent it to Aldo?"

"Your father!"

Anoush sat down at the table where the envelope, Tavid's weapons and paraphernalia were before her.

"Look in the leather pouch."

For a moment, Anoush gazed at Tavid and focused again on the items on the table. Anoush took the leather pouch and pulled out its contents.

---

[1] Armenian: "Little Devil."

She pulled out the envelope. As she opened it the four visas to Cyprus fell out. Looking at Tavid apprehensively, she pulled out the letter. Seeing her father's handwriting, tears filled her eyes, her hands shook and her gasp choked back a sob.

"*Nareg Armenian School. Larnaca, Cyprus SE. Dear Baron Tavid, you have been invited with your family to come to Larnaca and become a part of our Cypriot community. Enclosed are your visas. May you have a safe journey.*"

Anoush blinked back tears and looked at Tavid for help.

"Look at when it is dated," Tavid instructed.

Anoush could not answer.

"Aldo says grandfather has bought a vineyard. He grows grapes and sells wine..."

"Stop it!" Anoush cried. "He is dead! I saw his body. You saw him. We buried your grandfather. Why would he do this to us?"

Tavid let her process the drowning emotions. He began to describe the story that Aldo had told him at Eftendelians. He recited his grandfather's plan to impersonate a physician, to find a suitable imposter, the execution of the sham, placing the body near the Turkish command post, killing the old commander Yesil he had been paying off, and finally why Yervant Yacoubian, her father, had left for Cyprus leaving his family behind. Repeatedly, Anoush rebutted with the same questions Tavid had put to Aldo. This time, Tavid gave the same answers.

The elements within Anoush were so distraught that all she could do was lie down on a cot next to the table and curl into a ball as if regressing back to her childhood. She closed her eyes and began to cry.

Moments later, Stepan walked back into the room and saw his mother crying. Flashing an accusatory look at Tavid he sat down next to her, stroking her long black hair curling it between his fingers as a child would. He looked over to Tavid for an answer.

"Now what did you do?"

It was easier explaining to his younger brother. As he repeated the story, Stepan's reaction was quite different. No questions, no doubt of his older brother. Elation showed on Stepan's face.

Anoush sat up, wiped the tears from her face and as she looked at her Stepan, she could not resist his addictive smile.

"Twice in one day, Mayrig! When are we leaving for Cyprus?" Stepan asked. "How will we get there?"

"In the spring we can leave from Constantinople by ship," Tavid replied. "Aldo's brother will come for us and take us to Cyprus."

Anoush tried to process. "What will we tell everyone? Why we are leav…"

"No! No one must know! Tell no one of this, ever. We will just disappear one day. That is it! There are spies, jealous people. If Kalkim Bey were to find out, I am sure he would kill us all. It cannot leave this room. Swear it!"

Anoush and Stepan both nodded. And for a moment, she felt as if her father had spoken.

Tavid repeated his concern, "Not even the girls. No one. Not a soul."

Tavid grabbed a towel, stood up from the bath and dried himself, but had no clothes to change into. Feeling embarrassed to ask his mother for anything, Tavid stood there for a moment with the towel wrapped around his waist. Finally, Anoush stood up having found new energy, and asked Tavid if there were going to be any other surprises this day. Tavid thought for a moment and answered slowly.

"Yes, there is one more thing. I did not forget to buy your spices this time," he smiled.

Anoush's eyes widened sarcastically as if this could have any significance now. She went into the adjacent room for a moment and returned with fresh new clothing for her son.

"These are not my clothes. Where are my clothes?"

"They are at the cemetery, buried!"

"What? You buried my cloth…"

"Yes, yes. Vartabed thought it would be symbolic. Burying something of yours. Something with your scent." She shrugged, smiling.

"How deep is the grave?"

"Never mind! It is late, are you still hungry?" Anoush asked.

Tavid just smiled.

"Good. Then sit down while I prepare something light for all of us to eat."

Tavid considered his mother's cooking unmatched except for Seta Eftendelian's but he dared not make a comparison out loud. Tavid thought of how the food and meals were simple in their village compared to Constantinople, as was the lifestyle. He missed this and loved the simplicity of his village.

Anoush's meal was simple: lavash,[2] goat cheese, olives and fresh fruits still in season. She called the others who all sat at the table. Anoush had Stepan say a quick prayer and they began to eat.

"Karoun, why did you leave the farmhouse?" Tavid asked.

Karoun did not answer right away.

"It seemed like you had been gone for a long time and I was worried it would get dark before I would find my way here."

"Did anyone see you on your way here?"

"Luckily, I did," Stepan interrupted. "I was hunting out by the edge of the forest when she came through. I cannot believe you left her alone up there."

"She was not supposed to…"

Karoun cut Tavid off. "I was alright. I had the dogs with me at the farmhouse."

Stepan gave a scolding look at his brother but Tavid brushed it off.

"Karoun, did you close the door of the farmhouse?"

She nodded.

"She told me one of your dogs is pregnant. Karoun says they are beautiful!" Varsenig said.

"I thought you were afraid of dogs?" Tavid teased.

"No, I am not!" Varsenig scolded.

Tavid shook his head and glanced at his mother.

Later, with the help of the two girls Anoush cleaned up after the meal while Tavid and Stepan went out to unpack the horse. Tavid was tired and decided to bring the bags in for the night and go through them in the morning. Promptly, Anoush had everyone off to bed including Tavid. Anoush had put a hemp-filled cot on the floor next to Varsenig's.

The family did not fall asleep quickly. Anoush thought of her father and son both coming back from the dead in a single day, but still wondering why her father had not yet returned home. Stepan dreamt of being with his older brother and learning from him. Varsenig whispered questions to Karoun about Constantinople, Karoun trying to answer without getting too emotional.

Tavid, however, exhausted from the day's activities, with a full stomach, had no more thoughts looming in his mind, and fell fast asleep.

---

[2] Armenian: unleavened flatbread.

"In a world of a thousand years ago, the village of Tchingiler would be much the same. Silk would be traded for items not found in the village. Fruits and vegetables would be plentiful. Goats and sheep would be commonplace. There would also be a wide variety of personalities in the village making for an interesting life. I yearn for this type of place again. Where life is clean, not muddied by the sale of opium and guns to pay off marauders. I believe I have found this place on the island of Cyprus. And I hope my family agrees."

– Yervant Yacoubian

CHAPTER 21

# My Father's House, A Den of Thieves

TAVID HEARD SOMEONE AT THE door but could not get to it in time to hold it closed. It opened and in walked Tahir followed by his father, Captain Kalkim Bey.

"Where are the guns, Hyevan?"

Tavid could not answer.

Tavid heard his mother and siblings in the next room and so did the two Turks who smiled at each other.

"Where are they?"

*Why are they here? he wondered. What day is this? What time is it?* Tavid's mind faded as the captain walked up to him. He was not who Tavid thought he was. It was his grandfather, Yervant.

"What are you doing? What are those bags on the floor, Hyevan?" his grandfather barked as he went to grab Tavid's face.

Tavid, pushing his head back into the pillow, woke up to see his mother standing over him touching the cheeks of his face.

"You slept well?" she asked.

Tavid's heart was pounding. He took a few deep breaths and smelled breakfast. He nodded and smiled at his mother.

"Good. Get dressed and come have some breakfast outside. Everyone else has already eaten."

She left Tavid clearing the dream from his mind. He laid there for a moment longer, closed his eyes and as he drifted, he heard voices as someone arrived outside, talking loudly.

"Not again," he thought, still half-asleep.

The door opened as his eyes did. His heart pounded.

"Shoon shahn vortee es![1]" bellowed the vartabed, shaking his head and fist at Tavid.

"This morning when they told me you were alive, I did not believe them! So I came to see for myself."

He stood in the doorway as if waiting for an explanation. Tavid approached the cleric, whose face softened as he held Tavid by the shoulders then embraced him.

"It is good to see you alive, hokees.[2] But I am still angry with you. How could you do such a thing to your family, to your mother?" Then the vartabed whispered in Tavid's ear, "My soul never really believed that you were dead."

The two heard Anoush calling them to join her outside for breakfast. Both hurried outdoors to enjoy a meal of thick dark coffee, warm sweet mulberry teas, dried flatbreads, madzoon[3] and fruits. As they ate, Tavid explained what had happened over the past month and the two listened intently. He found himself as before embellishing parts of the story and leaving other parts out so as not to be ridiculed or scolded by his mother or the vartabed. And when he came to the part of his journey where he arrived at the farmhouse in the mountains, he remembered the weapons and spices were still there. Again, he remembered this morning's dream. Throughout breakfast questions were asked. Questions Tavid tried to answer honestly.

"How many times did you visit Eftendelians? What did you do to irritate them this time?" his mother asked as the vartabed grinned sheepishly.

"What are your intentions with Karoun? How long is she going to stay here until you take her back to her family? How am I going to explain to the village that we have a young beautiful girl living with us?"

---

[1] Armenian: "you son of a dog."
[2] Armenian: "my soul."
[3] Armenian: yogurt.

The vartabed repeated some of the questions Tavid's mother asked if the answers were less than complete. Tavid stared at the vartabed when his mother was not looking.

"I have already had a long discussion with Karoun, Tavid." The vartabed waited to see if Tavid would start squirming but Tavid kept on eating then looked up at the vartabed.

"So tell me, was I wrong?"

The vartabed sipped on his rich coffee, then responded, "I feel very bad for...for her parents. I know by now they realize they have made a grave mistake and are being tortured by it. Karoun appears to be very happy and clear in her mind as to how she feels about you. I hope you feel the same for her?"

"Yes, I do. Are you surprised?" Tavid's mother began to smile.

"What kind of life can you give her with your travels to Constantinople and your chaotic lifestyle, selling opium on the black market, dealing with hooligans and the like. What kind of life is that for a young beautiful girl like her?"

Tavid snickered, "Mayrig told me that you had said that you wished you had a hundred Tavids living here."

"Ohf! I was just trying to comfort her," he said, trying unsuccessfully to hide his smiles with his coffee.

"I know you are half joking and being half serious. I can only tell you that things are going to change drastically in the future. That I promise."

"Well, I expect to see you all in church this Sunday. And do not try to skip communion this time!"

As the three continued to enjoy breakfast and their companionship, Tavid noted that autumn was changing the face of the land surrounding the village. Even though the morning sun was warm and the soft southern wind felt like an early summer breeze, the olive and mulberry orchards behind their home at the foothills of the mountains were changing color. The light winds of autumn played with the falling leaves. Snow was visible on the highest peaks, especially Mount Olympus. Tavid had missed his home yet was now faced with the ominous feeling he might never see this place again. Gazing back at the vartabed, he saw changes in him as well. Changes of age and stress. And life and death.

"Tavid, most of the village knows that you are back and alive. And many have asked me if I would find out if you have anything to sell."

"Ahn-Shoosht![4] Quite a few things I have. When should we meet?"

"Tonight, if you are able."

Tavid nodded.

"Good. We will meet as usual in the rectory."

The vartabed held his hands around Tavid's face, then kissed his cheek.

"If only your grandfather could see you, my son."

With that he got up, thanked Anoush for the meal and said his goodbyes.

"I have to go to the farmhouse this morning, Mayrig. I left the spices and other things there. I will take Stepan with me unless he has chores to do."

"Other things? What other things? Guns? Weapons?"

Tavid smiled. "Of course, Mayrig."

Anoush seemed impatient.

"He will want to go with you. Yes, take him."

Tavid got up to prepare to leave for the farmhouse. Calling his brother, the two of them saddled horses and shortly were on their way.

The short trip was exhilarating for Stepan. He was happy to see the farmhouse, play with the dogs, and help his brother pack up the horses with the guns and the spices for their mother. As they left, Tavid thought perhaps it would be wise to bring more supplies to the farmhouse in the near future, in case there was a need to leave the village this winter or before they left for Constantinople in the spring. When they returned, Karoun and Varsenig offered to help and took the spices into the house as Tavid and Stepan unloaded the weapons. Karoun appeared content with just being there, but Tavid yearned to spend more time with her. But his self-made chores were getting in the way.

"I have a surprise for you, Stepan. I am giving my rifle to you."

"What? Did you buy a new one?" Stepan was eager to have his gift in his hands.

"In a way," Tavid said as he pulled out their grandfather's rifle.

"It was our grandfather's. Aldo had been holding onto it for the past months."

Tavid handed the weapon to his brother to inspect.

"First chance we have, we will go hunting in the forests, or at least practice shooting and accuracy."

---

[4] Armenian: "yes, of course!"

Stepan's eyes beamed with excitement. "Can we go now?" he asked eagerly.

"Not today, Stepan. Not today."

As they finished, Tavid placed the weapons back in the hemp bags, leaving them on the floor in the house. He then hesitated, remembering his dream. Grimacing he picked up the bags and with the help of his brother hid them in the stables.

Evening did not come soon enough for Tavid. Throughout the day curious villagers stopped by the house, interrupting Tavid's chances to be with Karoun. Tavid had no desire to greet the crowd.

"Why do they not just leave me alone? Am I some freak that they have come to see?" he asked his mother.

"No. It is just their nature. They put their noses into other people's affairs. It has always been like that here. And I am sure it is like that in other villages as well. You really cannot blame them."

Tavid let out a deep sigh, looked out at the horizon and to his relief, dusk was near. It was almost time to leave for Gadar.[5] Anoush again indicated her disapproval. Karoun followed suit.

"Why do you have to sell weapons? Let people go into the city or elsewhere and buy them."

Tavid shook his head. "But I sell them guns that will fire when they need to use them. You know there is junk everywhere for sale," Tavid explained.

Anoush turned away refusing to hear any more and bade him to leave.

Karoun looked so beautiful in the last glow of sunset he had a moment's hesitation, and left before he could look at her again.

The night was cool and fresh as he passed through his village. Even the smell of smoke billowing from fireplaces had a sweet scent that wafted from the dried woods of fruit trees long past their ability to bear fruit. The crescent moon and the stars were awakening, both illuminating the watchful snow-packed peaks now sleeping like white-haired guardians tired from another day of sentinel duty.

Tavid stayed off the main streets. He guided his horse with its guarded cargo through some overgrown alleyways to the rectory next to the Cathedral Gadar. Lighted candles and lanterns burned inside, and Tavid heard sounds of conversation. He circled around to the rear of the rectory, securing the reins of his horse to a rusted iron hook embedded within the stone façade. He flung the bags of weapons over his shoulder and entered

---

[5] Armenian: apex, top of a mountain, perfect, pure. The name of the cathedral in Tchingiler.

the rectory through a service door that the vartabed always left open for him. A dozen or so men were inside. Most appeared very young or very old.

"Greetings, Tavid!" a tall scrawny man by the name of Vahé Vasakian bellowed.

"I was very surprised to hear you were alive!"

"As we all were," chimed in the heavily bearded Kristapor Sakalian who had come with Vahé Vasakian to the rectory.

Tavid continued to walk into the room and slung the heavy bags of weapons onto a large cloth-covered wooden table in the center of the rectory's central hall.

"You are still seeing my mother?" Tavid inquired. He did not give Vahé time to answer, "I am surprised to see you and Kristapor here."

"We would like to talk to you, Tavid. We heard you were coming tonight so we thought we would…"

Again Tavid interrupted him and turned away to talk to the small crowd gathering behind him.

"First things first," he said irritated.

"The rules are simple. I sell first to those who have not bought weapons from me in the past. Then what is left I will sell to those I have sold to before. All pistols come with at least forty rounds, rifles come with about fifty."

Tavid pulled out each weapon and laid it on the table.

"All are clean, without rust and in good working order," he uttered as buyers scrambled to examine the goods.

Tavid greeted the vartabed and thanked him for his hospitality. The vartabed seemed troubled, and without a word shifted his gaze to the two men who initially greeted Tavid. Tavid did the same.

"They want me to talk to you, Tavid, to convince you to help them."

Tavid shrugged, "Kristapor is a good man, but the other one…"

"That is true. But have you ever killed an Armenian?"

A look of puzzlement fell on Tavid's face. Then he smiled.

"Not yet. Someone you have in mind?"

The vartabed shook his head. "But they do."

Men were examining the weapons and some began asking questions and prices in reference to the items for sale. Tavid in turn would first ask what and why they wanted such a weapon, and for what they planned to use it. To some this was a foolish question to what was an obvious answer.

However, Tavid always found someone with a unique and often depressing reason. Some who had never fired a gun before would admit they would only use the weapon to defend themselves as a last resort.

He noticed an older, poorly-dressed man standing next to two baskets away from the others, waiting as if he were not allowed to view the weapons. Tavid stared at him for awhile but the old man would not meet Tavid's eyes. Tavid wondered why he behaved as an outcast compared to the others. There were no divisions or classes among this group. Tavid approached the man and at first said nothing to him. Finally, the old man looked up at Tavid.

"Are you here to purchase a weapon, Baron?"

The old man nodded. "I am hoping there will be something left after everyone is finished."

"Why must you wait?" Tavid asked.

The old man sighed. "Well, I am old and poorer than most. But I still am able to provide for my family. I...I have hoped that if there will be a stray rifle left I might be able to barter with you."

"What do you have to barter with, Baron? And why do you need a rifle?"

"Mostly to hunt small animals to feed my household. My rifle is old and rusted. I am afraid to use it any more. And to barter with, well I have what is inside these baskets." The old man removed rags on top to reveal their contents. One bag was filled with fresh vegetables and fruits from his garden, the other with a combination of preserves, dried fruits, flatbreads, and a small bottle of distilled spirits.

Tavid smiled. He led the old man by the hand, pushing some of the others away to find a rifle, a lighter model that would be easier for him to use. He found one and handed it to the old man, who examined the rifle, smiled and nodded with approval of the barter. He gave Tavid the two baskets. Others looked on and wondered what Tavid had traded for, but he placed the rags back on top of the bags and set them away from the crowd.

Others had chosen their weapons. Some continued to haggle for a better price. However, most knew from the past that Tavid's prices were fair. In less than thirty minutes the buyers had purchased their weapons and had begun to leave.

Again, Kristapor approached Tavid.

"There are a few rifles left over. Would you be willing to give them to me, and I in turn will pass them on to some of the Fedayees[6] in need of weapons?"

"What are you saying? Fedayees? Operating around here? There have not been any in this area for over ten years."

Kristapor shook his head, "Since the war, more have joined their ranks. I swore my allegiance after the soldiers came here last month and conscripted about fifty men into the Turkish army."

Tavid looked over to the vartabed who nodded in affirmation.

"Did you not notice that most who came here tonight were either very young or older like myself? They took all they could find. They were in their twenties and early thirties.[7] You were lucky you were not here."

Tavid shook his head in defiance. "Yes, they are lucky I was not here. And for the rifles, if there really are Fedayees in this region have them come and get the guns themselves. Why do they need you and...your friend Vahé to provide weapons for them?" Tavid asked sarcastically.

"That brings me to why we came here to see you tonight. May I speak of this now?"

Tavid finally succumbed to Kristapor's humble pleading. He explained how he and Vahé Vasakian had been procuring weapons over the past few months, knowing that there was a campaign to enlist and train more Fedayees. Rumors had swept the villages of increasing Turkish aggression, the burning of shops, and the murders of Armenians and other minorities to the east.[8] Then Kristapor mentioned the word "Cheté."

"Stop there! What do you know of them?" Tavid demanded.

"We have contacts in Bursa. They say that the Turkish government has emptied the prisons and armed the convicts under the pretense of needing army recruits. But we feel that these Chetés are being armed for another purpose."

---

[6] Arabic: One who sacrifices himself. Paramilitary. A group of civilians organized in a military fashion. Armenians used the word to mean "field worker" or "freedom fighter" as well as the former meaning.

[7] August 22, 1914: The male population between the ages of 20 and 45 is conscripted by the Turkish armed forces. (Source: www.genocide1915.info.)

[8] August 18, 1914: Looting is reported in Sivas, Diyarbekir, and other provinces, under the guise of collecting war contributions. Stores owned by Armenian and Greek merchants are vandalized. 1,080 shops owned by Armenians are burned in the city of Diyarbekir. (Source: www.genocide1915.info.)

Kristapor backtracked and answered. He had been hiding acquired weapons at a southern farmhouse on the outskirts of the village through the permission of its owner. But the guns had disappeared.

"We have proof that the farmer sold the guns to some merchants in Yalova,⁹" Vahé said as he walked into the conversation. "He needs to be killed."

Both Tavid and Kristapor in unison looked at Vahé Vasakian. Without expressing a word, they both conveyed their irritation of his interruption and gestured for him to move away.

"What does this have to do with me? Go kill him yourself if that is what you have decided, or have one of your Fedayees do your dirty work."

"We have tried. He has dogs and we just cannot get near him. He… knows you. You would be able to catch him offguard."

Tavid laughed. "Who are we talking about?"

"Crazy Aram!" Vahé barked from behind.

"What? Delibash¹⁰ Aram? You must be joking. He is one of the most honest men I know. And what does he say about all this?" Tavid argued.

"He denies everything, yet he has no explanation as to what happened to our weapons. He claims someone must have stolen them," Vahé added, again breaking into the conversation.

Kristapor hesitated. "Can we count on your allegiance with us, Tavid?"

"Are you both crazy too? You come here to ask me to kill a friend because you think he sold your guns?"

All were silent.

"My allegiance is to my family and friends."

"But are we not also your friends, Tavid?" Vahé asked abruptly.

Tavid could not contain his anger any longer.

"Friends? Here, let me show you one of my friends."

Directing his anger at Vahé he reached into his boot, pulled out his unsheathed dagger, and slammed it blade-first into the residing table. On the other side of the room, the vartabed dropped his head in helpless disgust.

"Here! Here is one of my friends!"

Only an echoing of the blow could be heard in the now silent rectory. After a long pause, Tavid's anger subsided.

---

⁹ The port city on the banks of the Sea of Marmara, 20 kilometers north of Tchingiler.
¹⁰ Turkish: crazy.

"I will go see him. Not to do your bidding, but to find out what has happened to your weapons. I will report to you, Kristapor, and only to you what I have found."

Kristapor nodded, grabbed Vahé by the arm before he could say anything else and the two left. The vartabed walked up to his table topped by its new imbedded ornament.

"Aboush![11] Get your dagger out of my poor table. I make sure to cover it with thick blankets beforehand so that your guns do not scratch it, then you go and do this!"

Tavid apologized, pulled the dagger out of the table then handed the vartabed the monies he had collected for the weapons. The vartabed kept about half, and handed the rest to Tavid.

"Are we going to have another funeral after you visit Aram?"

Tavid shook his head.

"Good! Tomorrow I will buy food and supplies with this money to help the families that lost their sons last month to the conscription. I will let them know it came from your generous donation."

Tavid sighed while looking at his half of the gun profits and then reluctantly gave it back to the vartabed, stuffing money into the vartabed's overcoat pocket.

"No, you will not. Do not tell them whom it is from. It will just breed jealousy and more hatred toward me."

The vartabed smiled and nodded while Tavid collected the leftover weapons and began to leave.

"See you at the services tomorrow, Tavid?"

Tavid did not answer and left through the service door. Gathering his horse, he loaded the bartered goods and leftover weapons. He thought he should visit crazy Aram right there and then while it was on his mind. But it was night, and he had promised Karoun and his mother he would not be late coming home. Tavid started toward home but then stopped abruptly. He needed to see Aram. He needed to see him tonight.

Crazy Aram farmed and lived south of Tchingiler. Rarely did he venture into the village. When he did, it was only for supplies or to attend holiday services at Gadar. Although married, for the most part he was a recluse. Tavid was one of a few people Aram enjoyed visiting with because of their mutual opinion of Turks, their handiness with weapons, and their inability to be submissive subjects of the Ottoman Empire.

---

[11] Armenian: idiot.

The crescent moon lit the way just enough for Tavid to find his way. He did not get but fifty meters from Aram's when his dogs sensed someone coming and barked for their master. However, no one came from the house or the large adjacent shed. A light flickered from the shed inviting Tavid toward it. The three dogs continued to bark and tried to cut off Tavid and his horse from reaching the shed. Tavid dismounted his horse and tried to quell the excited dogs by talking to them and holding his hands out to them. He knelt on one knee.

"Have you all forgotten me? "Soos! Hos Yegoor![12]"

The dogs cautiously approached Tavid, turning from threat to tails wagging but continued their barking as they recalled this friend.

"You three bark to scare everyone, but you are all babies and just want to play…yes, you are!"

After the dogs had licked his face and hands of any residual salt, Tavid stood up to see that no one had come from the house or shed. Accompanied by his three slinking hosts, Tavid entered the shed's open door to see Aram repairing what appeared to be a doll. He stood at a tall workbench with his back to Tavid. One of the dogs pranced over to his master to make him notice their guest. Aram did not turn and continued his work.

"I heard you were alive. Went to your funeral but did not really believe you were dead."

Tavid said nothing.

"Why are you here? Did they send you to try and kill me?"

"Of course," Tavid replied nonchalantly.

Still with his back turned to Tavid, Aram nodded his head in affirmation.

"But that is not why I am here," Tavid added.

Aram turned and faced Tavid. In his hands was a Mauser pistol.[13] Tavid smirked.

"I sold you that pistol, did I not? A beautiful weapon, though too large for me to carry around."

Aram, in his early thirties, was a Goliath in stature and girth even compared to Tavid. Partially cross-eyed from a scar traversing his right

---

[12] Armenian: "Be quiet. Come here."

[13] A semi-automatic pistol that was originally produced by German arms manufacturer Mauser from 1896 to 1937.

eyebrow, this black-bearded long-haired behemoth looked the part of one who should be labeled "delibash."

"Why are you here then? Only thieves and murderers visit here at night."

"Well, I have been called both those names in the past but there is no need for that tonight. I am here to find out what really happened to the guns they gave you and why you decided to help that idiot Vasakian."

Aram paused while trying to keep his composure. An uncontrolled emotion overtook him, starting deep in his stomach. Quickly working its way up into his chest and out his mouth, it spewed like a volcanic eruption. Delibash Aram roared in laughter and slammed his gun on the worktable. He walked towards Tavid and embraced his young friend.

"Do not crush me like you did last time. I could not breathe for a week!" Tavid pleaded.

Aram laughed even harder.

"Yes, that man is an idiot! But I am also an idiot for listening to him!"

Aram described what had occurred a few months ago. Vahé Vasakian had seen Aram during one of his trips into Tchingiler. He pleaded with Aram to help him hide weapons for his Fedayeen brethren. Later, Aram met Vahé and two Fedayees back at his farmhouse and together they buried the guns at the edge of the woods behind his shed.

"About a month went by and Kristapor came out here to retrieve the guns. We went out to dig them up and they were gone. Someone must have seen us when we were hiding them."

"I know you, Aram. You may be crazy, but you are not crazy enough to do this. You hate Turks maybe as much as I do."

"Ha! More!" Aram retorted.

"And your heart made your decision to help them. What about Vahé or the Fedayees? How do you know they really were Fedayees? How do you know Vahé did not sneak back here and take the guns?"

Aram shook his head. "Why? Why would he lie? Why would they bother with me if they wanted the guns for themselves?"

Tavid shook his head, not knowing the answer.

"What type of guns were they, Aram?"

"Russian. A few rusty pistols, but mostly rifles."

"Did they say where they had bought them?"

"No idea."

Tavid got up off the table and acted as if he was leaving. Then remembered something and looked over towards Aram's work bench.

"A doll? You were mending a doll?"

Crazy Aram smiled, looked over to his workbench and nodded.

"Arin[14] is pregnant."

"What? After all this time?"

"Yes, it is still hard for me to believe!"

Tavid, surprised with such good news went over to Aram and again embraced him without yielding to his strength.

"After almost fifteen years, Kreesdos[15] has finally granted us our only wish," Aram reflected.

"Come! Have a drink with me at the house. I have just made fresh mulberry brandy and have had no one to celebrate with!"

Tavid accepted, though thinking of his mother and Karoun waiting. Now he would be coming home late, smelling of spirits again. In the house, followed by the dogs, Arin warmly greeted Tavid. Aram asked her to bring two bottles of his home-distilled brandy. The two toasted and drank while Arin brought food for two of the most well-fed Armenians in the village.

In between toasts and leisurely eating the two talked of the stolen guns. Aram again described the poor condition of the weapons and his confusion as to why someone would steal them. Tavid promised to talk to Kristapor and clear his name. The conversation moved to the war and the happenings in the interior of their country.

"The Turks came while you were dead and took all the young men for their armies. I tell you the truth: we will never see them again unless they can somehow escape the first chance they have. And they are going to use this war as an excuse to take everything we have again," insisted Aram.

"My grandfather would say: *How fast our blood dries and is forgotten by time,*" Tavid reminisced.

Aram raised his glass. "To Yervant Yacoubian." Tavid's smile was genuine as he joined in the toast. He opened his mouth as their glasses clinked, and just as quickly changed his mind. "I...I must go. My mother. She will be worried—as usual, but I promised!"

---

[14] Armenian: Brave female.
[15] Armenian: Christ.

He slowly stood up hoping he was not too intoxicated to make it home. Aram insisted he take home the second bottle of brandy as a gift for his mother.

"Tell her of the good news here and she will not be as angry with you this time," Aram laughed.

Tavid rode at a gallop. Arriving home, Tavid secured his horse and quietly entered. All had gone to sleep apparently. All was serene with only a single lantern burning for him. As he went to lie down, he paused, seeing Karoun's cot near the kitchen. Smiling at her sleeping form, he crouched quietly next to her and leaned in to gaze at her inherent beauty and inhale her sweet fragrance. She sat up in an instant, startling him badly enough that he almost fell backwards. "Soos![16]" she admonished with a whisper. "I've been waiting for you." Tavid slowly leaned in again and kissed her. The brandy was strong and almost made Karoun dizzy from the smell. Her face twinged and nose wrinkled while she shook her head to get rid of the odor. Tavid could do all but hold back a laugh.

"You have been drinking again? Go to bed!" she whispered.

Tavid tried to explain but was too tired to try. He winked and obeyed his beautiful girl.

---

[16] Armenian: "Quiet!"

"I became a Fedayee when I was fifteen years of age. I joined
a group of seven others all from Tchingiler. For the most part
they were farmers that lived on the outskirts of the village.
My father was very proud when I was asked to join. I was the
youngest. And our leader was Delibash Aram's grandfather."
– Yervant Yacoubian

# CHAPTER 22

# Gifts to the Poor

ANOUSH WAS FIRST TO ARISE and began preparing breakfast for her family.
She saw Tavid sleeping in all his clothing including his shoes. In addition,
she noticed the unopened bottle of mulberry brandy on the table. Her
first thought was to take a stick and give her son a swift whack. Or maybe
douse him with cold water from the well. She thought of several ways
to punish her son but instead sat down next to him to watch him sleep,
wondering what he was dreaming. In sleep he reminded her of when he
was a young child. She did not easily influence Tavid, and what authority
she had over him was waning. Yet she now smiled at the sight of him and
how he had grown into a handsome young man. More importantly, he was
alive. And her father? She could scarcely contemplate the possibility and
impatience rose in her chest. Would spring ever come?

She left him to dream while she went back to her chores. Minutes
later as she occasioned a look out one of the back room windows, she
saw a group of men exiting the orchards and heading toward her home.
Apprehensive at first, she then recognized one of the bearded men as
Kristapor Sakalian, an old friend of the family. Anoush met them outside.

"Paree Looees,[1] Kristapor. Hrram-mets-ehk![2]" Anoush asked Kristapor and the other four young men to sit at the outside table.

"Have you had breakfast this morning?" she queried, watching each of them light up with pleasure.

"No, thank you, Anoush. We are just here to see…"

"What? Except for you, these young men look like they have not had a good breakfast in years! And since when do you not like my cooking?"

"Tsk. Herikeh![3] We come uninvited. You do not have to feed all of us."

"I seem to remember inviting you last night, Kristapor," Tavid said, as he had awakened and stumbled out the back door, catching the last part of the conversation. Eyes half-shut, breath reeking of warm digested alcohol, and medusa-like hair pointing in every direction he looked at his mother and smiled devilishly.

"So it is done. You were invited and you will dine with us. Is that right?"

While Anoush walked back into the house to prepare breakfast, Tavid examined the crew that had come to see him. He greeted each asking his name and where he was from. All were from the same city, Eski Shehr.

"Eski Shehr?[4] There are no Armenians down there."

"There are a few. They live on the outskirts of the city or in the surrounding countryside. Most are not openly Armenian though," Kristapor interrupted.

"If we had stayed there, we would have been conscripted by the Turks for the army. They took my father years ago and he never returned," interrupted one of the young men.

"The four of us decided to leave while we could and become Fedayees. We thought to come north to find other Armenians and…"

"Have any of you ever held or fired a gun?"

Their eyes scanned each other, trying to find an appropriate response.

"They have not gone through training yet, Tavid. Just young recruits," Kristapor explained.

"And who is going to train them? Dashnaks? Hunchaks?[5] Who is going to teach them how to survive?"

---

[1] Armenian: "Good morning."

[2] Armenian: a formal command used to welcome a guest to a home or to call guests or family to dinner.

[3] Turkish: "Stop!"

[4] Turkish city approximately 150 kilometers southeast of Tchingiler.

[5] Newly-emerging Armenian political parties.

Kristapor evaded the question. "That will all be taken care of. Our task right now is to obtain weapons and supplies and recruit at least a dozen men from each village in and around Tchingiler."

"Ha! You are joking. Where are you going to find these volunteers?"

"Someone needs to be ready to protect each village if the time comes again, Tavid. We have to be prepared this time," Kristapor explained.

Tavid shook his head and turned to see his mother coming with the first round of breakfast: golden teas, dark coffee, honey, and dried flatbread with various fruit preserves. As Anoush retreated for more, Tavid gestured for the hungry guests to take what they wanted. Anoush returned shortly with another tray containing dried fruit, madzoon[6] and soujouk.[7] As they ate, Tavid gestured to Kristapor to move to the far end of the table to talk privately. Kristapor's companions were too busy eating to notice.

"These are your Fedayees? Your local guards? More like a suicide band! What chance do they have against Turkish soldiers or the Cheté? Who is backing you up?[8]" Tavid whispered.

Kristapor shook his head. "I cannot answer that."

"Because you have no one, do you?"

Kristapor was cautious and still did not answer.

Instead, he said, "You are too young to remember the Sultan's massacres. We had no one to help then, only a few bands of Fedayees. A deterrent they were then and will be again," Kristapor lectured.

Tavid looked over at the four green mercenaries. They were Stepan's age, no more.

"I will make a deal with you, Kristapor. I will provide guns and supplies to these four Fedayees of yours. I will train them how to kill, maybe even how to survive…"

"And in return?"

"Leave crazy Aram alone."

Kristapor's eyes flashed.

"I visited with him last night. He did not steal your guns and unfortunately, he does not know who did. But he tells me that Vahé and two others knew where the guns were buried as well. Is it possible that…"

"No! Not possible. Vahé provided us with the guns in the first place. And the other two are sitting at this table. Aram must have taken them!"

---

[6] Armenian: yogurt.
[7] Multicultural: ground cured meat.
[8] As in "political party."

Tavid felt a flush of heat and anger as if from the steam of the hot-spiced teas just served by his mother. With gritted teeth Tavid slammed his fist onto the table, releasing his rage and frustration. Then, like frightened birds from a gunshot, the cups and saucers filled with precious liquids went flying in all directions.

"Ahnbeedann!⁹" Anoush smacked the back of Tavid's scalp with her open hand. "Behave. You will respect this house." Tavid had not heard her return. He deferred to his mother instantly, though red-faced.

Kristapor desperately attempted to hold back a smile, but as his eyes met Tavid's both broke out into infectious laughter that spread to the young men from Eski Shehr. Anoush shook her head, and then laughed with them. Tavid took his mother gently by the shoulders and looked squarely at her. "My mother, my Mayrig." The softness and affection in his voice were clear. Just as quickly, he turned back to Kristapor.

"I am telling you the truth. Aram did not take your guns. If anything happens to him, I will come after you, my friend. This idea of killing him has to cease."

Kristapor was not used to being threatened and was hesitant. Finally he took a deep breath.

"You are willing to train them and supply all that they need?'

Tavid nodded.

"For how long?"

"For as long as it takes for them to become real Fedayees."

"What if there were others who needed training?"

"What others are there, Kristapor?"

Kristapor turned away quickly, only to face Tavid again. "Are you willing to train others as well?" he repeated.

"One step at a time. Four is a good number to start with. Do not come to my home tomorrow with another dozen!"

Kristapor laughed, and agreed to this arrangement with Tavid.

"I will forget about Aram for now."

Over the next month, Kristapor trickled in eight more men to make an even dozen. All were young, inexperienced, impressionable and willing to learn. As with the first four, Tavid taught the new recruits to be self-reliant, crafty, and stealthy renegades. In time, they could track at night as well as they could by day.

---

⁹ Armenian: mischievous.

With the help of his brother Stepan, Tavid would take them north to the farmhouse at the foothills of Mount Olympus to hunt and practice with their rifles. To Kristapor's surprise, Tavid supplied each with Russian-made Mosin rifles, side arm and bandolier.[10] An almost-unending supply of weapons appeared to flow from him.

It was late fall now. Nights were becoming too cold for their outdoor activities and shelter. They decided it best to move these young Armenian patrolmen to Tavid's farmhouse for the coming winter months. There they would continue their self-sufficiency, their semi-nocturnal existence while waiting for instruction as to what might happen regarding the war.

By this time the government had censored all telegraphic communications and closed all postal services. The only news came from the rare traveler. Their stories were revealing and terrifying. Tales of murdered Armenian leaders, looting, rape, starvation and the spread of disease to the east permeated conversations. Occasionally there were rumors of released criminals called Chetés being supplied with weapons by the Turks inflicting these atrocities.

Small, secluded Tchingiler seemed immune to all these stories for the time being, and Tavid hoped that spring would come without incident. At Tavid's urging, Anoush began going through the family's personal items deciding what to take with them in the spring. One day she re-discovered a thick linen kerchief belonging to her father. On it, a poem was written, possibly when her father was Tavid's age. She gave it to Tavid who after reading it reflected for a moment, then placed it in his pocket. He dressed for the colder weather outdoors and left to find his students. The poem told of Fedayees of a generation gone by.

*Sleep by day to protect by night*
*Autonomous upon yourselves*
*Alone you are with your plight*
*Be wary of spies, traitors posing as friends*
*From them stay apart or meet your end*
*Your weapons are as children*
*Keep clean, dressed and dry*
*Kill only when essential*
*Then to escape you must try*

---

[10] A belt fitted with small pockets or loops for carrying bullet cartridges and worn across the chest.

*Have reserves and supplies*
*Hidden for you and your brothers*
*And a place to hide*
*They will come in numbers*
*For the few of you that still have your pride*

"Have I told you why everyone calls Armen Eftendelian 'Baron'?
It is a simple story. When he was younger he was always so
serious, always acting the adult, never relaxing, never letting
his guard down. He was like a old man at the age of eighteen.
And I think he enjoyed being called Baron even back then."
– Yervant Yacoubian

# CHAPTER 23

# Holy Eftendelian

ANOUSH WAS IN HER FRONT yard gazing at the newly snow laden peak of
Mount Olympus. It was a beautiful, crisp autumn morning and villagers
were out and about everywhere. For the most part though she ignored
their presence, wondering if she would ever see the autumn in Tchingiler
again. She considered why her father had not returned for them, what it
was like in Cyprus, and what scoldings she would cry to him when they
were reunited. As she drifted off into these thoughts, two hooded riders on
horseback approached her home from the north. As they arrived, Anoush
fell out of her dream. She looked at both the riders, priests in simple black
robes accented with bright silver crosses hanging from their necks. The
one priest looked straight at Anoush and smiled intensely through his
lengthy blondish mustache and early beard. The other looked away and
did not make eye contact. Anoush felt an odd sense of familiarity which
suddenly gave way to an erupting anxiety. Why had two priests come to
visit her? Had something happened that she was not aware of? Confusion
mixed in with the other emotions until the one priest spoke.

"Anoush Kaloustian, do you not remember me? Have I been away so
long that you have forgot…"

"Ahman Asdvasdz!¹ Aldo! Aldo Petrescu!"

Ha! You have not forgotten. Maybe it is my outfit that has confused you, eh? Do you also remember my shy companion here?"

As the other hooded figured slowly revealed his face, Anoush's mood changed from astonishment to disgust.

"You should not have brought him here, Aldo. It may not be safe for him," Anoush chided.

"Please Anoush, give him a chance to speak to you and the others. I promise you will not be sorry. I have been with this poor wretch for the past week and I tell you the truth, he is not the same man that your son and his daughter have told you of."

Armen Eftendelian dismounted his horse, followed by Aldo, and they slowly approached Anoush.

"Please Anoush, allow me to speak to you," a fatigued Armen Eftendelian asked.

Anoush stared at both of them with crossed arms, then ushered them both into her home. She sat them down but did not offer them any refreshments.

"I am listening, but it is lucky for you that my son and the others are not here right now. I do not know if you would get this chance at all."

With a heavy sigh, Armen Eftendelian slowly and deliberately emptied his heart to Anoush. He spoke endlessly as Anoush listened and slowly did not judge him any more.

"I have lost my daughter, I know that now. I have treated her poorly and hope that some day she will forgive me for the way I have treated her. And I am not here to bring her home, only to tell her how sorry I am for being an idiot all these years. I would like to speak to your son and apologize to him as well. He, he is a reflection of myself that I have fought against for years."

Aldo sat off to the side, snickering to himself and holding back the urge to interject. Anoush felt empathy now rather than disgust.

"I still do not know if they will talk to you. Or even if my son will let you see her. We have talked about this much and it always ends up with flames coming from my son's eyes. I tell you the truth, you are not safe here, Baron."

"Do not worry Armen, I will protect you," chuckled Aldo.

---

¹ Armenian: "oh my God!"

If Tavid tries to kill you, I will hold him down long enough to give you enough time to run..."

Aldo's mockery stopped abruptly as a gang led by Tavid walked into the room, laughing and playing. As Tavid saw and recognized the two visitors, he felt surprise followed by intense anger and quickly approached Armen Eftendelian.

"You should not have come here, Baron." Tavid paused but Armen Eftendelian was silent.

"Forcing your daughter to marry? Forcing your son into a profession he hates? Your children are going to grow up hating you! Is that what you want? Do you love your children? No, you just need to be in control, like your government friends. It is all about control, is it not?" Tavid's rage could be felt throughout the room. Armen Eftendelian was having trouble controlling his own temper as well and felt the urge to reach out and strike Tavid, but was able to control himself.

"How is it that you are so much like your grandfather? How is it that I was so much like you, when I was your age?" Armen Eftendelian suddenly got up and left to go outside, heading toward his horse. Karoun was frozen where she had entered the room with the others, taking in all that was said yet confused as Tavid was with Armen's rebuttal. She then felt the need to speak to her father and ran outside to see him. Outside though she could not think of what to say. She had planned this conversation over and over again in her head, but now nothing she had thought of to say made any sense. As her father turned to see her, tears escaped from his eyes. He wept, asking her for forgiveness. The two embraced as the others came outside as well.

"I did not come here to take you home. I came here to ask for your forgiveness. Everything that Tavid just said is true. Disgustingly true. I wish to apologize to Tavid, too, if he will let me." He looked up at Tavid for some type of answer.

With disgust, Tavid gestured to Armen Eftendelian to come back into his home. Allowing him to enter first followed by Karoun, he then grabbed Aldo by the frock, and dragged him back into the house and sat him next to Armen. To soften things up, Anoush rushed into the kitchen to obtain foods and drink to sooth these savage personalities and returned promptly, also not wanting to miss any of the conversation.

"So how is it, Aldo, that you and the Baron are such good friends now? Or should I ask, how much did he pay you to bring him here? Sikishmek Romanian." He muttered some profanities under his breath.

"Ah! What was I thinking!" Aldo exclaimed. "Yes, I could have bribed him for much money. But it was from the kindness of my heart that I brought him here. You should have seen this poor wretch when I delivered the note to him from his beautiful daughter. Even then he confessed to me like I was a priest, of all that he had done and wished he could reverse!" Aldo jokingly made the sign of the cross, and continued to tell the story of how it was his idea to come to Tchingiler and help Armen Eftendelian tell his daughter and Tavid how he felt.

"Plus, I had nothing to do and was bored as hell sitting and rotting on my brother's ship. Yes, we still have not been able to leave port. So I decided to come and visit with my new friend, the Baron."

Armen Eftendelian tried not to look too disgusted as Aldo told his tale. When Aldo was finished, Armen Eftendelian reiterated his many apologies, again repenting as if at some type of tribunal hoping for a light judgment. Afterward he paused and, looking apprehensive, reached under his frock and pulled out a stack of letters bound with tight hemp rope. Guardedly he offered these to Tavid.

"I know why you want to go to Cyprus." Armen paused trying to find strength to continue.

"I was afraid you would take my family from me," again Armen had to pause, trying desperately to hold back his emotions.

"What are you talking about, Armen?" Anoush asked.

"Those letters, they are about your grandfather, Tavid. They have been streaming in for months from Cyprus, from my wife's sister, Satenig. I have been hiding them from everyone."

Tavid looked at the bundle in his hands and handed them to his mother to review.

"Baron, what do they say? Is my grandfather alive?" Tavid asked impatiently.

"Yes, he is alive and doing well now, but when he first arrived in Cyprus he was incarcerated by the British military. There was some type of incident. I am not sure exactly what happened. But, being that he was in jail, he was not able to return and take you all back to Cyprus with him. The letters were urging you all, including my family, to find passage to Cyprus. He has even sent visas for my family." Armen paused.

"So, now that he is out of jail, why has he not come back?" Tavid questioned.

"Ah, that is easy! For the same reason that I am still here. No one can go anywhere with this war going on. He is stuck there and we are stuck here for now," Aldo cut in.

"I knew that if I gave you these letters, Tavid, that my family and yours would all have left and I would be alone. I would have been too stubborn to leave. And I am still not ready to leave my home for Cyprus. I still say it is too dangerous."

"Well, we will all see what happens by early spring. Who knows what events may occur that may change one's mind, eh?" Aldo grinned from ear to ear.

Karoun approached her father and sat down next to him, holding his hand. They looked into each other's eyes, Karoun expressing her forgiveness, her father expressing sorrow. The others gathered around and began to nibble on the refreshments. Stepan and Varsenig began listening to stories that Aldo continued to tell of their journey. But Tavid got up, not eating anything, and walked outside. As he gazed at his village and the surrounding terrain, a lone figure came from behind and wrapped her arms around him. It was not Karoun but his mother.

"I think you should let her go back with her father. I can only imagine how much her mother misses her. You can always go and check up on her, you know."

"What did he mean that he was just like me when he was my age? How could he have been anything like me? We are nothing alike."

"Hmm. When he was young, I seem to remember he was in ways quite similar to you, my son. Hard to believe, eh?"

"Very."

The two stood gazing at Mount Olympus, wondering what turn of events would be next in their lives as Karoun came outside. She also wrapped her arms around Tavid and his mother, and held them both tight. All three were as one knowing the other's thoughts.

"I miss you already, Karoun."

"I will miss all of you, terribly. You can come visit?"

"I will try. But the spring will not come fast enough."

Afterward, Tavid read aloud to all the letters his grandfather had sent. It was a healing and comforting time, to read these and to know that there was a reason he had not returned. Later that night, Tavid read over the letters again, pulling whatever message or feelings he could from the writings. Tavid slept poorly that night. Going over the letters in his mind and thinking of Karoun who would be leaving in the morning.

The next day Aldo, Armen, and Karoun prepared to leave for Constantinople. Tavid pushed to go with them for safe passage but his mother urged him to allow them to go on their own. Time would be needed between the two of them to help heal their wounds. Tavid made sure that Aldo and Armen were both heavily-armed under their frocks; he would not be there to anticipate potential danger to Karoun. Firepower eased his concern at least to a small degree. As the group prepared to leave Karoun crouched next to a tearful Varsenig, who had become deeply attached to Karoun. Tavid watched as Karoun pulled the doll that Tavid had purchased for her from her bag and solemnly handed it to Varsenig. She whispered into the little girl's ear, at which Varsenig mustered a smile and nodded. "I promise I will make her take her naps," she said to Karoun. Tavid looked on. A very sad boy-turned-man was letting his beautiful girl return to her home. But he would reunite with her soon, once and for all, if it was the last thing he did.

"Some call the church a sanctuary. But I tell you the truth, there are no safe places in this hell of a country unless you force it to be safe. It must be made second nature to always be on your guard or else you may just visit the true sanctuary before your time."
– Yervant Yacoubian

CHAPTER 24

# Revelation of God[1]

January 6, 1915. 0900 Hours

THE NIGHT HAD BEEN COLDER than usual and a light snow had fallen. Many were still asleep having attended the short midnight mass at Gadar,[2] the lone Armenian Cathedral in the center of the village. Other families like Tavid's would be attending the morning Mass and were already on their way to church to rejoice and pray.

Tchingiler was a pure Armenian-populated village. However, that had not always been the case. Established over three hundred years before in 1590, its oldest immigrants were a mix of Turkish and Armenian. Over the years, the Turkish population gradually decreased and by 1830 the village inhabitants were of only Armenian descent. The name of the village was derived from the Turkish word "Delibash Jengnilet" meaning "crazy-head fighter." It was named after Ouzoum Toros, Armenian hero of battles centuries gone by and forgotten, except by a few…

---

[1] All Christians had celebrated the birth of Christ on January 6. In the 4th century A.D., however, the Roman Catholic Church decided to celebrate Christ's birth on December 25 and the Feast of the Epiphany (Christ's Baptism) on January 6. Armenians still celebrate Christ's birth on January 6.

[2] Armenian: apex, top of a mountain, perfect, pure.

"Tavid! Just once! Just once I wish you would dress nice for church service and leave your guns at home, hokees!" Anoush complained as Tavid walked out of their home.

"If you put half the time that you do for those disguises of yours into dressing, what a happy mother you would have!"

"I feel naked without them. No one will notice; I will keep them under my coat. Besides, God does not care how I dress when I enter his house," Tavid professed.

"Yes, but you look so handsome when you dress well. Not when you look like this. Soon your younger brother will try to copy you."

Tavid smiled and looked ahead at Stepan, who heard his mother complaining.

"He already is, Mayrig."

Anoush sighed and shook her head. "He has his pistol with him? Delibash! Both of you."

At the church, Anoush briskly herded her family to the front. Unlike other cathedrals in Constantinople, there were no chairs, no pews. All would stand during the Mass. Tavid knew better than to hope for a short service, especially on the Day of Nativity. Watching the crowd, Tavid saw Delibash Aram arrive, pushing his way to the front on the opposite side of where Tavid and his family stood. When he saw Tavid, his mouth widened into a huge smile and he bowed his head in mock reverence. Tavid returned the gesture.

Tavid's mind was not on the service. He was thinking of Karoun, how he missed her, wishing he had not allowed her to leave last fall with her father. On two occasions he had attempted to travel to Constantinople but the weather had become severe earlier than usual. It had been months since he had seen her and possibly months before he would be able to leave again.

His trance was broken by the sound of approaching horses. At first he thought these were more worshippers arriving late, but the speed of the riders alerted him that something else was about to happen. Then before turning, he saw that the vartabed hesitated, followed by the choir.

"Good morning," a loud vulgar voice bellowed in Turkish inside the cathedral.

Tavid snapped his head to the back of the cathedral. A dozen Kurds from another village had arrived via horseback. Tavid recognized them to be from Ashiret,[3] outside of Kilidj, a port village northeast of Tchingiler. He knew this by their dress and use of blue to symbolize their freedom and the lake.

The Kurds, rifles high, brandished their weapons so all could see.

"Are you not going to invite us to share with your Christ? To pray with you. To share your offerings?" Laughter broke out amongst the Kurdish hooligans.

"We are here to share your gifts, I said!" Two of the Kurds carried large tightly-woven dirt-stained hemp bags.

"Do not be shy, my Ermenis. Give all that you have."

Tavid was farthest from the Kurds in the front of the cathedral. Then he slowly knelt down to the floor. Stepan followed suit. Pulling out both of his revolvers, he checked to make certain that both were without empty chambers. Tavid looked at Stepan, instructing him to do the same with his lone revolver. Anoush looked at her sons, pleading with them to put their guns away and go along with what the Kurds wanted. Varsenig was trying to be brave like her brothers, but was holding on tight to her mother for support.

Tavid shook his head at his brother.

"There are too many of them for just two of us, Stepan," Tavid whispered. "They will surely be able to get some shots off even if we were to hit every one of..."

Stepan looked over Tavid's shoulder, pushing Tavid to turn and see Delibash Aram through the chaotic crowd, smiling also as his huge frame kneeled down on the floor. In his hands was that same Mauser pistol with ten-shot clip he had obtained from Tavid years back. Tavid's eyes narrowed. He nodded his head to Aram. Then with his left hand he pointed to Aram, held up four fingers, and pointed to the Kurds on Aram's side of the cathedral. Delibash Aram smiled, shook his head and held up five fingers. Tavid shrugged his shoulders, then nodded.

"Stepan, you kill the two on the right. I will take the middle, and Aram will take the rest. I will signal when to shoot...ready, my dear brother?"

Stepan nodded.

Tavid looked over to Aram, nodded again, and the three slowly ghosted through the pandemonium toward the Kurds.

Most of the villagers did not even realize what had happened. Within seconds, bullets had struck all twelve Kurds. Some were dead, others just

---

[3] Free Kurdish tribes.

wounded; all were apparently neutralized. Delibash Aram had practically emptied his entire clip into the Kurds on his side of the now blood-stained cathedral. Each shot that had hit its mark had not only torn away their souls but large measures of their flesh. Tavid had shot simultaneously, with each revolver hitting each of the five Kurds with one bullet in the chest. Two of them spun and hit the cathedral wall behind them, and then slowly descended to the ground. Stepan had shot the last two, putting two bullets in each. Parishioners scattered throughout the cathedral confused, trying to escape where ever they could. Young women and children were crying or screaming uncontrollably. Some of the elders fainted where they stood; others were only dazed, having been witnesses to death and the sound of gunfire so many times in the past. Many eventually ventured through the main doors of the cathedral, hurdling over the dead or dying Kurds.

The smell of incense coming from the cathedral's altar had coalesced with, then was overcome by, the scent of gunpowder and blood. Tavid carefully eyed each of the bodies for movement, then headed cautiously out the large front doors of the cathedral where the Kurds had entered. He made sure none of their brothers were hiding outside. Tavid counted the horses, no additional men. As Tavid quickly turned back inside he nearly ran into two middle-aged women, arm in arm, standing close behind him.

"Curse you and your family! Do you expect us to thank you now for what you have just done? They will come and kill..."

Tavid did not let them continue their scolding. "Are you not tired of being stepped on? Not willing to fight for what is yours? No! I do not expect thanks from you or anyone. But I would rather die than accept the way they treat us." Tavid walked away seeing that Stepan, Aram, and now Kristapor Sakalian, who had also attended the morning mass with a few of the young Fedayees, had found three of the Kurds to be still alive. Kristapor Sakalian was crouched down by one of the Kurds who was facedown on the floor of the cathedral, going through his pockets. But as he turned the Kurd over, the half-dead Kurd was pointing a revolver into Kristapor's chest, a faint smile appearing on the Kurd's face just as he was about to pull the trigger.

Pow! The mauser fired its last shot as the Kurd's smile disintegrated into oblivion. Kristapor Sakalian stumbled up and backward into Delibash Aram, who had fired the shot.

"Be more careful the next time! So you do not get yourself killed...or kill the wrong person, eh?" Aram scolded.

Kristapor, coming to his senses, finally nodded in recognition.

Tavid, half-irritated half-amused at Kristapor Sakalian, put his pistols away only to pick up one of the Kurdish rifles and fire—making sure all the Kurds were indeed dead—then dropped the rifle to the cathedral floor. Instinctively he examined each of the Kurds for weapons, bullets, valuables or any other useful items. Taking one of the hemp bags that the Kurds had thrown to the ground earlier, he filled it with their belongings and collected the rifles with the help of Aram and Stepan. Hesitating, he stood up and walked over to the thick-bearded, shell-shocked Kristapor.

"Are you alright?"

Kristapor nodded.

"Take the rifles. They are in surprisingly good condition."

Kristapor agreed.

Tavid paused, then asked, "Why do you, as well as my students, not have your weapons with you today?"

Kristapor, embarrassed, did not answer. Instead he nodded, acknowledging his second mistake. He turned to retrieve the other hemp bag brought by the Kurds and collected the rifles, making sure to empty them of cartridges. Before Tavid had a chance to talk to his Fedayee pupils, he felt a warm hand on his shoulder. The vartabed had initially been comforting his flock after the event; now his expression went from consoling to irritation.

"I suppose I should thank you," he whispered in Tavid's ear. "But could you not have asked them to step outside first then kill them instead of spilling their blood all over my church? Who is going to clean up this mess?"

Tavid smiled, "Does this mean services are over now?"

The vartabed thought for a moment, then had his deacons usher all of the parishioners outside of the cathedral. Tavid found his sister and his mother, who had mixed emotions as to what to say to her son who was so much like her father. Tavid, staying in control, took their hands and escorted them out of the cathedral. Luckily the sun shone radiantly and the climate was mild for a winter morning. Gathering the holy communion from the altar, the vartabed followed his parishioners outside to offer communion to these imperfect souls.

*Let me at least try to cleanse them out here for The Holy Spirit to see,* he thought.

Partially-bloodied from examining the Kurds and smelling of gunsmoke, Tavid and the rest of his family—including Aram—were first in line to accept communion. The vartabed made sure each kissed the cross and took communion from his hand. After all had been purified to Tavid's delight, he ended the service early.

Kristapor and his Fedayees volunteered to dispose of the bodies and help with the cleanup.

It was time for Tavid to get the day back on track as much as possible, if only for his mother. Tavid knew that relatives would soon descend for Anoush's feast.

As guests arrived later in the day, the intoxicating smell of fresh breads, stewed vegetables and meats filled the household. Tavid was unhappy to see Vahé Vasakian. A tall lean man, Vahé had an oddly wicked appearance, enhanced by his dark clothing and the silver jewelry around his neck.

"Not good enough for our mother," he hissed to Stepan; he did not like the attention Vahé paid to Anoush at all. Stepan reminded him of their pact for the day. Tavid regretted it, but backed down.

"Tavid! Tavid! Again, it is a miracle that you are here! Who is watching over you? Which saints have you enlisted? Ha!" Vahé then quickly sought out others to greet.

Tavid grimaced, not only because of Vahe Vasakian's greeting but also from the scent of rosewater cologne coming from this man. The scent triggered fragments of memories that Tavid could not yet decipher.

All sat at a table that Tavid had set up in the larger of the two rooms. Tavid tried to stay busy so as not to be drawn into a conversation with the guests, but it was only a matter of time.

"Tavid! Come sit at the table with us. Tell us what has happened," his uncle insisted.

"What happened is done. This is not the day to be telling such stories," Tavid remarked.

"Nonsense! You must tell us," Vahé also insisted.

Everyone looked at Tavid in anticipation of his story. Possibly the wine he had been serving was already working its way into each guest's mind, enhancing their need of storytelling, jest and soon the meal. Tavid again told his story but was not as eloquent or long-winded as he had been in the past. In spite of that, most stayed focused on Tavid's face and words.

"Tavid, what happened when you left the Tokatlian Hotel?" Vahé asked. He pulled out some tobacco and lit a wooden match that reflected off his

necklace with a silver cross that shone briefly into Tavid's eyes. The scent
of rosewater again penetrated his nostrils. Tavid paused and thought for
a moment looking at Vahé, then looked away. He had purposely left that
part of the story out just in case his mother was listening from the next
room. With a sigh, Tavid retold the events that transpired after leaving the
Tokatlian Hotel, how the gendarmes took him and how through sheer
luck he was able to escape.

"That is difficult to believe, Tavid," his uncle insisted.

"Yes, I have to agree," followed Vahé. "But it would be easier to believe
after some more wine, yes?" Laughter broke out. The wine had taken
control.

After refilling the wine glasses, Tavid returned to the room full of guests
and heard them talking about Constantinople.

"I understand that you still travel there, Vahé?"

"Of course. I go there quite often. But not recently. The weather has
been unforgiving. There is still much trading to be done there, you know."

Tavid's uncle nodded.

"Are you still in the silk business?"

"Silk, dried fruit, leathers, anything that is needed," boasted Vahé.

Vahé paused to propose a toast to the hostess, Anoush.

He put his arm around her. Anoush blushed with a smile. Tavid tried to
hide his disgust.

"Tavid, do you still have any of that wonderful brandy?"

Tavid could not remember, for he had tried to block any of these past
visits from his mind.

"Ah, Tavid! Remember the Romanian brandy that you treated us to the
last time? Is there any left? Might we have some for another toast?"

"I...I am not sure. Let me go see," he replied. He went to the other
room to check the small cabinet next to a washbasin. He opened the
cabinet doors and saw the half-filled bottle of brandy that Aldo had given
him. Romanian brandy. Tavid read the words repeatedly on the bottle.
Romanian brandy. Tavid felt a rush of blood throughout his body. His
face flushed; the hairs on his arms and legs became erect. The scent of
rosewater, the priest-like cross. Now, Tavid remembered.

"I never had trouble with that skinny runt, Vahé Vasakian. I believe he was too scared of me to try anything when I was around. But after I faked my death, I believe he thought he would be able to get rid of the competition by eliminating my grandson. Big mistake."
— Yervant Yacoubian

CHAPTER 25

# Vasak[1]

*Pow!* A GUNSHOT INTENSIFIED IN resonance from the enclosed quarters as if a bolt of lightning had thundered within. Tavid had walked back to the table with both pistols in hand and shot Vahé Vasakian in the chest, but not in the heart. The bullet went through his torso, out the back of the chair and into the wooden wall behind. The impact and shock of the bullet pushed Vahé violently back into the chair; it would have flipped him over onto the floor if not for his upper thighs smashing into the bottom of the table. Reflexively he slammed forward, his face and hands thumping onto the table. Then he was motionless.

"You son of a bitch," Tavid muttered, followed by the trace of a smile. "By God's name what are you…"

"Sit down and shut up!" Tavid roared at the vartabed.

Tavid had also heard a crash in the kitchen and now his mother and sister were behind him. Anoush had a look of horror and bewilderment on her face, not unlike the rest of the guests. She walked into the room holding Varsenig, staring at Tavid hoping for an explanation she could swallow.

---

[1] Ancient Armenian history states that there was a Armenian by this name who was considered a traitor for siding with the Persians.

"Well, I was hired to kill a traitor and that is what I intend to do," Tavid said, now looking at Kristapor.

"This is crazy! What are you saying?" demanded Kristapor.

"This is the man who stole your guns, Kristapor. Not Aram. Knowing where they were hidden, he returned to Aram's stables and stole the weapons to sell in Constantinople. I know the man to whom he sold them. A Bulgarian who told me of an Armenian priest, a priest who wore a large silver cross sold him the guns, Russian-made, in bad shape. Rusty, were they not?" Tavid looked at Kristapor.

"Stepan!" instructed Tavid, "Search him for any weapons. Remember how I have shown you?"

Tavid stepped closer to the table, still pointing one pistol at Vahé Vasakian. "He is not dead yet, so be careful."

Stepan carefully searched the man but found no weapon.

"Nothing."

"Check his boots. Inside them."

Stepan got down on his knees and this time found a small two-round pistol and a short-bladed knife with scabbard. Stepan held them up embarrassingly to Tavid then put them on the table.

"Uhhh... black dogs... red eyes... chasing... help me.... I, I cannot breathe," whimpered Vahé.

"Can I see the pistol you took from him, Stepan?" Kristapor asked.

Stepan glanced at Tavid for permission. Tavid nodded. "Take the bullets out first Stepan."

He removed two bullets and handed the gun to Kristapor, who examined the pistol and with a look of disgust tossed it back to Stepan.

"What is it?" Tavid asked.

Kristapor paused. "I believe it is one of the pistols we gave to Delibash Aram to hide."

Tavid looked at Vahé, who was panting but also listening.

"Where did you get the pistol?"

Vahé did not answer, continuing to pant and look around the room.

"There is more," Tavid said, looking again at Vahé.

"You were at the Tokatlian Hotel when I was there. You must have seen me and slipped out to retrieve your gendarme comrades to come and arrest me. I realize now that I saw you standing outside, watching as they took me away. I saw the reflection of that cross of yours on your thin black silhouette. Like a ghost but I remember now."

Vahé Vasakian just shook his head, too breathless to speak.

"But what finally hit me in the head was the Romanian brandy. The Turkish gendarmes in Constantinople knew my name, that I was from Tchingiler and that my contact in Constantinople was Romanian, a Romanian merchant. That is where I am to blame." Tavid turned to Kristapor.

"Earlier this year my mother invited this devil over for dinner and I served him some Romanian brandy that was given to me as a gift. And I remember boasting about my Romanian friend. That is how he knew."

Tavid looked again at Vahé. "Now the question is why? Why did you want me dead? Because I refused to sell opium to you? Because I did not approve of my mother seeing you?" he said, staring at Vahé who was becoming ashen in color.

"Are you ... that ... stupid ... that you have to ask?" gasped Vahé. "You ... work with ... the soldiers in Bursa.... I work with ... the port commander. Strictly business. Besides, everyone ... hates Tavid Kaloustian. I was just ... doing everyone a favor." His eyes shut; his head rolled and sank to the table. "Black ... dogs ... red ... eyes ... stop, no..."

Then silence. Vahé Vasakian was dead.

Anoush's tears finally flowed without reservation. She looked at her son, shaking her head as she left the room. Varsenig followed.

Tavid put his weapons away and looked at everyone. At first he was silent, for he knew that even though he had taken care of the man that was trying to have him killed he had also terribly hurt his mother. Resolute in the outcome, Tavid tried to make light of the matter.

"Well, I guess we all know where he is going, Vartabed, I will bet not even you knew there were black dogs in Hell. With red bloodshot eyes, fangs probably dripping with..."

"Tavid! Now you shut up! No one deserves that fate."

"Hmm... No one? Not even the old Sultan?"

The vartabed waved his hand and nodded his head with reluctant assent. "No Armenian," he amended.

"What should we do with him?" Stepan as usual was curious.

"Who is going to tell his family?" Kristapor asked.

"I have no problem taking him and dropping him in front of his house and telling his family," Tavid mused.

"No! I will take care of that," interrupted the vartabed. "Just, if you could get the body to the rectory..."

"I will go with you, Vartabed. I feel partly responsible for his death," Kristapor said.

"We will take him to the rectory directly after dinner. Let us move him out back for now," Tavid proposed.

"Tavid, maybe we shall forgo dinner for tonight," the vartabed suggested.

"What? Well, that is up to you, but you are all welcome to stay. I for one am starving!" Tavid proceeded around to the other side of the table to remove the dead body.

The vartabed looked around, not knowing what would be more of an insult—to leave without having eaten or to stay and pretend nothing had happened.

Anoush, now being supported by Varsenig, walked back into the room and over to the vartabed. Still shocked and with a tremble she spoke. "I would feel much better if you would all stay for dinner. It is a shocking yet strange blessing what has happened." Anoush paused. "Perhaps the Vartabed can say some prayers for Vahé and his family. And for us as well."

"Jealous? Maybe I am jealous of him. Of that entire family. To be able to live and think as they do without fear, without remorse within. I…am not able to live in such a way!"
– Armen Eftendelian (The Baron)

# CHAPTER 26

# Eftendelian's

No one is safe.
January 7, 1915. 1600 Hours, Constantinople

"EVERYONE IS LATE, SETA. WHAT time did you ask them to arrive?" Baron Eftendelian called from the other room of their flat above the restaurant.

"They will be here. They are just late. Shant says he is always late."

"I hope they do not come," Karoun muttered under her breath as she helped her mother prepare dinner. Though her mother did not completely hear, she still sensed what was said.

"Karoun, your father promised. Do not worry. He has just invited them over out of respect. They are always asking about you."

"I do not care," Karoun sulked.

Seta gazed at her daughter. With mixed emotions she continued.

"I do know how you feel. What harm is there to meet this young man and his family?"

"I do not care about all the reports. Tavid is not dead. I know he is not."

Seta silently went back to preparing dinner.

"I pray that you are right. So many stories, Karoun, are floating into the city.[1] But why have you not heard from him? No letters. Nothing."

---

[1] November 9, 1914: News from the interior of Turkey reaches the Armenian community of Constantinople that persecutions already exceed earlier actions against the Armenians. December 1, 1914: Reports reach Constantinople that raids by irregular Cheté forces on the Armenian villages of Erzerum Province are continuing.

"We have gone through that before. Shant says the Turks are not letting any letters or telegrams into the city. Tavid said he would be back in the spring with his family. You will see."

Seta tried to smile, but was worried that Tavid and his family would never come as her daughter believed. But for now the current problem was preparing for the arrival of their tardy guests, the family of Daron Pashayan, the government official their son had been interning under for the past six months. Shant was to bring them to their apartment at the end of their work day.

More than an hour had passed. Dusk had descended and still their son and guests had not arrived. The Eftendelians began to worry. The government building was outside their sector, only a few hundred meters as a bird flies, yet farther on foot through the winding streets of Constantinople. Armen Eftendelian considered going to look for them, but after dark it was not reliably safe to leave their Protestant Armenian sector.

Two more hours had gone by when the entrance door of their flat was flung open. In staggered their son Shant, holding a bloody linen cloth to his face. He was alone.

Shant's parents converged onto him as if life depended on it. Seating him in the closest chair, the questions began.

"What happened? Let me see," Seta gestured to remove the bloodied cloth. Shant refused.

'Where are the Pashayans?"

Heart pounding, Shant just shook his head.

"There was a raid at the government building. Gendarmes and some bashibazouks.² They...they took all of the Armenian consuls."

"Took them? Took them where? What happened to your face?"

Shant could not answer and just shook his head. Karoun now was pushing her way between her parents to see her brother.

Getting through, she gently pulled away her brother's hand from his face to see the wound. Underneath was a deep and angry slash across his right cheek.

"I will get some clean linens and warm water," Karoun said as she hurried to the kitchen. She returned with the needed items and helped her mother clean and dress Shant's wound.

"They took Daron Pashayan and the rest of the Armenian officials. I...I do not know where. They beat them, beat them all and dragged them

---

² Turkish: hooligans, irregular infantry.

out of the building. I tried to stop them and a gendarme hit me, I think with a knife."

"What of his family?" Seta asked.

Again, Shant shook his head. "We were to meet them at their home before coming here. I did not go there; I have been hiding in the government building until night came and all the gendarmes had left the front of the building."

Armen Eftendelian pressed his temples as if to stifle an oncoming headache.

"There must be a logical reason for this. Why would they do this? Why?" Armen repeatedly asked himself.

For the rest of his family, the answer was deceptively obvious—the same answer that Tavid would have given if he were there.

Now, the Eftendelians sat together at their dinner table and ate solemnly. Karoun asked if Shant should be taken to an Armenian physician a few residences away to close the wound. Seta looked at her husband who was still trying to reconcile what had just happened to his beliefs and goals for his son, and also cope with the physical damage to Shant's face. Finally refocusing his attention, Armen agreed to take his son to the physician after dinner.

Karoun helped her mother clean up and went to bed early, only to stay up to write yet another letter to Tavid. Letters that were never answered. Letters that Tavid never received for Karoun never mailed them. Writing helped Karoun believe that Tavid and his family were still alive. The letters were cathartic, making it easier for her to sleep at night. Clearing her mind of all the thoughts that she wanted to say and did not want to forget. Hoping too, that some day she would be able to present them as a gift to Tavid from her soul.

And the nights passed quickly.

"What the Turkish government did to the Armenians during this war will be repeated time and time again. And if you go into the past you will see that is not a unique idea. To attempt to annihilate a race, take their land, their homes, their belongings, even their beautiful children and in time, the world forgets.... I will not forget."
– Yervant Yacoubian

CHAPTER 27

# Spring Havoc

Regional Ottoman Military Command Post,
Outskirts of Bursa
Easter Week, April 3, 1915. Dawn, 0750 Hours

ALMOST THREE MONTHS HAD PASSED since the half-frozen bodies of the twelve Kurds who were slain at the cathedral Gadar had been taken to the outskirts of Shak-Shak, a Turkish village resting on the shores of Lake Iznik. There, their bodies had been made to look like they were ambushed by local Turkish hoodlums. The deception appeared to have worked for no repercussions fell upon Tchingiler; no one had apparently traced the dead bodies to this small Armenian village.

At least, almost no one.

"But I am sure that Kaloustian killed them. All of them. You cannot continue to ignore this action, Captain!"

"Mustafa, do not even pretend that you are allowed to speak to me in such a manner! I see that you have waited until my son is not here to express your opinions. Why is that?"

Mustafa sidestepped the accusation, "But there is no reason to wait any longer. There is no spring crop of opium. It is all a farce! He has lied to us!"

Captain Kalkim Bey said nothing.

"My contacts in Bursa laughed when I asked of a spring cr...

"That is enough, Mustafa!" the captain yelled. "Your contacts are idiots!" Then regaining his composure, "Their information is never correct."

By chance, the captain's son Tahir walked in, unaware of the conversation at hand. Still, Mustafa continued his boldness.

"I understand that we have received additional orders from the Ittihad?[1]"

Tahir looked at his father who walked over to a desk where a confidential letter had been delivered earlier in the week. With a long sigh, he re-opened the envelope and paraphrased the instructions, looking only at his son.

"Now we are to enlist all male subjects between the ages of 18 and 58 years of age and transport them to the Dardanelles via the Sea of Marmara. Villages of Ermenis are also to be enlisted and transported, however, they are not to be supplied weapons or regular uniforms. All other Ermenis residing in our region are to be collected and transported south to Konia where further instructions will be given. Deadline to initiate transport: April 7th. All persons resisting are to be shot. Signed, Minister of War, Enver.[2] And so on, and so on."

Handing the letter to his son, the captain walked over to a window to view anything other than his anxious lieutenant.

"What are your orders, Captain?" Mustafa asked.

The captain did not answer.

"Captain?"

Looking at his two lieutenants, he came to terms with these new orders and his duties as commander.

"We will form three clusters of approximately eighty soldiers each. The first will be in charge of collecting Turkish brethren and Kurds, beginning in Bursa and then the surrounding villages, for enlistment. You will be in charge of this group, Tahir. The second group will collect Ermenis from within Bursa and again from the surrounding villages. I will start in Bursa and work my way north, ending up in Yalova where I will join with Tahir. You, Mustafa, will be in charge of collecting and transporting the rest of the Ermenis to Konia. We will leave in two days. Any questions?"

"What of Kaloustian?" Tahir asked his father.

Shaking his head he said, "There cannot be any exceptions this time."

"But, what of the opium harvest and his loyalty to..."

---

[1] The political party in power in the Ottoman Empire during WWI. Also known as the Young Turks.

[2] Ismail Enver Pasha, Minister of War, 1914-1918, Ottoman Empire.

"There is no harvest. And he has apparently been on a killing streak. He must be dealt with this time."

"'Dealt with?' You plan to kill him?"

"If he resists, yes; the orders are clear."

Tahir said no more. His father could see his son's rage building up. As he looked over to the smirking Mustafa he saluted his father and left. Mustafa stayed to ask several logistical questions, and then also left.

Now, alone in his quarters the captain sought a moment of solitary refuge. Sitting in a reclined chair, he smoked some half-dried tobacco, contemplating whether to lace it with the Ermeni's resin. But his moment of solitude ended abruptly as the anxious and now-paranoid Mustafa returned to alert the captain.

"He has gone to warn the Ermeni with two other soldiers! He must be stopped! What are we going..."

"Shut up, you babbling fool, you! What are you saying?"

"Tahir has just left the compound with two of his guards!"

"Idiot! He is doing nothing of the sort. He is just expelling some of his anger by riding."

"Captain, then why did he first stop at the supply post and take two days' rations with him? And the letter, he still has the letter from Enver!"

"Eshek,³" Kalkim muttered under his breath. "Alright. Take what men you need and bring him back. If you are able."

"Captain, do I have permission to..."

"No! You do not! Now get out!"

Mouth half-open, Mustafa quickly left the captain's quarters and hastily collected a dozen horsemen and supplies. In the midst of his rush to prepare and pursue Tahir, he suddenly stopped. He ordered his horsemen to double-check their supplies and to feed and water their horses before departing. Mustafa's anxious expression had suddenly been replaced by a sly smirk.

*Maybe,* he thought, *it would be better to let him make Tchingiler before catching up with him. Maybe something unfortunate could happen not only to him but to Kaloustian as well.*

---

³ Turkish: jackass.

"When my grandson told me of this young Turk who hated everyone including his father but somehow felt a connection with Tavid, I was not surprised. I have heard similar stories from my own father. Unlikely relationships between near opposites. It makes no sense but yet some how there is a connection. One might say God is playing games. I say his game has a purpose."
– Yervant Yacoubian

CHAPTER 28

# Spring Havoc, Continued

Village of Tchingiler
Easter Week, April 3, 1915. 1030 Hours

IN THE DISTANCE, A LONE towering thundercloud could be seen coming from the northwest. It announced its arrival, sounding like faint cannonfire in the distance being carried by its cool spring winds. Tahir, riding alone and half-slumped on his horse, made his way into the village of Tchingiler blood trickling down his legs leaving a tell-tale path. No Armenians greeted him; instead, they hid from sight until the wounded Turkish lieutenant passed. Overcome by their curiosity, they followed the lone rider toward Tavid's home.

Once there, Tahir rode clear up to the entranceway, calling out for Tavid while occasionally looking back at the small crowd of Armenians and beyond to the road from which he had just arrived.

A moment later a surprised young girl, Varsenig, cracked open the entrance door, recognized the soldier, then shut the door in fright. Varsenig ran out the back to the stables where Tavid was tending the horses. He was preparing to leave with his family in a few days for Constantinople and was about to meet Kristapor and his Fedayeen protégés for the last time. As he looked up to see her startled face, Tavid saw the horse and rider slowly coming around the house. The horse stopped as its rider fell to the ground. Pulling his gun from his waist, Tavid scanned the area around him before approaching the fallen rider. Tahir had fallen face-first to the ground and his exposed backside revealed blood from two bullet wounds. Tavid quickly knelt down and turned him over.

Tahir groaned in pain as Tavid struggled to shift his huge body. Trying to speak, it was more of a whisper.

"Sikishmek Mustafa came from behind and attacked us outside of your village."

"What? Why?"

"He…must have known…that I came to warn you…" Tahir muttered.

Tavid was silent as Tahir reached into his coat pocket and pulled out the official letter his father had received from The Minister of War. After describing these orders, he told of the conversation between his father and Mustafa, and what subsequent orders his father issued.

Tavid's mind raced.

"I did not hear any gunshots. How far from here were you attacked?"

"Three, maybe four kilometers. They wounded both of my guards. I ordered them to hold the devil at bay as long as possible. But I am afraid you…we do not have much time."

"How many are coming?"

"I…I am not sure. From the number of gunshots I heard, six, maybe a dozen soldiers. I should have killed him when I had the chance."

Tavid ran. He posted Varsenig at the front of the house, hidden to watch. His mother gathered what food and supplies she could. Stepan ran to the stables for weapons and the horses. Anoush brought bandages to Tavid, who tried to stem the bloodloss from Tahir's wounds. By now, Stepan had returned with horses. The two tried to help Tahir back on his horse but could not. Time was of the essence. Tavid decided to drag the Turkish lieutenant behind the stables, hoping he would not be found until he could come up with another plan.

"Just leave me! You do not have time to…"

"Shut up and help! We are going to hide you back here until I can come back for you."

Leaving Tahir behind the stable, Tavid called the rest of his family to return and then quickly sent them all including Stepan by horseback on the journey to the farmhouse. As Tavid ran inside to retrieve his rifle and bandolier, he watched his family clear the vineyards and disappear from sight before he left to encounter the now half-dispersed crowd. Tavid tried to explain the situation at hand and pleaded with them to notify the rest of the village of the advancing soldiers. Most retreated to the false shelters of their homes, locking the doors. He tried to yell warnings as he rode through the village, but his voice echoed down empty streets. As Tavid approached the cathedral Gadar in a frenzy, stray gunshots could be heard in the distance.

The vartabed was at his cathedral with Kristapor and his young men.

"Soldiers are coming!" Tavid paused to catch his breath.

"Why? What have you done this time, Tavid?" The vartabed displayed anger.

Tavid, still breathless, explained what had transpired at his home just moments before. Describing a plan of action he had Kristapor and his men split into three groups to take up positions in different strategic sections of the village, all with accessible escape routes and adequate concealment. Tavid's orders were given with such ferocity that not even Kristapor spoke. And, as fast as he was upon them, he left to try and halt Mustafa and his thugs before they could make it to the village. But once he approached his home, he knew he was too late. More than a dozen soldiers stood outside; the front door to his home had been kicked down, and Mustafa was standing in the doorway. Tavid could see the anger on Mustafa's face but could not discern the orders Mustafa was giving to his men. Most started up the road deeper into the village, but Mustafa and two others headed across the way toward the home of Tavid's uncle.

Tavid had to wait to encounter Mustafa until the passing of the soldiers riding into the village. He hoped that Kristapor and his men would be able to take care of the impending arrivals. As for Mustafa, Tavid intended to neutralize him now, once and for all.

Tavid approached his uncle's residence from the back side, which was a small, gardened terrace surrounded by a two-meter high stone wall. He could hear Mustafa's voice coming from within the terrace, as well as the whimpers and cries of his aunt and cousin Siran.

"I am sure at least one of your sons is a traitor. And traitors must be shot! Now, which one is it?" Tavid heard Mustafa shout.

A small opening existed within the stoned wall through which Tavid could peer. He saw that Mustafa had Tavid's two young male cousins up against the stone wall at gunpoint by two of his soldiers. He could not see his uncle but heard Siran crying from the other end of the terrace. Mustafa was addressing Tavid's aunt.

"Where is the Hyevan? Kaloustian! Where is he?" Mustafa pressed the young men, threatening them with his pistol as he kicked them to the ground. Tavid's aunt was hysterical.

Again, Mustafa bluntly questioned Tavid's aunt. "One of your dogs here is a traitor and he must be shot. Which one is it?"

The poor women, wide-eyed, only whimpered and knew not what to do.

"If you do not tell me which one is the traitor then I will be forced to have both of them shot! Now! Which one is it?"

Tavid could see a hint, a sparkle of excitement in Mustafa's face as he was enjoying this encounter: to be able to verbally torture this woman, to force her to choose which son would be killed. She stood frozen, watching in horror.

Now, crouched down, Tavid hid his rifle down in the spring grasses outside the stone wall and pulled out his two revolvers, checking that all chambers were packed. He crept closer so that he could approach the three Turks obliquely, blindsiding them. Quietly Tavid climbed up on the wall and lay prone, pointing both revolvers at Mustafa's pair of soldiers.

Tavid fired two shots from each revolver, hitting and killing both of the soldiers. Startled, Mustafa turned and instinctively raised a pistol to shoot but hesitated. Since Tavid was lying on top of the wall, he was camouflaged by his position. Tavid fired two shots to hit Mustafa's gun arm. The first shot missed, the second found its mark. Mustafa cringed in pain from the shot and involuntarily dropped his pistol.

"Have you been looking for me, Lieutenant?" Tavid asked, still lying on top of the stone wall.

Tavid yelled to his cousins to take the pistol and stand guard by the front door. Tavid climbed down off the wall into the garden and without hesitation approached the wounded lieutenant, only to firmly kick him in the groin. Mustafa fell to his knees.

Tavid ran to his aunt and Siran, who was holding his uncle. Seeing his uncle was alive, he turned to the wounded Mustafa.

"I am going to give you a choice, Lieutenant. Just like you gave this poor lady," pointing to his aunt.

"I can shoot you here in the heart so that your road to Jehennem will be quick. Or, I can shoot you here where if you do not bleed to death you might live, but you will not be a man anymore," pointing the revolver to Mustafa's groin.

Mustafa attempted to spit but Tavid's reflexes were too fast as he moved aside, then hit Mustafa in the jaw with his pistol.

"Make your decision or I will be forced to shoot you in both places!"

Without saying a word, Mustafa with his good arm pounded his chest over his heart.

Tavid smiled and pointed his revolver at the lieutenant's chest but did not fire. He held the gun still, pointed to Mustafa's chest. Moving the gun downwards, Tavid aimed at his groin and fired one shot.

Excruciating pain was followed by numbness and the lightheadedness of Mustafa's now hyperventilating and hemorrhaging body. Tavid knelt down again towards the lieutenant and spoke to him. "I have heard that you play such a game. Now I have seen. I am sure that if my poor hysterical aunt, even with the proddings or promises from the devil himself to save her other child, was able to somehow choose which son was to be killed by you that you would have shot not the one she had chosen but, in fact, the other. Just to see the horror on her face. Then you would have looked at her with surprise and asked *'Oh, the other one is the traitor? You meant for me to kill the other one?'* And with that, you would have had him killed as well."

Tavid ripped open the lieutenant's military jacket and pressed the barrel of his revolver to his chest.

"Oh…shoot you, here?"

"It is unfortunate that at times we have had to recruit and train young men overnight to become guerilla fighters. For the most part, it is not a profession that you are born into or that you make a career out of at an early age unless you are delibash. Occasionally you will happen across a soul that was born for the task, but many, if not most, must develop this skill as they would any other. It is not a forgiving profession; with one mistake your career could be over."
– Yervant Yacoubian

CHAPTER 29

# Lessons Learned

DISTANT GUNSHOTS SOUNDED IN THE direction of the village, only to be outmatched by a flash from an approaching thundercloud that would soon engulf the village with its towering mass and intensity. Tavid quickly removed the uniforms of the lieutenant as well as the other dead soldiers. Using twine brought to him by his cousin, he tied up the uniforms, goods, and weapons and threw them over the stone wall to be retrieved later.

"Come quickly, go and meet my mother at the farmhouse."

His uncle was in shock more than truly injured, so his wife and sons helped him onto his horse. They knew the way and left Tavid alone in the carnage as they headed through the forest to the farmhouse.

Tavid stole a look over the stone wall, climbed back over, grabbed his rifle and disappeared into the village.

Following the sounds of gunshots, Tavid headed stealthily into the village, avoiding the open streets. But soon he felt he was approaching too fast, getting too close, and he needed a strategy of his own. Crouching down by the side of a house, he felt blinded as if enclosed within a maze, unable to see where the soldiers were. Scrutinizing the sky, an idea came to Tavid as he searched for something to help boost him up onto the roof of a house. Seeing an old man staring at him in puzzlement through a neighboring open window, Tavid went to him and spoke urgently. The old man's face lit up with a burst of youthful aggression.

"Yes! There is an old, sturdy ladder in the bushes behind the house next door," the old man pointed. "We use it to clean the filth off the roofs. You do the same with it now. Find them and clean out our village!" The old man waved a fist in victory, then closed the window and watched.

Tavid leaped over to the back of the neighboring home and found the ladder just as the old man described. Shouldering his rifle, he took the ladder and placed it on what was the tallest house within sight. He climbed the roof and edged his way to the peak. As he reached and looked over the edge, the winds of the thundercloud announced the oncoming storm and hit Tavid full force.

*And the blind shall see,* Tavid thought as he squinted to peer at his village, as if he had just arrived late to a poorly-staged play that had already begun, sitting high in a balcony.

Tavid was able to spot the location of the Turkish soldiers and the hostilities. Kristapor and his crew had hemmed in what appeared to be most of the soldiers from two oblique sides and Tavid, just fifty meters away, could see the soldiers' backs as they fired in both directions.

Gripping his rifle, Tavid checked the barrel first for dirt, then the chamber and the bolt-action mechanism. He pulled out the stripper clip that held five rounds, inspected it, then placed it back in the rifle. At such close range Tavid would be able to hit each mark without difficulty. Before he fired he looked at his surroundings, then to his left and to his right.

*Where might you have to escape? Or where shall you climb next to change your angle of sight and fire?* he heard his grandfather Yervant advising him. To the right, he saw another taller home with a small stone chimney on one side that he would be able to use for cover. Focusing back on the Turkish soldiers, Tavid aimed and fired two rounds. After the first two shots hit their marks, the Turks realized that they were now being targeted from behind. Abruptly, they changed their positions.

Shouldering his rifle again, Tavid started to crawl back down to the ladder when there was a sudden crack of thunder overhead that resonated throughout the roof, as if Mohammed himself had clapped his hands for retribution. The shock of the blast caused Tavid to lose hold and he began an uncontrolled slide down to the ladder. With intense determination, Tavid quickly reached down, grabbing his dagger and plunging it into the roof, trying to grab hold before falling off. His blade jigged and jagged as

Tavid's weight pulled on it, making it difficult to catch hold and stay. With relentless pressure and the luck of his feet hitting the top of the ascended ladder, Tavid secured himself from falling. Taking a deep breath, he could hear the rain approaching, and within moments it was upon him and the entire village.

"Sikishmek!" he swore as he scrambled down the ladder.

Reloading his rifle, he hesitated to listen to the rain and continuing thunderclaps. The gunshots subsided and Tavid's curiosity forced him to get back up and move to his next roost. While climbing up on the next house, he could hear family members within the home whispering faint profanities at him. Tavid smiled and ignored their prickly kisses. Once at the apex of the roof he was surprised to see three Turkish soldiers retreating into the orchards outside the village and running at a fast pace.

Kristapor and his men were triumphant at the retreat. Tavid quickly swept his range of sight to the left where two more soldiers were trying to outflank Kristapor and his preoccupied young soldiers from the other side.

"God damn it, Kristapor! Turn around! Why are you just staring at the chickens?" Tavid yelled as he aimed and fired a volley of rounds at the two soldiers. Kristapor and his men looked back toward Tavid, startled. One of the Turkish soldiers fired a round at the group. Kristapor and his men returned fire instantly, killing both.

Quickly turning toward the three trying to escape into the forest, Tavid adjusted the sights of his rifle for the distance.

"Nearly one hundred meters now..."

Tavid fired, hitting the first soldier in the upper leg. Tavid adjusted his sights and fired again, dropping the second soldier then the third.

Pleased with the accuracy of his grandfather's Karabiner rifle, he took a deep breath and looked over to Kristapor and his men who were still watching Tavid on the rooftop. As Tavid turned to look back at the orchards where the downed soldiers were, he saw one of them now running with a limp toward the safety of the forest.

Tavid hurriedly took aim and pulled the trigger, only to hear a soft click. The stripper clip was empty having spent the five rounds, and Tavid had to reload while he watched the lone Turk approach the safety of the forest.

"Two hundred meters!" he said aloud as he wiped the rain off his face and adjusted the sights to take aim. The soldier had just reached the forest's camouflage and disappeared. Tavid stared into the trees and brush trying to see anything that moved, and then fired all five shots.

He repeated the gesture once more, trying to see and feel the bullets rip into the forest, searching for an unseen target until he felt his rage turn to frustration.

The havoc of gunfire seemed to end as fast at it had started. And as quickly as the thundercloud came and drenched the village, it had moved on to the next village. Tavid licked the salt-laced moisture from his lips and mustache. His body was soaked from the rain and sweat as he slowly descended off the roof, trying to decide whether to take one of the dead soldier's horses to ride into the forest. Torn between this option or riding up to his farmhouse to verify the safety of his family. And then there was Tahir. He concluded that one wounded soldier without a horse had escaped and could possibly reach his comrades in a few days, if at all.

As he closed in on Kristapor and the others, Tavid saw the soldiers kneeling down with their backs toward him. As he came closer, he saw that one of the Fedayees had a bullet wound to the chest and was gasping his last breath. Tavid walked away.

"Aboush pahn muhn eh…!" Tavid muttered as he reviewed the dead Turkish soldiers' bodies, making sure they were all indeed dead. After which the small band approached him.

"He is dead," one of the young Fedayees stated.

"I know. I know. What the hell were you all doing just watching the three soldiers run away?"

"They dropped their weapons and were yelling, pleading with us not to shoot," one of them squeaked.

"And the two soldiers that were coming upon you from behind, what were they pleading?" Tavid asked sarcastically.

None answered. Kristapor then spoke.

"Their friend is dead, Tavid. They still have hearts, and unlike you, death still holds great pain and shock."

While having the attention of the small band, Tavid softened and again lectured them, for the last time, on the rules of warfare as taught to him by his grandfather along with the rules of confrontation and survival. Tavid ordered them to remove all traces of the soldiers and their horses from the village and to bring them up to the farmhouse as soon as possible for concealment.

At first, the young Fedayees were at a loss until the determination on Tavid's face registered. They must go on.

---

[1] Armenian: "this is a stupid thing!"

"Do not forget the two chickens out in the orchards. Make sure they are dead!" Tavid ordered.

Many of the villagers had come to the small battle zone to see what had happened. Tavid saw the vartabed behind a small crowd. Focusing on him alone Tavid walked to him, as did Kristapor.

Kristapor greeted him and explained the events as if the vartabed was more than a religious leader. Tavid at first just stood and watched their interaction.

"Why were they here, Tavid?" the vartabed asked again.

"I have already told you. And more will be coming. I suspect when this group of soldiers and their lieutenants do not show up at their encampment tonight, they will target us first to see what has happened."

Staring at each other, Kristapor and the vartabed remained silent for a moment.

"If I were you, I would contact whoever is backing your young Fedayees and ask for a garrison of soldiers so that there is not a massacre here in a few days."

"There will be no massacre if there is no trace of fighting taking place here." The vartabed seemed certain.

"We will take the soldiers and their horses to your farmhouse as you suggested," Kristapor then stated.

Tavid nodded, then gazed at the intensity of the sun. He thought for a moment.

"No. No, I have a better plan, Kristapor. Have your men meet me at my home with the soldiers as soon as you can."

"What are you planning?"

"Just bring them. And hope there are no more informants in our village."

With that Tavid left for his home, making a quick stop to retrieve the uniforms he had bundled and left outside of his uncle's terrace. Arriving at his uncle's house, he saw they had not yet left for the safety of the farmhouse. They were in the midst of packing two donkeys with everything imaginable from their home. At a loss for words, Tavid ran to the stables behind his home to see if Tahir was still alive. Not only was he alive but was stumbling, trying to get back on his horse. When he saw Tavid, he gave up and handed the reins of his horse over to Tavid as he slumped to the ground.

"Have you come here to kill me now?" Tahir almost requested.

Tavid grabbed the Turkish soldier by his collar and put his face within inches of his.

"You need to sit back here and hide until I come for you. Or else you are going to get yourself killed. And what the hell is your problem letting Mustafa get the best of you? The next time you try to save my life, do me a favor and do not get yourself shot! Now… Now I have to save your goddamned life! So sit here and shut up!"

Tahir sat back, a smirk almost overriding his pain.

"I do not know what I was thinking. I thought if they killed you that my father would then have to find someone else to supply us with all those gifts we get from you. And he would put me in charge of this and I would have to come back to this stinking…"

"Will you just shut up before I do kill you myself? And why is it I don't?" Frustrated, Tavid left to meet the others in front of his home. What he was about to do next would seal his future, pushing him down a road he had been waiting to travel for months.

"Take the soldiers off their horses and remove their uniforms and any rings or jewelry they may be wearing."

Kristapor was irritated with Tavid's commands. "Do we really have time for this? We are petty thieves now?" Tavid stopped what he was doing and walked over to Kristapor.

"I am going to burn my house to the ground and we are going to burn the bodies of the soldiers with it. Their uniforms, even though they look and smell like they need delousing, can help later. Remove the jewelry so that there is no chance that the burnt bodies will be recognized."

Kristapor thought for a moment. Tavid was correct, once again. "But we will need a hot and sustained fire to do the job right."

Tavid smiled as he signaled to Kristapor's men to prepare the bodies. Within a short time he had removed countless personal items as well as cooking utensils, blankets, fine woven rugs, and the like. With the help of Kristapor and some of the Fedayees, four of the horses were set up as pack animals to take as many of Tavid's family's belongings as possible.

As the Fedayees spread the bodies throughout the house, Tavid took what kerosene was available and started to drench not only all of the bodies but the entire home. Realizing what he was doing, paused to look at his home for the last time. He walked through the now half-emptied rooms and at the walls, then walked out the back and looked out at the orchards. Soon his sorrow turned to anger as he walked back into his home to finish what he had started. With the light of a match, the cleansing began.

"I am never coming back here," he whispered to the walls of his home. "Never."

Tavid watched the house slowly smolder. As the intensity of the heat mounted, the power of the fire intensified as an upward wind blew harder and harder, until the roar and the deep amber flames engulfed the old wooden home.

The vartabed walked up from behind. "What of the message we are sending to anyone able to see or smell the smoke, Tavid?"

Tavid shook his head. "By the time the curious have arrived, the bodies will be reduced to ashes and we will be gone. I would suggest you tell your flock that the Kaloustian family was burned in their home."

Tavid now posed a question to the vartabed. "What will you do when the soldiers come for the entire village? You are welcome to come with me and my family."

"No...no, I will stay here. If the soldiers come as you say and kidnap us, then I will go with the rest of the village. But all will be notified regarding what may happen, and they can choose to stay or hide in the mountains as these young men will be doing," said the vartabed, looking at Kristapor's men.

The vartabed began to walk away and bid Tavid a safe journey to Constantinople. He stopped, returned to embrace Tavid, and whispered, "Worry not. It is the church and its brethren that are backing the Fedayees."

"What?" Tavid whispered back, barely able to be heard over the sounds of the hissing fire. "So that is how you have been investing my money? How many men do you have?"

"Not enough. Not nearly enough," said the vartabed, shaking his head.

"Goodbye, Tavid. Take care of your family and your dear mother. I will miss her." And he left.

Tavid gathered the four loaded horses tied end to end, said his goodbyes to Kristapor and his men, and pretended to leave for his farmhouse. Instead he went back to the stables to see if he would be able to retrieve Tahir by himself. Luckily the Turkish officer had been resting and even with his wounds, the two were able to get him mounted on his horse. Tavid tied the reins of Tahir's horse to the back of his caravan, then gave Tahir some opium resin for pain, instructing him not to take too much.

As they left for the farmhouse, Tavid turned occasionally to view the peaks of the flames, the rising pillar of smoke, and to make sure Tahir had not fallen off his horse. Tavid tried to continue at a fast pace.

At last, he reached the farmhouse, where his family had arrived. They had set up a fire and unpacked their belongings. Upon seeing the Turkish soldier they at first felt disgust, but then realized that the reason they were still alive was because of Tahir. Tavid helped Tahir dismount his horse and propped him up next to the barn. Taking a short break himself, he saw that Varsenig was sitting cross-legged on the ground surrounded by his two dogs. Chobanig and Keil were licking her face and trying to get their long noses underneath her arms so that she would pet them and stop paying attention to the pups in her lap.

"Babies? The babies?" Tavid asked softly, and walked over to see. When Tavid called his two dogs they glanced at their master, but remained at Varsenig's side looking intently at her lap. Nestled together, the small balls of fur were playing and scratching, nipping at her hands and dress. Varsenig looked up at Tavid with such joy, like a new and proud mother. Tavid watched and smiled, and reached down to greet their new puppies.

Suddenly, sounds of laughter caught Tavid's attention. To his astonishment, he heard the voice of Tahir, laughing and humming an old childish Turkish song.

"Ahhh, Hyevan! How long will this heaven last that you have given me?" He started to laugh and coughed repeatedly in obvious pain.

Everyone gazed at Tavid for an explanation.

"I think he took too much of the opium resin I gave him," he stated.

"Why have you brought all of our things from our home? We could have done that tomorrow or the next day," his mother asked.

Tavid looked away from Anoush, trying to find a way not to tell her.

"Hyevan!" slurred Tahir. "You did not tell me what has happened to my spineless cousin, Mustafa?"

"They are all dead," Tavid answered.

"Dead? Ha! Good then! My revenge has been fulfilled! And by an Ermeni no less! It is time to celeb…"

"Tahir! Listen to me! Your wounds need to be taken care of. Is there a physician back at your encampment?"

Tahir was silent in thought. "Yes, there is. But he is a butcher. You might as well kill me now if you are going to take me there."

Tavid remembered an old friend of his grandfather's, an Armenian physician in the port city of Yalova, about twelve kilometers to the north.

"There is a French missionary hospital in Yalova. I know an Ermeni physician there. I could take you there, but they are not in the habit of treating Turkish soldiers."

Tavid went to one of the four horses and removed the uniforms, separating Mustafa's uniform from the rest. Then, handing it to his mother, he asked her to clean the bloodstains and dirt as best she could.

"Can you ride?" Tavid asked, turning to Tahir.

"Ohf! And I am becoming so relaxed laying here now. And the pain is much better. We can go tomorrow."

"No! We have to go now! Can you ride?"

"Sikishmek! Of course. Of course I can ride. Agh! Do I smell that bad that you must get rid of me so soon?"

"Yes, you do," answered Varsenig from behind.

Tavid chuckled and added, "Dead fish in a desert are more pleasant. We will leave in a few moments."

Anoush had beaten Mustafa's uniform on a stone table. She turned it inside out and placed it on top of the wood-fired stove stoked with timber. Being careful not to burn the clothing, she moved it around as if preparing lavash.[2]

"I think I have killed anything that may have been living in these clothes. There was something moving in them but it appears to have been killed or escaped. I hope it is not hiding in one of the pockets."

"Stop it!" Tavid paused. "Did you really see something crawling?"

"It was moving quite fast. Maybe I should cook these a little more…"

"Ohf Bahbahm! I need to wear that uniform into Yalova."

"It is not safe for you to go there openly during the day!" Her joking had quickly ended.

"Yes, I know. I will be a lieutenant and will have Tahir with me. I should be able to move around without difficulty."

Anoush then handed Tavid a wrinkled scroll. "This was rolled within the inside pocket of this uniform."

Tavid opened it and read to himself. It appeared to be an edict in Turkish. Tavid started to shake his head, and then handed the scroll to his mother who at first read to herself then paraphrased aloud in Turkish.

---

[2] A traditional Armenian flatbread.

"All Ermenis to place their valuables in the church? Lock up but leave the keys in the door? Everything will be safe…safe until we return from Konia after the war?"

Anoush shivered, frightened. "Tavid, what choice do they have now back at the village?"

"No choice. I do not know what will happen…or if they will survive," Tavid said with apprehension.

In the background Tahir began his childish song again, which gave Tavid second thoughts about taking him to Yalova. Tavid's mother finished reading the scroll and walked up to Tavid with anguished eyes; mother and son said nothing. Tavid shoved the scroll into one of his bags before changing into Mustafa's ill-fitting uniform. He also pocketed some lire and vials of resin, then strapped on his weapons.

"It is time, Tahir." With the help of his younger brother, Tavid lifted Tahir to his feet and hoisted him on his horse. Swaying in his saddle in almost a circular motion, the drugged lieutenant almost fell to the ground. Tavid got on his horse, grabbed Tahir's jacket and held him in place.

"How are you going to make it all the way to Yalova like that?" Stepan asked.

"I have another idea. I just need to get to the village down the path. And I will be back tonight. Just remember, Stepan, do not shoot at me when I return thinking that I am a soldier!"

Stepan returned a slightly arrogant look and offered a wry smile.

Tavid and Tahir traveled on the poorly-marked path toward the Turcoman village for a kilometer. The old forest trees again formed a canopy above the two. As they exited from the forest to the beginning of a road, Tahir began singing again. However, once the village was in sight, he fell silent and his posture perked up and became stable on his horse. The two rode up to Tavid's befriended Turcoman who was resting in front of his farmhouse. As they came closer, Sinasi ignored them. Riding right up to where the Turcoman sat, Tavid greeted him, "Is the uniform not becoming on me, my friend?"

Confused at first from hearing Tavid's voice, Sinasi raised his head to see his smiling neighbor. Returning a confused smile, Sinasi asked his purpose, still hesitant to acknowledge that he recognized the uniformed pair.

"We are only disguised as soldiers so that we may travel without delay. Soldiers shot my companion and I am taking him into Yalova. I am afraid he will not make the journey well on horseback."

"I see. And what of the soldiers that you encountered?"

"All dead."

The Turcoman stood up. "So then, you will borrow my cart to haul your poorly-dressed friend into Yalova. We will harness both your horses, leaving your saddles here for the time being. Have you dressed his wounds?"

Tavid nodded.

"I should like to look at them nonetheless."

The two helped Tahir off his horse and, with some difficulty, guided him down onto trampled grass next to the farmhouse. Rolling him over, Sinasi undressed the wounds for inspection. Shaking his head, he instructed Tavid to hold Tahir on his side while he entered his farmhouse.

"This is not a good place to..."

Tavid quickly placed his hand on Tahir's mouth.

"Do not say anything stupid. Just be silent and we will be fine," Tavid whispered.

A moment later Sinasi returned with two jars, one with clear spirits of alcohol and the other with raw honey. Kneeling down beside Tahir he began to clean the wounds with the spirits, packed each wound with the raw honey, and finally replaced the bandages. Tahir grimaced, yet stayed silent throughout the process.

"It would be wise not to pretend to be soldiers the next time you pass through the village," Sinasi warned.

Tavid nodded and thanked the Turcoman for his generosity and counsel. Sinasi and Tavid harnessed the horses to the cart and placed Tahir on a bed of straw inside. Sinasi escorted them to the edge of the village and waved them off, repeating his admonition.

Once they were out of sight from the village, Tahir began a new song now filled with Turkish profanities inspired mostly by the return of his pain.

The skies had clouded once more on the road to Yalova. Fortunately, they arrived without incident, but Tavid, seeing the waterfront district and the swarms of soldiers, hesitated at the outskirts.

"Tahir... Tahir! Listen to me. Are you still alive?"

"Yes of course! Have we arrived?"

"There are soldiers everywhere. Do not forget that I am not Ermeni!"

"And that you were shot by a soldier turned traitor."

"Of course, of course. Do not worry!"

Tavid rode into the waterfront district, heading straight for the French missionary hospital. Many looked upon them as they approached and asked what had happened. For the most part, Tavid waved them off without explanation. There was no need since today he was a lieutenant and outranked most of the curious. Pulling up in front of the gated hospital, Tavid tied the horses' reins on a small adjacent tree. He helped Tahir from the cart. Guards within the gates watched as Tavid grasped the wounded Tahir.

"Why are you bringing your wounded here? Your hospital is up by your encampment near the government buildings."

"Tell Panos that a friend of his needs help," Tavid insisted.

Reluctantly, one of the guards entered the hospital. After what seemed to take forever as Tavid held Tahir from falling over, the hospital door opened and out peered an older white-haired and heavily-mustached man with surgical garb and cap. Tavid took off the military fez he was wearing so that he might be recognized. As he did, the doctor squinted, made one disdainful remark to the guard, and left.

"He is not happy," said the guard. "Follow me."

He led them in through the gates and into the hospital. Tavid and the guard placed Tahir on a gurney and wheeled him into a large, windowed room sterile in appearance with crude medical equipment.

"Stay here," ordered the annoyed guard and left.

"Ugh! This is torture!" Tahir squirmed and moaned, trying to find some position of comfort.

"Do not say anything stupid when they…"

But it was too late and Panos walked in, followed by a nurse.

"Do not say anything stupid? Is that what I heard, Kaloustian?" Panos interrupted, speaking in Turkish.

"I was just…"

"Why is it whenever you decide to come and visit, something bad happens? Do you remember the last time you were here?"

Tavid looked away from Panos, biting his tongue to stifle a laugh.

"Daughter of the chief surgeon here? What were you thinking?"

Tahir let out a chuckle and a snort, followed by a painful uncontrolled coughing spell. Tavid started to laugh as well.

"Yes, yes, very amusing. What have you dropped on me now? You with your officer uniforms."

Tavid shook his head. "My friend here has been shot in the back. Can you help him?"

Panos's facial expression changed to one of urgency, and his attention turned to Tahir coughing and writhing on the gurney. Turning him over, Panos removed Tahir's jacket, shirt and bandages to find the two bullet wounds.

Panos and his nurse examined Tahir with precision. Tavid sat on a stool in the corner of the room watching them work.

"We are going to have to take you into surgery, friend of Tavid," Panos told Tahir in Armenian.

"Panos, he does not speak Armenian," Tavid said with a sly grin.

Panos looked over at Tavid, then back to Tahir.

"What?"

"Well, I may not be a Turkish officer but he really is. Actually, he is the son of Kalkim Bey, the commander in Bursa. You have heard of him?"

Panos's face paled, more so than Tahir's. Grabbing a stool, he sat down and began to laugh nervously as the color came back into his face.

"Kalkim Bey's son! Are you crazy bringing him here? If he dies while under my care and the Bey finds out...forget about this hospital being under French jurisdiction. He will burn it down and slaughter us all!"

Tavid nodded, "But if he lives..."

"Yes, if he lives... Now, explain to me how you have a relationship with such a Turk."

Still speaking in Armenian, Tavid explained what had happened that day in Tchingiler and what information Tahir had brought with him.

"Are you telling me that this son of the Bey risked his life for you? Ridiculous! Why are you lying to me?" Panos was becoming angry.

"I am telling you the truth. But I agree it makes no sense unless you know this Turk. He hates everyone, his subordinates, Kurds, Armenians, even his father. But for some reason, he does not hate me. He is always saying that we are alike. I tell him he is full of shit."

"Well, whatever the truth is, it sounds like you may owe him your life. This war is an excuse to murder, steal and drive us mad. I almost hate living here as much as the Turks hate us. I should just pack up my instruments and..."

Composing himself, then switching to Turkish, Panos turned his attention to Tahir, asking him some questions, explaining why he needed surgery for his wounds. He sent the nurse to prepare the operating room. With Tavid's help, he wheeled Tahir outside the operating room.

"You can wait outside."

Tavid shook his head. "Unfortunately, I have to leave. There are some…"

"Oh of course! Of course! I can always count on you to drop off a bomb and leave before it explodes. Go then! Yervant is yelling profanities in his grave right now."

Tavid desperately wanted to tell Panos that Yervant was alive but held his tongue. Instead, he leaned down within centimeters of Tahir's face. "Do whatever they tell you here and listen to this doctor. He is to be trusted. If you do not, I am going to come back here and kill you myself."

"Ha! I thought you were going to give me a goodbye kiss, getting so close to me!" Tahir laughed and again started coughing. "Do not worry about me, Hyevan. Go and get your family out before my father comes. And watch your back, better than I…"

Before he could finish the nurse returned, wheeling Tahir away.

Panos questioned Tavid. "Hyevan? Is that what he called you? Appropriate. Wild, uncontrollable… I am surprised they have not tried to kill you until now."

"I was worth more to them alive."

"And what was he saying about you going away? Where are you going?"

Tavid did not answer.

"So then, this is a final farewell?"

Again, Tavid did not answer.

"I see. Yes, it is wise not to trust anyone, and if Kalkim Bey came here and began to torture me as to your whereabouts, I would probably tell him quite quickly. But since you are not talking, I will…" Panos paused for a moment. "If I were not here when Kalkim Bey came for his son, or if you were in need of the assistance of a physician on your journey to…"

Tavid's pause was long as he contemplated. Finally he said, "Yes. Yes! I am sure my grandfather would be…have been…pleased if you were to come with us. I do not know exactly when. Be prepared to leave at a moment's notice. There will not be time to waste."

"When I heard that there was an Armenian surgeon working at the French missionary hospital in Yalova, I decided to have a visit with him. The French were known to be skilled in the art of surgery and I thought it might be a good idea to know this fellow. Well, the first time I went to visit, they would not let me in. So I went into Yalova, purchased hot coffee and sweet baklava[1] and tried again. We have all been good friends ever since and whenever I would pass through Yalova I would stop in and visit. Always making sure to bring coffee and baklava!"
— Yervant Yacoubian

CHAPTER 30

# Short Return

THE SWARMS OF TURKISH SOLDIERS continued their incessant droning as he left the hospital. Tavid questioned whether the time was right to search out Haig Navasart, his water transport back to Constantinople. But there was no choice. He must make contact now. He could not bring his family here hoping that Navasart would be in port at Yalova and not in Kukukcekmeca on the north shores of the Marmara Sea.

Leaving the horses and carts, Tavid made himself scarce as he walked through the back roads and alleys of the small port city. Reaching a busy alleyway of traders and merchants, he stood tall and walked down the alley corridor which led him straight to the water's edge. Stopping at the end of the alley where it met the street, he scanned the area for soldiers, especially officers, and searched for Haig Navasart's boat. Finally, he spotted it in along the crowded docks. As he watched, a man approached, looking straight at him.

"Congratulations are in order I see. You have been made a lieutenant," said the man in Armenian. Tavid was momentarily startled, then a grin crossed his face.

---

[1] Multicultural: a rich, sweet pastry made of layers of filo pastry filled with chopped nuts and sweetened with syrup or honey.

"I was too busy watching for you by your boat."

"You are slipping!" Haig admonished.

"I do not have much time. I have eleven passengers and eight horses that need transport to…"

"What! Eleven? With eight horses? It is not safe to leave during the day."

"No, not now. Not today. In two days. We will come to this place at nightfall."

Haig nodded. "I do not have enough room for all the horses. Five is the most my ship can hold. And my price is going up with all this 'cargo' of yours."

Tavid agreed, and reaffirmed that he would return in two days.

Retrieving the horses and cart Tavid rode back up to Keles and the mountain villages. The sun had disappeared from sight, with only its reflection remaining on Mount Olympus' peak. The illumination intensified as Tavid's path converged with the brilliant rays on the mountainside. Then as if a candle was snuffed out, darkness fell.

Before arriving at the Turcoman village Tavid removed his Turkish garb. As he passed through Sinasi's village over the stone streets, there were no activities except within the private confines of the homes which emitted faint smells of tobaccos and mountain teas mixed with the smoky aroma of the smoldering fires warming the inhabitants. Sinasi was sitting outside of his house, barely visible in the darkness.

"Tavid! It is you! Let me go and light a lantern now so we can unbridle the horses. How has your friend fared?"

"I am not sure. I have left him in the hands of an Ermeni physician at port. Is there anything I can do to repay you for your help, my friend?"

Sinasi put his hand up, shaking his head. "I have done nothing more or less than you would have done for me."

Tavid thanked his friend, mounted his horse, and left for his own farmhouse.

He was relieved to see his family and relatives settled into their temporary dwelling. The farmhouse had warmed from the fire smoldering in the stove, and a second fire in a pit outside had also been stoked. Everyone had enjoyed a meal prepared by Anoush. His uncle and cousins sat with Stepan around the outdoor fire drinking peppermint teas while Anoush, his aunt, and the girls cleaned the tin utensils and dishes in the adjacent mountain stream. Varsenig played with the pups scampering underfoot, vying for her affection.

The scene was peaceful for a change, but Tavid's thoughts flashed back to the letter Tahir had given him and the decree his mother found in Mustafa's inner coat pocket.

After securing the two horses and feeding them food and water, Tavid took some sheepskin blankets from the farmhouse and joined the men in the crackling warmth of the bonfire.

"We were asking earlier, what if more Turkish soldiers are near and see our fire here?" Tavid's cousin Kerop wondered aloud.

"We are safe for now. They will not willingly come up here."

The warm fire and the comforting blankets were the onset of Tavid's sudden fatigue. He stared into the golden embers as they flickered bright, then faded to be as black as the carbon they had become. With a notable rhythm, the embers seemed to dance throughout the pit. Tavid imagined these to be the lamps of his village that could be seen at night when viewed from the mountain above. Alternatively he thought these were souls within the village trying to survive, only to fade with time.

*Why are they all asleep?* Tavid thought to himself. *Why am I different?*

Suddenly, a large crash sent a spray of sparks flying up from the pit. Startled from his half-sleep, Tavid saw Varsenig getting ready to throw a second and third piece of wood on the fire.

"Mayrig says you will not keep warm if your fire dies. She wants to know if you are hungry."

Tavid shook his head. "I am too tired."

Lying down next to the now-stoked embers, Tavid closed his eyes as he thought of what his sister had just said and whispered to himself, "My fire will never die."

"It is very important to stay calm in the heart of a battle and use the brains that God has given you, not your strength. A wise and patient fighter will live to battle again. And do not forget about the art of diversion."
– Yervant Yacoubian

# CHAPTER 31

# Beginning the Final Journey

TAVID TRIED UNSUCCESSFULLY FOR THEIR final two days to convince his uncle and their family to travel with them for the long-awaited reunion with Yervant—and a new life, free of fear. But their fears of traveling to an unknown island leaving their homeland of centuries, and their ignorant belief that all would be back to normal soon blinded them to the truth. Finally, there was no more time. With Stepan's help, he packed up four horses with their belongings. At last, tonight's dusk would signal their departure to reach Yalova by night.

"Your farmhouse is the safest place to be right now. You should just stay here with us, Tavid," his uncle insisted.

Tavid shook his head. "We have been through all of this a hundred times. We are leaving and so should you. All I can say to you is, I will tell Haig Navasart to look out for you. And do not go back to Tchingiler!"

"Time will heal and all will be the same again," his uncle said. "It has in the past and will again. You will see. By summer you will be back." His uncle was certain.

"No, you will not see us again, uncle."

"Stubborn! Just like your grandfather was. Could not tell him anything!"

"It is you who are being stubborn, Uncle. You risk much for little gain. Tchingiler will not be the same; you choose danger and fear over family and a new life. If I of all people recognize that it is time, then it is surely you who are the stubborn one."

It was time to leave. Tavid helped Varsenig on one horse. She carried a wide bag made of hemp sheltering two pups that she had been able to wean from their mother. Varsenig's face beamed with excitement, though not for the journey but for her two furry gifts. It would be her responsibility to care for and mother the pups. Tavid helped Anoush on another horse after she had said her goodbyes. The small caravan took off down the forest trail.

Entering the Turcoman village, Sinasi was nowhere in sight tonight. Few people were outside. Down the mountain trail Tavid and his family traveled through the darkness. Reaching the outskirts of the city, Tavid left the road and tried to maneuver his family as close to the hospital as possible without being seen. Leaving his family behind momentarily, he proceeded on foot to the gated hospital grounds and entered secretly over the fencing. Finding a door near the back of the hospital, he forced the lock with his clasp knife then ghosted the hospital corridors, listening, searching for Panos. Instead, he found a Turkish officer in a private room. The officer was pacing the room with a stiff gait. As he turned and looked up, the officer saw that he was not alone.

"Two bullets and he still could not kill me, that piece of shit! He is lucky you got to him before me. He would have regretted coming out of his mother's womb!"

"He did not have a mother," Tavid retorted.

"Ha! Yes, you are right, Tavid! Now you must do me another favor. Get me out of this place!"

"Forget it! Not until the doctor says you are well enough to leave. You have only been here for two days. I am surprised you are able to walk around already."

"You do not understand! Every day he has two of the largest and ugliest nurses pick me up and walk me around. Ugh! It is horrible. And they smell like they have not bathed for years!"

"You? Complaining about someone else not bathing? I must meet these two."

"I am going to go crazy if I have to stay here much longer!"

"You can leave tomorrow, Lieutenant," a voice said from behind Tavid. It was Panos.

"Panos. Are you ready to go?" Tavid asked in Armenian.

"Yes, but there may be a small problem. Kalkim Bey is in Yalova. Arrived just today. They have increased security down by the harbor. What or who do you suppose they are looking for, eh?"

Tahir interrupted. "Speak in Turkish! What are you saying about my father? You do not have to hide anything from me!" he howled.

"Calm down, Lieutenant. If your blood pressure rises too high you may start to bleed again and then you will have to stay with us even longer."

"I am tired of doing nothing."

"Sometimes it is enough to be alive." Tavid did not have time for Tahir's whining. "He is here in Yalova. And he probably thinks you are dead. Panos, he must go or we may all be dead."

"Risky for infection, but there is no more bleeding. Wounds can fester from inside and..."

"Yes, yes, I understand. You must let me go now!"

"What will you tell your father about me?" Tavid asked.

"You? You are dead."

"Who killed me?"

"I did."

"Ha! He is not going to believe that. He knows better."

Panos interrupted, "Just tell him the truth. Tell him exactly what happened?"

Tavid and Tahir looked at each other, and agreed.

"Panos, who can take him to his father? Maybe his two nurses!"

"Yes, that is a good..."

"No, No! What are you trying to do to me, drive me insane?" Tahir sat down to calm his nerves.

Tavid winked and nodded at Panos to continue.

"No, Tahir. I insist that they accompany you back to Kalkim Bey. It is for your own good. I will prepare a small parcel for you to take so that you may change the dressings once a day. Now if you wait here I will have everything prepared for your departure."

With that, Panos left the room.

"Give your father my best when you see him. I must be on my way as well, for it is time for me to escape again. May the doors of Jehennem be locked tight and rusted shut by the time you appear before them, Tahir."

Gritting his teeth, Tahir refuted, "I will see you again some day. And remind me not to do you any more favors!" Profanities then escaped in whispers.

Tavid left in search of Panos, who had just finished giving orders for Tahir's dismissal and escort. Going back to his office, Panos had his travel bags packed and ready. Relieved of the tedious duty of managing Tahir, they left via the rear of the hospital grounds and through a hidden gate for which Panos had a key. Reunited with a very nervous Anoush, Tavid secured Panos's bags on the horses and the group headed stealthily toward the harbor. The wind was picking up and the smell of rain blew in from the northwest off the sea. Before long, it began to rain. Pressing harder, they finally reached the alley corridor that led to their rendezvous with Navasart. This time, Tavid saw soldiers milling about the dock and on the main harbor street. Tavid halted. A family, traveling in bad weather by cover of night, would be an instant target.

The steady drizzle continued, and where most would have covered their heads or sought shelter Tavid closed his eyes, extending his head upward to welcome the hundreds of droplets that kissed his face. As the rain renewed him, Tavid's mind raced. It was as if the elements were trying to tell him something. One large drop fell on his forehead, obliterating all the droplets that clung to his skin. Then, he opened his eyes, smiled, and knew what to do. Walking back to one of the horses, he rummaged through a bag, gathered some explosives and cautiously kept the fusing dry under his coat, carefully hiding the stash from Anoush.

"What are you doing?" Anoush whispered anxiously.

"Just wait here until I return."

Then, turning to Stepan he ordered, "If by chance I do not, go straight ahead and seek out Haig. He will be waiting by the docks." Tavid left without another word.

How agonizing it was for Anoush to have a son who had no concept of his own well-being. How many times could she withstand the thought of her son getting himself killed? These thoughts raced through Anoush's restless mind. From experience, she became resolute that if her son was destined to die, there was nothing she could do to change his nature. All she could do was pray for him and stay focused on the rest of her family.

An explosion rocked her thoughts and the streets before them. Soldiers raced away from the docks toward the blast. Stepan kept them hidden and cradled Varsenig, who clutched the doll that Karoun had given her. They waited for Tavid to return, but there was no sign of him. Eternities seemed to pass. Then, Stepan became resolute.

"We must go forward now while the soldiers are gone. Quickly."

They walked to the opening of the alleyway off the harbor. The street was dark and empty now. No one was about except a figure of a man standing at the highest point on his boat, trying to see what had caused the explosion on the other side of the harbor. The man glanced into the alleyway where Tavid's family stood. Seeing them, he quickly came down off his boat and approached the alleyway.

"Paree eereegoon![1]" Haig greeted them in Armenian. Are you Kaloustians?

"Yes!" Stepan announced.

"Hurry then."

*But not without Tavid!* thought Anoush, anguished.

"Where is Tavid? Did he blow himself up again? How many lives does he…"

"Do not say that! He will be here. We must wait for him," Anoush implored Haig.

"I will wait as long as I can, but if the soldiers…."

Haig Navasart paused as he heard someone coming but could not see from where or who it was. Without any warning, a figure darted out from the black alleyway so quickly it startled everyone on the ship.

"What are you waiting for? Go!" the panting Tavid insisted.

Quickly they pushed off from the harbor and into the Marmara. Instead of starting the ship's engine, they raised the sail so as not be noticed from shore. The wind from the light storm carried them far from shore in the wink of a drunken man's eyes.

---

[1] Armenian: "Good evening."

CHAPTER 32

# First Reunion

TAVID HAD PAID HAIG NAVASART beforehand in case there was need for urgent action upon arrival at Kukucekmeca, a port located at the northern edge of the Marmara Sea within Constantinople. He had also inquired if Haig had ever sailed outside of the Marmara Sea, specifically through the Dardanelles and into the Aegean.

"It has been years since I have been to the Aegean and the Mediterranean. Sailing those seas is nothing like the calm Marmara. The larger the ship, the better your chances," Haig said with a knowing smile. "My vessel is too old and too small to venture such seas."

After two nights and a day of travel on the Sea of Marmara, their timing for arrival could not have been better. They had arrived at the port of Kukucekmeca before dawn with enough time to unload, pack the horses, and make their way to Tavid's apartment under the guise of darkness. The two-day journey had been uneventful due to the misty weather, poor visibility on the seas, and the sharpness of their captain who stayed clear of shipping lanes and other vessels. The winds were swift and kind, blowing due east, making for speedy travel without the use of the boat's deafening steam engine.

*You know, it has been years since I have seen your mother. I will pray for all of you to have a safe journey there and back.* Tavid remembered Ana's words as he had left Constantinople last autumn. Tavid looked forward to seeing her, but another woman was on his mind as well.

The small group arrived at Tavid's apartment just as dawn pierced the sky. Darkness had hidden many sights and details like the harbored warships to the southeast at the entrance of the Bosporus to the Marmara Sea and the Turkish troops stationed to the west of the port of Kukucekmeca. Remarkably, much of the northeast sector was the same as it was when Tavid had left Constantinople months before. Europeans, especially Germans, filled this sector, engaging in trade, business, and now war. Germany allied with the Ottoman Empire. Turks, for the most part, stayed out of this sector and treated its residents with neutrality.

Tavid situated the horses in the stable at the rear of the one-story building. He was eager to surprise Ana with the arrival, albeit brief, of his family. But Ana heard the commotion, rushing outside to greet the party. Ana joyfully embraced Anoush, praising God's mercy on all and praying for everyone's continued well-being. She rushed to embrace Tavid and the others. Although she had never met Stepan or Varsenig, she treated them as her long-lost children. Panos was also a stranger to Ana, but she welcomed him warmly.

Tavid, with the help of Stepan and Panos, situated the horses and removed the heavy belongings from their backs. After unlocking their apartment door, Ana opened a window to remove the stagnant air and prepared a fire in the central stove. Making several trips, Tavid and the others brought their belongings into the apartment.

"After this, it will not take long to warm up your apartment. You settle in with your family now while I prepare some breakfast for you."

Anoush, not used to having food prepared for her, hesitated then accepted Ana's hospitality, though she still offered to help prepare the meal.

"You are in my house now. Settle in and then you must rest," Ana insisted.

Soon they were sitting down to a satisfying breakfast. As they ate and conversed with Ana, a restless anxiety crept inside Tavid. He could wait no longer. He must see Karoun. Excusing himself, Tavid announced he must make a few arrangements and would be back in a few hours.

"You are going to go see Karoun? Can I come too?" Varsenig blurted out.

Tavid, rolling his eyes, did not answer but his mother knew that Varsenig had guessed correctly and smiled at her son. "Perhaps we should all go!"

Tavid did not answer. He searched his bags for a change of clothing, something without the scent of their journey. "Go, son. And tell them we look forward to seeing them very soon."

Tavid set out on foot to the Eftendelian's restaurant, traveling on lonely shallow streets, some dark and filthy alleys in the back of the markets. As Tavid made his way to the Eftendelian's back entrance and heard the first clanging of pots from the back kitchen door, he felt his heart start to race. He took a deep breath to calm his nerves and smelled the enticing aromas. Slipping in, he headed straight through the kitchen. Before he reached the doorway Karoun came walking into the kitchen, arms filled with dirty dishes. Focused on balancing her load, she did not see the young man who stood before her. Startled as she sensed the obstacle, her eyes met his and she lost her balance, dishes crashing to the floor. Tavid was also startled and stepped back to scan the display of broken dishes in front of him. Smirking at Karoun, he tried to think of something witty to say. Before he was able to, Karoun's eyes began to tear and she stood there looking at Tavid. He quickly stepped around the chaos and went to her. Ignoring customs he put his arms around her; her head fell onto his chest and she held on tightly. Tavid could smell the alluring scent of her black hair and kissed the top of her head.

"Karoun, what has happened?" Karoun's mother heard the crash and hurriedly entered the kitchen. She saw her daughter with Tavid and her facial expression changed to surprise and joy. Walking over to the two Karoun's mother embraced both Tavid and her daughter, kissing them both.

"We were worried, no word for so long! Have you brought your family? Is everyone well?"

Tavid nodded. "We arrived this morning."

She led Karoun and Tavid outside and up to their apartment above the restaurant.

Karoun's older brother, Shant, appeared from the bedroom upon hearing a voice he had almost forgotten. It had been almost a year since Tavid had seen Karoun's brother. At first, Shant seemed uncomfortable to approach his old friend. Solemnly, with a downward gaze, he walked up to Tavid.

"Shant! How is my favorite brother of my favorite girl?"

As Shant looked up, a scar on his left cheek bone was prominent. It had changed Shant's appearance, even his personality.

"It is from the gendarmes the day they came for my consul general at the government building. Almost dead he was before they took him away. I…I was lucky."

Tavid felt confused because he was unaware of these events. He felt the rage swelling within him trying to escape. Repressing his emotions, he said nothing at first. Yet, the colors of hatred were overflowing on the surface of his skin determined to escape by any means, even through each breath exhaled.

By reflex, Tavid attempted to touch Shant's scar with the back of his right hand. Abruptly backing away at first, Shant then relaxed, allowing Tavid to touch the deadness of the scar. With this, Tavid regained his composure.

"It does not look as bad as you may think, my friend. No. In fact, I am jealous. It makes you look strong, a man to be respected, even handsome."

Tavid reached down into his pocket and pulled out his clasp knife, opened it and held it up to his own face.

"Do you think you can get away with trying to be better-looking than me?" Tavid put the knife to his own face, pressing the blade onto his skin to the point that his skin was about to succumb to the pressure, as if to cut himself in the exact same place.

Shant, with a look of horror, slowly grasped Tavid's knife hand and held on firmly, followed by a calmness, then a smile. Something he had not been able to do since the incident at the government building.

"Still you are crazy… Only you could make me feel good about such a thing." And they embraced as brothers should.

Completing the family circle, heavy steps could be heard walking slowly up the outside stairway to the apartment door. Seeing his family with Tavid, Armen Eftendelian stood motionless in the doorway for a moment before closing the door behind him. He saw happiness on the faces of his family that he had not seen for months. Even his son appeared as though his recent trauma was erased.

"It is good to see that you are still alive, Tavid."

"Thank you, Baron."

"He brought his family, too! They just arrived this morning," Karoun said with excitement.

But Baron looked old and tired as he fell into one of the chairs. As he rested, Seta sat down next to him.

"Any news on the consul general?"she asked.

Baron shook his head, and began to prepare his blackened pipe with some tobacco.

"Nothing, no one knows where they are or if they are even alive."

Tavid glanced at Karoun and sat down with Baron, looking intently at him.

"What are you staring at? Hasn't my son told you what has happened?" Baron raised his voice.

Tavid shook his head. "Just that there was some incident with a consul general."

A heavy sigh issued forth before Eftendelian continued. "Not just any consul general. They took Daron Pashayan, a most influential man, highly respected by most Armenians and Turks alike. They…took all of the Armenian consuls. I have been trying to find word of their whereabouts, what fate has become of them all."

Tavid looked over toward Shant, waiting for him to tell firsthand of the events that occurred a few months back. Shant was a bit hesitant, then told a vivid story of the events as if they had occurred only yesterday. Tavid listened intently, watching the reactions of the Baron as the story was retold.

"I would be glad to help you, Baron."

Baron just stared at Tavid, shaking his head and inhaling from his pipe. "I am afraid they have all been killed."

Tavid nodded his head. "And did you think I was dead as well?"

Normally this was an invitation for an argument, but Baron did not accept. Only continued to fill his surroundings with smoke and focused on no one.

"Why have you not brought your family with you?"

"We have just arrived and they are resting. The journey was long, as you know."

"I would very much like to see your family. Would you bring them over tomorrow morning for breakfast?" Seta requested.

Tavid agreed.

"Speaking of which, you must be hungry. Come and sit at the table with my two children and I will bring something for all of us."

Tavid spent the better part of the morning with the Eftendelians, talking about his village, family and the events that had occurred over the past six months. Seta watched and enjoyed the happiness Tavid brought out in her two children. When it came time for Tavid to return to his family there was a sign of distress in both Karoun and Shant, which Tavid sensed.

"How is it that you can still worry about such things? I will be fine and will be back in the morning with my family. It will be an enjoyable day as many more will be."

"Trust the Turk? Share power with him? A voting assembly with
Armenian representation? A voice in the Ottoman government
for Armenians? Do not be a fool! I may not know much of politics
but I know Turks. And the more power you appear to have, the
more representation you strive for, the more your voice is heard by
them, the heavier their sword will fall upon your neck! You would
have a better sense of reality if you smoked resin for a living."
– Yervant Yacoubian

CHAPTER 33

# Breakfast with the Eftendelians

BY WAY OF THE ALLEYWAYS, Tavid led his apprehensive family to the
Eftendelians. Seta had requested they come to the restaurant where a table
would be waiting.

Without incident, they arrived at the back kitchen entrance. Tavid's
mother suddenly grabbed her son by the back of his hair before he was
able to enter the kitchen.

"You are taking us through the servant's entrance? Have you no respect
at all for your family?"

"Your father would always come here through the back. It was good
enough for him."

"My father, my father. Do you copy everything he did? Are you going to
leave your family some day, too? We are going through the front door!"

Reluctantly, Tavid followed his mother around an adjacent building
to the front of the restaurant. They were quite late and when they came
through the front entrance, Seta and Karoun were tearfully relieved. Seta
embraced each and every one of them, tears slowly running down her
face. They were contagious, for Anoush began to weep as well. Karoun
followed her mother's gestures and greeted each of Tavid's family with an
embrace, followed by a kiss on each cheek.

Seta led them to a large table in the corner of the restaurant opposite the kitchen where Baron and his son Shant were waiting for their arrival. The greetings continued while Tavid studied Baron, visually sweeping the interior of the restaurant and the exterior through the front windows. All seemed quiet, as if the world were at peace. Anoush had her sons sit on either side of Baron and Shant. Seta and Karoun brought out trays of the most aromatic foods before seating themselves at the table. Seta made certain her daughter sat next to Tavid, and she sat next to Anoush. Now Tavid had Baron on one side and Karoun on the other, which made him feel uneasy until Karoun began to speak to him.

"We were worried about you and your family when you did not show up at first this morning."

"We were very tired. Slept most of the morning," Tavid explained.

"It is good to see you, Tavid. And your family."

"Much better to see you," Tavid insisted.

Baron's thoughts were elsewhere and he only partially listened to the conversations at the table until he unconsciously interrupted his wife and Anoush.

"Cyprus? You are still planning on sailing to Cyprus in the middle of a war? Ha! You are crazy. It is much safer here in the city."

"I disagree, Father," Shant retorted, keeping his gaze away.

Seta added, "Armen, would it not be wonderful to visit my…"

"No! It would be suicide to go out on the open seas. Any fool can tell you this. You must all be out of your minds!"

The conversation ended. Tavid turned to his mother, winked and smiled. "We still have some time before we are supposed to leave. Events or circumstances can always change."

After a long breakfast Seta invited Tavid's family upstairs to their apartment to relax, digest their food, and continue visiting. Tavid noticed Shant's uneasiness as soon as he walked out of the restaurant, nervously looking for something or someone who was not there. Tavid walked behind him and slid his arm over his shoulders, at which Shant recoiled.

"It is just me, Shant. So…what have you been doing for the past few months? Working in the restaurant, I assume?"

Shant just nodded. Tavid saw shades of fear in Shant's expression.

"You must have respected him very much, this Pashayan."

Shant could not look at Tavid.

"I would like to meet this man some day," Tavid added.

"I...I wish you could, but I do not think it possible. Do you think it is safe in Cyprus? Safe for Armenians?" he whispered.

Tavid nodded.

As they entered the flat above the restaurant, Seta enlisted her son and Tavid to help her bring in additional chairs from another room so that there would be enough seating in the main room. But as she did, she pulled Tavid to the side after her son had left the room and began to whisper. "You see how Shant is not the same?"

Tavid nodded.

"Ever since they came and took the consul general, he has been having nightmares and is afraid to walk anywhere, even in our own sector. Maybe if you spent some time with him..."

"Of course. I understand. I will need an excuse to get him out of the apartment."

They both thought for a moment.

"Ahhh, I will send you to market to pick up some food for us all. Now, pretend not to know of this."

"Please tell your daughter so she does not think I am ignoring her," Tavid said, chagrined.

Seta agreed, patting Tavid's cheek with approval. Tavid walked out of the room with a large chair and sat next to the others.

As the two families sat and relaxed, Seta and Karoun served teas and thick coffee for all. Then Seta initiated her plan.

"I just remembered some things I forgot to get at the market this morning. Shant, do you think you could go for me right now?"

Shant had a look of surprise, almost horror.

"And why not take Tavid with you?" she added.

"Yes, the walk will do us both some good," Tavid said, smiling at the apprehensive Shant.

"I will go too," Stepan announced.

"Yes, you come too," Shant said, uneasily.

Seta went to get a list of needed items. Returning, she handed the list to Shant and the three left the apartment, leaving behind a disappointed Karoun.

"Karoun, can you remember the last time I was able to get your brother out of the house?"

"I know, but..."

"I asked Tavid to do this for me. He asked me to make sure you knew this so you would not think he was ignoring you," Seta explained with a smile.

"Such a difference we have, Seta. I wish my son would stay home more often while you are trying to get yours to leave!" Both mothers laughed, turning to Baron, who was surrounded in a mist of pipe smoke and again apparently in deep thought of something or somewhere other than the conversation at hand.

# The First Reality

Constantinople, Spring of 1897

ON A FLAT ROOFTOP NEAR the north central sector of Constantinople, where the Bosporus rips into the land from the Black Sea and splits the city in two, a lone figure sat silently watching dusk turn into darkness. Black tears fell from his face, hitting the roof with a silent intensity.

In the distance the silhouette of an arched bridge could be seen, traversing the Bosporus strait. And from this bridge turned gallows hung three bodies whose souls had escaped days before, twirling and swaying above the waterway as if influenced by its flowing currents.

The figure on the rooftop watched until neither he nor the bridge with its victims could be seen through the darkness. He slowly left the rooftop and approached the bridge through the city's maze. Crossing in silence and darkness, he freed the hanging bodies into the river's currents below, never to be seen again. Then, once more through the darkness, this lone silent figure left, but could not himself escape.

The sun never seemed to rise the following day, for before dawn had its chance to awaken the city, spring rains with distant thunder had stolen its task.

For Yervant Yacoubian, the sounds of the rains came as a soothing remedy for sleep. He had been awake throughout the night, unable to stop the images of his three lost companions or the events that had taken place over the last few days. Safe within the confines of his apartment the rains seemed to cleanse his mind, washing away the thoughts he had been unable to remove. His eyes closed, and he slept through the storm and most of the day.

A dream of oceans with sky-blue waters and islands with powdered sands was cut short all too early by pounding on the door. As the dreamer's eyes opened he quickly sat up, but at first did not open the door.

"Yacoubian! Open the door!"

Recognizing the voice of his younger comrade, he jumped up and did just that.

"Armen! I...I thought you were dead?" Yervant exclaimed, and tried to embrace his friend. Armen Eftendelian pushed him away.

"I escaped by the skin of my teeth! You and I are the only ones, Yervant. The rest are now dead!"

"I know. I know. I do not understand what went wrong."

"I did not like the plan from the beginning! Not enough men, not enough time. I do not know why I let you convince me. There would have been other times, other chances!"

Yervant closed the door of his apartment, then sat back down in a chair next to the stove to warm his hands. His long black hair and beard almost covered his facial features as he looked up at the now silent Armen Eftendelian, who could not think of anything to say and began to cry.

"Yervant, I cannot live like this anymore. It seems that whatever we do to avenge the dead, our situation worsens. There must be a better way."

Yervant looked up at his friend. "The Sultan has killed thousands. Tens of thousands right here in the city.[1] How do you deal with a devil like that but to send him back to hell where he belongs?"

"But it is not working! We failed again, and what of our friends, eh? They were all young like myself and believed in your words. No, I cannot be a part of this anymore! I must find another way, my own way to deal with the Turks."

With this Armen Eftendelian began to leave, and as he did Yervant stood up.

---

[1] October, 1895: Organized genocide takes place in Constantinople and Trebisond. In 1896, 300,000 Armenians are massacred in Constantinople.

"You and your father have always been very close. I pray this always will be."

Though frustrated in appearance, a resolute expression came over the face of the young man. And with that, he departed.

Yervant Yacoubian turned, and sat back down next to the stove in his apartment and began to think of his two grandsons back in Tchingiler. Before long, his mind raced back to the horrific events of the week. How his overconfidence had allowed him to convince not only some of his closest companions but himself as well to attempt the assassination of Sultan Abdul-Hamid, the ruler of the Ottoman Empire. Retribution, he thought, for all the Armenians the Sultan had massacred in Constantinople over the past two years. The grenades he had tossed under the Sultan's carriage as he left his palace in celebration of the Islamic New Year had exploded prematurely, killing one of the assassins. Then, as the others had tried to recover from the explosion and escape, two had been shot and killed by the Sultan's guards. The Sultan had commanded that the three dead bodies be hung from the arched bridge that spanned the Bosporus for all to see and scorn as a message to those who opposed his rule.

Yacoubian searched deep within himself to find answers and a resolution, only to realize that none would be given. He needed only to return now to Tchingiler.

"One cannot give up their beliefs and goals just because the
road is unknown or filled with obstacles. You must persevere
and clear your mind to find your way. For if you give up,
all that is left is the shell that your soul inhabited."
– Yervant Yacoubian

CHAPTER 35

# Shant's Reality

As the three young men—Tavid, Stepan and Shant—left the apartment
flat, Stepan put his arm around Shant. "We will protect you, brother," he
said with confidence, flashing his huge infectious smile. Shant pulled away.

"Shant, where is the market we are going to?"

"Up this street and to the north. About a ten-minute walk."

"Hmmm, very close. And the consul building?"

Shant looked at Tavid, confused.

"The consul building, it must be very far away," Tavid added.

Shant shook his head, "No, it is just past the market, less than half a
kilometer but to the south. I would pass by the market when…" Shant
stopped, giving Tavid a sharp, ominous look. Shant continued, "…pass the
market on my way there… We cannot go there, Tavid! It is not safe."

"The market is not safe?"

"No, not the market, I mean…the consul building. It is not within the
sector!"

Tavid thought for a moment, and nodded his head in agreement.

"You are probably right. It would not be safe even dressed as Turks as
we are."

"It is too bad about this Pashayan. You must not really care about him that much," Stepan added in surprise.

Shant stopped in place, letting the two Kaloustians walk ahead as the obvious anger began to build.

Tavid's face lit up. "Ahhh, now Shant, take that rage you are feeling toward us and direct it to the gendarmes who stole your mentor."

Walking back towards Shant, Tavid fed off Shant's rage. "Come now, let us at least say we tried."

Shant looked at the ground, then at Tavid and Stepan. Finally, he followed it with a nervous laugh.

"For months I have been afraid to leave my own home and now…now I am going to do something that I never thought possible. What would happen if I had to live with you for more than a few days?"

"Not sure. Convince your father to come to Cyprus and we will find out. Now come and show us the way to the consul building."

Shant was still hesitant, but led the way past the market within the Armenian sector. Tavid stopped to review the wares of street vendors along the way.

"Tavid! Let us go! Why must you stop at all of these? My thoughts of where we are going are making me crazy!"

"We have nothing but time, Shant. And how can you just walk by all of these delicious things? Look at these breads and…"

"Ahmahn, Asdvadz![1] We just finished eating! I cannot even think about food right now," Shant begged.

"Tavid, buy some of these black olives and this white cheese here," Stepan said, ignoring Shant's pleas.

"And some of these hot peppers to add some taste, eh?" Tavid smiled and looked back at Stepan, then to Shant who was perspiring.

After paying a vendor, Tavid first thought to sit by the street side and break open the bread and its complements but could see Shant's anxiety and decided it best to hold off and continue toward the consul building.

To an outsider, no clear markings revealed where the sector ended and a new sector of the community began. Building architecture did not abruptly change. Though slowly one could see the change in the inhabitants, whether it was their dress, accent or mannerisms. One with a keen eye might notice a difference in the cleanliness of the streets or the apparent wealth of the vendors' wares.

---

[1] Armenian: translates as "oh my God!"

Tavid noticed all these changes. Not that they were now in danger, but Tavid slowed his step and became even more aware of his surroundings.

"How much farther, Shant?"

"You can see the top of the building over the storefronts to the right. We will turn down the next street which will take us to the front of the building."

"What is behind the building?"

"Behind? Some storefronts and a small market. We would occasionally buy some foods there for the consul general."

"Armenians?"

"What? Oh…some are. It is mixed back there."

As Tavid and the others came to the next street, they could see the front of the consul building a short distance away. The building itself appeared dark and lifeless, showing no activity within or out. Shant, seeing the building, sighed and his apprehension amplified.

"Dead," Shant muttered.

"Maybe. But things are not always as they appear," Tavid said. "Let us go down to the next street. I would like to walk around this building before going inside. Are there entrances other than the front?"

"A service entrance that opens into the market area."

"Good. We will go to the market."

Around they went down narrowed streets. The market behind the consul building was similar to the one they had passed back in the Armenian sector but smaller and less congested, almost quiet even with the seasonal spring produce being sold. The combined aromas of the meats, spices and baked goods could be tasted by all who normally would approach, drawing them to this market. Tavid thought it odd for such a market to be so quiet. As they came closer Stepan began to wander on the opposite side of the street, looking into the store windows at their different wares. Tavid and Shant stayed where they were, examining the consul building ahead. Suddenly, a figure walked out the back of the consul building, his first gaze on Shant showing some recognition. Reflexing, Shant looked back and with a shudder turned his head and backed into a storefront doorway to hide.

"Tavid, that is him!" Shant tried to whisper.

Tavid looked towards this man. "Pashayan?"

"No! The gendarme! The one who…the one who cut me and took him away."

Tavid continued to look at the approaching figure, who was not dressed as a gendarme but more like European officials. Their dress and appearance reminded him of the two gendarmes he had killed at Aldo's store last autumn.

"Look at him again. You need to be sure, Shant. Now, come look!"

Tavid's urgency forced Shant to pull away from the shadows of the storefront and peer out at the approaching figure. As they did their eyes locked with recognition and Shant quickly pulled himself back into the shadows, nodding his head.

"Yes, I am sure. I am sure. What are we to…"

"Soos![2] He is coming to us. Do not move."

Calmly Tavid opened the bag of foods he had purchased back at the market in the Armenian sector. He pulled out some of the hot peppers and started to eat them.

"Mmm! These are hot!" Tavid whispered as his mouth filled with saliva, trying to protect him from the spices attacking his palate. Now the figure was close enough for Tavid to see and he could tell he had recognized Shant. The figure reached underneath his coat with his left hand to reveal a revolver. Tavid turned his head away as if ignoring the approaching gendarme.

"You! Come with me!" the Turk commanded, standing about two meters away from Tavid. Tavid pretended not to hear or acknowledge his presence.

Revolver in hand, the Turk took two steps toward Tavid.

"Ermeni!"

Without expression and focusing on the revolver, Tavid swung his open left hand, grabbing the top of the gendarme's pistol. Spontaneously the gendarme fired, pulling the trigger of his pistol, yet only a dull thud could be heard. The webbed skin between Tavid's thumb and forefinger lay now between the hammer of the pistol and its bullets. The gun could not fire. Tavid quickly looked from the pistol to the gendarme's face and spit the hot peppers into his eyes, instantly blinding him. Quickly with his free hand, Tavid grabbed the gendarme's throat and dug his fingers in like claws, cutting off circulation and squeezing his windpipe shut. The gendarme desperately tried to break free of this stranglehold. As he did Tavid buried the heel of his right foot on the toes of his victim. Unable to withstand another shock, the gendarme opened his eyes and gasped

---

[2] Armenian: "Be quiet!"

unsuccessfully for breath. As the gendarme continued to pull the trigger of his handgun, Tavid held on tight with his hands and steadily pressured with the heel of his foot until the gendarme went limp. Dragging him to the shadows of the doorway Tavid dropped the gendarme who slumped to the floor. He removed the pistol still hanging from his now-bloodied hand. Clamped tight like a dead animal whose only reflex after death was to hold onto its attacker. When he lifted the pistol's hammer, more blood flowed from the puncture wounds.

Shant was visibly shaking and vomited into the doorway. Stepan had come from across the way, seeing what had occurred.

"Stepan, break me off a piece of the bread in the bag!"

Looking at his brother as if this was an odd request at this time, Stepan obeyed his older brother's demand. Tavid took the bread, taking the soft inner portion and placing it on his wound, then ingested the rest.

"Sikishmek! Those peppers are hot! I hope this bread helps. My mouth is on f…"

"What in Jehennem was that?" Stepan insisted.

"He was the one who attacked Shant and took Pashayan."

Stepan searched the gendarme's pockets even before his brother asked.

"Why…why did you kill him? Maybe he could have told us what had happened to the consul general," Shant asked weakly.

"Could not let him get away with what he did to you, never mind the officials. And where there is one gendarme, there are most likely more." As Tavid looked over towards the consul building he said, "That is why this market is so quiet. They must be using that building."

Tavid looked around and peered inside the storefront where they stood. The store appeared to be vacant with only sparse merchandise. Tavid checked the door which was unlocked, yet stuck from lack of use. Grabbing the dead gendarme by the collar he forced the door open and dragged the gendarme inside. Shant and Stepan followed, closing the door behind them. Placing the gendarme up against one of the walls out of sight from the front store windows, Tavid surveyed the inside and walked to the back where he found another entrance into an alleyway. But as he tried to open this door it also was stuck. Something was blocking the door from the outside. Tavid gave one more push and as the door flung open, he saw someone had been sleeping off a drunken or opium binge against the door. Tavid saw an obese figure of a man lying by the side of the back entrance profaning towards Tavid through slurred lips and half-cocked eyes. Tavid grinned as he gazed at the man and scanned the rest of the vacant alleyway. Grabbing the putrid fat man by his pantlegs Tavid tried to drag him inside the store, only to accidentally pull his pants off and in the process fall backwards through the back door onto the floor.

"Stepan! Shant! I need some help back here!"

First Stepan then Shant came to his aid to find Tavid sitting on the floor laughing as he viewed the pants in his hands and the fat man in the alleyway.

"Come and help me drag this drunken gendarme into the store. He is too heavy for me."

Stepan quickly responded, but Shant did not.

"Does he have a pistol?" Shant asked.

"Good for you! Now you are thinking. But he cannot even see straight, let alone find his weapons. Check for a weapon, Shant."

Shant tentatively searched and seemed proud to find a small pistol. With great effort, the three dragged the reeking fool to the back of the store.

"Shant, find a lantern or a candle so that we can see this gendarme better."

"Skishmk... uhhh... give! My pant uniformmmm..." The gendarme tried to stand, but with a mild push on his shoulders from Tavid he slumped back to the floor, bumping into a metal pan catching water from a leak in the ceiling. Tavid had an idea and spoke in Turkish to his brother, asking him to bring the other gendarme into the room. While he did, Tavid took the metal pail and its now half-spilled water and dumped it on the gendarme's head.

"Ahhh! Skishmk! Whaaat are you doing?"

Tavid found some old rags smelling almost as bad as the gendarme, took them and vigorously wiped the gendarme's face and scalp.

"I need you to wake up, my friend! We have someone here we want you to see." Tavid held the fat gendarme's head up by his scalp and pointed it towards Stepan and the dead gendarme he was dragging in.

"Some Ermenis have killed this gendarme. Do you know him?"

The gendarme's eyes widened when he saw the face of the dead gendarme.

"Ahhh! Erdem! Erdem! You killed him!"

"Sarsakh![3] No, we did not kill..."

"Who are you?

---

[3] Turkish: idiot.

Tavid twisted the gendarme's scalp so that it would now point towards his face.

"Cheté…"

Starting to hyperventilate, the gendarme had a new look on his face. A look of terror.

"We are looking for the Ermenis that killed your friend."

The fat gendarme nodded.

"Where did they take the Ermenis that were in the consul building across the way?"

A confused expression overtook the gendarme's face.

Tavid turned the man's head so that he could see the consul building through the storefront windows.

"The Ermenis from the consul building that were taken away this winter…where are they?"

The gendarme nodded his head and tried to catch his breath. Tavid let go of his scalp.

"Some are dead. The rest…the rest being held in the old cattle storehouse near the prison. The Southeast prison near the port.

"Which storehouse?"

The gendarme shook his head, still trying to catch his breath.

"There…there is only one…you will see…"

Tavid smiled and looked up at his two companions, satisfied with the results of the interrogation. Tavid took his gun out and clubbed the gendarme on the back of the head, knocking him unconscious.

"Stepan, did you find a knife on the other gendarme?"

"Yes." He gave it to Tavid.

Tavid asked Stepan to lay the first gendarme on the floor and, with knife in hand, thrust it through the dead gendarme's chest into his heart.

"What are you…"

"Just wait, my brother. Just wait and watch. Here now, help me with the fat one. Let us roll him over onto his comrade."

With much difficulty, the three were able to accomplish a most odious task. Tavid then took the hand of the fat gendarme and secured it to the imbedded knife.

"Yes, I see now! But what of the fat one? Are we to let him live?"

"We will leave both doors open and his pants outside the front door. The other gendarmes will find him and most likely kill him for us. Shant? Are you ready to go back home now?"

Shant was still a little pale but seemed freer, as if a bit of confidence had been restored. He smiled.

"What about the storehouse?"

Tavid chuckled. "Not yet, Shant, not just yet. Let us go back and tell your father the good news. And on the way back let us think of a good plan!"

"At times I wonder what I have created with my grandson. I remember when I was his age, I would tell my father and grandfather of our 'adventures' as a Fedayee. And at times they would just look at me with astonishment on their faces. I would ask if I had done something wrong and they would break from their trance, approving my actions of course but telling me not to tell my mother of such things. Now I know how they felt."
– Yervant Yacoubian

CHAPTER 36

# Re-awakening

JUST AS THE WAIT SEEMED interminable, Seta heard footsteps and laughter coming from the stairs. The door burst open revealing three happy oversized boys, wrestling and pushing their way up the stairs. Seta was visibly relieved to see her son Shant with a smile returned to his face.

"Boys! Boys! It took you so long, for just a few things?"

"Just having a little fun, Mayrig," Shant answered.

"And we bought your groceries," Stepan piped in.

"And we stopped at the consul building," Tavid whispered as he walked by Seta, who gasped.

"What? Why did you go there?"

"Go where?" Baron injected.

"They went to the consul building!"

"Ohf, Bahbahm![1] What business did you have to go there? Can you not see that my son is…"

"Hayrig,[2] I am fine! I am glad we went. Thanks to Tavid, we found out where Daron Pashayan is."

With this, Baron stood up with questioning amazement.

---

[1] Turkish/Armenian slang: "my father!" Used in the same way as "oh my God!"
[2] Armenian: father.

"How could you find out such a thing?" Baron demanded.

But his son did not answer, and looked to Tavid to answer his father.

Karoun walked up to Tavid and took his hand.

"You are bleeding," she said, and made Tavid sit at the table while she went to get some alcohol spirits and a dressing from the kitchen.

Baron came and sat at the table across from Tavid, motioning for his son and Stepan to come and sit with them. Anoush said nothing but secretly hoped that the reformed-but-still-formidable Baron would reprimand her son for whatever had happened. As Karoun attended Tavid's wound he told the sordid story of their shopping excursion. Baron listened, surprisingly quiet. And when it came to the part where they found out the whereabouts of the Armenians from the consul building, a heavy sigh left Baron's body as he nodded his head with hesitant approval of the three young men's actions.

"I am sorry, Baron, they should never have gone there. Please forgive my Adapsoos³ son for..."

"No, I will not. Because I approve of what they did," Baron said, matter-of-factly looking at Anoush. "It is something I should have done myself, but have been blinded by my own stubbornness."

Tavid smiled at the never before heard words of approval.

Baron stood and paced the room. Tavid spoke candidly. "These Armenians may still be dead, or half-dead including Pashayan, but if they are still alive I have an idea if you are interested, Baron."

Baron gestured for Tavid to continue.

"I will disguise myself as a Turkish officer and go to the storehouse. I will tell them that one of my Armenian informants is missing and that he was working at the consul building. I could have falsified papers made allowing the release of Daron Pashayan. On the other hand, if the storehouse is lightly guarded we could just kill all the guards and free the entire lot!"

"Shades of your grandfather." Baron shook his head. "But your first idea, to go as an officer with papers ordering the release of the consul general. It should be a German officer, not a Turkish officer. And you are too young to be an officer other than a lieutenant, eh?"

Baron thought for a moment, then looked at Seta and smiled.

"May I take the boys out for a walk again, Seta?"

"Where? Where are you going?"

---

³ Turkish: stubborn.

"To the sanctuary."

Seta had a calm yet concerned look on her face. "You have been fighting yourself for years, Armen. Are you sure you want to do this?"

Baron smiled affectionately at his wife. "I am not saying that I was wrong all these years. Just that maybe it is time for a...temporary change." He went to his wife, embraced and kissed her, to the confusion of everyone else not familiar with Baron's past.

"Let us go, my young men! We have a plan to work on."

Out the door the four left, leaving behind an even more frustrated and confused Karoun. Noting her frustration, Seta sat her down and began to tell her of when her father was as young as her brother, Shant. Stories that had never been told and almost forgotten until now. Tales of a young, voracious fighter who in many ways paralleled Tavid Kaloustian in skill and stubbornness. And the circumstances that had changed her father to become what he was today.

"When Armen Eftendelian put his mind to it, he was a brilliant
strategist. Present a problem to him and he would be able to
suggest numerous plans of attack. It is funny how as a restaurant
owner, he used this same skill to create the most delicious foods
and found ways to get all Armenians to come to his restaurant!"
— Yervant Yacoubian

# CHAPTER 37

# Strategy of an Armen

DUSK WAS DESCENDING UPON THE Protestant Armenian sector of
Constantinople as the four left the flat. Their destination was in a
neighboring sector, a short walk where they would find the Central
Protestant Church and its rectory, Father Steinhauer, and his deacons.
An indisputable leader of the German Missionaries of Constantinople,
Steinhauer was respected not only by the Armenians but also by numerous
German citizens living within his jurisdiction. Specifically, Armen
Eftendelian sought the help of Father Steinhauer's deacons.

As they walked Baron talked of Father Steinhauer and how he had
helped keep their sector safe the past two decades from angry mobs of
Turks agitated by the former Sultan through German influence.

"Baron, if you knew he was an ally why did you wait so long to seek
their help?" Tavid asked.

"We had asked Father for help months ago, but because of the political
implications of the war and the consul generals, he was told by the Turkish
government that these consuls were all spies plotting with the Russians
against Germany. But now I will seek help from his deacons in a different
way."

Soon they arrived at the Protestant Church with its adjoining rectory. A simple, plain building compared to others in the sector, its interior was adequate for a large congregation. However, it lacked the ornate architecture of other contemporary sanctuaries. Baron entered the church and headed to the left where a large doorway opened into an entrance to the rectory. Lounging inside was a lone deacon whom Baron remembered as Brother Ludwig. He looked up at Baron, showing surprise and joy.

"Armen! Brother Armen! This is quite a surprise!" he exclaimed, speaking in German.

"I apologize for coming without warning like this, but…"

"Nonsense! You and your family are always welcome." Standing up to embrace him, Baron introduced the three young men to the deacon.

"Come! All of you. Come and sit down. I will bring some coffee for us."

As the deacon scurried out Tavid looked over to Baron. "You speak German?"

Baron smiled with raised black eyebrows. "Of course. Don't you?"

A few moments later the deacon reappeared with a small tray carrying a large porcelain pot, cups and a small assortment of baked sweets.

"It has been much too long since we have seen you, Armen. Do not use the war as an excuse for not coming and praying with us, much less to visit. Now first, I want you to tell me why you have come here with these three young men. Perhaps they are interested in joining our holy mission?"

Baron shook his head and in Turkish translated what the deacon had just said. The three young men smiled and chuckled along with Baron.

"How is your Turkish, Brother Ludwig? My son and his friends do not speak German," he asked in Turkish.

"Very good, my Turkish is. After all, I have been living here now for some five years. Now getting back to the subject at hand, we are in need of young men like these for the mission."

"Regrettably, we are not here for that reason, Brother Ludwig. We have come with some goods news and to seek your help as well as the other deacons."

Again, Baron explained the incident at the consul building this winter and the disappearance of many Armenians who were well known to Brother Ludwig and the others. In addition, he reiterated how Father Steinhauer was unable to secure their release and how new information was discovered relating to their whereabouts today.

"I have a plan to secure their freedom. But I need some supplies from your cellars."

The deacon sat forward, taking one last sip of coffee.

"Well then, let us go there now and take care of business first. Then we can relax and visit with each other. And while we are down there you can tell me of your plan."

The deacon stood up, as did the rest who followed him through the rectory to a cellar door. Fetching two lanterns, the five headed down a steep stairway which led to the dark, damp cellars beneath the rectory. Tavid wondered what it was that Baron sought here.

Once in the cellar Baron began to describe his plan, to disguise himself as a German officer and with falsified papers, secure the freedom of the Consul General, Daron Pashayan. The deacon listened intently and while Baron was talking began looking through piles of dust-covered wooden chests and crates. Finally, finding the one he was looking for, he wiped the dust off the top with his shirt sleeve, opened it and pulled out what looked like several old German officer uniforms.

"I would say you will need to be at least a captain. Maybe a major." As he laid out the uniforms on a dusty table, Baron inspected each of the uniforms.

"Try it on. Let us see how it looks on you," Tavid said with a smile.

"Yes. Good idea," remarked the deacon.

"Let me ask you about your plan, Armen. Most German officers have an entourage traveling with them. A lone officer traveling at night will seem suspicious as well as dangerous."

"I will be with him disguised as a Turkish lieutenant, pretending to be his escort and translator," Tavid replied.

"Yes, that is fine, but not enough. You will need at least two more escorts in German uniform. Preferably, ones who look German like myself. And I know just the two that will come with you," said the deacon with a smile.

"I did not come here to ask you to risk your..."

"I know, Armen. I know. But I am tired of sitting around here not being able to help anyone. I may be a deacon, but I used to be a soldier. Please allow me this honor."

Baron nodded and again embraced the deacon.

"And I have another problem with your plan, Armen. Why are you only trying to free one man when there may be others?"

"Yes, I have been thinking about that, but have not come up with a clear solution or one that will not further endanger all of our lives."

"I see what you are thinking. It could also start a large-scale manhunt, an excuse for the government to imprison even more innocents or pose further restrictions and sanctions on us all. For this one we must see how hot the fire begins to burn before knowing how to proceed."

The deacon brought another dust-covered chest. This one was smaller and bound with braided ropes made of hemp. Placing it on a table he untied the ropes, opened the chest and began to lay out its contents on the table. Tavid and the other two young men were totally surprised.

"You will need to protect yourself, Armen. And more importantly, you...we will need to be silent in our protection."

On the table, the deacon had laid out a cluster of German weapons comprised of standard issue army pistols, bayonets, and two Mauser semi-automatics. There were other items Tavid had never seen before. Handguns with some type of oversized cylindrical pipe added to the end of the barrels, riddled with symmetrical perforations.

"Are these what I think they are?" Tavid said with excitement as he picked up one of the handguns.

"Silencers. You have never seen a silencer before?" Baron asked.

Tavid shook his head. "How quiet are they?"

"They are adequate," said the deacon. "They seem more to change the sound than silence it."

Tavid nodded. "I would be willing to trade two of my guns for one of..."

"Take it. And if our plan succeeds and we are able to escape ourselves, I will expect you to bring it back one day soon—of worship!"

Tavid thanked the deacon and started to inspect the firearm by disassembling its parts checking for rust, dirt or malfunction. Baron also took a handgun with silencer and a bayonet. As Shant and Stepan went to grab some of the weapons, Baron smacked their hands.

"These are not for you! I have another task for the two of you." Baron explained they would be the watchful eyes on the outskirts of the Armenian sector where they would help with the distribution of the subsequent freed consul generals.

Stepan looked to his older brother to step in and counter the Baron's edict.

"I am sorry, Baron, but Stepan is coming with us. And as far as Shant goes, he, out of all of us, should be there to free the consuls."

Armen Eftendelian normally would have balked at Tavid's remarks and a huge argument would have ensued. But this time, he had a thoughtful look on his face. He turned to his son to answer.

"You want me to come with you? Carry a gun? Kill gendarmes like you do?"

"Well, you may not have to kill anyone. But it would be nice to have you with us. And I am sure the consuls will be proud to see you," Tavid responded.

Stepan put his arm around Shant. "Do not worry, Brother, I will protect you again," and he flashed his infectious smile. A weight seemed to lift off of Shant's shoulders as he nodded his head.

"But I want two hand guns in case one does not work!"

"Good thinking!" Tavid praised.

Armen Eftendelian found himself unable to hold back his emotions, and with tears in his eyes embraced his son.

Moments later the group was back on track.

"When will this happen, Armen?" the deacon asked.

"Tomorrow night. That gives me a day to think of the plan and obtain falsified military papers ordering his release."

"Perfect. Where shall we meet and at what time?"

"At my restaurant by 17:00 so that we will have enough time to review our plan and set off by dusk. You remember where the restaurant is?"

"Yes, yes of course. Brother Viktor will come with me as well. He will be very excited to come and help. I know he will be disappointed that he missed seeing you today."

Baron bowed his head. "Brother, it means much to me that you are willing to..."

"Herikeh![1] Would you not do the same for me? And in an imprecise way, is this not why this mission is here?" The deacon smiled and began to put away the leftover weapons and uniforms. The five then left the cellar, talking for more than an hour.

Finally, Baron began to show signs of fatigue. The deacon recognized Baron's weariness and ordered him to go home and rest for the next day would be long and tense. They bid their farewells and left into the night.

---

[1] Turkish: "Stop" or "Stop that."

"It is easy to get side-tracked when you are a person of many abilities. I would have preferred that Tavid focused strictly on getting to Cyprus. But these are for selfish reasons. And I am even more guilty of this phenomenon. This whole business of leaving for Cypress. My detour into prison. This huge war. It is obvious now to me that there is no predicting what events will happen when you change your path in life."
– Yervant Yacoubian

CHAPTER 38

# Execution

RETURNING TO THE EFTENDELIAN'S at such a late hour, the Baron insisted that Tavid and his family stay the night. By breakfast he was asking that they stay another night, since their plan to free the consul generals was about to transpire. Tavid had to leave early that morning to retrieve additional weapons, his Turkish officer's uniform and a myriad of official papers he had confiscated recently. He hoped these would be useful to help falsify orders for Daron Pashayan and possibly others. He stopped in to see his landlady Ana, then Panos, reassuring them that they would be returning the next night.

After his return to the Eftendelian's he spent the morning at the now-closed *Azadamart*,[1] the leading Armenian newspaper in Constantinople where the falsified orders were processed. Later when the deacons arrived, the four went over their plan of action.

In the afternoon, Tavid was able to spend much-needed time with Karoun. Even though she and her mother were working in the restaurant,

---

[1] March 31, 1915, *Azadamart*, the leading Armenian newspaper in Constantinople is closed by an order of the government issued through the office of the Police Commissioner of Constantinople, Osman Bedri. Three hundred Turkish pounds in the petty cash box were stolen. The printing presses were removed to the Ittihad Press.

business was slow and Tavid was able to shadow her and pretend to help in the kitchen. Occasionally they were able to steal a moment alone. Tavid joked and spoke of many things with Karoun, though not the one thing she was hoping to hear.

"How important am I to you, Tavid?"

Tavid smirked, took her open hand and held it on his face.

"Can you not see how I feel? Do I have to tell you? Can you not tell from my actions? See my soul?"

Karoun began to blush. He put his arms around her to hold her tight, not letting her go for quite a while.

"No. You do not need to tell me. I do know how you feel. But…it would make *my* soul smile with warmth to just hear you say it, even as a whisper," Karoun said softly.

The restaurant closed early in preparation for the night ahead. Returning to the apartment flat, the two deacons had arrived and together with Baron, Shant and Stepan, they were already dressed in their uniforms, looking dauntingly official.

"Shood uhreh,² Tavid! Dusk is almost upon us. Get dressed and we will go over the plans one more time," Armen Eftendelian ordered.

Tavid quickly changed into his uniform and equipped himself with twice his normal cache of weapons. Afterwards Baron again described the plan of action.

"Remember, we will be unyielding. We must make them cower by our ranks and their ignorance. Confidence, ruthless bravado and ego are everything for tonight."

"And if that does not work, I will try to bribe them," Tavid said slyly.

"This is no time for jokes, Tavid!" A German major does not have to bribe Turkish soldiers. We have papers and we will outrank them. And remember, if I start yelling in German, you are to translate it as you see fit for the situation."

Tavid nodded in affirmation and asked, "Are you all armed? What weapons do you have?"

The two deacons had standard issue Mauser rifles, and in their coats they carried one pistol with a silencer and a Mauser automatic with extended clip. Baron carried two pistols, one draped on the outside of his uniform in a swing holster and the other concealed under his coat with a silencer. Shant and Stepan both had a pair of handguns. The plan was

---

² Armenian: "Hurry!"

discussed further until Baron was satisfied. With resolution, Baron kissed his family goodbye and ordered Tavid and the others out of the apartment.

"If everything goes as planned we should be back within three to four hours. Look for us to return at that time by the cross streets near the southeast sector," directed Baron.

Seta did not know if she should be happy or sad at the possibilities. Anoush knew all too well the night they faced. However, the plan was set into motion and there would be no turning back.

On their way to the southeast prison several thoughts were going through Baron's mind, questions that he wanted to ask Tavid.

"Did your grandfather ever speak of me, Tavid?"

"In what way, Baron?"

"About my past...about my relationship with him when I was about your age."

Tavid thought for a moment. "Only that he has known your family for a long time. That you are a better man than you pretend to be."

"Nothing else, eh? Nothing about...how I was just like you? Thought the way you did? Was going to school to be a chemist until..." Baron hesitated. Tavid stared and said nothing, waiting to see if Baron would finish.

"Did he tell you of when we tried to assassinate the Sultan?"

"Yes! He told me that story but he has...had never mentioned you in regard to this. Were you part of that?"

Baron retold the events that took place years before from his perspective as Tavid listened intently.

"I did not know these things, Baron. Perhaps my grandfather was afraid to tell me these things, so I might also find my own way."

"You know, Tavid, since his faked death you have done just that. No two men are entirely alike, even you and your grandfather. I had also asked him not to share my past with others, so he may have been just honoring my request."

Baron again seemed distant with dreams until they came close to their destination.

"There it is, Baron. The southeast prison. Now where could the storehouse be?"

"Carry on as planned. We will walk in one-block circumferences until we find the building."

They circled the prison twice before spotting a two-story building whose broken windows were smothered shut with nailed boards. Two guards were stationed at the entrance. As they waited a block away, Tavid circled the building checking for other guards and entrances.

"Nothing. No guards. The other doors have all been barricaded shut," Tavid reported upon his return.

Baron nodded. "Any questions, my friends?" But none were asked as Baron walked toward the front of the storehouse and his guards. The sluggish guards saw the small entourage coming forward and they sprang upright and alert.

"What is your business here?" one of the Turkish officers demanded.

"Since when do you address a major in the German army with that tone and language?" Baron stated with a frigid tongue.

Hearing German being spoken, the guard blinked his eyes and studied Baron.

"Forgive me, Major. In the darkness I did not see who you were... Please state your business, Major," The guard spoke back in broken German to Tavid's surprise.

"I am Major Jonas, military attaché to German Intelligence within Constantinople. Here are my papers." The guard examined the papers, then handed them back to Baron. The guard glanced at the two German escorts and then at Tavid.

"And what is your business with the Major, Lieutenant?" asked the guard in Turkish.

Tavid smiled at the Guard and at first did not volunteer an answer. He slowly walked up to him until his face was just inches away.

"If the Major was not here under my care, I would have your tongue removed for speaking to me in that tone of voice."

The guard visibly blushed and nodded his head.

Tavid continued. "The Major here has papers securing the release of one of your prisoners. An Ermeni spy who was arrested from a consulate building this winter. We have reason to believe he is being held here." With that, Baron handed the guard the extrication papers which were reviewed as Tavid leaned in very closely, trying to make him nervous.

"Are the papers in order, Comrade?" Tavid asked with gritted teeth.

"Perfectly, Lieutenant, but..."

"But what?" Tavid snarled.

"Ehhh...many of our prisoners have died over the past few months."

Tavid asked harshly, "Are any of the prisoners still alive?"

"Y-yes."

"Well, what are you waiting for then? Open the doors!"

The guards jumped and unbolted the set of doors. The opened doors revealed the stench of death in the poorly-lit interior. A vast empty storehouse with only bodies of men riddled the floors of packed dirt and decaying hay. Many of the bodies were lifeless; others showed signs of still struggling souls.

"Bring your lanterns in here!" Tavid growled at the guards. "How are we supposed to see if you have killed our informant in this darkness? Sikishmek!"

Baron at first tried to hold back a grin from Tavid's performance. But upon seeing this scene, he now had no such trouble for the ruins of his humanity lay before him within these chambers. As he looked around the blackened storehouse, a sinking feeling engulfed him. Maybe he was too late and Daron Pashayan had passed from this life miserably.

Each of the guards carried two high-wicked lanterns shining brightly in the storehouse. The guards led the way as Baron followed his two guards, with Tavid in the rear. One could barely breathe from the stench as they walked from one end to the other. Tavid felt his rage building again, but he was able to suppress his feelings for the time being. Row upon row they walked, inspecting every prisoner for Daron Pashayan. On the second pass, Tavid noticed an older white-haired man who appeared familiar but whose face and jaw were grossly swollen. The old man sat crossed-legged on the floor, and as Tavid passed the old man looked up at him, a spark of recognition filling both their eyes. Tavid stopped dead in his tracks, blinked his eyes for at first he did not believe who he was seeing. The old man tried to smile from his recognition of Tavid, however, his face twinged in pain from the obvious swelling. The eyes of the old man then pleaded for help. Eyes that belonged to Malachi from the apothecary. Yahudi Malachi.

Tavid turned from Malachi and slowly addressed the guards. "This old man here, what has happened to his face?"

The guards stopped to look, as did the others.

"That one is only a Jew. Always talking. Could not get him to shut up until I broke his jaw."

Tavid nodded and began to walk away from Malachi toward the entourage. With his hand under his coat Tavid slowly walked past Shant, Stepan and the Baron, then pulled out his revolver with its silencer and shot both guards in the head. As they fell to the ground one of the kerosene lamps broke open and began to burn furiously on the floor, mixed in with the old hay.

"Aboush! What are you doing?" Baron's voice swelled in anger as they tried to quell the fire.

"Look around you, Baron! They have all been tortured!"

"Hayrig!" Shant interrupted. "Whether Daron Pashayan is here or not, we cannot leave anyone here. Tavid is right…"

From an adjacent row another man turned hearing the conversation and slowly stood on his feet.

"I…I am Daron Pashayan. Who seeks me out and comes here to kill these devils?"

Shant turned to see a pale, emaciated Daron Pashayan. The mist that clouded his mind when he entered the storehouse was lifted and new hope streamed through his veins.

"Shant? Who is with you in that German uniform? Praises to God, what is happening, my young man?"

Shant embraced the consul general and quickly explained the situation. "It is my father! And friends, but …"

Baron interrupted, "Now! We must leave at once. The missing guards will be quickly noticed." Baron turned to give orders to Tavid, who was with Malachi helping him on his feet.

"Tavid! Tavid I want you to take Daron Pashayan out of here and get him back to the sector now!" Baron ordered.

"Hayrig! I've got him," Shant insisted. Stepan stepped to Shant's side. "We've got him."

Tavid knew Stepan was ready. "Go! You know what to do!"

Baron started to protest but Tavid said, "I am going to take this one with me as well, Baron," physically picking up Malachi. "You make sure the rest are with us."

"Yes. And then I will burn this place down with the kerosene lamps!"

Tavid added. "And take the guards' guns and pass them out to the prisoners."

"Yes, yes, Tavid. Now go!"

Checking the outer streets for any movement, Tavid hobbled under Malachi's weight, following Shant and Stepan with the consul general. Tavid panted, as close as he could get to quiet haste, finally stumbling out of the storehouse into the night. Hearing an animal howl, he stopped behind a tree, resting Malachi in the fresh air. Malachi's broken jaw left him unable to speak but he waved Tavid to leave him and go. Instead, Tavid uttered the same animal cry. Moments later Stepan appeared, helping Tavid bring Malachi to Shant and the consul general. Shant proudly presented a merchant's cart. With Malachi aboard under Tavid's power and Shant and Stepan helping Pashayan keep pace, the master and his green young soldiers vanished into the night.

"Turks are ruthless when it comes to their enemies. They are
not merciful killers but embrace the art of torture. Not just
to Armenians but for all of the subjects that are under their
rule, including other Muslims at times. I believe they adopted
their religion out of convenience. Turks are Mongols who were
without a faith. After they conquered many people and lands
they adopted a religion that best benefited their quests."
– Yervant Yacoubian

CHAPTER 39

# Freedom

ONLY TWO HOURS HAD PASSED when the group re-entered the Protestant
Armenian Sector with the rescued men. Gunfire could be heard in the
distance from the southeast. Not uncommon in the city during these
times, but Tavid was concerned for his companions.

Once back at the apartment, Tavid left Malachi and Pashayan in the care
of Seta and Anoush. He wanted to search for Baron and the others, but
before he was able to leave he heard footsteps coming up to the apartment.
The door opened and in walked Baron.

"Thank God!" Seta sang, rushing to her husband. However, Baron's face
grimaced and he looked pale as he held his right hand beneath his officer's
jacket. Tavid noticed a pool of blood forming on the floor where Baron
stood and Tavid jumped up to help Baron sit down in one of the lounge
chairs.

"Baron! What…"

"Tavid, let me borrow your hand. Mine is too tired to hold pressure any
more." Baron took Tavid's left hand and slid it underneath his jacket. Tavid
felt the pulsing wound in Baron's chest. When Baron removed his fatigued
right hand covered with blood, Seta shrieked.

"Shant! Are there any doctors close to here, or a hospital where we can take your father?"

Before Shant could answer, Baron shook his head and gestured for Shant to ignore that request.

"It will not help, Tavid. Press tight on the wound with your hand so that I may have a few moments to talk to you all. I...I have lost much blood and was lucky to even make it back here," he said, grimacing from the pain.

Seta, Shant, and Karoun all knelt before Baron next to Tavid.

Staring at them all, Baron smiled. "Well, I do not remember the last time I was able to get all of your attention so quickly." Baron started to laugh but his pain brought a solemn look to his face.

"I was the last one out of the storehouse. There...were at least a dozen or so who were able to walk. We...we ran into some soldiers about a kilometer from the warehouse. At first, they did not see us, but unfortunately some of the prisoners could not move with much speed. I tried to help them hide in the shadows. I was not quick enough. A bullet hit me in the chest. I think most of the prisoners escaped, but I am not sure. How is Daron Pashayan?"

"He is here, Armen." Seta barely was able to speak.

"Now. Tavid...do you love my Karoun?"

Tavid, not expecting such a question, was momentarily stunned.

"Do you love her?" he repeated.

"Yes, Baron, I do."

"Karoun...do you..."

"Yes, you know I love him, Hayrig, but why are you doing this? We need to take you to a doctor!"

"Tavid, tell her...tell her for me."

Tavid paused for a brief moment, then as the words drifted from his lips tears began to flow from his eyes. "He is dying, Karoun. It is a fatal wound he has."

Satisfied with this explanation, Baron continued. "Tavid, I expect you to marry my daughter, but I pose one condition. That you take my family to Cyprus with you and the marriage takes place there." Baron tried to eke out another smile.

"As you wish, Baron."

"And stop calling me Baron! I am now your father for the next few moments. And you are my son."

"Not just for a few moments, Bar... Hayrig, forever."

Tavid could feel Armen Eftendelian's heart racing and becoming faint.

"Come! Give your father a bachig[1] so I can take it with me and show Christ and make him jealous."

With tears in their eyes and on the edge of hysteria, each kissed Baron on each cheek. Baron looked at his loved ones.

"I love you all. Take care of yourselves." And with that, Baron slowly closed his eyes and his head sank to his chest.

A cold shiver of revelation overtook Tavid, for he felt Baron's soul leave his body, confirmation to him that some day they would be reunited. Tavid recited a prayer to himself that he had learned as a child from his own father. He kissed the top of Baron's head and removed his now bloodied hand. As he did Baron's family took Tavid's place, held their dead father and husband, weeping and grieving for some time.

Tavid washed the blood from his hand before helping his mother attend to the needs of Malachi and Daron Pashayan.

"You will both rest here tonight, and in the morning I will take you both to a physician here within the sector," Tavid said to each of them.

"Armen should have never risked his life for me. Why? Why did he do it? I have never known him to do such a rash thing." Daron Pashayan was trembling.

"I believe it was something that he could not live with. You stood for everything he believed in. He did what his soul commanded him to do and he died knowing that the one man he believed in was now free," Tavid preached.

Daron Pashayan began to weep upon hearing these words.

"My son, I will be fine. Take me to my family if you will tonight. They live not far from here," Daron requested.

Tavid finally agreed and told Daron to first rest and eat so he could regain some strength.

Malachi, on the other hand, was in worse shape from his broken jaw and had not been able to eat what little food he was given. Anoush found some blankets to warm him and she boiled some water and made a warm moist poultice to reduce the swelling and draw the poison out of Malachi's face. Sipping some warm tea with honey, Malachi appeared to be somewhat comfortable, yet still unable to speak.

---

[1] Armenian: kiss.

"I will seek out your grandson, Ari, tomorrow. Is he still at the Tokatlian Hotel?" Tavid asked.

Malachi nodded.

"How long were you there, Malachi?"

At first Malachi slowly shook his head, then held up one finger followed by a hand gesture.

"One month?"

Malachi nodded again.

Tavid then looked over toward the Eftendelians sitting with Baron. He felt the fatigue of the evening overtake him, and made himself a cup of hot tea as well. Afterwards Daron was ready to leave and be with his family. With tears in his eyes, he asked Seta to forgive him and embraced each of the Eftendelians, for he felt guilty for Armen Eftendelian's death.

Tavid helped him out of the apartment and down the stairs. But as the two left in darkness, Tavid could feel the imploring eyes of Baron Eftendelian and his spirit following him.

"I am not afraid of death but look forward to this next adventure.
Not that I want to die this day, I have too much to do still! But I
look forward to seeing old friends, including Armen Eftendelian.
I am sure that we will both call each other vulgar names when
we are reunited, he will yell at me, telling me how stubborn I
am and I will call him a fool mixed with my favorite Turkish
profanities. Afterwards we will embrace. For we will have an
eternity to enjoy each other's arguments on life and death."
– Yervant Yacoubian

CHAPTER 40

# Preparation

EARLY THE NEXT MORNING, THE deacons from Father Steinhauer's parish
had arrived and taken Armen Eftendelian's body to prepare for the private
funeral services. Tavid was also able to retrieve Panos from the apartment
to come and assess Malachi. But It was early that evening before Tavid was
able to travel to the Tokatlian Hotel in search of Ari.

Dressed this day as a European, Tavid entered the Tokatlian Hotel. As
luck would have it, Ari was there preparing to leave as Tavid walked in.

"Ari!"

Ari looked up without acknowledging Tavid.

"Is it safe to talk to you here?"

"We have nothing to talk about, Ermeni," Ari answered in a disgusted
voice. "Go and leave me…"

"I have found your grandfather!"

A look of mixed emotions filled Ari's face and stifled his tongue. In
a low voice, Tavid concisely described the details of the events that had
occurred the night before. With sighs of relief, Tavid could see his words
breathed life back into him. He escorted Ari from the hotel and the two
walked briskly to the Armenian sector, back to the Eftendelians. On the
way Tavid described the events from the day before in greater detail and

the medical attention his grandfather received. Almost in tears, Ari could not find words to express himself adequately. Soon his thoughts drifted to the recent conversations of Turkish officials who had been at the hotel.

"Tavid, we have learned much at the hotel from the bragging of Turkish officials in their meetings with the Germans."

"But just now at the hotel you told me that we have nothing to talk about. Must I come with good news before you are willing to give me the bad? Will a Jew ever think of an Ermeni as a friend?"

Ari, now able to smile, said, "Do not try that with me, Tavid. My grandfather has told me how you trust no one no matter what their creed. Now, let me speak of what I know."

Ari described overheard conversations from the past few weeks, including confirmation of the mass execution of Armenian soldiers within the Ottoman armies, the release and arming of convicts in the interior of the Ottoman Empire and the turning of them loose on Armenian communities. He also reported the widespread looting, rape, starvation, and spread of disease. Also, the formation of Cheté bands employed by the government to carry out atrocities such as the torture and assassination of Armenian leaders and intellectuals.[1]

"Compared to the rest of the country, Constantinople has been relatively spared, likely due to the presence of Europeans. That is apparently all going to change within the next few weeks," Ari added.

"What is the government going to do, stir up the mobs in the city again to massacre all the Ermenis like they did twenty years ago?"

"No. I think they are going to use the Chetés this time with no regard to what the Europeans see or have to say. And they have already taken away the rights of the Europeans here in the city. It is just a question of time now."

"What will you do, Ari?"

"I feel safe at the hotel. I reside there now all the time. It would seem odd for the Turks to raid and destroy a place they enjoy. My grandfather will stay with me, though hidden out of sight."

Soon they were back at the apartment and the reunion of Ari with his grandfather. Malachi reminded Tavid of when he returned home to his village of Tchingiler last autumn after his family had thought him to be dead. Ari stayed the night, and the next morning Tavid escorted Ari and Malachi back to the Tokatlian Hotel. Embracing each of them before

---

[1] http://www.armenian-genocide.org.

leaving, he informed them that he would be leaving Constantinople soon and they might never see him again. Sadness returned to Malachi's face as he again embraced Tavid, still unable to speak.

"Take care of yourself, Malachi. I will send news when I reach my destination."

Tavid left, not looking back and not looking forward to his return to the Armenian Sector. It was Sunday and he was to go with his family and the Eftendelians to Father Steinhauer's church for the private memorial service for Karoun's father.

Tavid borrowed some clothes from the Eftendelians to wear to the service after Anoush pleaded with him privately to dress with respect for Baron. Leaving their apartment, it was apparent from the people on the street that many of their friends and restaurant patrons were aware of Baron's passing and tears could be seen on many faces as they passed. A dozen or so relatives, mostly from Baron's side of the family, were at the church as well as several deacons including Ludwig and Viktor who had escaped harm two nights before.

Tired as he was, Tavid sat in one of the pews and closed his eyes. He thought of the inscription over the altar in the sanctuary,

*Christ is risen from the Dead*
*Blessed is the Resurrection of Christ*

His thoughts turned to Baron's soul as he fell into a light, uneasy sleep.

He found himself in a forest similar to those that existed on the outskirts of Tchingiler. As Tavid walked, the sun found passage through the huge canopy of trees and intermittently illuminated his face. He looked down at the forest floor only to see bodies scattered throughout whose faces were all familiar. Faces from the past and present; those from his village and those who were with him today.

"Why do you seek the living among the dead?" came a voice from the forest. The sun became even brighter and Tavid squinted. Now this light came not from the sun, but from a youthful-faced woman with pure white hair.

"They are not dead," Tavid answered, staring at her.

"Come with me, Tavid."

"No. I am not ready. They need me still." But Tavid could not move as the woman drew close and kissed him.

Tavid startled to see Karoun above him, drawing away from his lips as the sunlight pierced the sanctuary's windows and shone on his face.

"Mayrig told me to wake you. They are going to start the service."

The service began shortly, followed by a burial service at a cemetery on the sanctuary grounds. A communal dinner followed overseen by two deacons, Ludwig and Viktor. After a long day the Kaloustians and Eftendelians left the sanctuary for their respective apartments with feelings of emptiness and regret.

Tavid tried not to think of Baron's death and to focus on escaping to Cyprus. But the events were still too fresh in his mind. Only time could help now.

"When I was Tavid's age, my conscience was asleep. I could kill
without hesitation or remorse. It was an act that I was comfortable
with, never having second thoughts. But when we had my
daughter, and then later with my grandchildren, well, things
slowly began to change. It was not as easy to kill, especially if the
victim was younger. I found myself hesitating and this became
dangerous. Or the death of a child in the village would bring
on emotions that I did not have before. But I am glad for these
changes and growth, as I know will happen with my grandson."
– Yervant Yacoubian

CHAPTER 41

# Rendezvous

FOR THE NEXT TEN DAYS, Tavid roamed the port where the Bosporus met
the Black Sea, searching for the arrival of Costel and his ship. *"Costel will
be back in Constantinople early spring. He is going to be sailing to Athens but first
he can take you and your family to Cyprus. Who knows, maybe even I will come
along…"* Tavid remembered Aldo saying. Tavid hoped it was not too early
to expect Costel's return to Constantinople.

As the days went by, Tavid remembered what Malachi's grandson Ari
had told him. In the back of his mind, Tavid's senses felt an increasing
tension building in the city. He had heard rumors of persecutions already
starting in other smaller Armenian sectors around Constantinople not
under the protection of the Protestant Church. In addition, stories
continued from infrequent travelers or from foreign missionaries fleeing
the east, telling horrific stories. One missionary spoke of barely escaping
one such event where, in an Armenian Cathedral, the Turks massacred
over a thousand Armenians, suffocating them all with smoke from burning
carpets and mats soaked with petroleum piled around the exterior of the
building.

As the days slowly passed for Tavid, he felt a desperate urgency to
find an alternative passage to Cyprus. Initially Tavid had been quite busy

directing his family and the Eftendelians in preparation of their trip; what items to bring with them and what to leave behind or sell. Falsified documents for the Eftendelians were obtained by Tavid from sources who knew him and had bought his resin in the past, all too eager to barter their trade. With the official document he had obtained from Tahir, the counterfeiters were able to design near-perfect documents authorizing passage to the Marmara Sea through the Dardanelles.

Three more days passed. Tavid walked the port's northeast pier searching for signs of his noticeably absent Romanian brothers. Entering the least congested section of the older and decaying pier, he noticed an older sailing vessel of great size, seemingly out of place compared to its surroundings. For a moment Tavid stood there admiring the boat, wondering what it would be like to sail such a large ship. Though these dreams had temporarily carried him away from the tensions that had plagued him since Baron's death, Tavid was still aware of his surroundings and sensed that he was being approached from behind. Quickly turning, he pulled out a pistol from under his coat.

"Ahmahn![1] Do not shoot! We surrender!" The men dropped to their knees with hands in the air pleading with Tavid to spare their lives.

Tavid returned his pistol to its place of rest under his coat and scanned the pier for others. He chuckled as he grabbed both men by their collars, pulling them to their feet and embracing each of them as if they were long-lost brothers. Aldo and Costel had seen Tavid admiring their ship and thought to sneak up on him from behind.

"Ha-haah! As we can all see, we are all still very much alive!" Aldo put his arm around Tavid as they turned towards the vessel.

"You were admiring our new ship?"

"This? This is yours? What happened to the other?"

"Long story. Aldo's fault, so we borrowed this one. Ahhh and it is much faster, especially when the winds are swift!"

"My fault? It was not my fault! It was my sarsakh[2] wife's fault!"

Tavid smiled as Costel began to laugh. "And I cannot wait to hear you retell that story to Tavid. Ha-haah! Now, let us find some place to have breakfast and talk of our escape!"

The two older Romanians, with arms around Tavid, walked to a small and quiet restaurant. Sitting in the back, Tavid asked the proprietor if there

---

[1] Turkish: translates as "oh my!"
[2] Turkish: idiot.

was a back door and where it led. Smiles of remembrance came upon Aldo's face as he watched Tavid's actions.

"Just like your grandfather! I am looking forward to seeing him as well," Aldo remarked.

"I am surprised you came, Aldo. I thought that you would have stayed with your family."

"Are you crazy? And miss out on such a trip? Never!"

Costel smiled. "Maybe you should tell him what happened, Aldo."

"What? Nothing happened...just that...mmm, I shot a police chief." Aldo could not hold back a smile.

"Tell him the story or I will!"

They sat down and Aldo recounted a lively tale that had occurred in the spring one evening when he returned home to Constanta[3] from a month-long trip involving the sale of black market goods outside of Bucharest.

"And so I return home one late evening and quietly enter my home so as not to awaken anyone. As I am looking for my sarsakh wife, I find that she is in bed with another man! I pull my pistol out and start yelling at this half-naked fat man as he grabs for his pants and tries to run past me out the door. I aimed and shot him right in the ass!"

"Ha-haa! Later we found out it was the police chief!" Costel added.

Aldo paused with a big smile barely showing his teeth through his thick blond mustache.

Costel continued. "Afterwards, the police chief issued a warrant for Aldo's arrest so he went into hiding on my ship at port in Constanta. But knowing that I was at port as well, they came down looking for Aldo and me. We barely escaped."

"What happened to your ship?" Tavid asked.

"I was just getting to that! They seized it! Took it from me! But while they were busy with my ship, my men and I stole the police chief's huge yacht! The one you have just seen! We sailed to Mangalia, just south of Constanta, bought supplies and headed south. Now, here we are, ready to escape again!"

Aldo asked what had transpired in Tavid's realm over the past winter, and for once Tavid was in no mood for more stories. There would be time for that in their new life. Tavid tersely turned the discussion to the journey, including the addition of the grieving Eftendelians and Panos.

---

[3] A port city on the coast of the Black Sea.

"Ahmahn! We did not know that you would be bringing your entire village with you!"

"I also have horses," Tavid added.

"What? Horses? Are you crazy? Your entire village and horses, too?" Costel cried.

"Can we not put them in the cargo hold?"

Costel swayed his head back and forth as if all these questions and details were making him dizzy.

"I suppose. But how many horses?"

"Only three. And two dogs."

"Ahhh, only three, eh? Who is going to clean up down there and what are we going to feed them? Dogs! What next, is this Noah's Ark?"

"They are my dogs for my little sister and they are coming."

"We will get those supplies today before we leave. Tomorrow."

"Tomorrow!"

Tavid explained the intelligence he had obtained from Ari at the Tokatlian Hotel. The Romanian brothers then agreed that the swift time frame was critical.

"I will inform my crew to get what we will need for the voyage, and to be ready to leave by mid-day tomorrow. We should load all of your belongings including the horses today so that there will be no delay," Costel explained.

Tavid agreed, and they decided to meet back at the ship within three hours. Tavid explained that he would be making more than one trip to port so as not to raise suspicion with such a large caravan traveling through the city.

"Remember, I will be wearing my Turkish officer's uniform from now on," Tavid reminded them as he stood up to leave. Aldo and Costel saluted in jest.

In better spirits, Tavid returned first to the Eftendelians to inform them that their passage had arrived and to prepare their things. Then he went to his apartment and informed his family and Panos. Excited yet uncertain, Anoush began to prepare their belongings. With the help of Stepan and Panos, Tavid started to load the horses. Moments later, Ana came to the stables.

"It is time, Tavid?"

Tavid turned, seeing the sadness on his landlady's face. He smiled and nodded.

"I am going to miss you and your family. Do you think you will ever return?"

"I am not sure. Perhaps after the war. I will write you to see how you are and to hear news of the city."

Ana nodded and went up to Tavid, embracing and kissing him as tears formed in her eyes, and then silently she walked away.

Most of the packing was already finished in case a hasty departure became necessary. Within an hour Tavid and the rest of his family were ready to depart for the port. It was now mid-day as Tavid guided his family with their belongings, making certain there was minimal outside contact through the maze of Constantinople. Once they arrived at the port the Romanians and their crew were ready to receive their passengers. Tavid introduced his family and Panos to Aldo and Costel, and they introduced their crew, all apparently related to Aldo and Costel. As they boarded the yacht, Tavid was able to coerce two of the horses into the cargo hold of the ship; the third he took with him to the Eftendelians.

"I will be back in approximately two hours with the rest of the passengers. Take care of my family and see that they are made comfortable," Tavid requested of Aldo.

"Ahmahn! You feel you have to tell me such things? Everything will be fine while you are gone. I will see that their quarters are prepared and they are treated like family."

Tavid smiled in gratitude and thanked Aldo. He left through the alleyways to the Armenian sector to the Eftendelians. Once there, he could sense the excitement; yet, there was a nagging fear about the events affecting their lives. The Eftendelians, too, had been prepared to leave at a moment's notice. When Tavid returned, they indicated they were ready to depart. With the help of Shant, Tavid packed the heavier baggage on his horse.

Seta tried to stay calm. "We have lived our entire life here, Tavid. So many memories, so many friends we are leaving. And our restaurant. It saddens me to see it closed, not filled with life and its aromas."

"Then you must think of this as perhaps a temporary trip. And after the war, perhaps we shall return. *'Our future is not engraved into stone,'* my grandfather would say."

Seta released a shallow smile, kissing Tavid on the cheek. "I will feel better once I see my dear sister. Now let us leave before I begin to cry."

Solemnly and discreetly the Eftendelians, led by Tavid, left their home of three generations, their life as they knew it and, in a very sad way, their beloved husband and father, Armen Eftendelian.

"Over the centuries, Armenians have been scattered throughout
the world to escape persecution or to find a land that is safe from
neighboring marauders. Before the Turks invaded our native
lands, it was the Persians, the Romans and many others. Do not
be surprised then if you are on a journey or in a new land and
one of the first souls you meet happens to be Armenian."
– Yervant Yacoubian

# CHAPTER 42

# The Last Day. The Last Hour

April 23, 1915. 2300 Hours

"TAVID! SEE BY THE MOONLIGHT! About five kilometers ahead! The
beginning of the Dardanelles," Costel pointed out into the distance.

"How long will it take us to pass through and into open waters?"

"The currents will be strong now from the spring rains. Without winds,
it could take us six, maybe eight hours, if we are not stopped."

"Who will stop us, the Turks or the Europeans?"

"I am not sure. Perhaps both. We will have to keep our eyes open."

Tavid, again wearing Mustafa's ill-fitting lieutenant uniform, walked
along the long starboard aspect of the boat, monitoring the northwest
shore about four kilometers away. All appeared to be quiet on land as well
as on the Marmara Sea as their ship's diesel tooled toward the Dardanelles
close to midnight.

They had left the Bosporus port of Constantinople early in the
morning. Hoisting a German flag which Aldo had discreetly obtained, they
also had Panos dress up in Armen Eftendelian's German uniform. It was a
measure that proved to be prudent. For as they entered the Marmara Sea,
the northern ports were riddled with Turkish vessels that turned a curious
eye to the yacht sailing by. However, with the German flag and Panos in his
uniform pacing the bow of the ship they easily made safe passage. Close

to midnight, they were about to enter the Dardanelle Straits and, from reports heard as far away as Romania, the Dardanelles had been closed off by the British at the southeastern entrance into the Aegean Sea. Tavid also heard these reports and hoped that the British who controlled the visas to Cyprus he had obtained would allow passage through the straits.

Entering the Dardanelles, the currents and the northeast winds accelerated. Costel quieted the diesel and had his crew raise the forward jib.

The hours went by slowly as they sailed through the straits, at first seeing no signs of Ottoman forces. Then through the moonlight, they saw encampments on the southeast shores, ghost-like in appearance from the reflection of the moonlight and apparent inactivity.

"Tavid, I have been thinking. We will not have any trouble with the Turks. They are only looking for vessels trying to come into the straits from the Aegean. It is time for you and Panos to change out of your uniforms."

Costel removed the German flag and hid it as Tavid and Panos went below and changed out of their respective uniforms. Finding the visas, Tavid put them in his pocket and returned to the deck.

"This is too easy," Tavid said to Costel.

"I agree. Much too easy." The moonlight reflected off the whites of Costel's eyes and his gleaming teeth. "Do not worry. We still have a long way to go. A very long way."

The orange traces of dawn showed the awakening of the sky and with it, Tavid could see the straits narrowing as they closed in on them from both shores with their protruding rock formations. Still, there were no signs of resistance to their passage. None until they reached the outlet to the Aegean, where the straits turned quickly to the east. As if they were about to enter the jaws of a monster, two ships larger than Tavid had ever seen were anchored yet appeared poised to attack.

"Destroyers. But I cannot tell whose they are," Costel said.

Then, without warning one of the ships came alive and began to signal the tiny vessel with flashes of lights meaning nothing to Tavid as Costel watched with the utmost attention.

"It is a French ship! They have ordered us to turn portside and anchor in front of her." Costel signaled back, acknowledging their message.

"French did you say? Tavid, I have a plan then," Panos stated with confidence, explaining that as a physician within the French Missionary

Hospital he had been given certain rights and privileges including free passage to France and its territories.

"Remember, my visa is French. I will tell them that I have commanded this vessel to secure my escape…and my family's escape." Panos smiled.

"But the ship has a Romanian registry," Costel stated.

"Do not worry about that, brother," Aldo interrupted. The French know that Romanians hate the Turks and the Germans!"

Aldo continued. "I will tell them that our destination is Cyprus. That we have family there. What do you think of this, Tavid?"

"It is as good a plan as any. I suppose we should not be wearing any firearms when they come aboard."

The group could now see a smaller vessel heading towards them. Using a bullhorn the captain from this smaller French vessel queried the sailboat's captain of their origin. Panos answered to their initial satisfaction and soon they were docked off starboard, and armed French soldiers accompanied their captain as they boarded the ship.

"Has not anyone told you? The straits are closed, gentlemen!"

Speaking in French Panos quickly apologized then introduced himself, presenting his papers and explaining the purpose of their voyage. Initially the captain listened intently, but then his face hardened.

"How is it that you were able to escape through the straits without a scratch from the Turks? Why would they not stop you unless you are spies?"

Panos replied that they were all Armenians and Romanians, that they had flown a German flag and posed as German and Turkish officers.

"Ermenis, you say?" The captain turned and walked up to one of his men, whispering in his ear. This sailor first considered all the passengers and approached not Panos but Tavid. But before the sailor began to speak, Tavid asked the first question.

"Are there many Armenians here in the French Navy?" Tavid asked the sailor in Armenian.

The sailor paused for a moment, then smiled. "A few. What is your name? Where are you from?"

"Tavid Kaloustian. I am from a village outside of Bursa named Tchingiler. Are you familiar with it?"

"No. Why are you here and where do you think you are going?"

Tavid shared a long and detailed account with the sailor. At first, the sailor's face was hard and without emotion. As Tavid continued to speak of the events that had occurred over the past few months, the sailor's face softened. Slowly, Tavid's mother and the others moved closer to the two, listening to Tavid. By the time Tavid finished, the sailor was close to tears.

With a long sigh, the captain turned to Panos.

"Do I want to know?"

"He has only described what we have been through for the past few months."

The sailor tried to replace his implacable façade as a French soldier and translated the conversation to his captain. Afterwards the captain shook his head, and ordered his soldiers to make a quick search of the vessel, who reported to their captain there was nothing of interest.

"It may be a hazardous journey to Cyprus. Do you have a French flag as well to fly?" the captain asked sarcastically.

"No, but if we may borrow one?" Panos smiled.

Sighing again, the captain turned to one of his men, ordering him to retrieve a flag from his boat and the book of documents. Moments later, the soldier returned, handing the item to his captain.

"I trust that you will treat this flag with honor and dignity?"

"Yes, of course, Captain."

The captain opened his book, looking for specific documents.

"I want you to take these as well. They are signed papers authorizing your vessel's passage through the Aegean to Cyprus. When you get there, if the British give you any problems, show them these as well. Now, what can you tell me of the Turkish encampments along the southern straits and the speed of the currents?"

Panos called Tavid to give a better description of what he had observed. After the captain was satisfied with the intelligence, he ordered his soldiers back on his vessel. He stopped and turned back to Panos looking at the rest wondering if he should utter a last thought.

"Stay far from the eastern shores of Turkey. We have spotted hundreds of dead bodies floating in the Aegean. The waters are sick with disease.

"Many have forgotten that the Germans were in bed with the Turks during this atrocity of a war. Do not tell me that the German military and advisors did not know or help with the destruction of my race. And after the Turks for the most part succeeded in their plans, what did the Germans decide to do some eighteen years later?"
– Yervant Yacoubian

# CHAPTER 43

# Uncertain Reunions

NEARLY TWO WEEKS AT SEA and only a few days from the western shores of Cyprus the exhausted, hopeful passengers could not see the pleasure of lounging on deck in the balmy breezes and healing rays of the sun. Their only thoughts were of what lay ahead and what they'd left behind. Even Tavid wished to feel ground under his feet. Karoun decided to present Tavid with the letters she had written over the past months and took the opportunity, approaching him as he rested on deck.

"I hope you like to read," she said, handing Tavid a small bundle of letters tied with a small hemp string. "Over the winter, I wrote letters to you but never sent them. So I held onto them. This seems like a good time."

Tavid smiled at Karoun and accepted the gift. He held the letters that were tightly bound, and at first did not want to disturb the writings but pulled out the most recent letter written in the form of a poem and read it to himself.

*Tavid, Tavid, where are you now?*
*I cannot find you, help me know how*
*I am forgetting all*

*Your face, your voice*
*Every detail no matter how small*
*Why do I forget these things?*
*Each day, each week*
*With much regret*
*Is it so I may focus on my family?*
*That I still have as of yet*
*Or there is no time to remember the past*
*As the future runs by us*
*Much too fast*
*The sadness of remembrance*
*Is though a happiness if not a ploy*
*For to remember what was*
*With what is and what may be*
*Is my only joy*
*To justify the focus on others I love*
*But hoping to see only you again*
*Stands far above*

"That was the last letter I wrote before I saw you again. It is, in a way horrible to forget, but... It is how we heal our wounds," she tried to explain.

Tavid continued to read the letters. After awhile, Karoun could see his mind was drifting from something he had read in the letters. Then Tavid spoke.

"It has been a little over a year since I have seen my grandfather and his image has almost completely faded from my mind. To see him again will be like a waking dream."

"I am sure it will be a wonderful dream, Tavid," Karoun said. "And I have not seen my aunt for almost the same amount of time. Of course it is nothing like your grandfather, but I know when I see her, it will be as if she had always been with us. Maybe you will feel the same."

As the sun rose three mornings later, Costel saw a large land mass to the northeast with mild terrain of green hills. He studied the huge island then reviewed his maps.

Also seeing the island, Tavid glanced at Costel for an answer. As Costel looked up again to the island, he knew Tavid was waiting for his judgment.

"We have come farther south than I expected. That is the underbelly of Cyprus. Now. I will change course and…"

Before Costel could finish, Tavid had him in a bear hug, swinging him around in circles, laughing as he did. Finally putting him down, he sought others to celebrate in the same manner. Aldo tried to evade him without success.

"Put me down, Hyevan! You are choking me!" Aldo pleaded. But Tavid just laughed and after releasing him found the others. He saved his beautiful girl for last and held her not as tight but for a long, long time.

Suddenly some of Costel's crew broke out with some music, using a tambourine, dumbeg and a small air flute. Now Tavid's smile was larger than life as he started to dance with Karoun but soon all, including a slightly bashful Shant, joined in on the celebration. Nearing exhaustion after a few songs, they all embraced and prepared for their arrival.

"Costel, are you sure it is Cyprus?"

"I am sure. But now the question is, what are the British going to say to us when we arrive at port?"

A lively discussion followed with the two Romanians, and soon Panos and Tavid joined in. Larnaca neighbored one of the two British military bases on the island that controlled southern Cyprus.

"The Turks are in northern Cyprus and the British keep them there from what I have heard. I am sure they hate the Turks as well," Costel stated with certainty.

"Forget about the Turks. What will the British think of us?" Tavid asked.

"I am sure they will want to see our papers. Possibly, we may need to propose a bribe here or there," Aldo said.

Costel laughed, as did the others.

As they approached the island of Cyprus from the southwest, its size continued to grow with unending shores blanketed with white sands and increasingly shallow blue waters. Buoys marked entrances through the reefs as they headed eastward down the coast. Finally, by afternoon Costel spotted the port of Larnaca based on his maps and its relation to the military base. Following the anchored buoys, Costel slowly navigated into port and headed towards one of the wharfs that situated near an ancient fort that guarded the city centuries ago. Coming closer to the dock, they saw British soldiers waiting for them.

"We will let you perform the introductions, Panos," Aldo suggested.

"And speak only French. No Turkish," Tavid added.

Nearing the wharf, Costel instructed Tavid and Aldo to jump onto the dock with ropes to secure their vessel. And once the lines were set and the sailboat was secure, a half dozen British soldiers signaled for all the passengers to exit the craft.

"Hmmm. They don't look like French citizens, yet they are flying a French flag," the British lieutenant said to one of his men in English.

"I don't suppose that any of you…French…speak English, do you?

Panos approached the lieutenant and began to speak French, but neither the British lieutenant nor his men understood.

"Just as I bloody well thought. Doesn't anyone know how to speak English in this part of the world? Round them up! We will have to take them back to see the commander!"

The lieutenant and his soldiers had hand-signaled for them all to accompany them. Tavid and the rest of the men helped the women down onto the dock. Varsenig had fashioned two leashes made from thick ropes she had found on board, one for each pup as she led them off the boat. The group walked down to the pier and into a large stone-faced, two-story building sporting a large British Flag.

"All right, gents and ladies. Everyone's invited, come on now, step lively, step lively, everyone inside and up the stairs. You too, pups. Refugees… bloody refugees in a yacht, ha! What will they think of next eh, men?" the lieutenant sang as they directed them into the building.

"Do you think the boat and our belongings will be safe?" Seta whispered to Anoush.

"I do not know. We can only hope."

"Say now, that didn't sound like French, dear lady. What language was that?" one of the soldiers asked, but Seta and Anoush stared at him then smiled.

"Stupid for me to ask, of course. Well the commander will find out. He always does."

Up a narrow set of circular stairs, the group walked silent among themselves as they listened to the unrecognized chatter of the British soldiers. At the top of the stairs they entered a large room mostly vacant except for a mixture of old wooden chairs and tables. Large windows facing oceanside streamed in light from the sun that was beginning to set in the southwest. Through these windows, they could see their boat and the British guards inspecting it.

"Now, don't go away, Frenchies. We'll be right back with the commander," said the last soldier who shut the door to the room and locked it from the outside.

"Well, what shall we do now?" Aldo asked his brother.

"Nothing, but wait. I hope that they have someone who can speak French. Tavid, as you can see they are going through the boat. Are they going to find anything that I do not know about to cause us trouble?"

"I was going to ask you the same. They will not find my weapons or anything of use to them," Tavid answered.

"Good. Now, let us wait and see what is to become of us."

A little while passed and Tavid could hear the rumblings of a group coming into the building and walking up the narrow stairs. Then, they heard the rattling of keys as the door was unlocked.

"Ahhh, remember me, gents and ladies? I've brought someone to see you now. Our dear Commander Borland. Ohhh my! We should have opened a window to get some fresh…"

"Lieutenant! I have a mind to place you on night watch with extra duties after this if you cannot learn to stifle that mouth of yours. Now shut up and stand with the rest of your men while I find out who these people are."

The commander reviewed Tavid and his clan, then signaled his attaché to find out if they had visas or documents identifying themselves. This was conveyed in French by the attaché who collected the documents to be reviewed. The commander, appearing bored, sat on one of the tables, and, through the windows, studied the yacht.

"A beauty, isn't she, sir?"

A long sigh came from the commander having to again listen to the lieutenant.

"I would like to get my hands on a beauty as she. With permission, sir, I'll find some reason on her that will let me…"

"Lieutenant! If anyone is going to take possession of that yacht, it is going to be me. In the name of his majesty's navy, of course. And don't you forget that."

"Ay ay, sir. But she is a beauty."

Suddenly, the attaché walked over to the commander with the documents.

"Commander, look at this. You're not going to believe this," he almost whispered.

"Oh, what is it now, Mr. Partriche?"

"Here sir. Look at these visas."

The attaché handed a group of the visas to the commander for inspection, then quickly handed them back to the attaché.

"You know I can't read this scribble, Mr. Partriche. So help me if you start irritating me as well."

"No sir, please, look at the names on these. They all say Kaloustian. Isn't that the name of Yervant's relatives he told us about?"

"What? Let me see them!"

The commander again reviewed the documents and suddenly a realization came over him as his face flushed and he looked up, scanning each face of the would-be emigrants.

"Oh, my God. More bloody Yacoubians," the commander muttered to himself. "Mr. Partriche, ask them...ask them if they have any relatives here on the island."

But before the attaché could pose the question, Tavid had sensed the nature of the conversation and answered the question.

"Yervant...Yervant Yacoubian," he said, his heart rising in his throat as he remained straight-faced. He stared at the commander, not knowing if this knowledge would better or worsen their situation.

"More bloody Yacoubians, Commander? This whole island is going to be infested with them," the lieutenant whined.

The commander again studied Tavid, got up off the table and walked up to him.

"Mr. Partriche, come and translate for me in French as I speak."

He began to ask Tavid some questions.

"Are you Yacoubian's grandson?"

Hearing the attaché translate the question, Tavid answered.

"Yes, and this is the rest my family."

"When is the last time you heard from your grandfather?"

"About a year."

"He had told me about you. And your family many times. I was curious to see if you would ever make it here to this island."

Tavid wanted to ask his own questions.

"What is the status of my grandfather here? Friend or enemy?"

Hearing the attaché's translation, the commander broke out into a roar of laughter.

"Your grandfather? A friend of mine? He is a pain. A toothache that I could easily do without! However, at times he can be quite valuable. Saved my bloody life on more than one occasion, he has."

With that, the commander smiled and looked over to his soldiers.

"Lieutenant! Be a good chap and fetch their grandfather. And tell the men to get off their boat and leave everything aboard. Now snap to it!"

Saluting as he left with a mumble, the lieutenant left with his men to retrieve Yervant Yacoubian.

"Mr. Partriche, tell them I have sent the men to bring their grandfather and that I would like them to wait here until his return."

Upon hearing these last two translations one could see a burden lift off of Tavid and the others. As if a truth had been revealed, a goal realized. Tavid suddenly felt remarkably at ease, which surprised him for he had not realized the tension that had been building up within.

Tavid noticed that the commander was getting ready to leave and quickly posed another question.

"I have horses in the hold of the boat. May I have permission to see to them?"

Panos translated through the attaché.

"Of course, of course. Take care of whatever you need to on your boat. By the way, where did you come to own such a craft?"

Tavid just smiled and shrugged his shoulders.

"Bloody stupid question, eh, Mr. Partriche? It is going to be hell having more than one Yacoubian on this island. I can see it now. Tell them I will be waiting downstairs until he arrives." The commander and his attaché left down the stairs.

Aldo, now laughing, his huge mustache hiding almost half his mouth, went to Tavid and embraced him.

"Did I not tell you? Everything is as I have said."

"As you have said? You were sweating more than all of us when you saw the British soldiers!"

"Yes, brother. I thought you were going to go hide with the horses when you saw them!" Costel chuckled.

They laughed, helping to relax the tension that had built within them. Tavid then walked over to his mother.

"Can you believe it? He is actually here."

As his mother tried to speak, the words would not come, and as she tried to smile, tears formed. There was nothing left for her to do but embrace and hold her son close for a moment.

"Do not yell at him too harshly, Mother. At least we had each other for the past year," Tavid said.

Anoush nodded. "He will hear what I have to say. Either today or the next. The sooner the better to help all wounds to heal."

Tavid and his brother Stepan went back to the boat to care for the horses. Costel accompanied them to inspect his boat to see if the soldiers had stolen anything. The rest of the family watched through the windows. In a very short time, they heard the rumblings of English chatter below, followed by a lone set of footsteps coming up the stairs. As they watched to see who would appear, it was an older, broad-shouldered man with long white wavy hair and beard contrasted by his dark complexion. He was dressed in old work clothes stained with colors of vegetation and black earth. The man stood at the doorway, looking about the room at the clan, and mist formed in his eyes.

Contagious as it was, others became teary-eyed as well. Yervant first went to his daughter Anoush and held onto her, kissing her face and stroking her hair. Next, he went to Varsenig, the two pups and the others. Anoush also introduced the Eftendelians, but Yervant remembered them all and smiled when he saw Karoun. Turning back to his daughter he said,

"You cannot know how it has been, living here without you."

Anoush hearing this, raised a subtle eyebrow in contempt for her father. "Where are my grandsons?"

Anoush, with her conflicted feelings, fought back emotion before answering.

"They are with their father," she said as she turned away to the window. "Both were shot as we were escaping Constantinople. Panos tried to save them but…we wrapped their bodies and had to bury them at sea."

Yervant was stunned. Aldo had to bite his tongue to stop from smiling. The room was silent. The others dared not say anything. Yervant sat down in one of the chairs for his legs weakened as he dropped his head. Covering his face with his hands, he began to weep again.

Anoush continued, "How dare you leave us? Do you know what we had to go through to get here? What your grandchildren have gone through over the past months? And when we found out you were alive…we could not believe you would have…just left us! What is the matter with you? This is more than being delibash! This was insane!"

Yervant wanted to explain how he had been in prison, how this is not how his plan was supposed to work, but decided to be silent and take the beating.

Anoush began to pace around the room trying to decide what else to say. She looked at the others who would barely meet eyes with her, all except Varsenig who stared at her mother with tearing eyes, shaking her head in protesting silence. Anoush's mood abruptly changed and she decided this was enough for now, and sat near her father watching him continue to be in pain.

A moment later there was again the English chatter down below and a pair footsteps again could be heard coming up the stairs.

"My word, Yervant! Crying again? You Armenians are too emotional! Pull yourself together, man!"

Yervant was too upset to hear the commander or the distant ruckus that was coming up the stairs. With a burst of energy Tavid and Stepan wrestled their way into the room, trying to race and falling on each other as they arrived, laughing and continuing to wrestle on the floor, not realizing that their grandfather had already arrived.

Tears half-blinding him, Yervant started and looked up as his grandsons blasted into the room. Struck with awe Yervant stared at them both, wondering if he was imagining this sight. Then looking over to his daughter with hints of rage in his face, he demanded an explanation for her cruelty.

"Perhaps I do not know what it was like for you, Father, but now you know what it has been like for me thinking you were dead, and not just for a few moments…for months."

His face quickly softened, now understanding his daughter's motive, and he bowed his head in guilt. Wiping the tears from his face, he turned to the two animals wrestling on the floor as Tavid had Stepan in a headlock.

"Dzo![1] Tavid! Stepan!" he said, trying to command attention.

Hearing a voice they had not heard in months, Stepan was the first to jump up and greet his grandfather, hugging him and showing his infectious smile.

---

[1] Armenian slang: "Hey!"

"Ahmahn, Azdvahdz![2] You are bigger that I am!" Tears again escaped from Yervant's eyes. Then he gazed at Tavid and felt as though he was looking into a mirror, seeing himself as he had appeared decades ago. Tavid smiled at his grandfather shaking his head, laughing and rushed to embrace him.

"I hope you have as many stories to tell as I do, Bahbeeg.[3] And a home big enough for all of us to live in!"

Tongue-tied at first, Yervant nodded. "We will match stories and our wits again. You will be surprised to see the home we will be living in, hokees.[4]"

"Well, now that you have been reunited with your family, Yervant, I was hoping I could ask just a small favor," the commander interrupted.

"Small favor? What is small favor?" Yervant asked in broken English.

"Well, I hate to intrude on your family reunion but remember Khan, the Turkish captain that has been trying to have me killed? My scouts have finally located his encampment and I only ask you to pay him a short visit. Maybe your grandson could do the honors this time. And then, of course, I would be obliged to keep my men away from your family's boat and treat them all as if they were citizens of His Majesty's Empire."

"I see. I see…three bullets then?"

"No no no! None of your traditional theatrics of revenge. Just bloody kill him and get it over with! Now, being that your family has just arrived, I am willing to give you three days to perform this small favor."

Yervant smiled as his eyes glistened and teeth gleamed, as a predator thinking of his next prey. Yervant translated the conversation to Tavid in Armenian.

"Three bullets? What does this mean?" Tavid asked.

Yervant smiled again. "You will find that you will enjoy the Cypriots here on the island, Tavid. If for no other reason than for their justifiable hatred against the Turks in the north. They have a custom here of retribution, where they will avenge their loved ones by shooting their victim three times. Once in each leg so that they cannot walk and in the groin, so that they cannot enjoy life." Shifting his gaze to Aldo, Yervant asked if he had given his old German rifle to his grandson.

---

[2] Armenian: translates as "oh my God!"
[3] Armenian: grandfather.
[4] Armenian: "my soul," an endearing name given to loved ones.

"Yes, of course! And what did I get in return for my faithfulness? Your grandson blew up my store!," at which point Tavid started to laugh.

"We have many weapons we brought with us, Bahbeeg.[5] These British are not going to care about this?"

Yervant turned to the commander and again in broken English confirmed that they would be given complete freedom to unload their belongings without hassle from his soldiers.

"Yes, yes of course. Or should I be asking what your grandson brought with him. A cannon, perhaps? Well, no matter. I hate to be brief but it is time for supper and I am to meet a most beautiful Cypriot woman I met just the other day. Keep me informed of Khan's demise, won't you? Good afternoon to you all!"

The commander, followed by his attaché, left down the stairs. Yervant and the rest were closely behind as they headed toward the yacht. The sun was now bright orange, descending over the ocean streaming wild colors on to their ship. When Yervant saw their vessel of passage he was in disbelief. Aldo proudly told the story of how they came to prosper with such a boat.

Yervant rode into Larnaca's port with a horse-drawn wagon. Tavid and Stepan had already removed the horses from the cargo hold and they all unloaded their belongings off the yacht onto the horses and the wagon. After an hour of checking to make certain they had thoroughly emptied the yacht of all belongings, the group—except for Costel's crew, who stayed with the yacht—rode north from port through the narrow stoned streets of Larnaca. Yervant walked arm in arm with his daughter as did Tavid with Karoun just behind, silently mimicking them.

At first, Tavid noticed the lack of colors as they walked through the city streets; the sun had faded all but the newly stone-built dwellings. Traveling farther into the city, they saw areas almost like small parks, where palm trees and other vegetation that Tavid had never seen before grew wild and engulfed adjacent buildings. In what appeared to be the center of the town was an immense Orthodox church that Yervant described to them as the island's most cherished site, the church of St. Lazarus. After his resurrection from the dead by Jesus, Lazarus elected to live out his "second" life as Bishop of Cyprus and was reputedly buried in a crypt under the main altar.

---

[5] Armenian: grandfather.

Walking by St. Lazarus they passed local inhabitants who seemed to know Tavid's grandfather and they all greeted him. Periodically he stopped and introduced each, speaking in the local language. Because of his popularity, their journey was halted along the way and nightfall came before they were able to arrive at Yervant's home on the outskirts of Larnaca.

Lanterns were brought to life before they unloaded the horses and the wagon. Excited yet exhausted, Tavid entered his grandfather's home. Even through the darkness, Tavid was awed at the size of the rooms, especially the kitchen and adjoining great room. It was as if an ancient giant had built the house with the tall ceilings and windows.

Throughout the night, stories were exchanged from the recent past. Strong black coffees and tall glasses of cool water served with Souzoukko,[6] Glyko,[7] along with sweetbreads. Even while the stories were flowing before dawn broke, Tavid and his family could no longer keep their eyes open and one by one fell fast asleep.

---

[6] A Cyprus specialty made by dipping strings of nuts in heated grape juice until the confection solidifies.

[7] Cypriot: preserves of almond, date, apricot, cherry, quince or grapes, always served with a glass of cold water.

"Yes, I am saying this to you: I am a very strong man; physically,
emotionally, in thought, and in soul. But if my family had
not succeeded in making it to Cyprus, I would not have
survived such a devastating blow. Have I learned from my
mistakes? Of course! Will I make new ones? Absolutely!"
– Yervant Yacoubian

# CHAPTER 44

# Sweet Meals, Guns & More Turks

TAVID AWOKE THE NEXT MORNING, neither by the streaming rays of warm
sunlight that pierced his grandfather's stone built home nor by the scents
of spring citrus forming in the groves just outside his grandfather's home,
but by the sounds of excitement from a visitor that had just arrived
with Tavid's grandfather. Yervant arose early and left to retrieve Seta
Eftendelian's sister, Satenig. On the way he stopped at the market to pick
up fresh produce, dairy, and eggs as well as local fish.

It was a happy, yet sad reunion as Seta sadly told of her husband's death.
Though Seta sat down with her sister and was able to give a more detailed
account of the events that led to Baron's end, the expression of these
events had its own healing qualities, helping her in a way to justify the loss
through knowing of Baron's peace of mind before he died. Yervant also
listened as Seta retold the story as she had the night before, and again his
memories returned of decades past and the loss of others.

Tavid got up slowly, stretching his tired body. He went to the window,
squinting his eyes until they accommodated for the intense brightness.
As he looked out over the landscape he saw citrus groves and vineyards
sweeping over tight hills, overshadowed by sparse green mountains. He
sensed an odd similarity to the terrain with his own village of Tchingiler,

but with differing foliage and climate. He wondered if the winters were cool or if snow ever visited the mountains here, and how his life would be or change. For a moment he longed for the familiarities of the past, his home, his way of life.

"Tavid, my aunt Satenig is here! Come and say hello."

Tavid hesitated. "What do you think of this place, Karoun?"

"I am not sure. I am worried that it is a dream and I will awake soon."

Tavid looked at her and smiled faintly. "The dream will stay and we will all forget where we came from after awhile, living here."

"Only if you choose to, Tavid." Karoun took Tavid's hand and guided him into the foyer where Karoun introduced a sleepy Tavid to her aunt.

Soon all were awake as breakfast was being prepared. Small chores were taken care of, all issued by Tavid's grandfather after he greeted each sleepy face with a kiss. The home was in disarray from the loads of belongings brought by all. In addition, the horses as well as the two pups needed care that morning. Yervant attempted to spend at least a few moments with each. Though, he yearned to spend more time with his oldest grandson, he felt drawn to Karoun and found himself at her side asking questions and telling of Cyprus. Tavid noticed this phenomenon, discreetly pointing it out to his mother.

The home slowly filled with the scents of burning fruit woods from the awakened Tonir[1] just outside for the baking of fresh breads. The faint smell of kerosene came from the cast iron stove in the kitchen.

Tavid took a moment to look through his grandfather's house again. More than twice the size of his home in Tchingiler, it was made mostly of stone except for the sun-bleached wood-framed windows, doors and rounded clay rooftop. Each room was simple yet overpowering, with tall ceilings and arched doorways. The floors were also made of stone with an almost polished appearance from use over the decades. As he walked outside, there was a second structure about fifty meters from the house. Odd in appearance for it was only half the height of what would be considered normal for any dwelling. As Tavid walked to the building, he saw a set of stairs that went into the ground leading to a doorway. While Tavid was considering the stairs he heard someone coming from behind.

"I thought the biggest mistake I had ever made was when I lost three of my closest friends while trying to kill the Sultan. Now I realize that I

---

[1] A cylindrical clay oven usually built within the ground in which food or bread is cooked over a bed of charcoal.

almost ruined my daughter's life and perhaps her family's by my deceit. I am an ignorant fool and can only hope that some day you will forgive me for my selfish stupidity." It was Tavid's grandfather, who had seen and followed him outside.

Tavid, being in good spirits this morning, gazed at the blue skies.

"It was a relief not to have you around," Tavid said matter-of-factly.

"Always trying to tell me what to do. A vacation that was cut short when Aldo informed me of the truth. But...this seems to be a nice place to live and I am sure you will need me to get you out of some trouble now and then." Tavid could not help laughing before he finished his sentence.

At first a blank look covered Yervant's face as Tavid's sarcastic revelation burrowed in and took hold; as he considered his grandson of the past, a knowing smile broke through. "There are many things I have forgotten about you, hokees. Including your wit. And with each remembrance, I am afraid I will feel joy and sadness for having missed so much of it over this past year."

Tavid embraced his grandfather, almost to comfort him and silently to grant forgiveness.

"Now come! I will show you what I do here," Yervant said eagerly.

He led Tavid down the stairs and into a half underground cellar filled with rows of huge wooden barrels held off the ground and in place with blocks of rough stone with natural light streaming in from the scattered windows above. Entering the room, Tavid's senses were filled with a cool and sweet intoxicating aroma. Tavid had never seen anything like this before and could not comprehend what its purpose was. Then a thought came to him.

"This is all resin? Aldo and others send their resin here, or are you..."

"Ahmahn! Resin? No, this is not resin. This is much better. This is where I make wine! Sweet wine that intoxicates like resin, heals wounds of the soul like resin, yet is loved, cherished and accepted by all. Especially the British." A feeling of a huge accomplishment enriched Yervant's face.

Tavid thought for a moment and nodded. "Different, but the same."

"Exactly! Now, come let me show you."

With that Yervant passionately showed Tavid around the cellar and began to describe the process of winemaking from beginning to end. As they toured the cellar some of the barrels appeared to be weeping a thick, dark, yet pungently sweet liquid which in ways resembled resin. As they both tasted, Tavid realized this was a substance with a different personality.

"Every three months, the Archbishop from Nicosia comes and blesses the wine. Everyone knows this and they say it deepens the taste and the journey of the wine."

"How much does he take with him when he leaves?" Tavid asked sarcastically.

"He...usually brings a horse and cart with him. And, of course, the blessing takes most of the day...and several liters." Yervant smiled again.

From the wine cellar, Yervant and Tavid heard Anoush calling for them. Like young children hearing their mother calling, they raced up the stairs. But outside waiting for them were three men unknown to Tavid, rugged in appearance with unkempt black hair hiding their darkened skin, rifles swung over their shoulders. Tavid hesitated, until Yervant continued up the stairs and greeted the three men in their own language. Even as he did the three stared at Tavid almost in disbelief as they continued to converse with his grandfather, who laughed at their not yet translated remarks. As their conversation continued, Tavid could only stare back at the three and wait. Finally his grandfather turned to him.

"They are the ones who have found Khan's new encampment. They are concerned he may not be there after tomorrow and they came as our scouts. We must go. And they are surprised at how much you look like me."

"How long have you known these three?"

"Eh? These? Ahhh, do not worry. They are all Cypriots."

"Do they not have spies here on this island? Is there no chance that they could lead us into a trap?"

Yervant began to laugh, then translated into Greek what his grandson had said. Laughter followed until Yervant finished with a final remark.

"They thought what I was saying was a joke until I reminded them I knew where each and every one of their family members lived and the friends I have accumulated on the island," he mused.

"I have told them we will meet them this afternoon outside of Dhali. After breakfast, we will prepare to leave."

The Cypriots left as Tavid and his grandfather went back to the house where breakfast was being served. With every step nearing the house, Tavid could smell the freshly made flatbreads and fish being cooked with butter and vegetables. Most had begun filling their plates with foods that covered a large stone table filled now with an assortment of cheeses made from goat's and lamb's milk, loukoumades.[2] Steaming flatbreads were heaped up into a delicious column accompanied by eggs and local sausages.

Tavid joined in, filling his plate with layers of food, simultaneously sampling small portions. As they ate Yervant told stories of the island, how it was a mere hundred kilometers from the Ottoman mainland. He spoke of the Turks who controlled northern Cyprus and the role of the British. He also spoke of the Armenians living in Larnaca and how this small community had been able to survive and flourish. The school and church had been constructed only ten years before.

After a filling breakfast and much good talk, Yervant was ready to leave for Dahli to meet the Cypriot scouts. He began to give out orders as he used to back in Tchingiler, listing items that would be needed for the undertaking. When Stepan enthusiastically asked what he would need to bring, his grandfather abruptly told him that he would not be going. Tavid's acute irritation now with his grandfather caused a change in the climate as he stood to give his own orders.

"Stepan is coming with us. I will need his help today."

Peering at the now sparkling eyes of his brother, he continued. "You will need your rifle and pistol with plenty of rounds. It is a sunny day so we will need dark linens to prevent the steel of our weapons from reflecting and revealing our position."

As Tavid spoke these words, Aldo began to stand up.

"Where are you going?" Tavid asked him.

"I am coming, too!" Then looking at Yervant, "If you think I am going to miss this tug of war, you are all mistaken!"

At first Yervant could not speak and was silent. Pride was swelling within him. For the first time since he had been reunited with his family, he found a spark of justification for his past deeds; he was seeing how his grandson had matured.

"What are you speaking of, you short Romanian? It is a relief to me seeing my grandson take over, as he should. You can stay here with the others."

The three then prepared to leave for Dahli on horseback, a ten kilometer journey first through the foothills as Dahli rested at the base of the Troodos mountains, though mild in elevation compared to the ranges back in and around Tchingiler. Tavid had unpacked his grandfather's

---

[2] Cypriot delicacy similar to doughnuts with honey.

karabiner, two of his pistols along with his dual knives. They dressed lightly and took additional clothing, for the climb through the mountain passes would invariably be cool and brisk. The women were saddened watching their men preparing to leave, especially Karoun as thoughts of her father came back into her head. She approached Tavid with a sense of fear and kissed him goodbye as if she might not see him again. Tavid sensed this.

"This is not an end but a beginning. As each day will be. Do not worry about me," Tavid said assuringly.

Soon they mounted their horses and left northward through the vineyards filled with the lingering scent of spring flowers and moist aromatic soils. The group talked of their future on the island and its influences.

Soon they arrived in Dahli in what seemed to be only moments after they left the house, and made contact with their Cypriot scouts. Tavid learned that most on the island could speak a fair amount of Turkish from the influence of the north. As it was a universal language for this group, Tavid asked that this be spoken, which at first disturbed the Cypriots. Tavid vowed he would learn their language, and a sense of pride overtook their reluctance to speak another tongue.

Continuing their travel through narrow mountain passes, one of the Cypriots described their target and the atrocities since the start of the war the summer before. He described how Khan would routinely send bands of soldiers over the mountainous border that separated Muslim and Christian regions to destroy the neighboring villages along a hundred kilometer border. Occasionally he would venture close to the British base north of Larnaca sending snipers in to kill officers with varying success.

As he portrayed in detail the specific atrocities of rape and torture these Turks committed in the villages, Tavid's hatred and rage began to build until he was about to erupt. He quickly galloped ahead of the rest as if to escape from this knowledge, only to find that it still sat firmly in his mind. From behind he could still hear the Cypriot continue to describe events of suffering and death that the Turks on the island had perfected so well.

The day lingered for Tavid. He longed to meet this Khan and pay retribution for his actions on the souls of his victims. Shortly before dusk the Cypriots slowed their pace as they neared the encampment of the target. They dismounted and tied their horses, and the three Cypriots led the small group up a steep ridge formed by a winding stream. Once they reached the top it revealed a valley on the other side where the stream also lived but was camouflaged within tall evergreens. Within this valley, Tavid saw the Turkish encampment, much larger than he had anticipated with over a hundred soldiers scurrying about like nimble ants getting ready to move their nest. Tavid scanned the surrounding highlands for a spot to roost and fire on his target. Seeing a band of trees to the right upon a ridge, he explained to the rest that he would climb to that point for a clear view and accuracy of shot.

"It will take me some time to climb to that point," he instructed Stepan. "Wait for me here until you see I am in position. Only cover my retreat by firing on anyone who tries to exit the valley through the stream's path. And make sure these old men do not fall asleep in the meantime!"

Tavid tried to make light of the situation, but his face was still flushed with rage. Even Stepan, despite his youth, recognized his brother's fury. He had also listened to the stories on the way. Tavid checked his pistols and rifle as he headed up the ridge but heard his brother calling him from behind.

As Tavid turned, Stepan silently held up one of his hands revealing only three of his fingers. Tavid focused on the hand then looked at his brother, nodding in confirmation and turned away.

"Hyevan!"

A second voice rang out again from behind Tavid. This time it was his grandfather, and as Tavid turned once more the Cypriot scouts held up one hand, revealing three fingers in solemn expression. Tavid paused for a moment and stared into his grandfather's eyes, then his brother's. He thought about how far they had come and all the events that had transpired. And how lucky he was. He went back and approached his grandfather slowly, never releasing his gaze, then embraced him for a good long time. Stepan quickly ran over not wanting to be left out, embraced them both.

"I promise I will never leave you again," Yervant squeaked out.

"I promise I will never let you leave again, Bahbeeg," Tavid retorted.

Yervant chuckled. "We are free now, you know? Not many get the chance to start their lives over again, at least not on this world. Let us celebrate our good fortunes every day, eh?"

Tavid kissed his grandfather on the cheek and then his brother. He wiped the mist from his eyes, then turned and continued toward the ridge of trees. He forced himself to clear his mind and open his senses. This was a familiar task in an unfamiliar landscape and any mistakes now could be lethal. He breathed in the air and scanned his surroundings as he trekked.

Reaching the site, he realized that he had picked a roost that was back-dropped by the sun, which glowed on the encampment like a leading ray pointing to the site of action. Using the scope of the karabiner, he searched for the commandant but at first was unsuccessful. Then a large portly officer exited one of the tents, giving orders to subordinate officers, slapping them around in the process. From the description of the Cypriot scouts, this was his target. Tavid methodically placed the scope back on his rifle, got into a stable position and searched again for Khan through the scope. But Khan was giving additional orders and was surrounded by several officers. Even though Tavid was nearly two hundred meters away, he could tell from Khan's gestures that he was full of a rage that was being thrown onto his subordinates. Finally, a clear shot was at hand. Tavid aimed at the commandant's left chest, palpated the trigger of his rifle but before flexing, he slowly dropped the barrel of his rifle and fired three shots...

# Epilogue

*do you now know me?*
*can you see into my life?*
*sense how I feel?*
*taste my surroundings?*
*and do you hate me as well?*
*despise me?*
*or am I a small part within you?*
*do you remember your father, grandfather, great-grandfather?*
*I do…*
*would they have known me?*
*seen me?*
*resembled me?*
*hated me?*
*or, embraced me?*
*clouded is life around me but clear is my sight and mind.*

# Chapter of Remembrance

Christian Genocide
April 24, 1915[1]

## Henry Morgenthau
## U.S. Ambassador to the Ottoman Empire (1913-16)

The below quote is from the book *Ambassador Morgenthau's Story* (the U.S. Ambassador to Turkey before WWI) and describes the torture, annihilation and deportation of the Armenian race within the Ottoman Empire during this time period.

Henry Morgenthau, *Ambassador Morgenthau's Story* (New York: Doubleday, Page & Co.: 1919), pp. 307-309, 321-323.

"One day I was discussing these proceedings with a responsible Turkish official, who was describing the tortures inflicted. He made no secret of the fact that the Government had instigated them, and, like all Turks of the official classes, he enthusiastically approved this treatment of the detested race. This official told me that all these details were matters of nightly discussion at the headquarters of the Union and Progress Committee. Each new method of inflicting pain was hailed as a splendid discovery, and the regular attendants were constantly ransacking their brains in the effort to devise some new torment. He told me that they even delved into the records of the Spanish Inquisition and other historic institutions of torture and adopted all the suggestions found there. He did not tell me who carried off the prize in this gruesome competition, but common reputation through Armenia gave a preeminent infamy to Djevdet Bey, the Vali of Van,

---

[1] Armenian Martyrs Day is commemorated on April 24th.

whose activities in that section I have already described. All through this
country Djevdet was generally known as the "horseshoer of Bashkale" for
this connoisseur in torture had invented what was perhaps the masterpiece
of all—that of nailing horseshoes to the feet of his Armenian victims.

Yet these happenings did not constitute what the newspapers of the
time commonly referred to as the Armenian atrocities; they were merely
the preparatory steps in the destruction of the race. The Young Turks
displayed greater ingenuity than their predecessor, Abdul Hamid. The
injunction of the deposed Sultan was merely "to kill, kill," whereas the
Turkish democracy hit upon an entirely new plan. Instead of massacring
outright the Armenian race, they now decided to deport it. In the south
and southeastern section of the Ottoman Empire lie the Syrian desert and
the Mesopotamian valley. Though part of this area was once the scene of
a flourishing civilization, for the last five centuries it has suffered the blight
that becomes the lot of any country that is subjected to Turkish rule; and
it is now a dreary, desolate waste, without cities and towns or life of any
kind, populated only by a few wild and fanatical Bedouin tribes. Only the
most industrious labor, expended through many years, could transform
this desert into the abiding place of any considerable population. The
Central Government now announced its intention of gathering the two
million or more Armenians living in the several sections of the empire
and transporting them to this desolate and inhospitable region. Had they
undertaken such a deportation in good faith it would have represented
the height of cruelty and injustice. In fact, the Turks never had the slightest
idea of reestablishing the Armenians in this new country. They knew that
the great majority would never reach their destination and that those who
did would either die of thirst and starvation, or be murdered by the wild
Mohammedan desert tribes. The real purpose of the deportation was
robbery and destruction; it really represented a new method of massacre.
When the Turkish authorities gave the orders for these deportations, they
were merely giving the death warrant to a whole race; they understood
this well, and, in their conversations with me, they made no particular
attempt to conceal the fact.

[Paragraphs omitted]

I am confident that the whole history of the human race contains no
such horrible episode as this. The great massacres and persecutions of the
past seem almost insignificant when compared with the sufferings of the
Armenian race in 1915. The slaughter of the Albigenses in the early part
of the thirteenth century has always been regarded as one of the most
pitiful events in history. In these outbursts of fanaticism, about 60,000
people were killed. In the massacre of St. Bartholomew, about 30,000

human beings lost their lives. The Sicilian Vespers, which has always figured as one of the most fiendish outbursts of this kind, caused the destruction of 8,000. Volumes have been written about the Spanish Inquisition under Torquemada, yet in the eighteen years of his administration only a little more that 8,000 heretics were done to death. Perhaps the one event in history that most resembles the Armenian deportations was the expulsion of the Jews from Spain by Ferdinand and Isabella. According to Prescott 160,000 were uprooted from their homes and scattered broadcast over Africa and Europe. Yet all these previous persecutions seem almost trivial when we compare them with the sufferings of the Armenians, in which at least 600,000 people were destroyed and perhaps as many as 1,000,000. These earlier massacres, when we compare them with the spirit that directed the Armenian atrocities, have one feature that we can almost describe as an excuse: they were the product of religious fanaticism and most of the men and women who instigated them sincerely believed that they were devoutly serving their Maker. Undoubtedly, religious fanaticism was an impelling motive with the Turkish and Kurdish rabble who slew Armenians as a service to Allah, but the men who really conceived the crime had no such motive. Practically all of them were atheists, with no more respect for Mohammedanism than for Christianity, and with them the one motive was cold-blooded, calculating state policy."

# Adolf Hitler
## Chancellor of Nazi Germany (1933-45)

The text below is the English version of the German document handed to Louis P. Lochner in Berlin. It first appeared in Lochner's *What About Germany?* (New York: Dodd, Mead & Co., 1942), pp. 1-4. The Nuremberg Tribunal later identified the document as L-3 or Exhibit USA-28. Two other versions of the same document appear in Appendices II and III. For the German original cf. *Akten zur Deutschen Auswartigen Politik 1918-1945*, Serie D, Band VII, (Baden-Baden, 1956), pp. 171-172.

"My decision to attack Poland was arrived at last spring. Originally, I feared that the political constellation would compel me to strike simultaneously at England, Russia, France, and Poland. Even this risk would have had to be taken.

Ever since the autumn of 1938, and because I realized that Japan would not join us unconditionally and that Mussolini is threatened by that nit-wit of a king and the treasonable scoundrel of a crown prince, I decided to go with Stalin.

In the last analysis, there are only three great statesmen in the world, Stalin, I, and Mussolini. Mussolini is the weakest, for he has been unable to break the power of either the crown or the church. Stalin and I are the only ones who envisage the future and nothing but the future. Accordingly, I shall in a few weeks stretch out my hand to Stalin at the common German-Russian frontier and undertake the redistribution of the world with him.

Our strength consists in our speed and in our brutality. Genghis Khan led millions of women and children to slaughter—with premeditation and a happy heart. History sees in him solely the founder of a state. It's a matter of indifference to me what a weak western European civilization will say about me.

I have issued the command—and I'll have anybody who utters but one word of criticism executed by a firing squad—that our war aim does not consist in reaching certain lines, but in the physical destruction of the enemy. Accordingly, I have placed my death-head formations in readiness—for the present only in the East—with orders to them to send to death mercilessly and without compassion, men, women, and children of Polish derivation and language. Only thus shall we gain the living space (Lebensraum) which we need. Who, after all, speaks today of the annihilation of the Armenians?"

## The 1915 Genocide

The below are referenced from http://www.genocide1915.info/history/.

**April, 1915**—Organized arrests of a large number of Armenian intellectuals and prominent national leaders in Constantinople and the provinces. They are deported to Anatolia and are slain on the way. The Armenian soldiers of the Turkish army are disarmed and massacred by the thousands. The defenseless Armenian population is exiled to the Syrian Desert and massacred by tens of thousands, slain by the Turkish army, the irregulars and the civilians were left to die of hunger and maltreatment. 1,500,000 Armenians are systematically obliterated by Turkish ferocity.

**April 24**—250 Armenian intellectuals and community leaders are arrested in Constantinople and sent to Chankri and Ayash, where they are later slain.

**April 24**—The editors and staff of Azadamart, the leading Armenian newspaper of Constantinople, are arrested and on June 15 are slain in Diyarbekir, where they had been transported and imprisoned.

**April 24**—The Armenian Patriarch of Constantinople and Zohrab, Armenian deputy in the Ottoman Parliament, petition the Grand Vizier, Said Halim, the Minister of the Interior Talaat, and the President of the Senate, Rifat, on behalf of the arrested Armenians of Constantinople. Although approached separately, all three give identical answers: that the government is isolating the Armenian leadership and dissolving the Armenian political organizations.

# ACKNOWLEDGEMENTS

How do you adequately acknowledge all those who have in some way helped in the creation of this novel? Not possible within this lone page! But here it goes. David Muzzin who was a very early reader of my notes, way before I knew what I was doing. He gave me encouragement and wanted to read more. Della Topouzian, Mae Derdarian, Lauren Thompson and especially Jodi Stanley, who have helped with the editing process. My brother Ara Topouzian who donated his music for our Kickstarter project. Elisabeth Veltman with Blue Pearl Strategies and Mark Stegeman with Stegeman Creative who were instrumental with the website design, production, and the cover art of the book. Troy Scott Parker with Cimarron Design and his expertise in typesetting. The local "Armenian Book Club" who read and critiqued the novel. All of our supporters who pledged our Kickstarter campaign. And of course, my family for tolerating my endless hours of writing.

# GLOSSARY

**Ahmahn!** (Turkish/Armenian slang): Oh my!

**Aboush** (Armenian): Idiot.

**Ahmahn, Asdvadz** (Armenian): Oh my God.

**Anbeedahn** (Armenian): Mischievous.

**Anshoosht** (Armenian): Of course.

**Armenians:** A nation and ethnic group native to the Armenian Highland. The largest concentration is in Armenia, having a population of nearly 3,500,000 most of which are ethnic Armenian. Because of a wide-ranging and long-lasting Diaspora, an estimated total of 3 million people of Armenian ancestry live outside of Armenia. As a result of the Armenian Genocide, a large number of survivors fled to many countries throughout the world, most notably Russia, Middle East, United States, France, Iran, Georgia and other parts of the world.

Christianity began to spread in Armenia soon after Jesus's death due to the efforts of two of his apostles, St. Thaddeus and St. Bartholomew. In the early 4th century, the Kingdom of Armenia became the first nation to adopt Christianity as a state religion.

Armenian is an Indo-European language isolate. The unique Armenian alphabet was invented in 406 AD by the scholar and evangelist Mesrob Mashtots.

The ethnic cleansing of Armenians during the final years of the Ottoman Empire is widely considered a genocide—an estimated 1.5 million victims—with one wave of persecution in the years 1894 to 1896, culminating in the events of the Armenian Genocide in 1915 and 1916. With World War I in progress, the Turks accused the Christian Armenians as likely to ally with Imperial Russia, and used it as a pretext to deal with the entire Armenian population as an enemy within their empire.

Turkish governments since that time have consistently rejected charges of genocide, typically arguing either that those Armenians who died were simply in the way of a war or that killings of Armenians were justified by their individual or collective support for the enemies of the Ottoman Empire.

**Baba** (Armenian slang): Father.

**Bachig** (Armenian): Kiss.

**Baron** (Armenian): Mister.

**Bashibazouk** (Turkish): Hooligan.

**Bastegh** (Armenian): Fruit rollup.

**Bosporus:** Strait that forms the boundary between the European part of Turkey and its Asian part (Anatolia). It connects the Black Sea with the Sea of Marmara.

**Bursa:** City in northwestern Turkey.

**Constantinople:** Now known as Istanbul; was the capital of the eastern Roman empire.

**Consul or Consulate:** A political title that is used for the official representatives of the government of one state in the territory of another, normally acting to assist and protect the citizens of the consul and to facilitate trade and friendship between the peoples.

**Dardanelles:** Narrow strait in northwestern Turkey connecting the Aegean Sea to the Sea of Marmara.

**Delibash** (Turkish): Crazy.

**Dzo!** (Armenian slang): Hey!

**Effendi** (Turkish): Name given to a man of property, authority, or education.

**Ermeni** (Turkish): Armenian.

**Eshek** (Turkish): Jackass.

**Fedayee** (Arabic): One who sacrifices himself. Paramilitary. A group of civilians organized in a military fashion. Armenians used the word to mean "Field worker" or "Freedom fighter" as well as the former meaning.

**Friesian:** Horse breed originating in Friesland, Netherlands. Although the breed's conformation resembles that of a light draft horse, Friesians are graceful and nimble for their size. During the Middle Ages, it is believed that the ancestors of Friesian horses were in great demand as war horses throughout continental Europe.

**Hay Allah** (Turkish): Praise God.

**Herikeh!** (Turkish): Stop!

**Hyevan** (Turkish): Wild animal.

**Hayrig** (Armenian): Father.

**Hokees** (Armenian): My soul (used as an endearing phrase).

**Jehennem** (Turkish): Hell.

**Gadar** (Armenian): Name of the church in Tchingiler. Translated in Armenian means 'perfect.'

**Hrammettzek** (Armenian): Come on in, welcome.

**Karabiner** (German): Rifle made by Mauser. Used in WWI and WWII.

**Kreesdos** (Armenian): Christ.

**Kukucekmeca:** Port city on the north shores of the Marmara Sea at Constantinople.

**Kurds:** A largely Sunni Muslim people with their own language and culture, most Kurds live in Turkey, Iraq, Iran. Before World War I, traditional Kurdish life was nomadic, revolving around sheep and goat herding throughout Turkey and Iran.

**Larnaca:** City in Cyprus inhabited by Armenians.

**Lavash** (Armenian): Flatbread.

**Mayrig** (Armenian): Mother.

**Madzoon** (Armenian): Yogurt.

**Marmara Sea:** Inland sea that connects the Black Sea to the Aegean Sea. The Bosporus strait connects it to the Black Sea and the Dardanelles strait to the Aegean Sea.

**Mount Olympus:** Rises 8,343 feet outside of Bursa.

**Ohf Bahbam** (Armenian): "Oh Father." A phrase used when something goes wrong.

**Ottoman Empire** (Turkey): Empire which lasted for 623 years until 1922.

**Paree Looees** (Armenian): Good morning.

**Paree Eereegon** (Armenian): Good evening.

**Pasha** (Turkish): A high rank in the Ottoman Empire, equivalent to the British title of Lord.

**Resin:** Opium.

**Sarsakh** (Turkish): Idiot.

**Sersem** (Turkish): Stupid, or idiot.

**Shoon shahn vortee es** (Armenian): You, son of a female dog.

**Sikishmek** (Turkish slang): Profanity.

**Soos!** (Armenian): Quiet!

**Soujouk** (Multicultural): Cured meat.

**Tonir** (Armenian): Underground cylindrical clay oven used in cooking and baking. The Tonir is used for cooking in Southern, Central and Western Asia, as well as in the Caucasus.

**Tavloo** (Armenian): Backgammon.

**Tokatlian Hotel:** Famous hotel in Constantinople.

**Tchingiler:** Armenian village of about 1000 families located outside of Bursa.

**Tilki** (Turkish): Fox.

**Toot** (Armenian): Mulberry.

**Vartabed** (Armenian): Celibate priest.

**Yahudi** (Turkish): Jew.

**Yalova:** Port city on the southeast shore of the Marmara Sea.

# CHARACTER LIST

**Ana:** Bulgarian. Tavid's landlady in Constantinople.

**Aldo Petrescu:** Romanian from Constantinople. Tavid's black market contact. Age: Late 30s.

**Aleksandar:** Bulgarian from Constantinople. Owns a brothel. Trades weapons for resin with Tavid.

**Aram:** Armenian from outskirts of Tchingiler. Also known as "Crazy Aram" or "Delibash Aram." Friend to Tavid Kaloustian.

**Arin:** Armenian. Aram's wife. The name translates as "brave female."

**Bey:** Turkish. A title for a chieftain, traditionally applied to the leaders with the simple meaning of "lord."

**Borland:** British commander at Cyprus.

**Cheté:** Members of armed irregular forces employed by the Ottoman government in carrying out atrocities against Armenians.

**Costel Petrescu:** Romanian. Aldo's brother.

**Daron Pashayan:** Armenian from Constantinople. Consulate. Mentor to Shant Eftendelian.

**Eftendelians:** Armenians from Constantinople. Own restaurant.
    **Armen:** Father (The Baron); late 30s.
    **Seta:** Mother; 30s.
    **Karoun:** Daughter; 16 years of age.
    **Shant:** Son; 18 years of age.

**Gabriel Kaprelian:** French Armenian sailor.

**Haig Navasart:** Armenian skipper who sails Tavid and others back and forth from the ports of Yalova and Constantinople.

**Ismail Bey:** Turkish Port commander, Village of Yalova.

**Ivanka:** Bulgarian woman who works for Aleksandar.

**Kalkim Bey:** Turkish commander in Bursa. Lieutenant Tahir's father.

**Kaloustians:** Armenians from Tchingiler.
  **Tavid:** 20 years old.
  **Anoush:** Mother to Tavid; late 30s.
  **Stepan:** Brother to Tavid; 16 years of age.
  **Varsenig:** Sister to Tavid; 12 years of age.
  **Yervant** Yacoubian: Grandfather to Tavid; 55 years old.

**Kristapor Sakalian:** Armenian from Tchingiler. Fedayee leader.

**Malachi:** Jew. Chemist who owns apothecary. Son's name is Ari.

**Mariam:** Bulgarian tailor who worked for Aleksandar.

**Mustafa:** Turkish lieutenant. Nephew of Kalkim Bey.

**Panos:** Armenian physician and French national working at French missionary hospital in Yalova.

**Partriche:** Commander Borland's secretary and translator.

**Satenig:** Seta Eftendelian's sister who lives in Larnaca, Cyprus.

**Sinasi:** Turcoman who lives in mountain village near Tavid's farmhouse.

**Tahir:** Turkish lieutenant. Son of Kalkim Bey.

**Vahé Vasakian:** Armenian from Tchingiler. Informant to Constantinople port commander. Tried to have Tavid Kaloustian killed on numerous occasions.

**Vartabed:** Armenian name for a celibate priest.

**Yesil:** Turkish captain who was replaced by Kalkim Bey.